By Michele L. Coffman

The Alpha Evolution Series

The Battle for Liberty Series

The Universal Guardians Saga

Veiled
Conspiracy

Book One
The Battle for Liberty Series

by

Michele L. Coffman

LAUNCHPOINT
PRESS

Launch Point Press

Copyright © 2022 Michele L. Coffman
Updated, Re-edited Second Edition with added content
First Edition © 2011

ISBN: 978-1-63304-229-2
Ebook: 978-1-63304-150-9

First Printing: 2022

Editing: Kay Grey, Judy Kerr
Formatting: Patty Schramm
Cover and Book Design: Lorelei

Launch Point Press
Portland, Oregon
www.LaunchPointPress.com

Dedication

To my children Ashley and Phillip for filling my life with meaning, my heart with love, and for always having faith in me. To my granddaughter, Michele, whose witty laughter engulfs my heart.

Wake up, dear souls, wake up I say
As reason calls out, each passing day.
Yet we are blind, and cannot hear
And with each day, so grows our fear.
Our hearts are weary, our eyes are dim
We're lulled to sleep, with each new whim.
Until the day, when terror strikes
And all our hopes are turned to frights.
We try to flee and escape our fate
But yet, alas, it is too late

~Elizabeth Leonard

Chapter One

May 12, 2030

Elaina Williams gazed at her watch. Five more minutes. The evening was late, after ten, and the sun had long since set over the vast skies of New York City. Career-making story or no story, Kim had wasted enough of her time. "If she isn't here in five minutes, I'm going home." *Home.* The calming image of her comfortable apartment made Elaina's feet stir on the pavement.

She shifted beneath the streetlight, cursing her own foolishness. Why had she agreed to this meeting anyway? Kim had always been flighty when they'd been together. Why should she expect different now? "Hell," Elaina muttered, "Kim's probably at that bar down the street, beer in one hand and a blonde on the other." Or if not that bar, some other. And if not a blonde—

A chill washed through Elaina at the picture she'd conjured all too clearly. Kim with another woman. Easy to imagine when she'd seen it before. In her own bed. The woman had been a blonde. All over.

"Damn, Elaina," she scolded herself, "it's been two years. Let it go."

Go. A good idea, she decided, and headed across the parking lot. Kim had sounded desperate on the phone earlier, but if her story had been so important, she should have been on time. Elaina didn't owe her anything, least of all more waiting in an empty park late at night, alone.

Kim had never been easy to predict, except for one thing: she thought everything was serious, urgent, life-or-death. Catastrophes and conspiracies. Even back in college, she'd been searching for the hidden patterns in the fabric of society. Politics.

Kim's passionate interest was probably what attracted Elaina to her in the first place, all those years ago, when they'd shared a dorm and dreams. Elaina was working toward a career in newscasting, her flashier girlfriend determined on the dangerous, exciting life of investigative journalism.

They were a match made in heaven. At least, that was what Kim had told her repeatedly, until several years later, when Kim decided to dirty Elaina's sheets with another woman's unsavory scent.

But all of that, Elaina reminded herself, was past and gone. The only reason she'd agreed to this meeting, at this stupidly clandestine location, late at night, was for the story her ex had promised her. And failed to deliver. "Are you surprised?" she asked herself and got in the Jeep.

As Elaina fastened her seatbelt, headlights from an approaching vehicle temporarily blinded her. A rusted-out pickup pulled alongside the Jeep, and Kim jumped out with a smile. "I'm glad you're here, I was afraid you might have left."

Elaina groaned, even more irritated. She glanced at Kim, perfect as ever, with her short hair and soft, sun-kissed skin. Should she bite her tongue, start her Jeep, drive away, or give Kim a piece of her mind first? Damn, Kim was sexy.

Kim could leap from bed ready to tackle the events of the day without having to run a brush through her dirty-blonde hair. Elaina, however, spent well over an hour in front of the mirror, not to mention the cost of the whole armory of necessary beauty products it took to tame back her long, dark-brown hair. She could, she thought, be at home brushing her hair, or soaking in a bath, or any number of things. Instead, she'd waited here for an hour, and Kim didn't even open with an apology. "I was just leaving."

"I know that look." Kim held up her hands in mock surrender. "I'm sorry I was late. I had this eerie sensation I was being followed, so I drove all around Manhattan."

Elaina shot Kim a disbelieving stare, biting back her impulsive retort. She sighed, feeling once again drained by this woman. Wishing to be done with Kim once and for all, possibly even salvage something from the long wait, Elaina reluctantly removed her seatbelt.

Slowly, she exited the Jeep. "What do you have? You said you had something big for me."

Kim glanced around as if to make sure they were truly alone. "Huge story, El, I really mean it. I have the story of a lifetime."

"Then why give it to me? Why not run with this 'huge story' on your own?"

Kim's laughter rang out crisply in the night air. "I didn't say I was giving you anything. I only said I would make it worth your while. No, I'm planning to sell it to the *Times*, but it's not quite ready yet."

Elaina gasped. The wretch! Calling out of the blue, making her wait alone, at night, in the middle of nowhere, and now this? She spoke slowly, keeping her voice low, even though she wanted to shriek. "Why am I here?"

Kim darted a quick looksee over her shoulder. "I plan on sharing the story with you, but not until I get the check in hand and I'm at the bank. Until then, I need you to hold onto something for me."

"Why?"

"I'm being watched, I can feel it." Kim quickly grabbed Elaina's arm. "I'm serious, El, and these people don't fool around."

Elaina struggled free. "I am going home," she said, "and taking a long hot bath. I'm tired, and unlike you, I have to get up early tomorrow and go to work."

Kim smiled, her lips slightly crooked. "Still upset I was late. Fine. Tell you what, I'll give you a small taste of information, and if it pans out, you help me."

Was Kim serious? Searching Kim's brown eyes, Elaina considered the offer. "What kind of information? Please don't let it be about the government implanting tracking chips into the brains of newborns. I still can't believe I almost fell for that one."

A mixture of pain and defensiveness fogged Kim's eyes, but she quickly recovered. "No, it's not, but for your information, that story is also real even if I haven't found anything solid on it yet." Reaching into her truck, Kim pulled out a cluttered daily planner. She flipped through a few pages then stopped. "On June eighth we will be hit by a financial collapse like nothing you've ever dreamed. Call it the Greatest Depression in human history. The Stock Exchange will close, maybe for the last time, and this will let loose a chain of events which will . . ." Kim paused, biting her lip. "I think I've given you enough for now. June eighth."

Elaina stood with her head cocked in disbelief, unsure of what to say, until finally finding the words, "How on Earth could you know that?"

"I have my source. However, this event is only the beginning. All of us going broke is small potatoes compared to what will be coming if we don't stop it."

"I really have no time for this, Kim."

"Hey, if I'm wrong, fine, won't be the first time, right? If I'm not, though, I want you to meet me back here on the evening of June eighth. I might even be finished with the story by then. Do we have a deal?"

Elaina briefly considered Kim's offer, remembering all the oddball theories that never panned out, then the few which surprisingly had. She shrugged her shoulders. "Sure, fine, Kim. Whatever."

Grinning, Kim took out a small, sealed package from the truck. "Keep this hidden. When I want it back, I'll let you know. Don't open it."

Elaina nodded her agreement but then frowned, unsure if Kim had finally lost it or not. But worrying about Kim wasn't her job anymore, was it? She climbed into her Jeep, set the package on the passenger's seat beside her, and stared at the brown wrapping. It was only a package.

The moment Kim's headlights vanished from site, Elaina pulled her Jeep away from the parking space, suddenly feeling she'd accepted something far weightier.

Chapter Two

June 8, 2030

"Car Fifteen on site."

The dispatcher's calm voice acknowledged each patrol car as officers reported their location and estimated time on scene. Panic ensued at a bank after the morning news informed viewers the stock market had crashed. The value of the American dollar was steadily falling. Banks and businesses who had the people's hard-earned money tied up in the now-depleted stock market, were locking their doors, one after the other, adding greatly to public hysteria. Similar events were happening all over the country. In this case, someone had shot a banker who was trying to get to work.

Samantha Kelly was one of the first police officers to arrive at the downtown bank in the heart of Kansas City, Missouri. She was making her way up to the top of the long line of stairs, taking two at a time, when she heard the approaching sirens.

She looked back, briefly catching a glimpse of the muscular officer exiting his black and white. Officer Jenkins was the last person Sam wanted to see. She rolled her eyes as she moved toward the swarm of spectators and her patiently awaiting sergeant.

"Officer Kelly, move these people back. I want a hundred-foot clearance all around," her sergeant instructed, before motioning to other arriving officers.

Shifting direction, Sam made her way to the crowd. Her green eyes were gentle, yet firm. She carried herself with an air of confidence which said she would push back when the need arose. She was medium built, standing just over five-nine, with an athletic, toned body, and shoulder-length, dark brown hair. Her high cheekbones and natural tan complexion came from the Cherokee on her mother's side, while her father had passed down a mixture of German and Irish, which gave her the stubborn streak and short temper.

The crowd moved back easily enough, giving her sergeant more than enough room in which to do his job. Several minutes later, Sam had the onlookers heading away from the area, except for a young woman who informed Sam she had seen the entire disturbing event.

The sergeant glanced over his shoulder. "Nice job, rookie," he said.

Sam kept her smile in as she pointed toward a lone woman standing nervously off to the side. "Sergeant, she witnessed the shooting."

The sergeant glared at the three uniformed men nearby. "Jenkins, take her statement. You other two need to find something productive to do, like go see if the detectives have arrived yet."

The sergeant's voice was deep, commanding, reminding Sam of one of her drill sergeants in the army. The three men dispersed, but not before Jenkins shot Sam an unappreciative grimace. Sam cheered victoriously—but without making a sound.

"Kelly, help Simmons with the guard's statement. I need to call the captain and let him know what's going on."

Sam nodded, heading off to where Simmons and the bank's guard were standing. She noticed the pale greenish color of the young guard's face and wondered if this man had ever seen a person killed before. Her heart went out to him.

After graduating high school, Sam had gone straight into the army, where she served for eight years as a Special Forces Communications Sergeant. Even after completing the extensive required courses, training in her field was constant. She was assigned to an ODA team from the 10th Group in Fort Carson, Colorado and deployed overseas more days out of the year than she was stateside. During various operations, Sam had witnessed friend and foe gravely wounded or killed. The first time was the worst, but gradually, she had learned to distance herself from the pain of it.

"I would say he was in his early twenties." The guard gave Sam a weak smile when she approached. "I don't think he meant to shoot him, either. I mean, the kid seemed even more scared than I was."

Simmons directed a sympathetic glance to the guard, before handing Sam the paper he had finished writing on. "Give this to Sarge. It's the perp's description."

Sam headed quickly back the way she came. As soon as she handed the information to her sergeant, he was on the radio to dispatch. Once he read the information off, the crackly voice of an older woman came on. "We have multiple reports of a riot forming down on Thirtieth and Grand. Captain wants you all to head back here pronto."

Sam followed her sergeant's glance up at the clear, bluish sky. The weatherman this morning had predicted a tranquil high of eighty-two, with light, patchy cloud cover by mid-day.

"It's too perfect of a day for this shit," he grumbled before shouting out commands to the rest of his officers.

She knew exactly what he meant.

The day felt like a week, if not two, and Elaina waited anxiously as the hours moved slowly by. She tried to reach Kim on her cell any chance she could, hanging up each time she reached voicemail.

How could Kim have known? Not just the event, but the exact date. Elaina had not believed in Kim's information—for the most part. Thankfully, she had listened to the little voice in the back of her mind that echoed, *what if?* She'd sold what stocks she had managed to collect throughout the years and withdrew her money from savings not more than two days ago. The sum wasn't a fortune by any means, but the twenty-three thousand dollars hidden in her apartment was nevertheless safe. Thanks to Kim.

She glanced up to her wall clock, feeling the dreariness of time as the second hand limped by. Thirty more minutes and she would be pulling her Jeep away from the station for a quick bite to eat. Two and a half more hours and she would be meeting Kim for what she hoped to be the story of a lifetime. One which took her from her job of finding and writing the news, to a seat behind the long shiny desk, reporting the news to the awaiting viewers.

Kim's story was her foot in. She could feel it. No more grunt work, no more going door-to-door for interviews on minuscule stories or standing outside in the freezing rain to show those watching how bad the weather truly was.

"Elaina, we need you to stay a little late tonight."

The voice of the young, energetic woman brought Elaina's eyes upward as she cursed silently for not locking her office door. "I can't tonight, I have a prior engagement."

The woman shrugged. "This came from the boss man, so you will need to take it up with him. Sorry," she ended, pivoting from the small, cramped office.

"Damn!" Elaina muttered, standing from her desk. "Of all the days for overtime."

She found her supervisor, and after receiving no sympathy from the scraggly-faced man, she managed to get the extra work done with little time to spare before her meeting with Kim. She thought about stopping on the way to grab a quick burger and fries, but didn't want to chance missing Kim, not to mention the unwanted calories she would have to work off later.

The night was a vibrant shade of bluish-black, as the natural light from the moon and stars glistened down onto this part of the park. The view stood animated as Elaina pulled her Jeep underneath the same hearty oak she'd parked by a few weeks prior. She saw no signs of Kim's truck anywhere in this section of the city park. This did not deter Elaina from turning off the engine and waiting. She would wait all night if she had to. Possibly call in sick to work the next day, an action she had never taken in her five years with Channel Seven News.

What story could be bigger than a major crash? She felt the excitement rise in her chest.

The passenger door flew open, and fear stifled her ability to scream. Kim moved swiftly inside, slamming, and latching the door quickly behind her, as if in great desperation.

"Kim, you scared the crap—"

"Start the Jeep and drive, El."

Elaina's relief disappeared when her eyes caught sight of what Kim was holding. "Is that a gun? Why do you have a gun? You know I don't like—"

"Damn it, El, drive!" Kim shouted, squinting over her shoulder in genuine fear. This alarm brought Elaina out of her hurt confusion, and within seconds, she had her Jeep moving away from the seclusion of the park.

Neither woman spoke for several minutes. Elaina guided the vehicle out onto the busy main road. Kim constantly gazed over her shoulder, and Elaina peered repeatedly at Kim.

"Sorry I snapped at you, El," Kim finally said. "I wasn't sure if I lost them or not." She relaxed somewhat and fastened her seatbelt.

"What is going on? Who's after you? Are you—" Elaina's voice cut off with a swift intake of air. "You're bleeding." She threw on the blinker to move to the right shoulder of the road.

"I'm fine." Kim motioned for her to continue driving. "The blood isn't mine."

"Not *yours*? My God, Kim!"

"No, I didn't do this." Kim pointed to the bloodstain covering the lower right section of her shirt. "They killed my informant earlier today and tried to kill me, but I got away. I've been hiding, waiting for you ever since."

"Who tried to kill you?"

Kim leveled her gaze on Elaina. "The less you know, the safer you'll be. I wouldn't have met with you tonight if I could've helped it, but I really need that package I gave you." Her eyes narrowed. "Please tell me you still have it."

"Of course, I have it." Elaina's voice came out defensive.

"Where is it?"

"My place, but—"

"Take me there now!"

Elaina yanked the wheel to the right, then slammed on the brakes.

Kim yelped, grabbed her neck, and glimpsed wildly around. Horns blared, followed by angry shouts, and the display of middle fingers from several outraged drivers. "Why'd we stop?"

"My Jeep, my package, so stop giving me orders!"

"*Your* package? Now, wait one damn minute! The package is mine!"

"Possession is nine-tenths of the law, so until you tell me what's going on—"

"I don't have time for this!" Kim spat.

"Make time!" Elaina was just as unmoving, her tone as determined, if not more so.

Kim stared angrily at her for several seconds, but gradually, her face softened. "El, I'm not trying to keep you out of this for my own personal gain, but for your safety."

Elaina had never seen Kim scared before. She looked exhausted, like she hadn't slept in days. "I only want you to talk to me. If you're in danger, maybe I can help."

Kim shook her head. "You don't understand, El. We are all in danger if I don't find a way to get this story out."

"Let me help you, then. After all, two heads are better than one." She threw Kim a light smile.

For a long moment, Kim didn't speak. She's weighing her options, Elaina thought and waited to learn what Kim's choice would be.

Finally, Kim nodded. "Fine, let's go to your place and get the package. I need to use your computer anyway to see what is on this." She held up a red flash drive, explaining her informant had given it to her seconds before he died.

"How did he die?"

Kim's shoulders slumped. "Doesn't matter, we can't help him. Let's just go. I promise to explain everything once we're in your apartment."

Touched by Kim's obvious grief, Elaina placed the gearshift in drive, checked to make sure the lane was clear, and eased the Jeep into the flow of traffic. By the time she pulled under her assigned carport, nearly an hour later, Kim was fast asleep.

Elaina didn't want to wake her, but the parking lot felt unusually dark and frightfully cold, unlike anything she had experienced before. A rustling in the bushes ahead made her ache for the safety of her apartment. She shuddered. "It's a rabbit, or squirrel, silly," Elaina said quietly as she breathed, a lump forming in her throat.

"It's not too late to change your mind."

The sudden sound of Kim's deep, groggy voice made Elaina jump. Shaking her head, no, she forced a smile before following Kim from the Jeep and toward the five-story apartment building. Elaina did her best to put on a brave front for Kim. She breathed a sigh of relief once they were upstairs, with the door to the apartment closed and locked.

"The computer is on my nightstand." Elaina pointed toward the master bedroom and then headed into the kitchen to make them something to eat. She prepared two turkey and cheese sandwiches with light dressing and grabbed two diet sodas from the fridge.

When Elaina entered the bedroom, Kim had the laptop powered on and was tapping on the keyboard. "Ah, good, I'm starving." She patted the empty spot on the bed next to her.

Elaina stopped mid-stride, uneasiness working its way in. The thought was harmless enough, but this type of careless thinking was what had ignited their explosive relationship in the first place. The last place she wanted to be with Kim was on a bed, especially her own bed. Elaina handed Kim her plate and cold drink, then pulled a chair alongside the bedside, giving her a good view of the screen.

"I need the package I gave you."

Elaina took a giant bite of her sandwich before heading to the hallway closet to retrieve the item from a lockbox. She handed the package to Kim and retook her seat. Elaina downed half her soda while she watched Kim unwrap the parcel.

Kim withdrew a black, leather-bound notebook, and two black flash drives. She placed them on the bed next to the red flash drive. Kim took a bite of her sandwich, washing it down with a swallow of soda, then grabbed the book and turned toward Elaina. "Where should I start?"

"The beginning is always a good place."

With a deep sigh, Kim said, "Six months ago, when I was doing some research on the financial corruption inside our government, I stumbled upon some information which made no sense to me." She snickered, a small humorless sound. "Since the information wasn't related to the work I was doing, I almost blew it off, but then I hit a dead end with my current story, so I decided to do a deeper dive on this." Kim withdrew several folded sheets of paper from the front of the notebook and handed them to Elaina.

"This makes no sense," Elaina said, after her third scan of the documents.

"That was what intrigued me the most, I think. I found out later the gibberish on those pages is a type of code, which I have been trying to break with help from my source."

"Who's your source? Or was . . ."

Elaina's face flushed, but Kim quickly answered. "He was a member of a private organization which recruited him prior to his discharge from the military. He was actually on the verge of being court-martialed until this group came in and somehow managed to clear his name."

Elaina was astonished. "How were they able to do that?"

"They're powerful, El, and very smart. I'm not sure who all is involved here. I'm hoping this will show me." Kim held up the red flash drive. Instead of placing it into the computer, she laid it on the bed beside her and retrieved the other two drives. "These devices hold various documents and files from the past sixty-five years. Everything from a detailed outline of this unknown organization's financial transactions to a sketchy outline of what they've done to our country so far, what they plan to do, and bits and pieces of their objectives. There's still a lot of intel missing, and some of the info has sizable gaps, but we have more than enough to get started. We're missing the actual names of those who are involved, and exactly what their endgame is. I'm hoping this flash drive will help shed some light on all the questions. My informant was working on this when they found him."

"What's going to happen to our country?" Elaina had the feeling she might have ventured into something she should have left alone.

"Life in the United States is going to get bad, El, and I'm not over-exaggerating. It's almost as if someone wants to wipe us out." Kim placed one of the drives into the computer and waited for it to load then handed the laptop to Elaina.

Elaina's eyes widened in disbelief as she examined the information before her. The data was patchy, but she was able to understand enough. The timeline started all the way back with the assassination of President John F. Kennedy in 1963, then on to the planning and funding of the deadly day at the World Trade Center in 2001. Including three failed attempts to overtake the White House, and the recession of 2008. By 2025 there had been multiple, high-level assassinations, anthrax attacks, bombings, the list went on and on. "How is this possible?" Her voice was nothing more than a whisper.

"They're not only funding terrorists, El, but it's almost as if some of these attacks are—I don't know, trial runs maybe."

"How did your source get a hold of this?"

Kim rose, stretching. "These people made a grave mistake when they enlisted my informant. Not only was he innocent of the charges the military filed against him, but he was a very patriotic man. He took the job because the money was appealing, and at the time, he had nothing better to do. Plus, having the charges disappear, whether he was guilty or not, provided him with a great deal of relief. He had no idea what all was going on, or what they were planning, until around the time I started snooping around."

Kim rubbed her eyes with the palms of her hands before continuing. "We happened upon each other and began working together to try to gather the information to expose all of this."

Elaina handed the computer to Kim. "So, who's involved and what's coming?"

Kim grabbed the flash drive and shoved it into the slot. She sat on the end of the bed next to Elaina's chair, and they scanned the information. The room grew thick with silence while they read.

As Kim scrolled through the detailed list, Elaina's insides quivered, as if her body were experiencing the effects of a sudden high fever. Everything she'd worked for, all of her life's accomplishments were now over. Gone. What was left was nothing more than fear. Terror spiraled Elaina into a void between reality and make believe. Her life was now a plot in a movie. The sort of near-future suspense story, which terrified viewers with the idea that this *could* come about. Just hopefully not in their lifetime.

"Oh my God, Kim, tell me this isn't really happening." Elaina covered her mouth with both hands, unable to tear her gaze from the screen.

"El, pack a bag. We're leaving." Kim jumped up, powered down the computer, and gathered up the rest of the items. She found a backpack in Elaina's closet and stuffed everything inside it.

Elaina's entire body grew cold, numb. She remained seated, watching Kim double-check her sidearm. She bit her bottom lip, unable to pull her gaze off the cold, black, life-ending weapon. It seemed as unbelievable as what she had read on the laptop.

Kim's expression shifted from determination to something softer. Not pity, not quite. "Why did I drag her into this?" she whispered.

Elaina figured Kim had not meant for her to hear the words.

"Hurry El, we have to go," Kim's voice was louder now. She pulled Elaina onto her feet. "Please, pack what you need, and we'll figure out what to do once we're away from the city."

Elaina nodded, fighting for what little courage she had left. She tottered to the hall closet where she retrieved the leather bag containing her life's savings. Before long, she had a second bag packed, and was following Kim outside.

"Start the Jeep, and I'll load the bags into the back."

As Elaina turned the key, her mind worked to grasp the sharp veer her life had suddenly taken. How long would it take for them to figure this out? Days, weeks, months? What about her job, her apartment? Thankfully, she hadn't found the time to adopt a pet. One less thing for her to worry about.

After Kim closed and latched the tailgate, Elaina observed her silhouette drift down the length of the Jeep toward the passenger door. Without warning, a distinct crack sounded, then a dull ping. Elaina jumped, unsure of the noise. Kim had paused. Elaina scoffed at her edginess the instant Kim's shadow moved again. "It's probably a low tire, silly," Elaina whispered to herself.

She followed the outline of Kim's figure, until finally the passenger door opened. "Do we need to add air to the tires? I have a pressure gauge in the . . ." Her voice trailed off at the glazed look of pain in Kim's eyes.

Kim tossed her weapon on the front passenger seat, her body swaying as if she was struggling to keep her balance. "Leave, El, please leave now." As she spoke, a thick dark substance trickled from the left corner of her mouth, down onto the front of her shirt.

"Kim, what's going—"

The second *crack* was louder than the first, a warm thick liquid splattered on Elaina. The copper aroma registered instantly in Elaina's brain. *Blood!*

She swiveled her head around in time to catch a final glimpse of Kim before her body fell lifelessly to the pavement. The upper-right side of Kim's head was completely gone. "Kim!" Her scream came out so high-pitched, the name was almost unrecognizable.

She fought hard with her seatbelt, trying to release it in an attempt to make her way to the fallen woman. A third *crack* whizzed by so close to her head, she felt a small breeze tickle the hairs on the side of her neck. The next *crack* hit the driver's window in a loud shattering explosion, seconds before Elaina saw a man crouched in the bushes a little over fifty feet away.

As if an outside force controlled her body, Elaina threw the Jeep into reverse and pressed the gas pedal to the floor. She slammed on the brakes within inches of hitting the parked car behind her. In one complete motion, she had the Jeep barreling forward toward the exit, unsure of anything other than the need to escape this nightmare.

Chapter Three

November 14, 2030

The reddish-brown liquid mixed with clear water pouring from the old chrome faucet. Elaina watched, as if in a mesmerized stupor, the slithering blend circle around the dirty white porcelain, before being sucked down into the rusty abyss. Elaina remained, hair wet, hunched over the sink in the bathroom of the shabby, rundown motel room. She listened closely to the effects of gravity as it forced the mixture of hair dye and water through the gurgling pipes beneath the sink.

She tried to recall the number of times within the last five months she'd dyed her hair a different color. Seven, or was it eight times? Did she really care? She wrapped a worn white towel around her newly cut and colored shoulder-length hair, then checked the parking lot through the musty curtains. They reeked of mildew and stale cigarette smoke, which seemed fitting to their repulsive plaid design.

Fifty dollars a night and no questions asked was better than she'd found in a long time. Good enough for her to consider breaking her own rule about how long to remain in one place. But there'd been so many close calls. So many disappointments, and so many lessons learned at costs she'd never have imagined she'd have to pay. They were determined to catch her, kill her was more like it, and they were pursuing her with unlimited resources. Their most effective method was plastering her face on nationwide news stations, stating she was wanted for questioning in Kim's death, which had directed suspicious glances, pointed fingers, and unwanted attention her way. By now, checking the curtains was habit. She knew the importance of concealment and the constant recalculating of her money. After five harrowing months on the run, she was down to nineteen thousand dollars.

Sighing, she sank onto the appallingly patterned bedspread to rest. Five hours could be no time at all, or an eternity, depending. She'd had more than enough of both, since that June night, when life had suddenly, impossibly, changed.

Don't think about it, she told herself. That way lay madness. Instead, she forced herself to concentrate on the meeting scheduled for later in the day. Marcus had seemed trustworthy during their two previous encounters. The first had been an assessment on both their parts. Light conversation, a fraction of shared information. The second, was to exchange more information, test the waters of trust and boundaries. But not all the information. Not yet. Elaina had given Marcus copies of the two black drives but held back the data from the red flash drive until this third meeting.

She still wasn't certain he believed her story. Nor was she sure she trusted him completely, though a friend who dated him two years ago, had judged him to be a moral man. A boy scout of sorts. Besides, she had nowhere else to go. His position in the FBI gave him access she couldn't have matched, even before being forced to run.

And now she was left with no other options.

As Elaina pulled into the deserted parking lot, she spotted Marcus standing next to his car, briefcase in hand. He made his way to her vehicle and climbed into the passenger seat.

"What's going on?" she asked, unsure if she wanted to hear his response.

"I researched the information on those memory sticks you gave me yesterday, and it checks out."

"Of course, it checks out. I wouldn't be in this predicament if it didn't." She was agitated but kept her emotions under control.

He shook his head. "It's gotten worse. You've been wiped from the system since then."

"Wiped?" Confusion and turmoil twisted through her, a new wave of fear taking hold. "What are you saying?"

He sighed heavily. "You no longer exist. Everything about you is gone. Your birth certificate, social security number, everything. Someone had to have known you contacted me, which means whoever is involved has high-level clearance, unrestricted access."

"They do." This added dilemma painfully sunk in. She took out a backup copy of the red thumb drive and handed it to him. "I have a driver's license and all my documents—"

"Worthless. They're nothing more than forgeries now." He pulled a laptop from his briefcase and loaded the device.

"My mother and father . . ."

The somber look he gave her cut her words short. Her blood went instantly cold.

"They're missing."

Her voice was almost hysterical. "What do you mean, missing?"

"Not dead, only missing. Elaina, I promise I'll do all I can to figure this out. Until then, I need to keep you safe." He glanced at the screen as the program finished loading.

"There is no safe place." Elaina turned her head away as her tears fell. She hadn't spoken to her parents since she came out to them in college. Her mother had made it clear if she opted for the gay lifestyle, they would have nothing more to do with her. Her father had remained silent throughout their intense argument, not having the courage to come to his own daughter's defense.

"It's worse than I thought." He closed the computer and placed it inside his briefcase. He retrieved a slip of paper and handed it to her. "Directions to my cabin in southern Missouri. It's well stocked, well hidden, and it doesn't exist."

Her words were as heavy as her chest. "It's all pointless. Why should I even bother hiding anymore—"

Marcus grabbed her roughly by the shoulder. "There's more at stake here than you, me, or your parents. Damn it, Elaina, I need you to keep it together. I know you're hurting, you're scared, but you have to remain strong."

She wiped away the moisture from her eyes and nodded.

"Good. Now I want you to leave for the cabin right away. Stay there, and when it's safe, I'll come get you. It could be a while before that happens. There's no phone, but if you must get a hold of me, I want you to find a payphone or buy a burner phone and call this number." He gave her another slip of paper as he opened the passenger door and stepped out. "If anyone other than me answers, then it means I'm dead. Stay off the internet and no cell phones. I don't want to take the chance of them tracing your signal. You're in grave danger, Elaina. I promise, I will do all I can to keep you safe."

"If you die, then what do I do?" The thought of losing her last hope was overwhelmingly disturbing.

His empathetic gaze was sincere. "I'm not sure who to trust after last night. If you can't find anyone else to help—if it were me, I would head to Canada, or perhaps Mexico."

➤◄

"The president has issued a freeze on all prices. Beginning next Monday, December seventh, at eight a.m., supplemental cards will be handed out at the designated buildings throughout the city for those who qualify. For further information, please call six—"

Sam heard the television cut off and she glanced up from the bills she was poring over. She sipped her drink and stretched in her chair as her sister lumbered into the kitchen.

Rachel pulled a can of diet soda from the fridge. "I thought cops were supposed to live off coffee, twenty-four, seven." She sat across from Sam.

Sam placed her iced tea on the table. "And I thought you were supposed to be doing your homework."

Rachel waved her sister off. "I'm almost done. I was watching the news for one of my assignments."

Sam patiently waited for Rachel to continue. Rachel was so much like their mother, easygoing, with a "take life as it comes" personality. Unlike Sam, who had inherited their father's hurry-up, no-nonsense attitude.

Rachel pointed to the pile of bills. "They're handing out food assistance cards on Monday."

Sam was amused by how well her sister had learned to avoid asking her questions directly.

"The president has ordered a freeze on all prices." Rachel ran her fingers nervously through her long hair. "It sounds like it's getting pretty bad out there."

Sam knew what Rachel wanted to ask her, but she wondered exactly how long it would take her little sister to ask it. She retrieved her glass and took a few more swallows. Still nothing.

"Two of my friends are moving next month. One's heading out of state to her grandmother's because the bank foreclosed on her parents' house, and another, her dad got laid off three months ago."

"We're fine." Sam kicked herself mentally when she noticed the worry in her baby sister's eyes. She should have said something right off, instead of making Rachel go through the nervous nudging.

Sam stood. She was twenty-six, nine years older than Rachel. When their parents died over a year ago, Sam had chosen to come home to take care of her little sister instead of reenlisting for another eight years in the army, as she had originally planned.

"I guess you're old enough to have a say in your own money." Sam motioned for her sister to stand.

Rachel followed Sam through their house, still holding her soda. She stood an inch taller than Sam, and her body structure was slender and delicate, unlike Sam's athletic build. Sam was beautiful, but Rachel's beauty was striking, radiant, the spitting image of their late mother.

Sam guided her little sister into their father's study, flipping the lights on in the rarely utilized room. She headed to the wall behind their father's oversized oak desk, where the grand family portrait hung.

Running her hand down the left side of the frame, Sam's fingers glided to the button, squeezing the spot where the latch was located. She motioned for Rachel to move a few steps to the side, before rotating the picture outward, revealing the high-end safe. "The combination goes in the order of age. First mother's birthday to the right, my birthday to the left, then your birthday back to the right."

The thick metal door swung out smoothly, revealing three expansive metal shelves. Each shelf was packed full of valuables and neatly organized. Large stacks of hundred-dollar bills lined the top. Antique coins, rare stamps, jewelry, and other priceless collectibles Sam had yet to go through, lay on the middle shelf. The bottom shelf housed the various certificates and documents containing the rest of their family fortune.

"Is this real?" Rachel breathed.

Sam tittered at her little sister's bewilderment. "Yes, it's our inheritance."

Their father had been an investment banker. Talented, foresighted, and cautious. Their wealth had come as a surprise to Sam, too. Swiss bank accounts, overseas investments, US holdings in several thriving businesses, and more durable wealth than she knew what to do with. Real estate, cash, and gold.

"You might want to sit down," Sam said. "We have a lot to discuss."

Chapter Four

September 3, 2031

Elaina added up the days on the calendar and heaved a sigh. More than nine months had passed since her arrival at the cabin, and the last time she had talked to Marcus was nearly three months ago. He said he was closing in on the organization, preparing to bust their scheme wide open, share it with the world. No more hiding for Elaina. Unfortunately, since the list of names, as with the information on the drives was incomplete, he needed more time to investigate this matter. Leave no stone unturned.

Her once-abundant cache of supplies was growing thin, and with no cell phone or internet providing her any means of news or connection to the rest of the world, she was restless. She did find a hand-cranked TV and radio combo, but it only picked up snow and one "all religion all the time" radio station. After an hour of listening to flamboyant preaching, Elaina could take no more. She vowed not to use it again unless in dire need. She had made a list of her required supplies the night before. She blew out the kerosene lamps, checked the fireplace, and stuffed her gun in the waistband of her jeans. Thus prepared, Elaina set out down the thick wooded hill to where her vehicle sat hidden over a quarter mile away.

Over the last several months, Elaina had grown to like this part of the Ozarks. The rustic wooded surroundings were beautiful, peaceful, and full of animal life. On the downside, being alone for so long was becoming almost unbearable. A generator was located in one of the two outer buildings, which she used to recharge her laptop every so often to watch one of the three movies she had saved on her hard drive. She tended to occupy most of her days with long walks or jogs throughout the area, reading the fifty plus mystery and crime fiction novels in the cabin, and becoming proficient with Kim's nine-millimeter handgun. She'd also found two hunting rifles and one assault rifle in the back storage room along with numerous boxes of ammo and an abundance of military rations. Marcus had obviously been ready for the apocalypse.

She wasn't worried about anyone hearing her shoot. Marcus's land went on for miles in every direction, with dense woodland encompassing all but one overgrown gravel road. The closest vestige of civilization was a small country town thirty miles away, a rustic town where she was heading today, and she was both excited and frightened.

The trudge to the vehicle was easy enough, but the thought of the return trip with all her provisions lay heavy on her mind. Maybe she could drive closer in. No, the risk of getting her only means of transportation stuck out here in the boonies was not worth the lessened legwork.

It will be good exercise, she thought as she removed the bulky camouflaged tarp covering her SUV. This ride wasn't as nice as her beloved Jeep had been, but in this area, the hail damaged body and putrid-green paint was less conspicuous, and the interior was roomier. The vehicle started easily enough, and within minutes, she moved along the overgrown grass and dirt trail onto the gravel road, windows down and radio blaring.

The drive didn't last long. She found a good parking spot behind the general store. Excitement built up inside her as she donned a tan ball cap and sunglasses, an extra precaution, before making her way to the battered payphone in front of the store. Thank God for vintage towns.

Marcus picked up on the first ring. "I was hoping you would call. I've been worried about you."

Elaina expelled a breath in relief. "I'm fine, but I'm going stir-crazy from all the solitude."

"You're doing great, Elaina. Stay safe for a while longer, and hopefully this all will be nothing but a bad memory."

"How's it going on your end?" She held her breath, praying for good news.

A lengthy pause filled the phone lines. Marcus said, "I've been hiding out for the last few weeks, to be honest. Seems someone wants me dead. Don't worry, though. I'm trying to locate a man who should hold the final pieces to all of this."

"I didn't think it would take so long. We have so much information now. Can't we go to the media?" She knew even as she asked the question this wouldn't be the smartest thing to do, but she was tired of being alone, desperate to reenter life.

"You don't understand, Elaina. I've discovered an organization, which I'm positive is run somewhere outside the United States. We have a vague list of what they plan to do, but not why, and an incomplete list of names of those who are involved within our own government. Acting without knowing the entire story, or exactly who all is involved, might trigger a chain reaction we're not equipped to handle. Could even get us killed, along with countless others."

Elaina finally hung up the phone, her hand lingered on the handset. Marcus was alive, which was better than she had feared some nights. Nevertheless, his investigation was taking too long! She decided standing around like an ice sculpture wasn't going to help, so she headed for the store. Mentally, she added a few bottles of whisky and additional soda to the list of the many canned goods she planned to purchase.

The store was larger than it appeared from the outside. She filled up the shopping cart within the first two rows, with more than half the list still to go. She debated whether to pay for the items, and return after loading them into her vehicle, or if she should try to maneuver a second cart alongside the first, when an attractive, older woman strolled up to her.

"If you have more shopping to do, you can leave this cart behind the counter and grab a new one. Jed lets me do it all the time." She smiled politely.

Elaina returned her smile. "Thank you." She was about to move up to the counter when the woman extended her hand.

"I'm Agnes Cooper, but most people still refer to me by my maiden name of Kelly. That's my husband, Phillip." She motioned with her head toward the man approaching from the far isle. He carried a robust watermelon on his shoulder, which he placed into their cart.

Once Elaina finished shaking their hands, Agnes asked her husband to take the overloaded cart up to the counter and grab Elaina a new one. He headed off after giving his wife a tender kiss of the forehead.

"If only I could get him to do the dishes," Agnes watched her husband depart. "You just move here?"

Elaina said, "Um, I'm camping close by. Sorry, I'm Amy, Amy Bishop." Elaina had an instant feeling this woman knew *Amy Bishop* was not really her name, and that the camping was also a lie, but thankfully, she was polite enough not to pry.

"My husband and I are going to grab some lunch at the diner down the street when we're finished. Would you care to join us? It might be a nice change from campfire cooking."

Elaina shifted uncomfortably, accepting would be a bad idea. She didn't know these people. They appeared friendly enough, and the idea of human contact was appealing, but she needed to stay under the radar. Coming into town for supplies, and to use the phone was dangerous enough. "I would love to, but I have things I need to do. Thank you for the offer."

When Phillip returned with her new cart, they said their farewells. Elaina finished her shopping, wishing she could have said yes.

The box was heavy, but Sam made no move to set it down. She was mesmerized by the television. Not that the newscaster was saying anything new, but somehow, hearing it all neatly summarized made it worse.

"The year and a half following the day marking the start of our second Great Depression, has brought sorrow and misery for many living within the United States. Businesses closed or gone bankrupt, countless people driven onto the streets unable to work, and others doing what they can to keep their families together as they hang on by a thread. The middle class is fading away, our social stratification now separating into the rich, poor, and poorer. Those who do have funds to protect face harsh choices as banks may close without warning and the government can no longer reimburse losses, but the rise in criminal activity makes the mattress no safer a place to keep savings."

The young man talking into the camera peeked over his shoulder toward an empty podium. "In spite of all of this, as the air of democracy blows, it has brought with it the hope and promise of one man. A man who has sworn to do all he can for the good of America and her people. He has promised drastic change, while pointing blame at the incompetent way government officials have squandered money for so many decades. He has a plan, a plan strong enough to raise the hopes of many, earning him the next place in the White House, and in our prayers."

The scene shifted to a waiting crowd gathered at the platform. A tall blonde woman in an expensive dark blue dress and winter coat approached the microphone. "President Adam McMullen swears in this day, the twentieth of January 2032—"

"Shh! Quiet, everyone, it's starting!" Steven shouted above the roar of commotion in the room, frantically searching through boxes for the remote to turn up the volume.

Sam perked up at Steven's words and she placed the box labeled 'Kitchen' on the massive oak table before turning toward the newly connected television. The room was full of off-duty cops and Rachel's college friends who had volunteered to help the two women, and Steven, move in.

Steven had been their neighbor, and Rachel's best friend, since the day their family had moved here from the Ozarks, when Sam had been barely a teen. Several months ago, Steven had arrived home after working the evening shift, to find his house robbed and his mother brutally murdered. Sam and Rachel were the closest thing he had to family, and both were more than happy to welcome him into their home.

Their Johnson County house had been too massive for everyday upkeep, especially with their busy schedules. With Rachel and Steven going to college in the city Sam wanted to move closer so they'd have less of a commute. They had received over three million for their parents' high-end home. The house was worth more, but the couple who bought it paid with a certified check, and the whole thing took less than a week to settle. After buying a modest three-bedroom residence overlooking downtown Kansas City, the sisters put most of the money in their overseas accounts.

"Pizzas are here!" Jenkins yelled above the clamor, making his way into the crowded room carrying a moving box.

Several of the college kids closest to the door rushed outside to retrieve the boxes of hot pizza.

"How much is the damage?" Sam asked.

"The kid said ninety-seven fifty," Jenkins said.

"Quiet everyone, I'm trying to hear!" Steven turned up the volume on the TV.

"Can I shoot him?" Jenkins placed his box beside Sam's on the table.

Sam snorted. "Better wait until after we finish unpacking."

Jenkins guffawed as he made his way to the kitchen to retrieve one of several six-packs of beer. When they first met, Jenkins had been the precinct's sexist dick who Sam couldn't stand to be around. The more they shared the same airspace with bullets flying past, she had grown to know the man behind the façade. He was more genuine than most, a huge teddy bear really. After handing Sam a beer, Jenkins passed out the rest to the other off-duty cops.

"Hey, we have beer!" shouted a tall, lanky, red-haired college kid. Sam had only seen him on one other occasion and couldn't recall his name.

"How old are you, son?" Jenkins narrowed his eyes at the young man.

"Twenty."

"Sorry, this drink is only for grown men. There's soda and lemonade in the kitchen."

"I've worked as hard as you have."

Jenkins pulled out his gun, holding it muzzle-end up so the adolescent could see it. "Well, I'm a cop and you're underage."

Sam chortled at how quickly the tall kid moved to the front of the room. "Put your weapon away and give this to the pizza driver."

Jenkins, still amused by his own humor, made his way out the front door.

"What do you think you're doing?" Steven asked.

Sam whipped around, heart racing in panic. She looked to the heavens in exasperation when she saw Steven rush over and retrieve the box Rachel was carrying.

Rachel's first boyfriend, her high school sweetheart, the father of her unborn child, had deserted her last month when he found out she was pregnant. The breakup had broken Rachel's heart, but she was a strong-willed woman, and Steven and Sam stepped up to help her through this hard time.

"Steven, it's only sheets and bedding!"

"Plus, she's only two months pregnant," Tashonda said. She was an attractive dark-skinned woman on the police force with Sam and Jenkins.

"I don't care, I am still the godfather."

"And mother," said a chunky kid grasping a box of pizza which he'd claimed as his own.

His remark set off a wave of laughter, and Steven gave the greasy-faced teen the finger.

"We officially have a new president," Tashonda said.

"Let's hope he can get us out of this mess," the teen mumbled between bites.

Tashonda waved away the beer Jenkins held out to her. Sam shifted awkwardly as Tashonda moved in next to her. "Need help with the unpacking?"

Sam smiled. "No thanks, I think we can manage the rest."

"Sure, we need help." Rachel threw Sam a wink.

"I don't want to put you out. Really, I'm sure we can manage the rest by ourselves."

Tashonda shrugged. "Can't blame a girl for trying."

"You can try with me any day." Jenkins smirked, moving to place his arm around Tashonda's shoulders.

"Not even if all the women on this planet mysteriously vanished." Her elbow caught him in his left side, making him gasp. She said her goodbyes and made her way out, as did several others. Jenkins trailed off after her, laughing.

"Ouch." Sam jumped the instant Rachel pinched her arm.

"Why did you let her go?" Rachel asked.

"No kidding, she's freakin' hot, and so into you," Steven cut in, as he reentered the front room. "You need to put an end to these meaningless one-night stands, Sam, and date someone with some real substance."

"I appreciate your concerns, but I have no interest in dating, so let's drop it," Sam retreated to her bedroom to unpack.

"Wow, she's never going to find love if she keeps pushing away all the good ones." Steven turned to Rachel. "Even though neither of you will talk about her past, I'm betting her very first girlfriend really did a number on her."

Rachel's solemn gaze followed her older sister down the hall. "In a way, she did," she said and left it at that.

Chapter Five

February 1, 2032

The winter was even more ruthless than the previous years had been. The last five months had not only brought strong winds, freezing rain, and record-breaking snowfall, but also silence from Marcus. Elaina needed to find out what was happening throughout the country, but more importantly, why hadn't Marcus rescued her from this place of solitude yet. Surely, he had plenty of time and resources to put an end to this world gone mad. So why was she still here? Maybe he'd forgotten her. Or maybe he couldn't remember where the cabin was located. She knew both excuses were absurd, but as isolated as this hillside was, she wouldn't have been surprised. Whatever the case, she required answers to her questions.

Elaina removed her wool pajamas and began her morning ritual of dressing in layers. She wasn't preparing to take on the frigid elements to shovel paths in the snow to each of the outbuildings, or to chop more wood, but simply to take a trip into town. First, she slipped on a set of insulated winter long johns, a recently heated pair of thermal socks were next. She pulled on blue jeans and a sweatshirt. She stuck her feet into hiking boots, then put on a thermal coat, stocking cap, her mother's handwoven scarf, and an insulated pair of work gloves. Feeling like the Stay-Puft Marshmallow Man, she was set.

She kept the sturdy cast-iron stove and covered fireplace burning, double-checking the wood pile before venturing out into the freezing morning air. Her outfit proved to be more than adequate as she trundled down the hill to her vehicle. Her feet crunched against the white blanket covering the ground, and twice she slipped, but each time she quickly recovered her footing.

Elaina was grateful the camouflaged tarp had prevented ice from collecting on the windshield, but the wind made a funnel of the thing as she struggled to fold it, increasing the already brutal chill stinging her cheeks. She slid onto the driver's seat and hurriedly closed the door, blocking out the wind. The engine made a slight groaning sound, the only sign of its brave but futile attempt to come to life. Elaina pushed the gas pedal to the floor and held it there while turning the key. This time a couple metallic clicks sounded followed by ominous silence.

Flustered, Elaina pulled the inside latch to pop the hood. She knew a few things about vehicles. Where the gas cap was located, how to check the oil, and the basics of adding air to a deflated tire. If any other automotive work was needed, Elaina had called the mechanic shop two blocks away from her apartment building and made an appointment. She no longer had that luxury. With the hood propped opened she surveyed the engine in the hopes something obvious, like a disconnected wire or a loose cap would present itself.

Dirty white mounds of foam covered the two wires fastened on the top edge of the battery. Was battery acid leaking out? She mumbled, "So much for a trip to town."

Elaina replaced the tarp over the vehicle. Seemed like her only option was to walk into town and purchase a new battery. By her calculation, it would take a good ten hours for her to make the trek and she'd need to leave early enough to arrive before the auto store closed. She could use a phone in town to call Marcus and then stay overnight at the one hotel before walking back the following morning.

The constantly changing weather was a concern. Getting stuck in the middle of a snow or ice storm was not appealing. She'd best not chance it. She really needed to talk to Marcus, but it would have to wait until the weather cleared up in a month or two. Until then, she had plenty of supplies to last her, including new books and DVDs to occupy her time.

She was grateful for the volume of purchases she had made on her last trip into town. There almost hadn't been room to fit everything into her over-sized SUV, but she had somehow managed to squeeze it all in. Combined with the stacks of military rations, and her rationing of the canned meat, beans, and chunky soups over the last several months, she wasn't going to starve. Lowering her head in defeat, Elaina labored up the hill to the warm cabin.

><

March 8, 2032, dawned with a chill in the air. Crime in Kansas City had almost tripled in the past two months, with no sign of slowing any time soon. The atmosphere in the city felt as if everyone had given up hope and begun an insane mission to kill one another. Sam was used to robberies, murders, and gang-related violence, but she was having a hard time wrapping her head around this new wave of brutality on the streets. Targeted bombings, random shootings in crowds, and extremist groups sparking bloody riots around town had become a daily scourge in her city.

By what Sam had heard from the media and her colleagues, this raging chaos was the same across the US. But she couldn't think about the problems of other cities, other towns. Kansas City had more than enough trouble to occupy her sleepless nights.

"Twenty-five college students in Georgia have been reported dead, many more injured." The anxious voice of the radio station's announcer incited Sam to push her squad car that much faster.

"Oh, my! This just in . . ." Sam turned up the radio to an ear-punishing volume. "We've received word of a gunman opening fire at one of the colleges here in Kansas City. We're awaiting confirmation and further details."

Sam knew the story to be true for she had received the call not more than ten minutes earlier and had been unable to reach her sister or Steven on either of their phones ever since. She steered her patrol car through a crowd of running students, toward the front of the main building on campus. She spotted Jenkins's car pull in ahead of her.

"It's been reported the first shooter in Georgia is dead. We've received confirmation he used some sort of explosive device on himself and those around him. No news yet on the number who've been injured or killed."

Sam flipped off her radio as she brought her car to a screeching halt. Sam unlocked and grabbed the shotgun from the holder, then jumped out and headed toward Jenkins. "Have you seen Rachel?" she asked, sounding almost hysterical.

"Calm down, Sam, or you're going to get yourself killed."

"Fuck calm!" Sam rotated toward the building.

Jenkins stopped her. "Sam, we'll go in. But first, you need to get your vest on, and take a few deep breaths."

Sam examined him briefly. Her gut told her he was right. She rushed back to the trunk of her patrol car for her bulletproof vest.

"Captain called," Jenkins shouted. He ushered students out as fast as he could. Several had blood covering their bodies and others helped carry out the injured. "He said to proceed with caution. There's a good chance the shooter has some kind of explosive device."

Tashonda and her rookie partner rushed up as they were about to head inside. "Are you doing all right?" Tashonda asked Sam.

Blocking out the terrifying images of her pregnant sister lying dead on the cold tile floor, Sam muttered, "Yes." She forced herself to focus on the task before them. Gripping her shotgun, she signaled to Jenkins she was ready.

"By twos. Sam and me up front, you and the kid follow."

Everyone indicated they understood. They made their way quickly inside the brick building and around to the base of the first set of stairs, each taking a position on either side of the area. When Sam and Jenkins moved forward, Tashonda and her partner rushed up to take their abandoned positions. They constantly checked behind them for any unexpected trouble.

They spotted the first dead student when they reached the top of the stairs.

"Crap," muttered Jenkins.

Sam looked from Jenkins to the motionless student. On closer inspection, she realized why Jenkins's tone was fraught. The red-haired kid was the same one he had denied a beer a mere two months earlier. Sam didn't recognize any of the other dead bodies scattered throughout the hall. Many seemed so young, giving Sam the impression this part of the campus was where the bulk of freshmen classes were held.

Jenkins motioned for Sam to take the far outside wall when they moved. She held up three fingers, counting silently down to one. Jenkins and Sam pivoted jointly around the corner, crouching low against opposite walls. They stopped at each of the doors along the way, and after inspecting the rooms, they directed any able students they spotted to move down the hall toward the main door. When they reached the third set of doors, Jenkins stopped, and scanned the area inside. He motioned for Sam to join him and the other two to stay back.

Sam and Jenkins shifted into the room. A small crowd of kids huddled in a far corner, and in the middle of the room, kneeling over a bloody, unmoving body, were Rachel and Steven. Sam's heart raced at seeing them both alive and unharmed. Jenkins quietly guided the rest of the students out as Sam examined the lifeless body.

"Rachel, get Steven out of here. I'll take care of Nathan," she muttered, the ache building in her heart. Nathan and Steven had been dating for close to a year, and seeing him lying there, was heart wrenching.

Rachel pulled the red, swollen-faced Steven with her as Sam felt Nathan's neck for a pulse. She didn't need the confirmation of her fingers, nor Jenkins's voice to tell her Nathan was already dead. She could tell by his ashen skin and the amount of blood pooled on the floor around him. Her partner touched her shoulder, bringing her back to the job at hand. She rose angrily to her feet to continue their search for other students and the perp or perps responsible.

They shuffled out, taking positions along the hall, stopping at each room. When they were two classrooms away from the end, all hell broke loose. A man jumped from the last room, screaming in a language Sam didn't recognize. He gripped the neck of a hysterical girl in one hand, the other held a raised automatic weapon. He sent two bursts of gunfire down the hall toward the cops, then dragged the crying girl back into the room.

Sam checked to make sure Jenkins was uninjured, then peered at the other two officers. Her heart skipped a beat when she saw Tashonda lying on her back, the rookie kneeling next to her. Just as she was about to rush to the unmoving woman, an earth-shattering explosion knocked her to the ground, and chunks of concrete and hot wreckage rained down around her.

Chapter Six

April 13, 2032

Sam arrived at the department after a long, tiring day in the city. Crime was at an all-time high. The president's public appeal last month didn't seem to have helped the situation much. Due to increased violence and deaths, the president declared a State of Emergency and banned the possession of firearms except for the military and law enforcement agencies. He'd said immediate incarceration would happen to anyone caught breaking this law and strongly urged citizens comply.

Her mood lifted at the sight of the petite woman heading down the hall toward her. Tashonda appeared healthy, cheerful. Her uniform hung looser than normal, but considering what she had been through, a little weight loss was to be expected.

"Did you miss me?" Tashonda gave Sam a seductive smile.

On any normal day, Sam would have evaded this engaging, highly flirtatious woman. Not because Sam wasn't attracted to her, but because she was. She had learned years ago, work and sex never mixed. Since that day at the college, when a bullet hit Tashonda in the leg, she'd been on sick leave, and Sam had worried. "Yes. We all did. How's the leg?"

Tashonda playfully narrowed her eyes. "Better, but you'd have known this if you came around to check on me."

"I sent you several care packages."

"Yes, with Jenkins. Thanks, by the way. Now he and my baby sister are dating." Tashonda arched an eyebrow.

Sam coughed away a laugh and avoided eye contact with Tashonda. When her cell phone rang, she gratefully held up a hand and politely excused herself from a conversation she really wasn't in the mood for. Her aunt started talking and Sam stiffened as she took in the grave news from her childhood hometown. Mister Dowell had been killed.

Her distress must have been obvious. Tashonda's question was layered with concern the moment Sam ended the call. "Is everything all right?"

Sam shoved her phone in her pocket. "That was my Aunt Agnes. One of my family's closest friends was shot and killed last night."

"Oh, I'm sorry. What happened?"

Sam shrugged. "She didn't want to tell me while I was at work, but she sounded pretty upset. I'm supposed to call her later tonight."

Tashonda placed a gentle hand on Sam's shoulder. "Let me know if you need anything."

"Kelly, Baker, meeting in ten minutes!" a male voice shouted from the other end of the hall. Both women acknowledged their sergeant, watching as he spun into the conference room.

"What's up with him?"

"Not sure. He's been like that for the past week." Sam smoothly played off a slight shoulder roll to the left, causing Tashonda's hand to slide off.

"Why do you constantly fight me on this? You know, you might find me irresistible if only you gave me a chance."

"It has nothing to do with you."

"Here we go." Tashonda said with attitude.

"You asked, so I'm telling you. I'm happy being single. I'm sorry, but I'm not in the market for a relationship of any kind."

"I'm not asking for the U-Haul truck, Sam. Just a drink. Hell, we can even make it coffee."

"Come on, you two," Jenkins called out, making his way down the hall. "We better get in there. I just got off the phone with the Sarge and he sounds pretty upset."

Tashonda gave Jenkins an annoyed glance before stomping to the conference room.

"You know, I don't think she likes me dating her sister," Jenkins said.

Sam followed Tashonda into the room. Sam didn't care one way or the other, she was only relieved Jenkins had shown up when he did. "She will, give her time."

The lengthy room was unusually quiet as they made their way into the crowded area and took the open seats in the back. Sam noticed eight men in dark blue business suits lining the outer walls. At first glance, she had them pegged for FBI agents, but something about the way they glared at her fellow officers told her she was wrong.

"What's going on?" Tashonda leaned over, whispering in Sam's ear.

Before Sam had a chance to respond, a tall man in a dark blue suit sauntered into the room. His hair was short, reddish-brown, and neatly tapered to the middle of his neck. The suit he wore had a slightly different cut than the others, showing off his slim waist and powerfully built chest. He made his way casually up to the podium in the front of the room.

Something about the man's eyes disturbed Sam.

"I'm Agent Brandon Clayton with the HTF. For those of you who have not been watching the news, this would be the Homeland Task Force. We are the agents assigned to this department. Our orders are to assist you fine officers with the implementation of the Homeland Protection Act. We will be with you for as long as it takes to put an end to this crisis. Please don't hesitate to let me know if there is anything I can do for you."

HTF agents began dropping thick books on the desks in front of each officer in the room. Sam and those around her jumped at the loud thumps. Without thinking, Sam peered over to the podium. Her body froze. Brandon was eyeing her like a starving lion glares at its prey. She had never seen a pair of eyes like his. They were cold, dark to the point of being black. If someone had asked her to describe them, she would have used words like disturbing, sinister, or maybe even evil. She shifted uncomfortably in her seat, opened her copy of the book seconds after it thumped down on her desk, and stared at the tiny, typed words, reluctant to look up again.

"These laws are absurd!"

The voice of a fellow officer brought Sam out of her daze, and she sat up in time to see the middle-aged man rise to his feet.

Brandon said, "I'll answer any questions once—"

"These provisions in your *so-called* Protection Act take away every constitutional right we as Americans hold dear."

"We *are* in the middle of a crisis—"

Cutting Brandon off, the officer addressed the room. "Flip to page thirty-nine."

Sam could tell by the grimace on Brandon's face, this didn't happen often. Pages rustled as everyone, including her, thumbed through the book. Everything was so crammed together she had no idea what he was referring to.

"Section A, Sub-part D, of law HPA thirteen-dash-seven." The officer began to read aloud:

"Any individual discovered to have broken any of these laws, attempted to undermine the provisions of this Act, in whole or in part, or is deemed a threat to the Government of this Nation can be detained for an indefinite period of time, without prior notification or elucidation to any other individual or party. The direct or extended family of said individual may also be incarcerated. In addition, the Government will have the right to confiscate any and all property and assets held by the individual or family, to dispose of in accordance with the Government's immediate needs."

The officer slammed his book closed and tossed it onto the desk beside him. "I became an officer to serve and protect. Not to become a member of the Nazi party!"

Brandon waved down several of his men who were moving angrily toward the officer. "I'm sorry you feel this way, but this Act was created by our government, and as a fine officer of this country, you are required to enforce its laws."

"Not anymore." He emptied his weapon, placed it and his badge on top of the book, and angrily exited the room.

A few of the other officers stood to follow suit. Brandon's voice was clear, unwavering. "In case all of you have forgotten, we are in a major depression. The unemployment lines, work lines, and bread lines you go by every day are not figments of your imagination. They're real. Families are being separated because of starvation and poverty. Please, I beg you to reconsider." Despite his empathetic tone his eyes held no sympathy. "Think about your children, and those who count on you for support, before you walk out that door."

Sam detested this man, but Brandon did get his message across. One by one, the officers slowly retook their seats. Sam didn't *need* the money, but she did feel a *need* to wear her uniform. Now, more than ever.

The meeting lasted for well over an hour. Once everyone had filed out, Sam made her way to the locker-room to change. She was halfway to the main doors in her civilian clothes when Brandon stepped from one of the larger offices.

"Ah, Officer Kelly, I was hoping I might run into you. Could you spare a moment? There are some things I would like to discuss."

"Actually I was on my way home. Could it wait?"

"It will only take a minute."

Sam paused for a few seconds before following Brandon into his newly claimed office. He motioned for her to take a seat in front of his desk and made his way around to his position of authority.

"I really must be—"

"Your name is Samantha?" He flipped through a file on his desk. Hers, she assumed.

Sam nodded, unsure why she was here.

"Several of the officers said you preferred to be called Sam, is that right?"

Another nod.

"Okay, it says here you were in the United States Army for eight years before becoming a police officer. An 18 Echo, Special Forces Communications Sergeant. Fascinating. Your unique military experience gave you an interesting skill-set, including parachute training. Oh, and also scuba diving. Interesting career choice for a woman."

Sam didn't respond.

Flipping a few pages, Brandon read deeper into the file. "In the two years you have been a police officer, you've earned several awards, including a certificate from the mayor himself."

"Have I done something wrong?"

Brandon closed the folder. "On the contrary, Sam, I was planning on giving you a promotion."

"What kind of promotion?" Sam shifted in her seat as Brandon moved in front of her and leaned against the edge of his desk.

"You are exactly the sort of person the HTF needs to help heal an out-of-control nation. You are tough, patriotic, a real go-getter, if I may be so bold." He motioned with a flick of his head over his shoulder. "Your file says you were deployed into combat zones, have been given two purple hearts, and a bronze star. Yes, I could use a woman of your caliber. How would you like to come work for me?"

Sam kept her voice level, her eyes trained on Brandon. "I like being a cop. Sorry, but I decline."

Brandon seemed slightly taken aback but recovered quickly. "Being an agent will more than triple your current salary, not to mention—"

Sam stood. It took some restraint, but she remained composed. "There's more to life than money."

Brandon grinned. "Oh, so you're one of those . . ." He moved closer to Sam, to the point he was invading her personal space. "There are other benefits that come with the promotion." His voice was low, his eyes hungry. He placed his right hand suggestively on Sam's shoulder.

Sam bit back the urge to deck him. She figured, with these new laws, striking a member of the HTF would probably earn her the firing squad. "I'm with someone, but thanks anyway."

Brandon smiled. He allowed his fingers to glide leisurely down Sam's arm before he withdrew his hand. "I guess we're done here, then."

As she was about to leave the room, Brandon called out, "Sam. It might take some finagling, but I eventually get what I want."

"Not this time," Sam muttered, leaving Brandon's office.

As HTF agents continued to work their way into police stations all across America, Sam could not believe how rapidly life in in the United States was changing. The once free air which soared throughout the nation was transforming into something thicker, dangerous. Her once beloved land of the free had converted into a police state. For Sam, the Constitution was feeling more like a discarded scrap of paper, than an affirmation of freedom and independence. She felt helpless.

The riots in the city grew steadily worse as the president announced new laws one after another. The three most recent laws were the least favorite by far. First, was a mandatory nationwide registration of every man, woman, and child. This law had unregistered immigrants taken away in handcuffs, no matter their age. Next, a mandatory curfew from nine in the evening, to five in the morning. Lastly, venturing outside the commute radius of forty miles from one's home address required proof of authorization, and was usually only granted for work reasons.

Sam, along with most of the other officers, often let people off with warnings when the HTF was not around, but if the HTF was present and the citizens were without the proper travel documentation, they had no choice but to immediately incarcerate them, even if the officers felt their excuses were justified.

On top of everything else, Sam had done everything she could to avoid Brandon over the last several weeks. She changed in and out of her uniform at home and always checked the shift schedule to see when Brandon worked. On days he went in early she waited in the parking lot for Tashonda or Jenkins to show before clocking in. Not that she was afraid of Brandon. Sam had every confidence she could kick his ass if needed. But she had no desire to place herself or her career in an uncomfortable situation. Thankfully, her preventive measures worked.

Today was the first day in a week she hadn't been called in early for riot control. She made her way down to the detail board with Tashonda and Jenkins, the three engaged in conversation. As usual, the topic involved Jenkins and Tashonda's sister.

"What is checkpoint detail?" Tashonda asked, reading from the board.

"Checkpoint detail is a new system we're implementing, from this day forward," Brandon replied from behind them. He gave Sam a covert wink before continuing. "Find the agent in charge, and he'll fill you in on where you need to be."

As they turned to leave, Brandon spoke to Sam, "Officer Kelly, may I have a word?"

Tashonda and Jenkins stopped.

"Just Officer Kelly. You two may go."

Neither Tashonda nor Jenkins moved. Sam gave them a warning look, letting both know not to press the matter. She followed Brandon into his office, keeping alert and at a distance.

Brandon shut the door behind him. "Officer Kelly, please take a seat."

Sam had known for some time now this moment would arrive. She sat, wondering whether she should hand in her weapon and badge now, or if she should wait until after she got in a few good punches. Sam decided to wait.

"I believe you're avoiding me."

Sam stared silently up at the arrogant man.

"Have you changed your mind about the job offer?"

"No, and I don't plan to."

"You know I could have you fired."

Sam jumped up, ready for a fight. She was sick and tired of being nervous about going to work every day. She wanted this to end, and she wanted it to end now. "Then fire me!"

Brandon raised an eyebrow, surprised by her outburst. His startlement was short-lived. "I like you, Sam. I'm not going to fire you. I was—"

"Threatening me?"

"Of course not. You have me all wrong." He moved closer. "I've never met a woman like you. So determined, so full of confidence in the way you carry yourself."

Sam's voice was low, angry. "What do you want?"

"Why, I want you, of course. I only need to find your weakness. Even though it's taking longer than expected, I can see you will be worth the wait."

His smirk felt like a slap in the face. Sam moved a step forward with her fist clenched. "You can go to hell!" she shouted.

"Is this foreplay?"

The door flung open, and Tashonda and Jenkins rushed in.

Brandon was outraged. He pivoted sharply toward the intruders, like a coiled snake preparing to strike. His dark eyes softened instantly as if a new personality had taken over, giving Sam the feeling Brandon's wiring wasn't up to code.

"We heard yelling," Jenkins glowered from Brandon to the heated Sam.

"Everything's fine. Right, Officer Kelly?"

Sam gestured with a jerk of her chin, too upset to speak.

"You see. Now if you three would leave, I have some work to do."

Tashonda spoke as soon as they were at a safe distance down the hall. "What's going on, Sam?"

"I can handle it."

"He's the reason you've been acting odd lately, isn't he?" Jenkins was clearly upset. "Sam, you need to see the captain, you can't mess around with these people, especially him."

"Don't you think I know that?" Sam felt bad at how angrily her words came out. He was only trying to help. "Listen, thank you both for your concern, but I'll handle this on my own. I'm not sure what Agent Clayton is capable of, and I don't want either of you or the captain to get into trouble."

Like with Jenkins, Tashonda didn't seem happy with Sam's response. Thankfully, she had enough sense to know Sam was right. "Fine, but from here on out, we'll do what we can to watch each other's backs."

Checkpoint detail consisted of blocking off streets and highways throughout the city in order to search every vehicle for firearms and travel paperwork. The detail was grueling as the three of them, with their sergeant, worked alongside four newly assigned HTF agents. Agents who became excited whenever they caught someone breaking one of these new laws. Sam wondered if the agents were paid a commission with each arrest they made.

"I need your papers," Sam informed a middle-aged man traveling with his wife and two frightened kids.

Sam examined the man's travel papers. Thankfully, the documents were in order. "Could you pop the trunk, please?"

"What do you want to see inside my trunk for?" His tone and the building stress on his face sent up warning flags. Sam peered over to where the HTF agents were tearing through two other vehicles.

"It's routine, sir. Are you carrying anything which would be considered illegal or unsafe?"

"No, we're only going to my brother's down south."

"Please pop the trunk."

He reluctantly did as she asked.

Sam walked to the rear of the car and searched through the luggage and boxes filled with the family's valuables. Right when she thought all was clear, the outline of an object underneath a sheet in the far corner caught her eye. She reached in and lifted the covering enough to see the tip of a rifle.

"Sir, I need you step back here."

Through the window, Sam observed the man squeeze his wife's hand. She waited while he climbed slowly from the car. Frightened, he made his way to her.

Keeping her voice low, Sam questioned the man. "Sir, why do you have this?"

"Ma'am, I'm a law-abiding man. I bought this item two days ago for this trip. We really are only trying to get to my brother's farm. With everything going on, I need to protect my family, don't I?"

"It's illegal."

"It's necessary."

Sam caught sight of one of the HTF agents staring at them with a scowl on his face. Without waiting, she muttered her warnings to the man. "Don't bring it back into the city. If you come upon another check-point, find some way to dispose of it, understand?"

"Okay." He wiped his brow with relief then hustled to the driver's side of his car. Sam saw the agent making his way toward her. She closed the trunk and moved up to the man's window, instructing him to leave.

"Hey!" She heard a shout from behind her as the car pulled away.

"They were clear," Sam insisted, glowering to the agent.

"My ass, they—"

A shot rang out. She and the agent spun with their hands on their sidearms.

"What the fuck are you doing?" screamed their sergeant to another agent. He rushed over where a biker lay sprawled on the ground.

"He had a gun!" insisted the agent.

"He wasn't going for it. You didn't have to shoot him."

The sergeant crouched next to the unmoving man. "He's still alive."

Everyone hurried to see.

"I can fix that." The moment the agent brought his weapon up to take aim at the injured biker, the sergeant drew his sidearm. Within a flash, everyone was pointing weapons at each other. Cops at the agents, agents at the cops.

"What the hell is going on here?" the captain roared.

Sam kept her eyes on the agent, her weapon pointed at his chest.

"I'm ordering everyone to lower their weapons now!" Brandon's words were hard, crisp, and his agents obeyed. As soon as they had their weapons holstered, the officers lowered their own.

The captain called in an ambulance for the injured biker, as each agent and officer gave their side of the story.

"This shit is getting out of hand!" the captain bellowed the second he got off the radio.

"Yes, it is!" Brandon hissed. "Next time your officers draw on my agents, I'll have them all arrested!"

"You saw it yourself! Your agent was going to shoot an unconscious man!"

"It's within his right, and we're in charge! I want everyone in my office as soon as this shift is over. This includes you, Captain.

Chapter Seven

May 1, 2032

The last of the winter storms passed through over a week earlier, followed by several warmer days and a few frostless nights. This gave Elaina the hope she needed to tackle the thirty-mile hike into town. She wasn't positive how heavy her backpack would be with a new battery crammed inside, so she packed light, with barely enough provisions for the round-trip journey.

The nine months since her last venture into town had been hard. Even with the disciplined way she had handled her abundance of supplies, she had less than three boxes of military rations left, all her canned and dry food was gone, and her numerous attempts to set small animal traps, had left her with empty snares for over a month. She followed the survival books to the letter yet seemed to be doing something wrong.

She left before first light, staying hidden within the thickness of the trees, but near enough to the road to prevent her from veering off course and becoming lost. Impressed by the time she was making, she allowed herself an unscheduled stop at the halfway point for a quick snack and her third potty break.

Even though she had worked out in the cabin throughout the winter months, a regimen of push-ups, sit-ups, and various calisthenics, her legs still ached from moving through the rough terrain. The foliage was thick and the steep Ozark hills didn't make the hike any easier. By the time Elaina finally made her way past the first building, her body was screaming out in exhaustion.

Dusk blanketed the quiet town, pushing Elaina to move faster. She was unsure what time the store closed and wanted to purchase a battery before using the phone. Afterwards, she would head to the small down-town motel for the night.

Something felt off as she trudged along the first of several houses lining the streets, toward the heart of the town square. Right before her last turn she realized what had caused her uneasiness. There were no sounds of laughter from children playing. No cars drove past, their passengers waving a friendly small-town greeting. All was silent, motionless, unlike her other trips into this once-spirited place.

She glanced around, as if for the first time noticing the cold, unfriendly houses standing on either side of the road. Several homes were empty, vacant of their former tenants. The rest had bars or boards covering the windows with no porch lights on. A chill passed through her. Either the temperature had abruptly nose-dived, or the harsh appearance of the town had drained all heat from her bones. Elaina pulled her jacket around her tighter.

Her inclination was to buy her battery and leave. The eerie atmosphere gave her pause. Had it finally happened? She'd prayed to a higher power to give Marcus the strength to halt the events, but now she was certain her prayers had gone unanswered. The fall of America had begun.

Feeling under her jacket for the security of the gun, Elaina quickened her pace. Her heart sank when she caught sight of the downtown square. The general store was not only closed, but an out of business sign was posted on the door. Thankfully, the auto parts store across the street was still open. She stepped inside and found an extremely limited inventory.

It took several minutes for the man behind the counter to determine which battery her SUV needed, and several more minutes for him to find one. She felt his eyes watch as she placed the battery into her backpack. Leaving the store, she made a beeline for the payphone on the main road.

She dug a handful of change from the front pocket of her jeans, placed quarter after quarter into the slot at the top of the black and silver mounted box, and dialed Marcus's number. On the third ring the phone was picked up, but instead of hearing the familiar voice on the other end, the line yielded complete silence.

She waited several seconds, wondering if the phone had lost connection. "Hello? Marcus, are you there?"

No response came. She hung up the phone and repeated the entire process again. "Marcus?"

"Is this Elaina? Sorry, Marcus stepped out, but he'll be back shortly." The sound of the deep male voice on the other end froze Elaina in place. "If you don't mind waiting for a second, I can run and get him for you. I know he's been anxious to talk to you for several months now."

The man spoke slowly. Playing for time? *If anyone other than I should answer, then it means I'm dead.* The memory of Marcus's words cut like a knife, and Elaina slammed the receiver down hard.

Marcus was dead, and they were trying to track her location through the phone. *Do they know where I am?* She gripped the booth for support. Her mind whirled. Her body felt weak, and she fought to steady herself. *How long do I have?* Her stomach knotted, causing her to fight down the urge to be sick from fear. She silently cursed herself, taking several deep breaths for courage.

Not wanting to linger in the open, Elaina made her way out of town. Her eyes kept a constant watch for any signs of movement around her. She didn't care night was falling, or the temperature had dropped several degrees within the last twenty minutes. All she wanted to do was to seek shelter in the safety of the cabin. Once there, she would plan her next course of action.

Today was the third day of May. Other than the weather, nothing was changing. Sam slouched through the front door and collapsed heavily onto the overstuffed chair in the living room with a long sigh. Rachel sat on the couch with Steven, where he spoke softly to his unborn goddaughter. Baby-talking words of praise inches away from Rachel's stomach.

Steven exchanged an unmistakable frown with Rachel, before swinging his attention onto Sam. "You're home late, is everything all right?"

Sam gave a weak smile and muttered sarcastically, "Oh, you know, yet another wonderful day with the HTF."

Rachel stood and left the room. As she walked out, Sam noticed how much her sister's baby bump was growing. Even with the world falling apart, and the baby's father fleeing from their lives, Sam was beyond happy Rachael decided to go through with the pregnancy. The thought of having a nephew or niece was exciting, and she would do everything to keep them safe. Rachael returned with a cold bottle of beer and handed it to her sister.

"Where did you get this?" Sam tapped on the glass. "Beer in a bottle. Have you been getting into the emergency fund?" She took a long soothing drink. There hadn't been beer in the house since the night they'd moved in. With the high prices and rationing, Sam denied herself this one small treat, refusing to dip into the inheritance her parents had left them. Instead, she spent her allotted mad money from her paycheck on baby items.

Rachel smiled. "Steven knows a guy who knows a guy, and if I wanted to get into the emergency fund then I would."

Sam grunted to Rachel as her eyes fixed on Steven. "You don't like beer."

"Yes, but you do, and with everything you've done for me, and with the strain you've been under lately, I figured you needed it."

Sam gazed at him, touched, before lowering her eyes to the drink in her hand. "So, you've noticed?"

"We both have, and we've been worried about you," Rachel said, reclaiming her seat on the couch.

"Sorry. I tried to keep the work stress away from home." Sam heaved a sigh. "I guess I didn't do so well."

Steven scooted his butt to the edge of the couch. "What's going on, Sam?"

She didn't respond.

"We're your family, please talk to us." Rachel's eyes were tender, reminding Sam of their mother.

Letting out a deep breath of air, Sam finally gave in. The weight hanging heavy on her shoulders seemed to lift as she spoke. She talked, in great detail, about Brandon and the stressors she was going through at work because of him and the HTF.

Once she was done, Steven angrily got up, replacing her empty bottle with a fresh one. "He can't do that!"

"Unfortunately, he can," Sam grumbled.

"Let's leave here, Sam. Steven and I have been talking about it. Let's sell the house and move to the farm."

Sam shook her head. This thought had entered her mind several times in the last month alone, but Steven and Rachel's education was important. "You both need to finish school."

"We can go to school in Springfield. We've already applied to the college for the next semester and," Rachel paused, jumping up to grab two envelopes from the kitchen table. "We both got in. It's around forty-five minutes from the farm and we can carpool."

Sam examined the envelopes in Rachel's hand. For a split second, she felt a wave of parental anger for not having been informed sooner of this plan. Then she remembered they were mature enough to make their own decisions.

"Is this what you both want?"

Simultaneously, they nodded.

Sam stood and studied the view of the neighborhood through the bay window. Several of the houses around them were empty, and a few had boards on their windows due to the growing vandalism throughout the city. She closed her eyes to the heartbreaking scene. She was tired of her once-beloved city. The violence and the ever-growing homeless population on the streets was disheartening. Yes, she was ready to leave. More than ready. "I guess a move might do us all a bit of good."

Sam was off work the next two days, giving her time to get the affairs with the house in order, along with gathering all their financial documentation and travel passes. At first, she had planned to give two weeks' notice at work, but the thought of being on the road, heading away from Kansas City and Brandon Clayton, was more appealing than Sam had first realized. She finally decided on a week.

What would she do for work when they arrived at the farm? The thought of applying at the police department in Springfield crossed her mind, but she wasn't keen on continuing a profession which forced her to work hand-in-hand with the HTF. She didn't want to be a farmer, this much she knew. She loved the land and the wide-open space, but she had worked it when she was younger with her father and Aunt Agnes. Even though the work was hard and fulfilling, running a farm was also lonely, and too tranquil for Sam.

When Sam opened the front door, new piles of packing boxes stacked along the walls in the front room greeted her. The view was amusing. Rachel and Steven were as ready to leave town as she was, if not more. She called out to them she was home, placed her weapon and holster on the table, and headed into the kitchen.

Sam grabbed a beer from the fridge and searched the house for Rachel and Steven, eager to share the exciting news. The realtor had called her less than thirty minutes ago. She'd found an out-of-town buyer for their house. A company in Chicago was purchasing homes in the surrounding neighborhoods to demolish. They believed transforming the prized landscape into condominiums for upper-class citizens would earn them a sizeable fortune. Citizens who were apparently unaffected by the Depression. Those were not the woman's exact words, but Sam read between the lines as the boisterous woman spoke.

They agreed to Sam's asking price. All she had left to do was go to the realtor's office in the morning before work and sign some paperwork to close the deal.

Sam didn't find anyone on the main or top floor of the house. Feeling cheerier than she had in a long time, she made her way downstairs to the finished basement, whistling an old nineties tune as she went. She stopped abruptly at the bottom of the stairs. The lights in the main room were off, giving the suggestion no one was down there. Sam placed her beer on the pool table and checked all the rooms, yelling Rachel's and Steven's names with a building surge of worry.

Heart racing, Sam ran up the stairs taking two at a time. She shouted into the eerie silence, retracing her steps through the entire house. Her search ended in the front room where she paced the area from the window to the door then back again.

The wall clock read five minutes to nine. Five minutes until the start of curfew. Sam was a police officer and allowed to venture out past curfew without a permit. Rachel and Steven were not.

As the clock struck nine Sam had her jacket on about to leave. The front door swung open. "Where were you?" Sam asked.

Rachel entered the house. Her gaze darted frantically around the room. "Has Steven come home yet?"

Sam fought to keep her voice controlled. "I thought he was with you."

"He was, but I left him at the college three hours ago to finish his transfer paperwork. I went to rent the moving truck, and he was supposed to meet me out front after he finished." Rachel was terrified. "Sam, a riot broke out at the school. I drove around for a while, but when it got so late, I didn't know what to do." Rachel stared toward the door. "I thought maybe he came home on foot or got a ride. I need to go find him." Her last remark was almost a cry.

Sam grabbed her arm. "No, I'll go. You wait here. If he comes home, you call me."

Rachel wiped her eyes.

"Whatever you do, don't leave the house," Sam said.

The first stop Sam made was the security building located on the college campus. None of their security staff had reported seeing a student meeting Steven's description after curfew check. Both guards promised to call Sam if they found him on their rounds. She swept the area twice in her truck and then drove toward her department.

Sam knew if they'd arrested anyone during the riot the detainees would be taken to her police station since the school fell under its jurisdiction. Sam parked in front of the building and entered through the main door. She was surprised to see the front desk stood empty. The halls were also deserted.

The building was far too quiet, giving her an inkling something bad had happened. Her gut told her to push on. The unpleasant feeling in her stomach drastically increased when she reached the stairway leading down to the holding level. She heard a muffled commotion coming from the closed door below.

Sam wasn't prepared for the horrific view when she opened the door at the bottom of the stairs. Three HTF agents surrounded Steven's bloodied, crumpled body lying on the floor. Their jackets off, sleeves rolled up high, they were enjoying the beating they were inflicting on the defenseless teenager.

Their laughter filled her with rage. Instinctively, Sam reached under her jacket for her gun. When her hand came away empty, the image of her weapon lying useless on the table at home flashed in her mind. She scanned the room for a weapon as one agent punched Steven hard on his swollen face, and another aimed a powerful kick to his stomach.

Sam rushed forward, grabbing a metal chair as she went. She hurled it with as much force as she could at the closest of the three agents. The man's high-pitched shrieks, combined with a cracking sound that followed, played like gratifying music in Sam's ears. She aimed a ferocious kick into another agent's kneecap, and he collapsed on the floor wailing.

The last agent standing surveyed his fallen comrades in disbelief. He narrowed his eyes at Sam with a smile rolling across his tight lips. "Little girl officer wants to play?"

Sam remembered this man, the agent who had watched her inspect the car with the rifle in the trunk on the first day of Checkpoint Detail. The agent she had pulled her weapon on, and who had his pointed at her.

She didn't hear the other agents enter the room until it was too late. Sam spun on her heels but had no time to react. A stout muscular man tackled her to the ground, then aimed two hard punches straight into her kidneys, she doubled over with pain.

"That's enough!" Brandon shouted from the doorway.

"But, sir, do you see what she did to our men?"

"Be quiet! I said everything happening here tonight is off the record. Now, put the kid back into his cell, and take Officer Kelly up to my office!"

Hands grabbed Sam's arms and two men lifted her onto her feet. She roughly shook them off before spinning angrily around to face Brandon. "What the fuck is going on!"

Brandon clicked his tongue. "Such language. Please follow these men and I'll explain everything to you when we're alone."

"Kiss my ass!"

Brandon motioned to the agent who was placing Steven into one of the empty cells. "I'll call you later tonight—either to kill that young man or to release him into Officer Kelly's care. Do you have a problem carrying out either one of those orders?"

"No, sir, I don't," the agent said. He threw a sneer in Sam's direction.

"Good, now, Officer Kelly, please accompany these men to my office."

Sam pushed past the men. She muttered, "I know the fucking way."

As she reached the stairs Sam overheard Brandon order his agents to stay put.

Brandon entered the office several seconds after Sam. "Please take a seat." He closed and locked his door.

Sam picked up the chair and threw it with all her force into the built-in shelves in the back of the room. It hit with a thunderous crash, bringing books, shattered glass, and splintered wood down onto the high polished floor.

"Feel better?" Brandon asked with raised eyebrows.

"Not yet," Sam said, taking two steps toward the amused man.

"It only takes one bullet to end the life of the boy downstairs. Do you really want to see that happen?" He leaned against the edge of his desk.

"What do you want?"

Brandon stared at Sam evenly. "You know what I want."

"I'm not for sale!"

"All right. I have your answer." Brandon casually stood and headed to the closed door.

The instant his hand touched the metal handle, Sam dropped her gaze. "You have no soul," she whispered, fighting down the urge to vomit.

Brandon spun to her, surprised. "Sam, I'm not your enemy. I care for you a great deal. You have no idea the lengths I had to go through to plan this night."

Sam glared, dumbfounded.

"Please understand, everything about you inspires me. I have sat in this room for hours upon hours thinking what this moment would be like."

"What do I need to do?" Sam didn't want to hear any more. She only wanted this night to end.

"Why, be with me, of course."

"Then you will let Steven go?"

"You have my word."

Sam swallowed a few times, taking shallow breaths. Doing her best to block the experience from her mind, she walked over to Brandon, unsure of what to do. Her chest ached. Her insides grew colder than ice as she fought down the cry building in her throat. She wanted to be sick, to strike out, and to run as far away from this soulless monster as she could and never look back.

Brandon leaned in, preparing to kiss Sam on the lips, but Sam pulled away. Brandon tried again, but his effort was met with the same ending. "Fine. We'll chalk it up as a business deal!" he spat. He removed his jacket and threw it onto his desk.

Sam felt ill as Brandon unfastened his shoulder holster, tossing it aside, angrily undid his belt, and unzipped his pants. He positioned himself against the edge of his desk and pulled Sam to him. She closed her eyes and brought her head down to the man's unfastened pants. Sam reluctantly lowered the top of his boxers and Brandon forcefully pulled them up, pushing Sam's hand away.

"Isn't this what you wanted?" Sam whispered.

"Fuck you!" Brandon moved around his desk and picked up the phone. "My own hand has more passion than you."

Sam rushed to him, a mixture of anger and fear spreading through her. She yanked the handset from his hand and threw the phone hard to the floor where it split apart on impact.

"How dare you—"

Sam shoved Brandon roughly against the wall. With one jerking motion, she tore Brandon's shirt open, sending buttons flying everywhere. She kicked buttons aside and dropped to her knees. Sam yanked his trousers down and covered his penis with her mouth, sucking hard, wishing to cause him as much pain as possible. She could feel Brandon's muscles stiffen with desire. Sam closed her eyes tight as unwanted tears slid down her cheeks.

Sam placed Steven gently into her truck, buckled his injured body in, and closed the door. She leaned forward, vomiting up everything in her stomach and then some. Refusing to look at the building, Sam climbed behind the wheel and started the vehicle. She drove as fast as she could to the hospital, while images of the last hour ripped through her mind.

"Damn woman, you're remarkable," Brandon had said after the deed was done.

Sam fastened her jeans and walked toward the door. Before she twisted the handle, Brandon's words tore through her. "What, no cuddling? Maybe next time."

Sam was livid. "There's not going to be a next time," she said through clenched teeth.

Brandon's laughter was straight-up sinister. "Oh, I'm afraid you're wrong, my sweet dyke."

Sam opened the door feeling sick. She didn't want to hear the sound of Brandon's voice ever again.

"I'd appreciate it if you made sure we didn't have to go through the trouble of bringing the boy in. There's really no telling what my agents will do next time."

Sam had slammed the door on the repulsive sound of Brandon's snickering.

She swallowed the urge to vomit again as she forced the disturbing image from her mind. Steven's raspy cough made her push the truck faster, speeding down the winding streets of the desolate city. Sam picked up her phone and called Rachel to let her know she'd found Steven and was taking him to the hospital. She also told her sister to go through the house and make sure all the doors and windows were secure. And finally, Sam instructed her sister to grab her weapon off the table and keep it within arm's reach until she returned home.

"What's going on, Sam?"

"Nothing, Rachel. I'll pick you up after I get Steven checked in."

The waiting room wasn't crowded and with Steven's condition and Sam's badge, the staff wheeled him into an exam room. Sam paced along the edges of the carpet separating the waiting area from the tiled walkway. After what seemed like hours, the doctor came out and informed Sam that Steven's condition was stable. Sam thanked the older woman, then headed to her truck to pick up Rachel.

"How is he?" Rachel asked as soon as Sam stepped into the house.

"Two cracked ribs, a broken nose, and his hand is smashed." Sam forced out a shaky sigh. "He's covered in bruises, cuts, and both of his eyes are swollen shut."

"What happened to him? Who did this?" Rachel asked.

"HTF agents. Please get ready and pack Steven a bag. I need to take a quick shower."

Sam ran up the full length of the stairs, taking two at a time. Not her usual charging from place to place but more of a retreat. Rachel followed Sam upstairs, determined to get an explanation.

The instant Rachel entered Sam's bathroom her shoulders fell. Sobs poured out over the sound of the high-pressured shower. Only one other time in Rachel's life she had seen her big sister cry. Twelve years ago, when Sam was sixteen and Rachel was seven, an experience Rachel knew she would never forget. Their parents had brought Sam home from the hospital, and like now, Sam was in the shower crying.

The scene played out in heartbreaking *déjà vu*, except Sam was now twenty-eight and Rachel was nineteen. Rachel opened the shower door and took in Sam's harsh movements, scrubbing her flesh. Her sister's eyes were red with tears. Rachel stepped into the shower, wrapping her arms tight around Sam. They knelt into a ball as they had so many years ago, except this time Rachel wasn't wearing her pink pajamas, but a soaked pair of maternity jeans and a drenched blouse. Rachel rocked Sam until her sister's cries subsided and her tears finally ceased.

Neither spoke about what had happened as they exited the shower, Sam finished getting ready, and Rachel went to change out of her wet clothes and pack Steven an overnight bag. Rachel watched in silence as Sam double-checked the security of the house before placing her weapon in the shoulder holster. The ride to the hospital was equally silent, and Rachel fought the urge to glance at her sister. She wanted to say something, to reassure Sam everything would be all right. Her big sister could overcome anything. She'd already proven this in the past. As she watched Sam's eyes, though, she could see, 'all right' was still too far away. So she remained silent. Unmoving.

"You get out here, and I'll go park." Sam stopped the truck in the circle drive around the emergency room entrance.

Rachel paused, but after glancing into Sam's eyes, she assented and climbed down from the passenger seat. She stood for a few seconds watching Sam's truck pull away.

Two long days passed before Steven was awake and back to his cheerful self. He complained often about the hospital food, so on this trip to see him, Sam sneaked in a large greasy cheeseburger with a side of equally unhealthy fries. Tashonda wandered in thirty minutes later carrying a five-pound box of chocolates and a get-well card signed by the entire precinct.

Rachel was pulling at the covers and adjusting the bed, when Steven asked the question Sam wasn't ready to answer. "How did you get the agents to let me go?"

Tashonda's hand hovered over the assortment of chocolates, her frown glued on Steven. "I thought you were caught in the middle of a riot. That's what Rachel told me, anyway."

Steven shrugged as he swallowed a hefty bite of cheeseburger. "No, I avoided the riot easily enough, but these HTF agents grabbed me when I was waiting for Rachel to return."

Replacing the lid, Tashonda studied Sam, even though she directed her query to Steven. "What happened next?" Her voice sounded calm, but her eyes were full of fury.

Steven used a wet wipe to clean off his hands. "They took me back to the station and beat the shit out of me. Didn't tell me what I did wrong, only pounded on me until Sam showed up." He waved a hand to Sam. "She came in and took out two before someone tackled her from behind."

"Then what happened?"

Steven shook his head, wincing at the movement. "I was in and out of consciousness by then, but I do remember some man telling Sam to go upstairs, and if not, I was dead . . ." Steven's voice trailed off, his eyes darting to Sam. "Was that Brandon? What did he want from you, Sam?"

Sam angled her body away.

"I'm going to kill him!" Tashonda shouted, bringing two nurses into the room.

Sam waved them out. She closed the door before pivoting to Tashonda. "Why? So, they can come after you and the ones you love?"

"He can't get away with this!" Tears filled Tashonda's eyes as she squinted at Sam.

"He can, and he did." Sam walked over to Tashonda. "He's crazy. Tashonda, you need to listen to me. Do you want what happened to Steven to happen to your mom or dad? What about your baby sister?"

Tashonda didn't say a word.

"We're leaving. I have almost the entire house packed, so once Steven can travel, we're gone."

She tried to hand Tashonda her badge and gun, but the woman waved them away. "He is crazy, we all know it. Do you think he will come after you once he knows you've left?"

"I'm sure of it," Sam said.

"Keep them. I have an idea." Tashonda left the room before Sam could stop her.

She returned over twenty minutes later and seemed less upset than before. "I called the captain. Spent most of the conversation calming him down and reassuring him you were all right. He's going to do all he can to help, including putting you on extended family sick leave. He said once this loses strength, he'll tell Brandon he has you doing some undercover work with narcs or the feds. Either way, you'll still be drawing full pay. Captain also said he wants you to call him if you need anything."

A knock on the door made them all jump. One of the nurses stuck her head into the room. "Sorry to interrupt. A flower arrangement was just delivered for you." She pushed the door wider and brought in a crystal vase full of long-stem roses.

"Who sent those?" Rachel asked, rubbing her swollen ankles.

The courier didn't give a name," said the nurse. She handed the arrangement to Steven and left the room.

"I guess Steven has a rich admirer." Tashonda's smile was clearly forced, but Sam appreciated the effort.

Steven removed the Get-Well card from the center. As he read, the curiosity on his face curdled into hatred. Steven threw the vase to the floor. Rachel shrieked as glass, water, and roses shattered and covered the tile floor.

The nurse rushed in. "What happened? Is everyone okay?"

Steven, face pale, somehow managed to form a smile. He held up his bandaged hand. "Sorry, I lost my grip."

The nurse surveyed the mess. "I'll call housekeeping."

Sam grabbed the card Steven held out to her. She read the note silently, and after giving Steven a brief glance, she read it aloud. "Dear Steven, hope you are feeling better. Please give our love to Rachel and her unborn child. Signed Brandon Clayton and the HTF Staff."

"He wrote that to let Sam know who he could hurt other than Steven," Rachel whispered, holding her stomach protectively.

Without saying a word, Sam exited the room. She returned ten minutes later and informed everyone the nurse believed Steven would probably be discharged tomorrow. "I'm going home to finish packing," Sam said.

"I'll come with you," Tashonda said, waving down Rachel. "You take care of Steven and try to get some rest. We'll be back when we're done."

Tashonda had called Jenkins and her sister on the way to Sam's, and with the added help, Sam had the rest of the house packed and loaded into the full-sized moving truck, and her sister's SUV hitched onto the back with a tow dolly.

"I didn't think we'd get it all in." Tashonda wiped sweat from her brow once she finally managed to shut the door on the Chevy four-door.

Sam handed her a slip of paper with her new address and her Aunt Agnes's phone number. "If you need anything, including a place to stay, please don't hesitate to get a hold of me."

"Is this an invitation?" Tashonda asked, with a tired, yet mischievous grin.

"I gave Jenkins the info and told him the same thing, so don't let it go to your head."

Tashonda inhaled sharply when Sam pulled her into a tight embrace. "Thank you for everything."

Tashonda was smiling when they pulled away. "Did you hug Jenkins, too?"

Sam grinned. "Actually, I did."

Chapter Eight

Unexpected Homecoming

The following day, shortly after noon, the three left the city. Rachel driving Sam's truck, Steven following behind in his old, foreign clunker, and Sam navigating the oversized moving truck, bringing up the rear to their tight little convoy. Sam suggested Steven leave his car behind, mainly because of the condition he was in, but also because the engine-rattling jalopy was unlikely to make the two-hundred-mile road trip, let alone be drivable for much longer once they were there. Sam said she would buy him another, more reliable vehicle as soon as they settled into the house. Unfortunately, he would not hear of it.

The normal three-hour drive turned into a nine-hour nightmare. They had to stop three times along the way to do minor repairs on the ugly contraption, including jump-starting it once in the town of Clinton. Several cusswords and half a roll of duct tape later, the raggedy caravan rolled down the long gravel drive.

Tired and hungry, Sam was irritated when she climbed from of the gas-guzzling truck, so she took a moment to breathe in the cool, crisp, country night air. She hadn't realized how much she had missed her childhood home until her headlights reflected off the bay window her mother had adored. Or the toolshed attached to the garage her father had spent many hours tinkering in. The wide-open pastures wrapped around acres of thick Ozark woods. Sam's parents had loved the beauty of this place as did she.

Their family's land surrounded a dense, tree-covered stretch of rolling hills, which was once the family gold mine when their third-great-grandfather was alive. The property extended for miles on all four sides of the vast hillside, which some of the locals argued was actually a mountain range. The house and land had passed down to them from their late father and rested in a valley on the south side of the mine, mimicking their Aunt Agnes's horse ranch located on the north side.

Their cousin Michael's land was to the east, and adjacent, sitting between theirs and Aunt Agnes's stead, was their late Uncle Sam's house along with more sprawling farmland.

When Sam and Rachel's grandfather passed away, he left the land to his three kids, which he divided evenly among them. Their Uncle Sam Kelly, whom Samantha's father named her after, had died a few years later, leaving no wife or descendants, only an empty farmhouse and well over two thousand acres that split once again between Agnes and Sam and Rachel's father.

Sam had often made her way through this land in her youth. She had explored it numerous times on horseback, quite often on a dirt bike or four-wheeler, and more times than she could count, on foot. She hungered for the opportunity to revisit all the places she loved.

"Sam, could you grab this bag for me?" Rachel asked, bringing Sam's daydream to a sudden halt.

Sam did as her sister asked, pausing long enough to place a soft kiss on Rachel's protruding stomach, before heading through the dark to the front porch.

The eight-thousand-square-foot house was extravagant. And unduly modern for a rural community such as this. With an open floorplan, shiplap in the master bathroom, and a baker's pantry off the kitchen, her father had gone to great lengths to find the right builder. Not counting the partially walled in attic, the structure stood two stories tall, with a fully finished basement. The attic consisted of a half-bath, storage room, and spare bedroom, which their mother had used for her office. The second floor held her parents' old master bedroom and bath, her bedroom, Rachel's bedroom, a guestroom, and a second bathroom. There were two more guest bedrooms on the first floor, each with smaller bathrooms of their own. Her late father's office and a substantial library catty-cornered the formal dining room, and a laundry room was located in the rear behind the state-of-the-art kitchen, where their mother had spent much of her time baking for school functions when she wasn't working. The basement consisted of their father's den, a game room for the girls, three more bedrooms, two full bathrooms, and a theater room where her father whooped and hollered during football season.

Their mother had complained several times during the building phase of the house, saying the place was way too big for their family. But their father had his heart set on giving his wife and daughters the best. After all, he was a successful businessman, and his wife a skilled surgeon. He argued how, not only was this investment well within their means, but a structure like this would provide a solid home for many generations to come. Sam had often thought the real reason was because he had silently hoped for more children. A lot more children.

Sam smiled at the memory of helping her father build the eye-catching wraparound porch when she was fourteen. She cherished the thought of his praise when he told her she'd make a splendid carpenter. He'd always been supportive.

"Sam, do you have the keys, or did you leave them in the truck?"

Rachel's question brought Sam to the present, and she blinked in surprise. How long had she been standing in front of the door? Still half-lost in memory, she retrieved the set of keys from her jeans pocket. The lock and deadbolt turned easily enough, and Sam followed the two inside.

"Oh, where is the blasted light switch?" Rachel moaned.

"Good lord, some memory you have. It's on the other side of the door by the coat rack. I'll head downstairs and flip the circuit breaker. Damn. Steven, can you grab the flashlight from my truck—"

Out of nowhere, a hard blow hit her face. Sam staggered backwards. Pain seared through her head. A loud crash next to her was followed by a shriek from Steven and his body hit the floor. Sam saw the faint outline of a figure rushing toward where Rachel was crouched, her body against the door, her arms protecting her stomach.

Sam sprang into action, hurling herself at the attacker, taking them both down to the hardwood floor. She punched the assailant seconds before a voice from the stairs above shouted "No!"

Sam wasn't sure who flipped on the lights, or how many people were in her house. She stood in a ready stance, with Steven and Rachel behind her. A frightened woman with long, auburn hair, hurried down the stairs and threw herself over a teenager with a bloody lip.

"Please, leave him alone!" she shouted.

The familiar voice caused Sam to look at her more closely. Her heart raced, confusion fueling her question. "Christina?"

The woman glanced up. "Samantha? Rachel?"

"Christina Dowell?" Rachel asked.

"I take it you all know each other?" Steven grunted as he climbed slowly to his feet.

Christina sprang to her feet and ran over to embrace Rachel. Sam bent down to help the boy stand. He angrily jerked his arm away and sneered at her. "I can get up on my own!"

"Mike be nice. This is Sam Kelly and her sister Rachel. They own this farm." She gave Sam a warm hug.

"She hit me!" He wiped the blood from his split lip.

"As I recall, you hit me first, attacked Steven, and were going after my pregnant sister."

"So? I thought you were breaking in." Mike stomped up the stairs.

Steven stretched out his back. "Sweet kid. He makes me appreciate my decision to not reproduce."

"He's been through a lot this last month." Christina's smile was warm, yet her eyes looked tired.

Sam watched Mike's march to the second floor to her sister's old bedroom, where he slammed the door behind him. At a movement at the top of the stairs, her gaze shifted. She noticed a set of eyes peering at her from the shadows of the landing. Is that a kid? she wondered. "What's going on here, Christina?"

"Maybe we should make some coffee," Rachel said.

"Good idea." Christina led the way toward the back of the house to the kitchen. She had the coffee on and proceeded to slice and warm some homemade bread, which she mentioned their Aunt Agnes had brought over earlier in the day.

Rachel dug through the refrigerator, bringing out a large jar of strawberry jam and a container of butter to go with the bread.

Christina said, "I'm going to go check on Mike."

Rachel fussed over Steven.

"For the last time, I'm fine," he insisted.

"What about your ribs? Are they all right?"

"Oh, for heaven's sake, Rachel, will you leave him alone?" Sam protested.

"I'm worried," Rachel sat next to Steven at the table.

"You worry too much. If he passes out or starts having seizures, then you can fret. Now who wants coffee?" Sam crossed to the counter where the coffee was in the final stages of brewing.

Christina returned. "I about had to hold him down to get the ointment on his lip." She paused to study Sam. "Looks like your eye will have a nice bruise by morning. Do you want some ice, or need something for pain?"

Sam said, "No."

Christina leveled her gaze at Steven. "Any new injuries you need me to fix?"

"How do you know these are old?" Steven asked. "That kid could have really torn into me before Sam popped him."

"Those cuts and bruises are at least a few days old by their color and how well they're healing, and I'm betting the bandage on your hand was done at a hospital or clinic."

Steven asked. "Are you a nurse?"

"She's a doctor," Sam said.

Christina's eyes widened. "How did you know?"

"Aunt Agnes wrote me when I was overseas, and you were close to completing your residency. She said your father was so proud . . ." Sam's words trailed off when she remembered what Agnes had told her of the recent death of Christina's father. "I'm sorry, Chris. I wasn't thinking."

Christina grabbed a coffee cup from one of the cabinets. "It's all right," she said. "Yes, Dad was very proud of me."

Sam watched Christina add a hefty amount of creamer and a generous portion of sugar, bringing the liquid up to the brim where it threatened to spill over. Christina had to take a couple of small sips before she could carry her cup over to the table without spilling any.

"Sorry, it's been a long day," Christina blushed under Sam's scrutiny.

Sam then remembered why they were in the kitchen in the first place. "What's going on here, Christina? Who are those kids?"

"What, there's more than one?" Steven sounded disappointed.

Christina nodded. "Yes, Mike, who you all have met is sixteen, and as you can tell, he's filled with a lot of anger and has trust issues. Billy, his younger brother, is ten. He's shy, but he has a good heart."

Sam exhaled with her eyes trained on the ceiling. She wasn't going to lie, having an angry teenager in the same house as her pregnant sister wasn't ideal. During these last two years, since life had turned to shit, she had arrested kids far younger than sixteen for doing horrific things to others.

"Their mother and father were taken along with a group of campers a month ago by the HTF. Aunt Agnes and I found the boys hiding in my father's barn the night we went to break into his house."

"Oh, those poor kids." The way Rachel touched her hand to her chest, reminded Sam of their mother. "Why were their parents taken by the HTF?"

Sam fought the urge to remind her sister one of those 'poor kids' had attacked them not more than twenty minutes ago. Sam respected the fact the boy was protecting his brother and Christina from possible intruders, but she couldn't get the image of Rachel shielding her stomach out of her head. What if she hadn't intervened in time?

Christina took a sip of coffee before answering. "They and the others were traveling from town to town to organize an uprising against the government."

Steven let out a long whistle. "I can understand why, but far too dangerous in the current climate."

Christina opened her mouth but closed it without responding.

Sam interjected. "What do you mean you and Aunt Agnes were going to your father's place to break in? Isn't it your farm now?"

"No," Christina said. "When he was shot by the HTF for going after one of the agents, the government seized the land and everything on it. Murder and theft are becoming routine with our government. If you break the law and get taken away, you lose everything. Possibly even your life."

Sam's mouth dropped open in disbelief. "He went after one of the agents?" She had known Mister Dowell since as far back as she could remember. Hell, she had even dated his oldest daughter. Even though he was a hardheaded farmer, he was also a highly intelligent man. He would've known better.

"Remember Todd Kirkwood?" Christina asked.

Rachel shook her head.

"His father owns the hardware store downtown, right?" Sam said.

"That's him," Christina said. "He's the sheriff now, and he was there the night my father was murdered."

"Murdered?" Sam was not sure why her question came out sounding so surprised. After all, she knew first-hand how heartless the HTF agents were. She had, as of yet, to work alongside one with even the slightest trace of compassion. Nevertheless, she had somehow hoped the new laws and unwelcomed changes would less affect life in the Ozarks. Evidently, this wasn't the case.

"Yes. He said my father was trying to stop an HTF agent from taking my grandfather's antique German rifle the night they came to confiscate all the weaponry. In the process, one of the agents shot and killed him."

Rachel sucked in a sharp breath. "Damn, I'm so sorry Christina."

Sam recalled the pride on Christina's father's face the first time he had shown her the heirloom from World War II, which he cherished deeply. Her muscles tightened with anger at the thought of Mister Dowell's unjust death. "Why didn't Todd stop it?"

Christina placed her cup on the table. "He said it all happened so fast. Plus, if he'd interfered, he would've been killed as well. And then the HTF may have even gone after his family. Dad wouldn't have wanted Todd's blood on his hands." She looked directly at Sam. "This country has changed, and the people around here have suffered so much loss."

The raw pain on Christina's face was too much to handle. Sam changed the subject. "When did you move here from New York?" she asked and sipped her coffee to mask her uneasiness. "Aunt Agnes said you were doing your residency in New York."

"I came home a year after finishing to be closer to my father. I missed being here, the slow pace of it all. It's quite different from New York where everyone is always in such a hurry."

"Have you been living here long?" Rachel asked.

"I've been here a little less than a month. I arrived home the morning after my father's death. I knew something was wrong when Agnes picked me up at the airport, instead of Dad."

"Oh, that's horrible." Rachel reached for Christina's hands, cupping them in her own.

"It has been hard, but it gets easier as time passes." Christina's eyes fixed on Sam. "I'm sorry we're in your house. With what has been happening around town, your place felt safer. It's close to your Aunt Agnes and Uncle Phillip, so when she offered, I said yes. I promise we'll find somewhere else to go first thing tomorrow."

"Absolutely not, Christina! We won't have it!" Rachel insisted. "This home is big enough for all of us, and then some. You all can stay here as long as you want."

"Better listen to her," Sam said. "She's exactly like our mother."

Christina turned to Steven. "I'm not sure how well you knew Mrs. Kelly but let me tell you, she was a force to be reckoned with. Even though their father's muscular frame had easily overpowered her elegant build, when their mother was upset, he toed the line." Christina patted the table between Rachel and Sam. "Your mother's the reason I decided to be a doctor in the first place. I admired her in so many ways."

Rachel's eyes brightened. "That means a lot, Christina. To both of us." Rachel paused, staring at Christina almost to the point of visual intrusion. Sam was about to clear her throat to snap her sister out of whatever she was going through until Rachel finally spoke. "You look so different than I remember, Christina. Not like you did when we were younger."

With the awkwardness lifted, Sam laughed. "That's because the last time you saw her, she was twelve with pigtails and pimples covering most of her face."

Christina narrowed her eyes at Sam. "I was fourteen, and they were freckles, not pimples."

"Oh." Sam tried to force her tired brain to recollect her memories from the past. "Didn't you have a lisp?"

Rachel straightened in her seat, also laughing. "No, Sam, she had braces." She shook her head to mock her older sister's useless memory. "I was only seven when we moved, but even I can remember that."

Sam shrugged. "A long time has passed." She then gave Christina her full attention. "I've really missed you."

"I sent you several letters when you were overseas, but you never wrote me back."

Sam felt guilty. "I know I should have. But your letters touched on memories that were too hard to deal with at the time. I still have them and the ones your father wrote, too."

"I knew it!" Steven was excited, as if someone had given him some deep, priceless secret. "You two dated! Am I right? Tell me I'm right!"

Out of the corner of her eye, Sam spotted Christina and Rachel exchange an uncomfortable look with one another. "No, Christina has always been like a little sister to me. I dated her older sister, Sarah." The name felt heavy as it fell from her lips. "She passed away several months before we moved to Kansas City."

"Oh," Steven said. He slouched forward with his focus going straight to his untouched slice of buttered bread. "I'm sorry, I didn't mean to—"

"You did nothing wrong, Steven." Christina assured him, even though her words were filled with concern. "How are you doing with being back here, Sam?"

Sam knew this question would eventually make an appearance, but she figured it would have come from Aunt Agnes and not Christina. And definitely not so soon. How disappointing. "To be honest, I was surprised when I first realized who you were. You look a lot like her." Sam swallowed a lump of sadness and did her best to perk up. "I'm doing fine. Happy to be home, actually."

Christina reached over and gently squeezed Sam's hand. Sam pulled her hand away and grabbed her coffee mug. "Time for a refill."

Footsteps echoed from above, breaking the uncomfortable silence in the kitchen.

"You're fine with taking care of two kids?" Steven sounded as if he too was ready for a topic change.

Sam gladly aided in this new line of questioning. "Christina was always bringing home strays. Granted, back in the day they were animals, not children. Do you remember the baby raccoon you rescued? Chip, wasn't it?" She topped off her drink and returned to her chair.

Christina grinned. "His name was Chuck, and as I recall he tried to follow you home more than once." Amused, she told Steven, "This is how it worked, I'd take in the animals and care for them. But the second Sam set foot in our house they'd gravitate to her. Like she was a magnet of sorts."

"I fed them better."

"Most people would not consider French fries or cheeseburgers healthier."

"I said better, not healthier," Sam said

"Anyway," Christina said, "every animal I rescued ended up over at Sam's and Rachel's one way or another. The outside of their house resembled *Mutual of Omaha's Wild Kingdom*."

"Mom was livid," Rachel chimed in. "Remember when Bambi the Third ate her green beans for the fourth time?"

Sam rolled her eyes. "If Dad and I were not there to stop her, I think Mom would've actually shot the poor thing—that is, if she could've figured out how to load the bullets into the rifle."

Steven's eyes were wide with disbelief. "Sam and Rachel's lovable mother trying to shoot a cute little deer. I don't believe it."

"Mother loved her garden," Sam said.

Steven asked, "What happened to Bambi One and Two?"

Sam shrugged. "Hunters probably got them. I know Aunt Agnes was always bringing us over deer jerky back then."

"Oh, that's horrible," Steven said.

"That's country life." Rachel smiled at him.

Even though she'd been away from the family land for years, Sam could see the pride in her baby sister's eyes.

Christina giggled. "Their Aunt Agnes is about as country as you can get."

"So . . . Christina," Steven asked, "is there any special someone in your life?"

She gave him a smile. "I have sort of been seeing a guy from Springfield for a few months now."

"Sort of?" Steven leaned forward.

"We've been on several dates, and he wants to move to the next level."

"Which is?"

Christina's face flushed. "He's been pushing me for breakfast in bed, but I don't feel we're quite at that stage yet."

Steven seemed perplexed. "You've been with him for a few months and you two haven't slept together?"

"I think it's very responsible," Sam piped in.

Rachel gave her a mocking look. "This coming from the woman who doesn't date at all."

"I date," Sam insisted.

Steven quickly joined in on the attack. "When have you ever gone out on an actual date, Sam."

Sam glared at him. "I date once, maybe twice a month."

"One-night-stands are not dating," Rachel said.

"I still think you and Tashonda should hook up," Steven said, with a playful grin.

"Who is Tashonda?" Christina asked Steven, clearly amused by the banter.

"A woman Sam works with. She's smart, beautiful, and very into Sam."

"Why don't you two date?"

Sam laughed at Christina's question. "Now, don't you start. As I told these two, work and relationships don't mix. I did that once in the military and it about got me killed."

"You need to let it go, Sam. Jump back in with both feet." Rachel stood.

Steven held out his empty coffee cup. "As long as you're up could you get me a refill. Please?"

"What does your boyfriend do for a living?" Rachel asked, returning with Steven's filled cup and a glass of milk for herself. She handed Steven his coffee.

Sam stood up and retrieved another slice of bread from the oven.

"He's in sales and marketing at one of the larger firms in Springfield."

"Impressive," Rachel said.

Doctoring her bread with butter and jam, Sam rested against the sink and surveyed the scene, focusing mostly on Christina.

Christina waved a hand. "He's done well for himself. But. . ."

"What?" Sam noticed Christina's frown.

"I don't know. As of right now, he seems . . . predictable. Way more mature than any guy I've ever dated. He has his life together, oh, and did I mention, he's ruggedly handsome? But we've only gone out a few times."

"Ruggedly handsome, sounds like another word for old and boring." Steven bit into his bread. He chewed quickly and swallowed down the bulk. "Next subject. So, did you all grow up together?"

Christina laughed, clearly liking Steven more with each passing minute. "Yes. I mean Sam and my sister met in kindergarten, but I didn't meet Sam until—"

Sam waved her arms frantically at Christina from behind Rachel, her movements and Christina's grin bringing her sister's head around.

"What?" Rachel asked, looking from Christina to Sam, then once again to Christina.

Christina smirked. "She doesn't know? Your own sister and you've never told her? Oh, now this has gotten juicy."

"Don't do it, Christina!" Sam tried to sound stern and failed miserably, yet her spirt soared in good humor. She sat at the table licking the remnants of her bread off her fingers.

Rachel's eyes glistened with mischief. "Spill it, Christina."

"We met at—"

"Christina, I'm begging you. If you have any respect for me at all, you'll keep your trap shut."

Christina smirked. "I've always had a great deal of respect for you Sam, even when we took baton lessons together." She covered her mouth with both hands.

"Sam. You took baton lessons?" Steven roared with laughter.

Sam snorted. "Gee, Christina. Thank you so very much."

Christina ignored Sam's dirty looks. "She was only in it for six months until Mrs. Pumpernickel kicked her out."

"What, Pumpernickel like the bread?" Steven continued to laugh. "What did Sam do?"

Christina was having way too much fun. "She popped Jacklin Carter in the head with her baton."

Steven laughed harder, but Rachel's brow crinkled at hearing the name. "Jacklin probably deserved it."

"She did, or at least your sister thought so." Christina said, enlightening Steven with the full backstory. "You see, my mother died when I was two, leaving me and my sister with my dad. He did a great job raising us. Better than great, he was a wonderful father."

Steven motioned that he understood.

"When it came to fashion sense, though, especially with girls, he had none. He was a simple farmer, after all. The outfits he got us were dreadful, but we didn't complain because he tried, and we loved him for it." Christina sighed. "That night Jacklin made fun of us and our clothes, and when I started to cry, Sam swung her baton and nailed her right on her head."

Sam swallowed her last mouthful of coffee. "Not very funny when Mrs. Pumpernickel ended up being my fifth-grade math teacher. Thank goodness it only took three weeks of class for Mrs. Pumpernickel to realize Jacklin was a bully who deserved a good hitting."

"Which you obliged quite often, as I recall," Christina said.

"Sam!" Rachel shouted and her face flushed. "You lied to me!"

Sam leaned back, feeling attacked. "How did I lie?"

"I showed you a picture I found after Mom and Dad died. The one of you in tights holding a baton, and you told me the outfit was a Halloween costume Mother had made you wear."

Christina tsked-tsked Sam. "You lied to your baby sister?"

"Badass Sam in tights," Steven said. "Were they pink?"

"Yes," Rachel said.

Steven pounded the table with his hand, unable to control his laughter.

Sam stood. "Thanks, chick. I owe you a big one." She raised an eyebrow at Rachel and Steven who were now imitating a feminine version of the tomboy Sam in tights. "This would be a good time for me to unload our overnight bags from the truck."

Steven held up a pretend baton and acted as if he was twirling it high into the air.

"Oh, do I owe you," she muttered to Christina before exiting the kitchen.

Sam awoke to cold and rain in the blackness of night. Her head was throbbing, and her body screamed out in pain at every little movement she made. Even the rapid blinking of her eyelids felt labored as she fought to wake up. *Why wake? Why not sleep until morning?*

She moved her head slightly, feeling the roughness of wet, muddy earth beneath her cheek. *Something is wrong,* she thought, squeezing her eyelids together as if this movement would help lift the fogginess in her brain. *Why am I cold and wet?*

The sounds from the insects in the woods filled Sam's bloody, rain-soaked ears, and fear built up deep inside her naked, quivering body. "Where am I?" she mumbled, but only a rough gurgling sound came out. She focused, trying to recall the events which would explain why she was soaked, naked, and in pain. She remembered driving to high school that morning after dropping Rachel and Christy off at their school. *But now it was night? How?*

She tried to move her arm, but the pain was excruciating, sending her breaths into a quick, shallow rhythm. She closed her eyes tight and tried to think. *Sarah was giggling over the conversation they were having as they pulled into the high school parking lot.*

Think Sam, think!

"No, Chris is young, her crush on you is normal." Sarah smiled and bent to place a kiss onto her lover's lips.

"Sarah," Sam mumbled. Then a flash of the drunken man on top of Sarah and her loud sharp screams devoured Sam's memories of the day, flooding her brain with the terrors of the night.

She willed herself to rise, her naked body twisting with unbearable pain. She bit hard into her bottom lip, producing a trickle of fresh blood, while her legs quivered under the weight they could not hold. She hit the ground hard on her knees, her lungs forcing out the word "Sarah" in one high-pitched scream. With every frantic, painful turn of her head as she glanced around for her partner who would not, or could not answer, Sam had to fight off the urge to pass out.

"Sarah, answer me!" She climbed back to her feet, forcing her weak legs to move, her heart pounding a threatening beat. It was dark here, where *the trees grew thick, preventing the moon from shedding its rays onto this part of Earth.*

"Sarah, please tell me where you are! If you can't speak, then try to make a noise, baby!" Sam stopped, leaning most of her weight against the side of a large oak tree. She strained her ears to detect the faintest of sounds.

She peered down at her pain-filled naked body, in hopes of assessing the damage, but it was too dark. She took in a few short breaths before pushing on. She focused her eyes forward, squinting into the distance, seeing the opening in the thick trees a little further away. Maybe Sarah had made her way out? Hope had her quickening her pace.

Her right leg caught on something hard, bringing Sam to the ground. She sprawled out on her face, fighting back the pain with a sharp cry.

Sam sat up in bed and gulped in air, filling her lungs. Her night-clothes clung to her as if she were back in the heat of the Middle East, surrounded by the desert landscape in the blistering oven of summer. A wave of reality washed over her. She wasn't injured now. She had not just survived the conflicts of battle but the childish effects of a bad dream. Only a dream, she thought, burying her face in her hands. Had she cried out loud in the throes of the nightmare?

She scanned the dark room and got her bearings. She climbed from the bed in a daze, but lucid enough to realize she was in the downstairs guest room.

She made her way through the smallest bedroom in the house and entered the bathroom. When she flicked on the light, she caught her reflection in the mirror. "Crap," she muttered, spotting her black eye.

Needing rejuvenation, Sam jumped into the shower. The cool water washed the remnants of the nightmare from her mind. After towel drying and brushing out her hair, Sam dressed in a comfortable pair of jeans and loose sweatshirt all set to take on the day. She checked her watch and was surprised it was only four in the morning. Up before the sun, she thought.

Sam moved through the dark, quiet house to the kitchen to put on a fresh pot of coffee. She jumped when something in the corner moved.

"Sorry, I didn't mean to scare you," Christina rose to her feet and flipped on the main light in the kitchen.

Sam was happy to see a pot of fresh-brewed coffee. "Couldn't sleep either?" She fixed herself a cup before taking a spot at the table across from Christina.

"I woke when . . ." Christina glanced away from Sam. "I got up to use the restroom and couldn't go back to bed."

Sam figured with her room being directly under Christina's, Christina had heard her cry out in her sleep. Christina was lying purely for Sam's benefit for which Sam was grateful. She sipped her coffee, enjoying the taste.

"Rachel is up in your parents' old bedroom since it's the biggest. Mike is in Rachel's old room. His brother is in the upstairs spare bedroom. Steven claimed the other spare bedroom down here next to the one you slept in last night."

Sam made no comment as Christina spoke of the arrangements they had made after she'd gone to bed.

"After breakfast, I'll move my stuff down to the spare bedroom so you can have your old room back."

Sam said, "Don't be ridiculous. You're already settled, and I like being closest to the front door anyway, just in case."

Christina's mouth curved upward. "Still like being the protector, I see."

"What do you mean?" Sam asked.

"Nothing . . . well not nothing. Sam, let's face it, you were always the first one to step in when someone we knew was being bullied or was in trouble."

"Hey, you two. It's awfully early to be up, isn't it?" Rachel entered the kitchen.

"We couldn't sleep," Christina said. "Plus, we live on a farm, and we country folk are supposed to be the first ones up."

Rachel protested. "Yes, but not two hours before the rooster crows."

Christina shrugged.

"You missed out last night, Sam," Rachel said. "We stayed up for several hours reminiscing after you went to bed."

"I'm getting old. Whereas you're still young and able to stay awake until all hours."

"Oh, brother," Rachel muttered before pouring herself a full glass of milk.

As soon as Rachel sat down, Sam got up. She downed the rest of her coffee and stretched. "The sun will be up soon. I'll see if Steven's ready to unload the truck."

"Need any help?"

"Sure, Christina, the more the merrier."

The morning move had been blessed with clear skies and everyone pitching in to do their part. Even Mike had shown up an hour into the unpacking of the vehicles and jumped right in. He ignored Sam the entire time, but since he was pleasant to Rachel and Steven, Sam didn't mind.

"No, Jed was apprehended the same night my father died. They seized his house and business as well." Christina's face was turning slightly red from the weight she was carrying. "Can we rest again?" she asked, and she lowered her end of the couch without waiting for Sam's reply.

Sam laughed and watched as Christina and Rachel plopped down in an exhausted heap on the sleeper-sofa, which sat on the lawn halfway between the rental truck and front porch. Rachel was tasked with only carrying items weighing less than ten pounds. In her late stage of pregnancy, the walking to and from was enough to wear her down.

Sam peered at the front door, wondering why Steven and Mike were taking so long to hook up the fifty-two-inch television in the front room. They'd mounted the bracket to the wall over an hour ago. With his cracked ribs, Steven couldn't do much. But every little bit helped, and he was good at organizing the rooms.

Steven had them move most of the old furniture from the house out into the yard, until they finished emptying the truck. Then they decided which items they'd take to the drop-off point in town, where it would be passed out to those in need.

"These days, the numbers of those left homeless around here are steadily growing," Christina had told them earlier that morning.

"They searched your father's house on the last day of firearm turn-in? Doesn't sound right." Sam claimed the open spot in the center of the couch. "I mean, taking people away in buses, with no word to anyone. So, the HTF didn't arrest you because you were not at your dad's house when they found the weapon, therefore you didn't break the law?"

"Yes, that's how Todd explained it to me. Your Aunt Agnes and Uncle Phillip's place was also checked the same night, but the HTF didn't find anything."

"I'll go get us something to drink," Rachel moved to hoist herself up.

"I've got it, you rest." Sam was quick to her feet. "I want to see what's keeping Steven and the boys anyway."

She made her way up the front porch, mulling over what Christina had said. The locals now in need were all people from her past, and the thought of what was happening to them was unsettling.

"Are you done yet?" Sam called to Steven as she stepped inside. She skidded to a halt when she saw Steven reclined on the couch with his feet up, remote in hand, and Billy cheering on his brother.

When the screen door slapped shut all three sprang to their feet.

Sam grumbled, "You've got to be kidding me."

That evening Rachel found Sam in the garage an hour after Christina left for work. "Want some dinner?" she asked, taking a seat on a stool close to the workbench next to Sam. "I made spaghetti and meatballs, figured the kids would like it."

Sam turned down the music on the radio and continued going through the stored containers of tools, organizing them on the multiple shelves her father had once used. "I'm fine, thanks. Has everyone eaten?"

"Yes, and now they're all engrossed in that game of yours. Death something."

Sam's insides tickled, remembering earlier when she'd found them playing the game instead of working. "Good. Those kids look like they've been through a lot."

"I know what you mean. Steven and I have already decided to take them shopping tomorrow in Springfield for some new clothes and necessities. I also need to head to the grocery store to stock up on food. You want to come?"

"No, thanks. I have a list of chores to do."

"Don't get too busy too soon because I have a favor to ask of my dear, sweet, mechanically inclined sister."

Sam lowered the drill and waited.

"Christina's Blazer is on the fritz. She hasn't had time to get it fixed and she's too stubborn to ask for help. The guy she's been seeing is taking her to and from work each day."

Rachel's kind heart never ceased to amaze Sam. She was truly their mother's offspring. "I'll put it first on my list."

Rachel watched in silence as Sam unpacked box after box, placing each item into its proper spot. "Planning on doing an ample amount of work in the near future, I see."

Sam shrugged. "I thought about it. Figured I might as well bring the farm back to life if we're going to be living here." Taking one of the shop rags down from the shelf, Sam dusted off the full-sized table saw. "Eventually I'll need to go into town and get a few new tools and parts to repair the tractor." Sam paused, eyeing her sister. "What?"

Rachel's smirk melted into a warm smile. "I'm happy. I've missed it here. And, I haven't seen you this relaxed in a long time. You deserve this, Sam. You really do."

The following day, Sam had moved Christina's Blazer out of the barn and positioned it underneath one of the oak trees in the front yard. While she was making the repairs to the vehicle, Sam explained her every move to Christina's new canine. Christina had found the dog wandering the hospital parking lot last week, probably a stray. She'd posted flyers in town and held off naming the mutt until she was sure no one would claim him.

Like all her past pets, Sam spoke to the dog as if she were speaking to a human. "Now, this contraption is a ratchet, and this piece is an extension which goes on the ratchet to help me get into those tight places." Sam paused, giving the lab mix a wink. "I'm sorry I said that very unpleasant word a few minutes ago. I rather lost my cool when I knuckle-punched . . . um, never mind. It won't happen again."

The dog's floppy ears raised slightly, and he tilted his head, making Sam wonder why anyone would abandon such an adorable creature.

"You know, a phone call, every once in a while, wouldn't have killed you." A voice floated from above.

Sam's smile broadened at the sight of the aged woman astride a tall reddish Thoroughbred with a black, well-groomed mane, and tail. "It's interesting how the phones in this day and age can not only receive calls, but also send them."

Agnes swung herself easily down from the horse and wrapped her niece in a tight embrace. "Fine, you made your point. You must've inherited your lack of conversing from our side of the family, as well as your good looks," she added with a sly grin.

Sam and Aunt Agnes had always been close. Agnes was the one who had gotten Sam through the hard times when she was first overseas, sending inspiring letters and understanding e-mails every few weeks. She was a formidable woman, with a strong heart and equally strong drive. This allowed her to perform the difficult chores of running a successful farm and still tending to her family.

Agnes was attractive in an uncomplicated, down-home way, with a firm figure and strong Irish features. Her dark-brown and silver hair was pulled back into a loose hanging ponytail. Sam could barely discern the effects of age on her aunt's features.

Agnes surveyed the hefty engine suspended in the air on a thick chain and pulley setup, which Sam had rigged up over the sturdy tree branch above Christina's vehicle. She laughed. "This brings back fond memories. Do you remember the first time you helped your father and me replace the engine on my Buick? I think you were eight, maybe nine."

"I learned many cuss words from you both that day. If Grandma could have heard how you and Father spoke to one another she would've been livid."

"I guess you forgot your dad and Uncle Phillip installed a lift in the garage the winter before you left."

Sam's gaze ping-ponged between her aunt and the engine a few feet from her. "Crap," she muttered remembering how long it took her to hoist the engine with Mike's help.

"Too late now."

"I'm close to being done anyway." Sam offered her aunt a cold beer from the cooler next to her toolbox.

Agnes declined. "I need to get home before dark. Your uncle is with the vet at the house. One of our mares is about to deliver, and I need to be there in case something goes wrong. Which reminds me, I brought over three good horses in case you need them around the farm. They're in the barn." She gestured toward the house. "Is Rachel inside?"

"No, she and Steven took the kids into town to go shopping. I don't expect they'll return until later tonight."

"Are you two all right with the kids staying here? I should have told you weeks ago, but we've had a lot going on lately."

"It's fine. We're getting along great. Mike and I butted heads when we first arrived, but we're better now."

"I'm impressed. It took more than a week before he and I got along. But then again, I don't have the patience I once had." Agnes placed her hand on Sam's forearm. "How about money? Do you guys need any?"

Sam explained to her aunt about the overseas bank accounts, holdings, and the valuables they had locked in the safe inside the house. With the sale of their previous house and their emergency fund, they also had close to seven hundred thousand in cash stashed in the safe.

"Good, I figured with your father's business sense he would have more than enough put away to take care of his girls. I'm also impressed you managed to get Christina to let you fix her Blazer."

Sam smiled. "Actually, she doesn't know about this yet."

Chapter Nine

Settling In

Elaina's heart fluttered uneasily as she paced inside the cabin. Every few seconds she sent a nervous glower over to the opened laptop, which rested in the center of the wooden table. The screen glowed bright in the middle of the dark room, casting an eerie assortment of shadows around where the light touched the darkness.

The timeline was not supposed to reach this point. Elaina's stomach tightened. She made her way slowly to the chair in front of the computer. Reluctantly, Elaina retook her seat. *How much damage has already been done? Is the devastation to the point where our country is lost?* She blinked away tears and reread the information for about the hundredth time. There were listings of hidden cells this group had planted throughout the United States to increase the crime rate and death toll of the American people. There had been bombings in targeted areas to take out massive amounts of citizens with single strikes. Riots, shootings, and biochemical offenses wreaked havoc. Some laws had been struck down and news ones enacted, weakening the strength and morale of the American people, while steering power and control to an unknown entity. Yet, they appeared to have planned this in ways to keep the challenging masses at bay. Much like the frog who did not jump from the slowly burning pot of water but allowed itself to be gradually boiled alive.

The taking away of weapons, unlawful search and seizure of homes and businesses, and the unconstitutional ways this group planned to enforce nationwide registrations and curfews, did not compare to what would follow.

My God, what of the camps? Elaina thought as she lowered her head to the cold hard table. *How far into this are we?* Her tears of worry and regret spilled from her eyes. *A year and a half gone, wasted. Marcus is dead, so now what am I supposed to do? Me against this mighty conspiracy to destroy America. I don't even know who is behind it, or who to trust. Is it too late for me to try another way to stop this? Should I wait here and hope for the best? Maybe they know where I am? Did they trace my phone call?*

Elaina fell into a restless sleep that night, clutching her pillow in one hand and Kim's gun in the other.

The next several days on the farm were overflowing with hard, yet exciting work as each person pitched in with transforming the house and land back into a fully functioning farm. Mike and Billy worked alongside Sam, fixing fences, burning overgrown brush, cleaning out the barn, and making other necessary repairs. The others scrubbed and cleaned the inside of the house, restoring it to the grand structure it once was. Aunt Agnes even did her part with helping her nieces. She made some calls and had several dozen head of cattle purchased and delivered to one of the larger pastures.

Traipsing along the freshly mowed lawn, Sam said, "Billy, you don't have to help. It's Saturday and other than caring for the animals, we try to take the weekends off."

"I want to help, Sam. Plus, I've never built a house before."

Amused, Sam bit the inside of her cheek to keep from laughing. "We're not building a house, only fixing up the guest house."

"Oh, that's right."

The two-story, four-bedroom house sat up against the base of the hill like the main house but was located over three-hundred feet past the barn. The outside had siding and high-end brickwork matching the main house, giving one the false impression the structure was in tiptop shape. The inside was old and tired and in need of much tender loving care.

The smaller dwelling was the original house Sam and Rachel's father grew up in. She recalled how the summer before they moved to Kansas City, Sam and her dad had worked on restoring the place for when out-of-town relatives came to visit.

"Why are we fixing it up, Sam?" Billy asked.

"If anyone needs a place to stay for a few days, they can stay here."

"Like the man who worked on the farm with us yesterday?"

The guy Billy mentioned had been the second person to arrive hoping to trade a day of work for food or money. Sam gave him both. "Yes, like him."

"I guess this would be better than sleeping in the barn."

"I guess so." Sam found the boy's endless supply of questions entertaining.

Unlocking the main door, Sam swung it open and pulled the screen door shut behind them. They'd loaded multiple stacks of wood, flooring, and drywall into the front room two days ago. The tools and hardware, they had put in the kitchen. Sam decided to wait on the kitchen appliances and bathroom fixtures until after they finished the rough-in stage of the house.

"Grab the radio, and I'll bring our tools upstairs," Sam said, and Billy rushed off happily to do his first task.

They dove in, ripping up carpet in each of the bedrooms, and sanding the old floors. Mike showed up a few hours later. "You were supposed to wake me up," he grumbled, placing one of the tool belts around his waist.

"I was going to, but you were out cold. I decided to let you sleep in."

He shrugged, wiping the remainder of sleep from his eyes. Sam had realized, several days earlier, Mike was not a morning person. He grumbled his responses when asked a question and occasionally appeared short-tempered if Billy talked too much. Fortunately, after the first hour or two of the morning, his mood became more pleasant—for a teenager anyway.

By noon, Sam had the radio tuned to a rock station and she and the boys were singing along. She enjoyed their upbeat conversations on topics ranging from their favorite foods to which state they liked living in the most.

"What about school?" she asked.

"We were home schooled," Billy said. "I didn't mind, Mom was a great teacher, but there weren't many kids to play with."

"We lost our house over a year ago, and have been on the road ever since," Mike added with an expression of one who had seen and been through more than he would have liked.

The music suddenly stopped. Sam stood to tweak the dial for the third time today, when the normally upbeat announcer came on sounding all worked up. "I apologize for the interruption, but I've been told a massive uprising is taking place outside the White House."

"What's an uprising, Sam?"

Mike shushed his brother and Sam turned up the volume.

After a slight pause, the man said, "Yes, it's confirmed. An armed group of citizens are trying to overrun the gates of the White House. There's still no word on the number of casualties, but apparently, the president is not at the White House. Stay tuned for updates. Now back to the music here on SMYZ, Springfield's number one place to rock."

Mike stared at Sam. "Dad said this would happen."

"What, Mike?" Billy asked. "What would happen?"

"A war. A civil war here in the United States. He said people will rise up and overthrow the government."

Sam flipped off the radio. "We're not at war, Mike. People do things when they're upset or scared but like with everything else going on throughout the country, this too will pass. There's no need to worry."

"They're attacking the White House, Sam."

Sam was concerned. Since they had moved in, she had almost forgotten how bad life in the United States was becoming. A few people had come by looking for a day's work or any food one could spare. The US was in a depression and hardship was to be expected, but hearing about an assault on the White House brought Sam to a new level of alert.

"Sam, are you okay?"

Sam smiled at the pair as she removed her tool belt from around her waist. Mike and Billy did the same.

"Why don't we forget this for today and let's do something fun."

"Like what?" Billy asked, his apprehension fading.

Sam shrugged. "I don't know, you tell me."

"We can go play Death or Glory," Mike said with a grin.

Billy piped up, "Let's build a clubhouse."

"Clubhouses are for babies."

Billy puffed out his bottom lip at his brother.

Sam poked Billy in the stomach playfully. "No, they're not, Mike. I had a clubhouse until I was fifteen. I guess it was more of a hideout then a clubhouse." Suddenly, a wonderful idea struck her. "Hey, do you two want to see it?"

Billy jerked his head to his brother. "Yeah, if Mike wants to."

Mike threw his little brother a wink. "I guess so."

Sam motioned for them to follow her. They stopped at the house to get flashlights, pack a lunch, and to tell Rachel where they were heading.

"Cool," Rachel said.

"Want to come?" Billy asked, overjoyed at the idea.

"No, I have some things to do, and Steven is going to the grocery store soon to pick up stuff for dinner."

"Where's Christina? It's been a while, she might like to see it again," Sam said.

"She was called away for her volunteer work. I swear that poor woman is always working."

Sam silently agreed. Several minutes later she led the kids out to the barn, motioning for the inquisitive dog to stay behind. They made their way to the over-sized tack room in the back, past the multiple rows of horse stalls.

"Is this it?" Billy asked, sounding let down.

Sam grinned. "Wouldn't be much of a hideout if it was."

She placed her backpack on the ground and moved several drums of feed to the corner of the room. Then she grabbed a knothole in one of the wooden floor planks. With a smooth motion she lifted an inconspicuous hatch revealing a set of stairs leading down into darkness. A weight system attached to the door from below, so it lifted relatively easily for Sam.

Both kids gawked at her.

Sam winked and flung her backpack over her shoulder. She headed down a flight of wooden steps. Billy flipped on his flashlight. A bright light emerged from below, along with the sound of Sam's voice. "The electricity still works!"

The brothers followed Sam into the unknown. Sam stood next to the many fully stocked shelves in the dusty, underground room waiting for Mike and Billy.

"That's odd." She inspected a large container of processed meat. "This item has been added recently." She replaced the can before moving down several rows to look at another. "These are all less than a year old."

She made a mental note to check with Aunt Agnes later about who'd been down here.

"This place is great," Billy said. "It's a real hideout."

"We're only at the entrance." Sam focused her attention on the boys. "Has either of you ever seen a gold mine?"

They shook their heads.

"Then you're in for a treat." She searched the shelves and found an old crate to sit on. "Take a seat." She motioned for the brothers to sit on the steps. "This old mine is full of history, dating all the way back to seventeen-ninety-two."

"That's a long time ago," Billy leaned forward on his perch.

"A very long time ago," she said. "When my great, great, great grandfather Sam Kelly first staked a claim here. Some would say he fell in love with the Ozark hills and its untouched landscape, while others insist Granddad Sam had a nose for gold."

"He had a gold nose?" Billy sounded confused.

Mike rolled his eye. "No, it means he could smell gold."

Sam beamed. "Exactly. The way my father told the story, Grandad Sam cherished both. Anyway, Granddad Sam struck it filthy rich, so they say. He took all his gold and buried it on his land somewhere so no one would find it."

"He didn't spend it?" Billy was beside himself.

"No one really knows. His true love was farming the land. It's a love passed down in my family from one generation to the next."

"Like to you and your Aunt Agnes. You two are farmers, right, Sam?" Billy asked.

Sam found herself at a brief loss for words. No one had ever labeled her a farmer, not even in school, even though she came from a family of farmers. She sat motionless deep in thought, and, then with much pride Sam nodded. "Yes, like me and Aunt Agnes. Hey now, we're drifting off course. Now, where was I? Oh yes, this mine was used from 1805 until close to 1850 for the Underground Railroad. Then—"

Billy raised his hand high in the air. "Where are the tracks?"

Sam gave him a quizzical look, not understanding what Billy meant. "What tracks?"

Mike laughed. "He thinks the Underground Railroad is an actual train."

"I see. It's not a real railroad, but what they called the movement to free slaves," she told Billy. "Do you know about people owning slaves and the Civil War?"

"The Civil War was fought to free the slaves, right?"

"That's one of the main reasons, yes. But even before the Civil War was fought, many people didn't believe one should own other people, so they would help slaves escape from states which allowed slavery, to other states where people could be free. Missouri was a slave state, along with many other southern states. People brought runaway slaves to our mine for food and a safe place to hide before continuing north."

"Oh, Mom talked about this before," Billy said.

Sam said, "This mine is extremely large and has several hidden entrances leading to different areas on our land. This came in very handy during those times. Later, many of the entrances were sealed during the Cold War by my grandpa and great grandpa, and the mine was made into a fallout shelter of sorts."

Billy frowned. "What's the Cold War? I don't know about that war."

"The Cold War went from nineteen-forty-seven to I think nineteen-ninety-one and was a very scary time for people in the United States. Our country and the Soviet Union were having problems getting along with each other. People here in the United States were afraid the Soviet Union would attack us with nuclear weapons. So, they prepared underground bunkers."

Leaping to his feet, Billy shrieked with delight. "We can stay here in the mine if there's another war. We have a lot of food, and we can shut the door and lock it so no one can get in."

Sam laughed. "That's a wonderful idea, but like I said earlier, this room is only an entrance." She stood. "Do you want to see the old family gold mine?"

Billy jumped in place with excitement and Mike stood, doing his best to ignore his brother. They followed Sam to the far corner of the sprawling, low-ceilinged room. She stopped in front of the last row of shelves, which housed many dusty survival items like batteries, flashlights, rope, and blankets.

"This mine is a family secret. You must both promise not to tell anyone about this place, understand?"

They nodded in unison and watched as Sam stuck her hand under the center shelf. A faint click echoed overhead. She pulled on the edge of the dusty shelf, swinging it, along with its fake backing, outward to reveal a metal door. "My father once told me a vast cave system connected somewhere through one of the lower tunnels. I've never seen it, but he said they figured it to be seven times larger than the mine itself, and there's an underground river flowing through one of the center chambers."

The brothers stood side by side, staring wide-eyed as Sam twisted the metal handle and pushed the heavy door open, revealing a dark passageway. She pulled a flashlight from her backpack, and the boys did the same.

"Are you sure it's safe?" Billy's voice shook.

Sam squatted in front of him. "My family has gone to great lengths throughout the years to make this mine very safe. If you don't want to go in it's all right. I can bring you back later."

Billy squared his shoulders. "I'm not scared, Sam. Let's go."

Giving the boy's arms a reassuring squeeze, Sam stood and led the way through the long, wide tunnel. "You see these supports?" Sam pointed her light along the walls and to the ceiling overhead. "They are solid steel and very strong."

"Do those old lanterns still work?" Billy asked. His light shining on one hanging from the ceiling next to Sam.

She peered up, puzzled. "I don't know. I've never seen them before. Aunt Agnes or Uncle Phillip must have added them." She reached up to take the lantern down from its hook, but realized the light was not an old, oil-fueled lantern, but electric. The lantern was attached to a thick black wire running along the shadows of the ceiling. They followed the wires and more lanterns through the tunnel, almost to where they had entered.

"I found it, Sam." Billy flipped up a switch.

Light filled the passageway.

Sam clicked off her flashlight and crammed it in her backpack. Her body froze as she observed the multiple sets of footprints on the dusty earth below. The kids' prints and hers were more recent and easily identifiable, but the other markings were larger, older, and the way they pressed into the ground told Sam they were from heavier people, probably men.

She moved along the tunnel, nearing the end of the pathway before the first opening of the mine. The instant she noticed the familiar imprints of combat boots in the loose dirt, Sam pivoted to the boys. "I need you both to go to the house and wait for me."

"But—" Billy said.

Sam deepened her voice. "Don't argue. When I'm done looking around, I'll come get you, but first I want to make sure it's safe."

She waited until the brothers left the tunnel. Once gone from sight, she slowly continued forward. She paused again, this time considering whether to head to the house for her weapon, but she figured grabbing it would only alarm Rachel, so Sam pushed on, trying to detect any noise or sounds of life ahead. She finally came into the spacious, unusually lit entryway, which she had used as her hideout for so many years.

The smaller wooden doors to the right and left were firmly padlocked as they had always been. The familiar warning, 'Danger do not enter,' was painted onto the surfaces but faded after all these years. The metal wall housing the broad door in front was not familiar. The door itself was standing slightly ajar and a dim light was seeping from the mine. Sam also noticed additional beams and supports had been added to the walls and ceiling.

What's going on here? She squinted behind her, debating again whether she should head to the house for her weapon.

The sound of far-off laughter brought her head around. She heard more than one voice, definitely male, two, maybe three. Sam moved forward, crouching next to the slit in the door to try to get a glimpse of what, or who, was on the other side. She did not see any movement in the mine ahead but did spot multiple boxes and crates lining the outer walls.

Retrieving the knife from her backpack, she took a deep breath, and quietly made her way in. She remained low, shuffling to the first set of unlabeled containers, which she used as cover from the unknown individuals further ahead. Unfastening the strap around the handle, Sam unsheathed the survival knife, and worked loose the top on one of the wooden crates. Prying up the lid, Sam inspected a crate full of large metal trays of ready-to-eat meals. When she felt safe to go ahead, Sam rushed to the opposite wall, to the next set of crates. This container held old-style, green-and-black camouflaged military uniforms, with several pairs of black combat boots.

She continued moving down the mine, passing several branches and turnoffs. Sam had gone this way once with her father to her aunt's house as a fun little excursion when she was younger. Back then the trip had felt safe, exciting, unlike this experience her heart was pounding through now. Sam was filled with uncertainty and fear.

Along the way, she uncovered so many crates of food, clothing, and even first aid items. A stash of supplies a small town of people could live on for years. But why? She was not ready for the next few rows of wooden boxes, which displayed in fine print, 'Property of the United States' over the top and sides. Prying the lid off, Sam grimaced at the sight of Claymore mines. The next lid she opened revealed brand-new M-16 and nine-millimeter weapons, stacked neatly inside. She peered at the wall across from her where slightly smaller crates sat, "AMMO" in bold dark letters stamped across the wooden slats.

Feeling the hairs rise on the nape of her neck, Sam grabbed her knife and spun, facing two men. They had to have come from a side tunnel. The first man was well-built with a five-o-clock shadow covering his face, the second was tall and slender, with thin-framed glasses, giving him the appearance of someone who belonged in an office behind a computer, not in an old mine filled with military supplies. Both were dressed in camouflage uniforms and had M-16s slung over their shoulders. She locked eyes with the first man, noticing his expression change from peaceful to alarm in a matter of a second.

"Don't move!" He pointed his weapon at her.

The skinnier man did the same, which is when Sam noticed neither weapon had magazines loaded. She flipped the knife in her hand and raised it in one smooth motion, ready to throw it. "I don't want to kill either of you, so please don't make me."

The larger man's voice cracked slightly. "We have guns, you only have a knife." He tried to give her a grin of confidence as he aimed at her chest.

Sam squinted at their weapons. "Those work better when they're loaded."

"Crap, I told you I'm not ready for this," the skinnier man complained, his gaze holding nervously to Sam's upraised knife.

"Quiet, Kevin, I need to think."

"Listen." Sam moved slowly, lowered her knife, and placed it into its holder. "Why don't we all calm down and talk this out."

With a great sense of relief, the larger of the two nodded. The second he lowered his own weapon, his eyes shot to something past Sam's right shoulder. The sound of running feet made Sam spin seconds before two more men were on top of her position.

She aimed a high kick at the right cheek of the first man. The blow sent him crashing into the row of crates lining the wall. Crouching, she spun her leg low, sweeping the legs out from under the other. The flailing man landed hard on his side, sending a cloud of dust into the air.

Sam twisted toward the first two men, who were coming for her. She had scarcely enough time to duck away from the butt of the larger man's weapon. She sent a hard right punch straight into his groin, doubling him over onto the ground. The one called Kevin moved in, his stance uncertain. He brought his leg up toward Sam's stomach. Sam sidestepped easily enough, giving his kick nothing but air, and she pushed the off-balance man into the pile of broken crates where the first man had landed. Sam felt the presence of another attacker, maybe two. She turned right as a shoulder caught her in the gut, driving the air from her lungs. In one heap of tangled limbs, she and the unknown attacker crashed to the ground.

Sam rolled, brought her head up, and sent her forehead into the nose of a middle-aged man wearing jeans and a Kansas City Chiefs hoodie. The man spun off her with a wild screech, dripping fresh blood everywhere. Fighting for air, Sam scrambled to her feet. Unsure of who was coming next, she managed to avoid the blow of someone's fist. She threw a punch, feeling the impact as her knuckles struck hard against the guy's ear.

"Leave her alone!" Billy's cry echoed around the tunnel.

Sam's heart fluttered in panic, and she swirled in time to hear the high-pitched scream of one of the men and to see Billy go flying to the ground landing in a small heap.

"Billy!" Mike rushed to his brother, reaching him the same moment Sam did.

"What is all of this?" The voice of an older woman sounded from somewhere behind Sam.

Sam yanked Billy to his feet. His mouth was swollen and bleeding, but he stood up straight, as if ready for another round.

"Stay behind me!" Sam shouted. She jerked her knife out, ready to protect the two kids with her own life if it came to that.

"I demand to know what's going on here!" The older woman spoke again, and something in her voice was alarmingly familiar. Sam leaned forward, trying to see her face.

"Samantha Kelly?"

Confused, Sam lowered her knife. "Mrs. Pumpernickel?"

"Joyce, do you know her?" asked one of the men who was helping another to his feet.

"Yes, I know her! She owns this land and six men against one woman is not a fair fight! You all should be ashamed of yourselves!"

Sam heard footsteps of others approaching from deeper in the mine. She stowed her knife, before speaking to the stout man closest to her. "Did you hit him?" Sam asked, pointing to Billy.

"I didn't mean to—he bit my leg. I didn't know he was only a kid."

Sam cleared the distance between her and the man. "He is only ten!" She put all her strength, all her anger, and all her weight into the punch she aimed at the big man's face.

They both landed hard on the floor.

"Samantha Kelly! Enough!" Mrs. Pumpernickel's voice bounced off the mine's walls.

"Sam, what are you doing here?"

Sam whipped around. She glared at her Aunt Agnes. "I could ask you the same thing."

"Billy!" Christina ran up to the bleeding boy. She surveyed Billy's gash before twisting to Sam. "Why did you bring them down here?"

"Tee didn't. Tam told us to go to da house, but we didn't listen," Billy informed the onlookers through a mouth full of blood.

Agnes said to Sam, "Let's get you guys cleaned up and we can discuss where to go from here."

Mrs. Pumpernickel placed her hands on her hips. "I see you still like causing a ruckus, Ms. Kelly." She motioned with her hand at the damaged boxes and equipment littering the floor of the passageway.

Sam opened her mouth to speak, but closed it, feeling suddenly like a guilty fifth grader standing before her stern math teacher.

Mrs. Pumpernickel gave a loud "humph," before falling in behind Christina and Billy. Agnes didn't say anything, only aimed an amused grin to her confused niece.

Following the group down into the mine, to the fourth branch on the left, Sam paced well away from her old math teacher for fear of getting one of her many lectures. The branch opened into a room the size of their barn, with numerous cots scattered throughout. Three metal desks sitting side-by-side were the focal point and the group gathered around one. Two narrow passageways past the cots and several metal storage cabinets and shelves full of medical supplies were snugged up against the wall around the cavernous room.

Christina and Agnes, with the help of Mrs. Pumpernickel, tended to the injuries from the brawl. "She really worked you men over," Agnes said, dabbing ointment on the cut over Kevin's right eye.

Sam shifted uneasily when she spotted a woman lying covered on a cot on the other side of the farthest desk. The woman looked seven, maybe eight months pregnant to Sam, and possibly a few years older than Rachel. A bulky white dressing covered the woman's head, with a circle of blood in the center. The woman stirred slightly, blinking her eyes open.

Sam asked, "Do you need anything?"

"No." The woman brought her hand up to her forehead, as if the slight head movement caused her pain or discomfort. "I'm fine, thank you." She closed her eyes once again.

Sam stared a few seconds longer, then went to Agnes. "Why are these people here?"

Agnes held up a finger to Sam and spoke to Mrs. Pumpernickel. "Joyce, maybe you should take Billy into the conference room and get him something to drink. I would like the rest of you to return to your posts." She tossed a dirty wad of gauze into a nearby trashcan. "Mike and I will clean up the mess in the passageway, and afterwards, I'll send him up to the house to bring Rachel and Steven down here." Agnes placed her hand on Sam's shoulder. "Now, you let Christina examine your hand. We can talk later after I get everyone together."

About thirty-minutes later, Agnes returned with Rachel and Steven in tow. Soon after, the oversized chamber of the mine, dubbed the conference room, began to fill with people Sam had known since birth. Aunt Agnes explained how the mine was being used as not only a safe haven for those in need, but a staging post for a planned uprising. Sam's dreams of running from the chaos in Kansas City to give her sister and her unborn niece or nephew a chance at a normal life, vanished in a dizzy haze of instability.

"This is suicide!" Sam said to Aunt Agnes. "These people are farmers and simple town folk, not the military."

"We farmers and simple town folk are Americans as well, Ms. Kelly," Mrs. Pumpernickel shook a finger in Sam's direction. "Our rights are being stripped away, and our loved ones are being slaughtered or captured by our so-called *government*! They killed Christina's father in cold blood on his own porch! They have stolen homes, businesses, and lives. For no reason! I'm not waiting around to be next! No American should!"

Sam's shoulders drooped under the weight of how real the idea of a war was for her childhood community.

Mister Douglas spoke, not with the venom Mrs. Pumpernickel held, but with a solemn certainty. "Sam, our forefathers fought a tyrant many years ago to ensure our rights and freedoms in this land, and they wrote a constitution to uphold those freedoms. It's not only our right, but our duty as free Americans to protect these liberties."

Sam held nothing but respect for this older man. He used to play chess with her father out in front of the general store every Sunday.

"Mister Douglas, I went to school with your son. He's still in the Marines, is he not?" Mister Douglas nodded proudly. "Aunt Agnes, Michael's in the Army over in Africa, right?" Agnes bobbed her head in agreement. "These are the people you'll be fighting against. Your sons and daughters, your friends, and neighbors. You will not be fighting a tyrant on the other side of the ocean, but people you love and care for right here in your own backyards."

Mister Douglas rose to his feet holding his faded fedora in his hand. "Sam, we've already discussed this." He swung his arm to encompass Agnes and the other community members. "We've all sent word to those in the military, telling them it's time to come home. But if they decide to stay in, then it is what it is. My boy would understand."

Agnes spoke plainly to her niece. "Sam, we could use you and your combat training to help get us ready. We have a few ex-military combatants with us, but though they are skilled people, they're not spring chickens anymore, and they don't have the recent combat experience you have."

"Don't ask me to do this. Using the mine, I'm fine with, as long as Rachel and Steven are. However, I won't help you prepare for this slaughter."

Rachel stood "Sam, Steven and I have talked it over, and we have no problem with the group using the mine. In fact, we would like to help if we can. Maybe assist Christina in the hospital, or—"

"Do you realize how dangerous this is? And for God's sake, Rachel, you're in your third trimester."

Rachel squared her shoulders. "I'm not a child, Sam, and thank you for the heads-up. I didn't realize I was pregnant. Now I know the reason the diets aren't working."

Her comment brought a stifled giggle from Steven and a few others.

Sam was consumed with worry and anger. "This isn't a joke, Rachel!"

"No, it's not! Which is why we must do something! Oh, and for your information, being pregnant doesn't make me useless, it makes me even more determined to be a part of this. What future will my child have if we do nothing?"

Agnes calmly held up both hands to silence Sam and Rachel. She said, "Christina could use the extra help, and we'd appreciate it, Steven. I do have to agree with Sam. Until your child's born, Rachel, you should avoid the stress of the medical wing as much as possible. Still, there are many other things we can use your help with."

Frustrated, Rachel eyed her sister. They stared at one another for some time before Rachel retook her seat.

Sam stewed over Rachel's decision. She wanted her sister as far away from this madness as humanly possible. At this point, returning to Kansas City was pulling at the restless parts of her mind.

Todd Kirkwood cleared his throat. "Sam, I felt the same way you do, until I saw first-hand what was happening to innocent people. All I ask is for you to think about it. If you change your mind, we would be fortunate to have your help."

"You're a coward, Samantha Kelly!" A tall, teenage boy yelled out from the center of the room. "You don't deserve to be here!"

Mike was the first to his feet, followed by several others who appeared as outraged as Mike. "Who said that?"

"I did!" A dark-haired teenager moved toward Mike, who balled up his fists and took a threatening step forward.

Calmly, Mister Douglas said, "Son, if I was you, I'd keep my mouth shut about things you know nothing about. Samantha Kelly is anything but a coward." He looked at Sam, his voice sounding sympathetic. "Teenagers think they know everything about everything. Don't pay him any mind, Sam. We all know you, and we understand what you're going through, because we've struggled with the same doubts."

"I'm sorry, but I don't feel this uprising is the answer." Sam gestured Mike to his seat. "I'm not prepared to point my weapon at American soldiers, or intentionally take another American life." With that, Sam left the crowded room.

Rachel followed her out. "Sam, no one here wants this to happen, but it's happening whether we like it or not."

Sam spun with her hand waving toward the room filled with their family and neighbors. "Rachel, can't you see how traumatizing this will be for everyone? I remember the first time I killed a man. I thought I was going to shrivel up and die inside. What got me through was Aunt Agnes telling me to take all my pain and doubt and place it in a box deep inside myself. To focus on the people fighting next to me and to know with each enemy I killed, I could be increasing the chances of sending them home safely to their families." She searched her sister's eyes. "How would I justify this? How could I see myself through killing people I once called my countrymen? How could they?"

"Sam, you need to open your eyes to what's going on around us. We no longer live in the same country you once fought for."

Chapter Ten

Martial Law

Elaina pulled back the wooden floor panel. She placed her laptop inside the opening, along with a shoebox containing the flash drives, notebook, paperwork, and most of her money. She replaced the panel and swiped a hand across the floor several times, removing any trace of the slats being disturbed.

For the last week, since making the phone call to Marcus's number, Elaina had been hiding out, too scared to leave the only home she had known for over a year. She had replaced the battery in her SUV the moment she returned to the cabin, only to find out the vehicle still wouldn't start. She was trapped in the woods and certain that death was coming for her.

She was sick of waiting, sick of pacing the cabin, tired of rereading the information on the computer screen, cowering at every little noise outside. Even the crackling from the fire at night unnerved her, making it hard for her to settle into a full evening of rest. She felt drained, spent, and unable to take the solitude of the cabin any longer.

She could either give up or make another trip into town, buy a new car, and drive up to Canada. Not one to give up, the choice of going to town won out. She'd need to acquire new identification, and somehow, make it over the border. But that could wait until she was on the road driving away from here.

Once she acquired a vehicle, she planned to return and grab her things, including the now-hidden drives and documents, which she would drop off at one of the local news stations along the way. What else could she do? She had nowhere else to go, no one else she could trust. She needed to pass on the information, and with any luck, the story would find itself in the right hands.

Elaina stuffed her backpack with snacks, a few water bottles, and four thousand dollars cash for the purchase of anything reliable with four-wheels. She tucked her pistol in the front waistband of her jeans, concealing it under her jacket, and set out. Eyes open for any sudden movements, Elaina traveled as fast as she could toward town.

The weather had greatly improved this week, since her terrible trip for the battery, but she was too worn down to enjoy the improvement. She felt suddenly weak, cowering behind her failure. She wasn't giving up, she was accepting defeat, Elaina rationalized internally, attempting to ease her growing guilt. If she were giving up, it would mean she had strength left to fight, but emotionally, she had nothing left to keep her going. Giving up would have been six months ago.

I have lost everything, she thought, pulling her jacket tight around her. *My parents, my job, my life, even my ex.* The chill passing through her was not from the cool May winds, but her own hopelessness, as she zigzagged between luscious green trees and bright wildflowers.

She stopped halfway through the woods for a quick bite to eat. The dried peaches tasted like dust in her mouth. She tucked the half-eaten package into her backpack and went onward. She was close enough to the road to hear vehicles go by, but far enough away to remain undetected.

I cannot do this, her mind silently shouted once she reached the edge of town. She closed her eyes tight, and then opened them again and squatted inside the tree line. She was several blocks away from the area where she had noticed the used car lot on her previous trips, but the idea of being out in the open for even that short a distance was unnerving.

Why was she so scared? Was it the fear of dying? Was she so selfish to value her life over those who have already died to try to put an end to this nightmare? Did she consider her existence more significant than the people who might live if she was able to expose the truth? Calming herself, Elaina stood, taking in large mouthfuls of air.

Do not think, Elaina, just do it!

Her feet moved. Before she knew it, she was standing in front of the used car lot, unable to remember much of the fast walk that brought her there. She surveyed the empty slab of asphalt, feeling an alarm go off in her head before her mind registered the problem. *They've closed!* The reality sank in. There were no cars, no trucks, no vehicles of any kind. Her eyes darted anxiously from one end of the lot to the other. Even the double-wide, old mobile home they had converted into their office was gone.

Feeling lost, she spun from the deserted parking lot and scanned the street, hoping she was at the wrong place. Her breath caught in her throat when she spotted a black, government-looking SUV with dark-tinted windows approaching from the other end of town. The vehicle crept along the street. Assessing?

Without thinking, Elaina crossed the road and traveled the way she had come. She fought to keep her pace casual, herself calm, but her heart pounded rebelliously inside her chest. She could feel sweat droplets form on her forehead and dampness coated the palms of her hands as she continued onto the first side street.

Only two more blocks, she thought, giving herself a little bit of hope. She sneaked a look over her shoulder when she was partway down the block. At that exact moment, the shiny hood of the black vehicle entered her line of sight. She quickened her pace, focusing on the line of trees dead ahead as she strode toward the end of the long stretch of brick buildings.

She made it halfway across the street when everything around her, including her own breath, felt frozen in time. A second SUV appeared around the corner ahead of her, blocking her route. A short siren-burst sounded from behind her. Red and blue lights flashing, the revolving colors reflected off everything around her.

Run to the right! her mind shouted, and Elaina did. She sprinted as fast as she could, blocking out the sound of tires peeling on the concrete behind her. She ran toward the first yard she came to, and somehow cleared the chain link fence in a fraction of a second. She could hear the angry shouts of men, ordering her to stop, but she kept going, not daring to take a glimpse for fear the movement would slow her down.

She dashed toward the last row of houses, heard the *crack* of a weapon firing, and a loud metallic *ding* from a near miss rang in her ears. Elaina hurdled over a picket fence, jerked around yard ornaments, coming close to tripping on a three-foot tall candy cane. She saw the second vehicle pull to the end of the street from the corner of her left eye, and she knew if they cut her off before she reached the section of woods ahead, her life would be over.

She pulled out her weapon without slowing her pace and took aim at the front driver's tire forty feet away. She pulled the trigger three times, feeling the kick from the pistol. The second bullet found its mark. The SUV jerked to the left, smashing headfirst into a robust tree, standing unmoving in the middle of the neighboring yard.

Elaina stretched out her legs and raced swiftly across the street and up onto the brush-covered embankment. The sound of another shot echoed from behind her, and a sharp painful sting burned deep into her right side, seconds before she found cover in the thick patch of trees. She pushed herself forward, spinning her arm around, and squeezed off two more rounds, unsure of their mark, trying to put as much distance between her and whoever was in pursuit.

Branches snagged at her hair and clothes, uneven terrain threatened to send her off balance, and all sense of direction was lost as she pushed deeper and deeper into the forested area. The sounds of running footsteps faded behind her. Without warning, the ground under her right leg vanished, sending her face first down a steep hillside as twigs and rocks cut her face and hands.

She heard the loud splash as she was fully submerged in the depths of cold moving water. She kicked her legs frantically; her jeans, sweatshirt, backpack, and jacket clinging heavily to her body. Genuine panic sank in as the current whipped her around under the water, forcing her downstream. Her lungs burned for a much-needed taste of air, but she couldn't discern up from down.

When all hope was lost, and her muscles twitched with exhaustion, Elaina reached out with her hand and grabbed hold of a rough, unmoving object. A tree branch. She gripped it with both hands and pulled with all the strength she had left, dragging herself from the water. She gasped, swallowing mouthfuls of sweet-tasting air.

Minutes felt like hours, while she worked her body along the low-hanging branch until at last she lay in a cold wet heap on the muddy earth, with overgrown brush all around her. Even though she was freezing, she did not move for some time, every muscle in her body ached with burning pain. When she was finally able to move, Elaina stood and then realized her weapon was gone. She searched around. No sign of her gun, no doubt it had been swept downstream. Elaina was unsure of where she was, but she knew she needed to keep going, because more importantly, she was unsure of where *they* were. She clawed her way up the hillside with her eyes and ears on high alert.

As soon as she hit the top of the hill, excruciating pain from her side shot through her, causing her to double over onto her knees. Gazing downward, Elaina spotted the blood covering the lower side of her sweatshirt and jacket, and her mind raced. She pulled her shirt up revealing a dime-sized hole to the far-right side of her stomach, directly across from her belly button, with a trail of watery blood seeping out.

"Crap!" she muttered. Bleeding to death in the middle of nowhere was not an option. What of the items she had hidden in the floor of the cabin? If she died, then their deadly secret died with her.

Trembling, Elaina stood, and removed her jacket. She tore off a piece of the lining and pushed it into the wound as hard as she could to slow the bleeding. She bit down on her lip, stifling a scream, as tears slid down her cheeks. The pain was greater than anything she had ever experienced in her life. Several minutes passed before she was able to continue in the direction she thought would lead her back to the cabin.

Sam had the coffee on, and eggs and sausage frying in the skillet, by five the following morning. Rachel made her way into the kitchen. "You're cooking, what's the occasion?" she asked, giving Christina's dog a pat on the head.

"For your information, I don't need an occasion to cook for my family. Now check on the biscuits."

Steven and Billy entered next, discussing the new game Steven bought at the store the day before. "Want to play after breakfast?" Steven asked.

Billy appeared excited for a moment, then his face went blank. "I'm working on the guesthouse with Sam today."

Sam did a visual assessment of Billy's busted lip. The swelling had gone down, but the bruising on someone so young still made her jaw clinch. "I was hoping we could take a break today, if you don't mind."

Billy started to smile, then cringed with pain when his grin stretched his healing lip. "I don't mind."

After the boy devoured his breakfast, Steven said, "Hey, Billy, why don't you go get dressed and then we'll play."

"Okay!" Billy took off like a rocket.

As soon as Billy was out of earshot, Steven lowered his next bite of runny eggs and sausage. "I think it would be best if we don't tell him what we're actually doing in the mine. He's only ten and it might be too complicated for him to understand. I thought about saying we're helping people who've lost their homes, which technically isn't lying."

"That's a good idea," Sam said, and Rachel agreed.

Steven fiddled with his fork. "Also, Rachel and I wanted to talk to you about this next semester, Sam. With what's going on in the country, we want to hold off on school until after Rachael has the baby."

Sam worked the spatula under an egg and flipped it in the skillet. She finished the sausage and added bacon to the pan. "That's probably a good idea. I know you guys are old enough to make your own decisions, whether it's about school or what's going on in the mine. Please promise me you'll be careful."

Several minutes later Mike trudged in, his head low as he poured the last of the coffee into a mug. Without being asked, he made a fresh pot, while stealing glances Sam's way.

Sam could tell something was on his mind, but she kept her thoughts to herself, and her attention on the stove. "Do you want some breakfast, Mike?"

Mike said, "Yes, please."

"How do you want your eggs?"

"Any way I can get them. If you manage to save a yolk or two, I'd be grateful. I fed the horses this morning and cleaned out the stalls. If you want, I can help you with the guesthouse today."

Sam studied him for several seconds before speaking. "We decided to take the day off. I have to go into town later for more horse feed and would appreciate some company."

"Sounds doable," Mike said. He headed to the kitchen table but came to a sudden stop. "Sam are you afraid to fight?"

Rachel and Steven sat in silence, watching Sam. "Yes, I am, Mike. But I'm not so much scared of dying as I am of seeing those I care for in danger. I'm also terrified of ending the life of another American who is only doing what they think is right."

Mike took a step closer to Sam and lowered his voice. "That's what's scaring me, Sam. I want to fight, for my parents and because I feel it's the right thing to do, but I've never killed anyone before."

"You're too young, Mike."

"I'll be seventeen next month," Mike said.

Billy came and announced, "I was getting ready to load the game, but Christina wanted me to tell you the president has issued a nationwide marital law. Does this mean everyone has to get married?"

Steven scrunched his face. "I don't know, I've never heard of such a thing."

Sam, spatula in hand, swiveled toward Billy. "Do you mean martial law?"

The group, as one, erupted in movement and joined Christina in the front room.

The news reporter seemed stressed, and his voice sounded strained as he spoke into the camera. "The president is activating all members of the Armed Forces, including those in the Reserves and National Guard branches. Soldiers already stationed overseas will remain at their current posts until further notice. The president insists martial law will be the safest and most effective way to bring our ever-growing crime wave under control by having more soldiers on the streets. Citizens shouldn't worry, everyone should continue with normal everyday life knowing the soldiers are there to protect them." He paused as he read the information before him. "The soldiers who fail to report to their assigned units immediately, or leave without proper orders, will be declared AWOL, and they'll be dealt with swiftly."

The reporter placed the sheet of paper he had read from on the anchor desk and brushed a hand over his tie. He looked directly into the camera and his tone became more upbeat. "Bingo will be held tonight at eight at the Westside Nursing Home for those who wish to come."

The woman sitting next to him jumped in. "Ah, Leonard—correction—bingo's not until tomorrow and it's at seven."

Sam returned to the kitchen. She had been in the military long enough to know what was coming. She'd witnessed martial law firsthand in a third world country. All the lives lost, the destruction, the mass hysteria, the total control of a whole nation of people, virtually overnight. Sam sat at the table. "Martial law, you've got to be kidding me."

Christina had followed Sam into the kitchen. "It's happening, Sam. Whether we want it to or not. Come with us, we'll find out more tonight at eight."

"At eight, what do you mean?"

"Leonard's in the movement. The line about bingo was his signal to let everyone know what time the meeting is. Like Agnes said, you're welcome to come whenever you change your mind."

Thirty minutes after the others had left for the meeting, Sam restlessly paced the living room. She wished she could have talked them out of being involved in the group, but they needed to make their own decisions. The only thing left to do was to hope for the best.

Billy had begged Christina into allowing him to go and play with some of the other children he met in the mine the night before, leaving Sam to face the eerie stillness of the home-front alone. She pressed the power button on the remote, switching off the television before heading into the kitchen. She stuck her head aimlessly into the fridge.

She cursed and flung the refrigerator door shut. "It's going to be a long night," she stomped through the living room, unsure of how to bide her time. She glowered at the barn through the oversized bay window. Sam gritted her teeth in frustration and grabbed her keys, motioning for the dog to stay. She headed outside to her cherry-red, extended cab truck.

Sam started the Dodge Ram, flipped on the headlights, and spun the truck around with the front end pointing down the long gravel driveway. Destressing would take some time.

The thought of finding an open lesbian club and having an evening of unattached sex crossed Sam's mind once or twice as she drove aimlessly down the road. She knew the chances of a club still being in business were slim to none. Not since the curfew had gone into effect. Who wanted to leave a club and be home by nine? Or take a chance of getting pulled over by the HTF after having even a sip of alcohol?

Sam had no idea where she was going, but she didn't really care. Being on the road and away from the farm was all that mattered. She needed to get some distance, to think, blow off a little steam. Have a moment of me-time before returning to the stresses that waited.

Eventually, she pulled her truck into the only remaining gas station in town, where she bought a cold six-pack of soda, and a box of chocolate iced doughnuts to help lighten her mood. As the older man behind the counter rang up her items, Sam, in a split-second decision, added a pack of cigarettes and a disposable green lighter.

Several minutes later, Sam sat in her truck in the parking lot of the gas station staring down at the unopened pack, as her fingers fidgeted with the lighter. She took up smoking soon after getting out of the hospital when she was sixteen, to help her cope with the trauma she was going through. She finally quit when her parents died, with the support of her sister, and the much-needed pills from her physician, while swearing to herself she would never take up the horrid habit ever again.

It's only one, she thought, removing the wrapper from the top of the pack. The first inhalation of smoke felt as if her throat and lungs had suddenly caught fire and sent her into a coughing fit which lasted for more than fifteen seconds. It didn't take long for the familiarity of the old habit to work its way in. She smoked the first cigarette, then lit another.

By the time the sky grew completely dark, Sam was parked behind the old, deserted train depot with less than half a pack of cigarettes left. She would need to stop and buy something to cover the smells in the truck and on herself before Rachel got close to either.

Tossing the most recent cigarette butt into an empty soda can, Sam decided it was time to leave. Her hand hovered over the key when the sound of multiple vehicles approaching the dead-end area gave her pause. Her eyes held tight to the thick outline of trees and brush as warning bells clanged in her head. She had no way of knowing who was coming, but she knew the locals didn't venture into this unused part of town.

Sam started her truck and moved behind one of the old, half-standing, lean-to structures toward the rear of the depot. She shut off the engine when she heard heavy reverberation from several huge vehicles blowing into the area. They moved with purpose—and not because they had taken a wrong turn somewhere along their travels.

The view wasn't great from her position, so she switched off the dome light and eased the driver's door open. Sam exited into a crouched stance and shuffled forward, taking up a position behind a pile of old boards and a mound of overgrown weeds. She counted seven prison buses with blackened windows, and four semis pulling what appeared to be troop trailers. At least their drill sergeants called them this when she was in basic training many years ago. In reality, they were giant cattle trailers converted into compartments with handrails throughout. Enough room for eighty plus soldiers to squeeze snugly in next to each other. Standing room only.

Sam eyed a rugged man exiting the lead bus. "I get first dibs on the women!" he shouted. Hearty laughter brayed from several others filing from the vehicles.

Sam counted eight men in all, each of them bearing a loaded automatic weapon. The brightness of the multiple headlights allowed her to see the men were dressed in uniforms comparable to Army fatigues. Except their outfits were solid black, instead of camouflage green, brown, and black, and most had never seen the underside of an iron.

"Lock it up!" the commanding voice of a large, stocky man caught everyone's attention, including Sam's.

His slab of a face was unwavering, even when the sound of a train's whistle cried off in the distance. She noticed the other men around the vehicles grew oddly excited at hearing the echoing call. Sam was mystified. Trains no longer stopped here, not since before she was born. She shifted uncomfortably, all appearances informing her tonight would be different.

A second blow of the whistle, but still no lights appeared from the space between the woods nestled on either side of the tracks. She heard metal grinding down on metal even before seeing the glow of the slowing locomotive coming around the bend ahead. Sam leaned in and strained to see through the darkness.

As soon as the train appeared, the men took strategic positions around the area. Sam assumed they were somewhat trained and familiar with working together. Their hard expressions reminded her of hungry drill sergeants waiting for their new company of troops. The man who seemed to be in charge remained off to the side, watching his subordinates, and calling out commands.

The train stopped and the boxcar doors clanged open, chilling the blood throughout Sam's body. What unnerved Sam was the terrified faces of men, women, and children who stood packed in the metal containers, visibly too frightened to move. They gripped each other tight.

Sam could tell the people on the train were not criminals, yet the armed men pulled out ramps and forcefully herded everyone from the train, directing them roughly onto the awaiting vehicles. The eyes of the captives were wide with fright, their faces pale in the headlights. The soldiers placed the men onto the cattle trailers and the women and children were ushered onto the buses, several weeping, pleading for their freedom.

Sam remained unmoving, mouth agape, unsure if this scene was real or a horrible dream, as confused and terrified kids were pulled forcefully away from their fathers. The little ones calling out to them for protection.

"No, please. I need to stay with my family!" a middle-aged man begged the guard who was yelling repeatedly for him to climb into the trailer. The man reached out for his wife's outstretched hand. The guard smacked the butt of his weapon into the man's forehead. Even though Sam was about a hundred feet away, she was certain she heard crunching as the weapon made contact. The man dropped straight to the ground.

"No. Father!" A tall, red-haired, teenage girl screamed and rushed to his side.

Sam was worried the blow might have killed the man. With great relief, she saw him slowly move his legs. The guard who had exited the vehicles first when they arrived, stormed to the melee. He yanked the girl to her feet as a few of the male prisoners helped the bleeding man to his.

"Don't worry, honey, Daddy will be fine." The guard pulled the girl over to the bus. "If you want, I can be your daddy now."

His comment earned laughter from several of the other guards. Without realizing it, Sam was on her feet. How long she had been exposed? Her anger grew into rage. She fought down the suicidal urge to rush forward and fight with no weapon to try to free these people.

Luckily, her voice of reason prevailed, and she hunkered down behind her pile of cover.

Several more train cars were unloaded in the same fashion. Sam calculated a rough estimate of three hundred women and children and maybe four hundred men. More than enough bodies to rush a group of eight. Yet, who would want to be the one to charge soldiers holding automatic weapons?

She climbed into her truck when the convoy of vehicles pulled out. Keeping her lights off, and remaining a safe distance behind, she followed. The convoy stayed to the gravel roads, and to Sam's good fortune, she knew this area inside and out, allowing her to slow her speed without losing them.

The dense trees in the area blocked any glow from the moon. She kept her vehicle as much in the middle of the road as she could, while leaning forward, hoping for a clearer view through the fog of gravel dust and blackness. What I wouldn't give for a set of night vision goggles right about now, she thought. She swerved her truck on the gravel road narrowly missing the ditch.

She steered her truck around a curve, close to the entrance to her Uncle Sam's old farm, when she spotted taillights from the line of trailers breaking off from the rest of the convoy. Puzzled, she watched them take a paved road leading in the opposite direction from town. The buses continued on the gravel road, in the direction of the old quarry.

Sam stopped and weighed her options, then followed the buses. She remained a good distance behind the line of vehicles carrying the women and children. They drove on the gravel road for ten more minutes, giving Sam an idea of where they might be heading. She slowed as she approached the top of the next hill on the off chance she was right. The moment her truck reached the top, Sam's eyes caught sight of the brake lights from the last vehicle. The bus gradually swung to the right, through a newly constructed security gate.

She backed her truck off the road, trying for as much concealment as possible. Sam threw her jacket on and searched through the full-size toolbox mounted on the truck bed. Finally, she found her binoculars and crept into the woods, quiet as a mouse, to see what she could see.

The distance to Christina's old farm took longer than it should have. Sam wasn't sure what level of perimeter defense was in place, so she was extra cautious on her approach.

She came to a stop on the hillside overlooking the familiar valley. The once thickly wooded area surrounding the farmhouse was now a vast open stretch of gravel and chain-link fencing. Dense tree-covered Ozark hills enveloped three of the four sides. Several high-powered spotlights shone down on the encampment, encasing the area in a bubble of brightness, unseen past the towering hillsides. Multiple tents and metal buildings had been erected around Christina's old farmhouse.

Sam moved to a position halfway down the hill, alongside the remains of a fallen tree large enough to provide her ample cover and a decent vantage point. Adjusting her high-powered binoculars, she focused on the growing commotion. Shouting uniformed men forced the frightened women and children off the buses and into semi-organized groups as they clung tight to one another. Sam watched, helpless, while the soldiers separated the prisoners and directed them into the military tents.

Two well-built guard towers had been erected on opposite corners of the encampment. Each was positioned to have a perfect view of the enclosure for the armed men perched twenty feet up inside the wooden structures. She didn't see any heavily armed bunkers or defensive positions other than the two towers, but several armed men walked the fence line.

A disturbance near one of the corner tents caught her attention. Two of the guards antagonized a teenage girl while several of the other armed men watched, clearly enjoying the victimization of the child. Sam couldn't hear what the men were saying to the frightened teenager as they pushed her from one to the other laughing the whole time. Their twisted game ended when the leader shot two rounds into the air above them. He barked out several commands then stalked to the farmhouse, slamming the front door behind him.

Sam closed her eyes and lowered her head to the cold ground, unsure of what to do. She was one unarmed being against a small army. A twig snapped close by. Her heart pounded. She remained still and waited. Her breathing was shallow, almost silent, as the figure of a man passed below her position with his weapon raised.

Chapter Eleven

The Encampments

The tranquil, reddish-blue hues of morning were peeking up over the green, flourishing trees. Wrapped snug in the warmth of two patchwork quilts, with a fresh cup of hot chocolate in their hands, Rachel and Christina rocked slowly on the front porch.

"Did it seem like Sam was still upset with us? Maybe I should try to call Aunt Agnes again?" Rachel dabbed a tissue at the corner of her eye.

Christina placed her hand on Rachel's arm. "Sam will be fine. She's a smart woman and can take care of herself."

"Sam doesn't act like this, Christina. She always calls me if she'll be out all night, even if she's pissed." Rachel inspected the length of the driveway. Her lips quivered and a fresh wave of tears fell.

"I found Mike passed out on the couch next to Billy." Steven stepped out on the porch, closing the screen door behind him. He wrapped his blanket around his body and sat on the porch-swing across from where the two women cuddled together. "I put Billy to bed and threw some blankets on Mike."

Christina's phone made a sound.

Rachel watched in silence as Christina hurriedly checked the text message. "It's from Mrs. Pumpernickel, I need to go." Christina stood.

Within seconds Mike rushed outside, somewhat off-balance. "I received a message to report down to the mine—"

A shrill beep cut Mike off, and Rachel snatched her phone and read the text. "Me, too."

They rushed inside and discovered Steven's phone had received the same message. "Something big must be going on." Steven grabbed his jacket from the coat tree. "What are we going to do with Billy?"

"Take him with us. We can keep him in the medical wing." Christina donned her jacket. "Mister Douglas told me they finished hooking up the ventilators yesterday."

Mike said, "I'll go get him ready."

Within ten minutes, the group entered the mine. They were surprised by the vast amount of movement and commotion outside the conference room, but not as surprised as when they finally made their way through the crowd of onlookers. In the center a mud-covered Sam leaned over a map showing a detailed image of the terrain in a fifty-square mile radius of town. She appeared to be pointing out places to Aunt Agnes and a handful of others.

Rachel hurried forward. "What's going on? We've been worried sick over you." Rachel threw her arms around Sam, then jerked away. She spoke with her fisted hands on her hips. "Sam, have you been smoking?"

Sam's eyes were bloodshot and unfocused as if she were trapped in deep thought.

"Are you sure you want to do this, Sam?" Agnes asked, her features reflected apprehension.

Without hesitation, Sam gave her Aunt Agnes a firm nod.

"We're behind you one-hundred percent, Sam." Mister Douglas patted her on the shoulder.

Christina and Rachel each flashed their confusion to one another.

Steven piped up, "Sam, what happened? What's going on?"

"We're about ready to explain the situation to everyone." Agnes guided Sam toward the exit. "Why don't you all take Billy down to the medical wing, and I'll get everyone else settled."

"We won't be long," Sam said to Agnes, then motioned for Rachel and the others to follow.

After securing Billy safely with two volunteers Sam and her followers retraced their steps through the passageway.

"Sam, will you talk to me?" Rachel asked.

"We're carrying out a mission tonight."

"So, you're in the group, Sam?" Mike asked with a grin.

Sam offered the teenager a weak smile. "Someone needs to keep an eye on you."

Frustrated, Rachel heaved a sigh. "Will you please stop avoiding my questions?"

"There's a lot to this, and I promise you'll find out shortly. If you don't mind, now I would like to speak with Steven alone first."

Rachel stood, not saying a word. Her eyes showed confusion, even hurt that her sister would rather talk to Steven than her. But Christina grabbed her hand and Rachel followed her and Mike to the conference room.

"What is it, Sam?" Steven asked.

Sam could hear the concern in his voice as he stared at her, unknowing. She smiled in hopes of easing his worry. "Everything's fine Steven. I'm merely covering all of the bases."

"I'm listening."

"If anything should happen to me, then I want you to get them as far away from here as possible. There's plenty of money in the safe, and Rachel has the combination. Canada would be my choice, but I leave it up to you."

"Sam, what are you talking about?" Steven's voice was insistent.

"Please promise me you'll look after them if anything should happen to me."

"Sam, you know I will, but nothing is going to happen."

"Of course not, but there's peace in knowing my loved ones have a back-up plan, just in case."

"Um . . . Sam, Steven, Agnes told me to come get you two."

"Thanks, Mike." Sam knew Steven would take care of Rachel, with or without having been asked. "I guess we better go."

Steven went to find Rachel and Christina, and Sam made her way up to the front with Agnes.

"Everyone, settle down, please." Agnes waited until the soft murmurs and whispers ended before she continued. "Thank you. Now, I know you're all wondering why we called you here this early, and I do appreciate everyone showing up so quickly." Agnes's voice carried through the room. "We have all known for some time things were getting worse, which is why we joined together in the first place."

Many shouted, while others mumbled their agreement. The room grew silent again. "Unfortunately, the time for planning has passed. We must act now."

The room filled with cheers, and Sam's heart twinged. These people were not soldiers. They had not seen the bloody edge of battle. Never had it stared up at them with its razor-sharp teeth, bringing with it the promise of pain and or death. Even though all here were more than willing to seek out justice, most were untrained for a fight. Sam knew she had made the right choice on who would be going tonight.

Agnes held up her hand. Silence descended once again. "Most of you know my niece, Samantha." Several clapped, others whistled. "She has learned the government has transformed the Dowell farm into a camp where civilian women and children have been imprisoned. We have reason to believe there's another camp in this area for the men, though we have not been able to find it yet."

Anger spread like wildfire, and a male voice shouted, "I knew this would happen."

An elderly woman spoke in a shaky voice, "Just like Hitler and the concentration camps."

"Please, everyone." Agnes held up her hand once more, but few noticed, too fueled by their own outrage.

Mister Douglas brought a fist down hard onto the surface of the table, the sound of the impact silenced the group. His glare was stern. "I don't believe Agnes was finished." He gave her a nod to continue.

"We have come up with a plan to attack the camp, and God willing, free everyone there. Now I'll hand this over to my niece and she'll walk us through the details."

All eyes were fixed on Sam. She moved forward, not daring to look in Rachel's direction. "First, I would like to take this opportunity to ask you all to really think about if you truly want to be a part of this." She scanned the room, making eye contact with many of her neighbors. "We're only a handful of citizens who are preparing to go to war against a powerful government with thousands upon thousands of trained soldiers under its control. Any one of you can leave now, and we'll more than understand."

Sam paused to give those in the room a chance to leave. Nobody moved. She was sad they stayed and proud of their choice at the same time. "I didn't want this to happen. I love my country. Going against one's own government should never be a decision a person makes lightly, but when a government goes after the innocent, then I say it's time for a new government. With what I witnessed last night, I feel by being here, I'm doing my duty as an American citizen, and I'm saying *no more!*"

The room rang with loud echoes of applause and cheers. "We have chosen to rise up against a corrupt government no longer functioning for the welfare of its people, but *against* the people, and they must be stopped." Sam raised her chin. "Nonetheless, we must be smart, cunning, and we will need to cover our tracks as much as humanly possible. We must organize and pull together to see each other through this safely. We will continue with our daily lives as if nothing has changed. We will train hard and do all we can to unite with and help others along the way."

"When are we going to attack the camp?" The teenage boy who had called Sam a coward the night before shouted out.

"Tonight, and we've already assigned the team."

"What if we want to be on the team?" Someone else asked.

"I'm sorry, but the team's been hand-picked due to prior military experience. We still need help preparing the mine ready for when we return."

"I want to fight!" the teenage boy insisted, and half the room erupted in an uproar of agreement.

"Have you ever killed anyone, son?" Mister Douglas narrowed his eyes at the young man. "Could you rush over to the screaming person next to you and shove their bloody innards back inside their mangled body, while at the same time being shot at?"

The boy remained silent under the older man's gaze. His expression twisted sideways in disgust.

"If you or anyone else goes out there, untrained and half-cocked, then you'll not only risk getting yourselves killed, but also the people on your team, and possibly those citizens we're trying to save." Mister Douglas glared to the hushed room. "I do not plan to die tonight."

Sam agreed. "Several groups like this one have already been slaughtered or captured because of arrogance or impatience. The more precautions we take, the better we become, and some of you might come out of this difficult time in one piece, if you're lucky."

"Who's going?" A young woman by the exit asked.

Sam noticed the concern in her sister's eyes. She could tell Rachel knew she would be going but thinking it and hearing it were two different things. "The team will be Mister Douglas, Todd Kirkwood, Frank Johnson, and myself. We have acquired four school buses, which we'll use to transport the captives. But we need volunteers to get everything operational before we arrive."

"What do you need, Samantha?" Mrs. Pumpernickel called out.

Sam grabbed one of the lists from the table. "We'll need sleeping and bath accommodations in areas of the mine with working ventilation already."

"I'm a master plumber and George, he's a carpenter. Give us three others and we'll see it's taken care of," a man standing toward the front of the room spoke.

Over half the room raised their hands and Mrs. Pumpernickel chose three out of the group. She went up on the platform to the desk, took out paper and pen, and unlike the other lists with Sam's chicken scratch handwriting, she wrote their names in pristine penmanship.

Sam said, "We need to move all the weapons and explosives out of the pathways and secure them in a separate room." Several more raised their hands. Mrs. Pumpernickel pointed at four, before jotting down their names. "The largest entrance into the mine is through Uncle Sam's barn, but it's been sealed off. I think we'll have the space to bring the buses in through there, but we need to open up the entrance."

Agnes smiled proudly when Phillip stood. "Sam, I can help with that. My backhoe is in good shape, but I'll need several individuals to assist with reinforcing the supports once we get it open." Sam nodded to her uncle as Mrs. Pumpernickel selected eight strong-looking individuals.

Sam went on until they had enough volunteers to help with organizing the food and water supplies, getting the medical wing together, erecting several lookout posts throughout the area, and setting up communications from the mine to the buses, and to the people on lookout.

"If you notice we're being followed, call it in. We have an alternate spot designated if things don't go as planned."

Once Mrs. Pumpernickel finished with the list, she handed the sheet to Agnes. Agnes double-checked the names then asked Sam if she had anything further needing addressing.

Sam figured now was as good of a time as any. "We must focus on organizing this group if we want this to work. I suggest we elect a committee to oversee specific jobs. Such as training, supply, medical, communication, maintenance, finance, but more importantly, security. I assume you're all parked at my Aunt Agnes's."

Almost the entire room indicated they were.

"Overly conspicuous, and at the present time with these new laws, this many people gathered in one area is illegal."

Sam and the three other members of the night's team made their way through the southeast passageway, coming out into one of four newly constructed rooms in this part of the mine. Numerous shelves and containers lined the reinforced walls, each packed with different types of weapons and equipment. They had enough firepower to supply a large garrison, maybe two. Frank Johnson told Sam their group had gotten the items over the last several months, and more were on the way.

"I have my connections," he gave Sam a sly smile. "Not only was I a Ranger during Desert Storm, but I was also in charge of supply at times due to my, shall we say, thriftiness."

Sam searched through several of the containers. "Tonight might go better than expected." She ran her hand over a long-barreled rifle with a high-powered scope mounted on top. "An M82A1 fifty caliber semi-automatic sniper rifle. Not bad for bringing down helicopters or low-flying aircraft."

Frank raised his eyebrows skyward. "I'm impressed, Sam, you know your weapons."

"To an extent." Sam said, "This rifle will be too much firepower for tonight, I'm afraid."

"Ah, don't worry, little missy, I also have several of these." He moved to where Douglas stood and unlatched the top crate.

Sam whistled. "Whoa! You have the M-40A3 Marine sniper rifles. Yes, these are an excellent choice for tonight."

"Correct, and I must say, you're very knowledgeable for having a communications background."

Sam grinned. "My job was a bit different than you think. Plus, I love my weapons."

"I'm glad you two are on our side," Todd remarked, eyeing the multiple shelves.

"Douglas, you were a sniper, right?" Frank asked.

"That was an awfully long time ago, Frank. Now I only shoot at deer and elk when the season rolls around."

"I built a firing range in the cavern behind the armory. Let's say we all brush up on our skills before going over the plan once more." Frank spread his arms out wide to Sam, Todd, and Douglas. "Choose your weapons and I'll get the ammo ready."

Elaina caught her breath when her footing threatened to give way as she stumbled down the hillside. Her body felt weak, feverish, causing the wound in her side to ache even more. She wanted to stop and rest, but the bad guys knew she was somewhere in these woods, and she had to find her way to the cabin before they caught her.

The bleeding had stopped sometime during the night. But without food or medical supplies, Elaina was sure her strength wasn't going to last much longer. If only she could find somewhere to rest for a while, to build a little strength, then maybe she would make it. She had less than one full bottle of water left in her backpack after using one this morning to flush the dirt out of the bullet wound. She drank sparingly, even though her dry, scratchy throat demanded more.

She took a few shallow breaths before willing herself forward, using several of the trees she passed for temporary support. Her mind wandered, and she almost giggled remembering how often in the cabin she'd wished for the normal, everyday comforts to which she was accustomed. Her queen-sized, pillow-top bed, sturdy cast-iron bathtub, electric stove, microwave, television, and radio. In contrast, now she was wishing for the simplicity of the cabin and her few worldly possessions inside.

A moan escaped through her pursed lips, and her gaze slowly lifted. She halted in disbelief, her tired eyes squinting to focus as her body swayed. Ahead, past the edge of the dense forest she had trudged through all night, and beyond a wide-open pasture, stood a magnificent farm. She had to blink twice to make sure it wasn't a mirage or a hallucination brought on by the fever.

After surveying the area, Elaina moved forward as fast as her legs would carry her. She fell once on her way over the first wooden fence but had enough strength to clamber to her feet. It took her some time to cover the remaining distance to the barn, but once she made her way inside, she discovered the trip was more than worth it.

The building was well cared for, and as she stumbled further into the high-ceilinged building, she noticed only three of the stalls housed well-groomed horses. They made a little ruckus at her presence but settled once she headed toward the back. She found a spacious room, with several canisters of horse feed, equipment, and four polished western saddles. The whole barn smelled of hay and leather and the soothing aroma made her weary head ache for slumber.

Across from the tack and feed room, Elaina found what she had been praying for. A cozy room which held a sturdy wooden desk, matching cabinet, fully stocked refrigerator, microwave, leather couch, and a table with four matching chairs.

Her heart skipped a beat when she opened the first door of the cabinet, revealing a white box labeled *First Aid,* giving her hope for survival.

Night had fallen early, thanks to a new front of storm clouds making their way into the area. Sam had managed to get only a few hours of sleep as visions of the captive women and children played over and over in her mind. The four team-members dressed in solid black military uniforms, with matching military boots and gloves, courtesy of Frank Johnson's black-market connections. They had smeared black camouflage paint on their faces and necks, then completed their outfits with black stocking caps and tiny headsets for communication with one another.

"We might be under-trained and unprepared for this mission, but by God we look lethal." Mister Douglas grinned as he climbed from the bus.

Sam felt the face paint pull when she tried to smile at her three companions. Yes, she thought, we do look sharp. Let's hope we perform that way. "Remember your jobs and we'll make it out in one piece. They're not expecting anything to happen, so their security is minimal. Consider this a good refresher exercise for future missions."

Todd said, "Like I told you earlier, I have little combat experience, but I'll do my best.".

Douglas slapped him hard on the back. "I'll have you covered, son. Keep your kills as quiet as possible, and your mind focused."

Sam flipped on her headset. "Let's go." She slung her M-16 over her shoulder, fixed the suppressor onto her pistol, and added the attachment of additional wipes.

Todd did the same.

When they were a quarter mile from the encampment, Douglas and Todd veered to the left, while Sam and Frank continued on a course to the right, heading for opposite ends of the compound. They remained quiet and alert as they moved, while keeping as hidden amongst the trees as possible.

They trudged to the top of the hill and Frank inspected the terrain. "This spot's good, Sam. Far enough away so it should lessen the noise some," he muttered. He removed the M-40A3 from around his shoulder and placed it in a fixed position on the ground, with the front leg supports propped up onto a medium-sized rock. He attached the suppressor to the end, tossed his headphones on the ground, then secured a comfortable firing position at the rear of the weapon.

A loud *crack* from a snapped twig echoed in her ears, causing Sam to crouch down beside Frank.

"He's thirty feet to your right, Sam," Frank whispered, motioning with his first two fingers.

She scanned the vicinity where Frank gestured. She spotted the shadowy outline and raised her pistol. Her target moved casually along to the right of their position. Normally, with this type of weapon, Sam fired straight on. With the suppressor and extension, instead she adjusted her aim a tad higher and to the left to ensure a perfect shot. She took in a lungful of air and let out half before holding her breath and squeezed the trigger until the slack was gone. She aimed for the target's chest and fired. A light *whooshing* sound, followed by a barely audible *pop,* and the shot found its mark.

"Good girl."

Sam breathed slowly out before speaking into her headset. "Todd, we're in position."

"Copy that, Sam, we're good to go," Todd said, giving Sam the signal to move out.

Sam placed a gloved hand on Frank's shoulder, before setting off down the hill toward the well-lit camp. She kept her body low, pistol ready, her eyes inspecting the trees for any sign of movement. When she was less than fifteen yards from the ten-foot-high chain link fence, she spotted a second figure leaning against the base of a thick, over-turned tree. Sam moved closer, taking steady aim as she readied her body to fire. The shot was perfect, sending her next victim face-first to the ground.

Adrenaline surged through her body. She crouched against the tree and gave Frank the ready signal via her headset. She didn't think about the fallen body next to her. He was dead, and she had a mission needing completion. She'd learned to distance herself. Learned to control her emotions.

Sam squinted at the tower at the exact moment she heard the distinct *crack*, and the soldier high on his perch, jerked in slow motion before collapsing straight down in a heap. His corpse conveniently hidden by the sides of the wooden structure. She studied the camp for movement. The suppression on the sniper rifle was disturbingly louder than she hoped. Thankfully, the camp remained motionless.

She pushed forward to the fence, choosing a spot nestled within the shadows of the closest tent. Removing the metal cutters from the side cargo pocket on her pants, Sam cut out a hole in the fence and squeezed through. She took cover along the rear of the tent, her senses on high alert.

"Sam, hold up for a moment. I see two guards moving toward the front of the tent to your right. Not sure which way they're heading yet, so don't move."

Sam did as Frank instructed, keeping low, her breathing steady. The commotion that followed caused Sam's blood to boil. Women from the next tent shouted in protest, before a loud *smack* silenced them.

"So, help me, I'll put a bullet in anyone of you if you don't shut up," growled a man's voice. A second man snickered in a twisted sort of way, which made Sam's skin crawl.

"You, stand up!"

"Hey, I get first pick this time, you had it last time!"

"Fine, then pick one and let's go!" The man sounded irritated.

"I want her."

"Damn. You over there, stand up!"

"Please sir, don't do this. They're only children."

More sinister laughter. "Once a girl develops tits like these, she's no longer a child. Now move!"

Clenching her jaw muscles, Sam shifted along the edge of the tent, halfway toward the front to try to get a better view. Her eyes caught sight of four individuals exiting the tent. Two of them were men from the train depot last night, along with the tall, red-haired teenage girl who had cried out for her father. The shorter, dark-haired girl, Sam didn't recognize. By her appearance, Sam figured the child wasn't a day over sixteen. Sam bit back her anger at seeing the men pull the frightened girls toward the house.

"Frank, see anything?"

"No, Sam, only those two assholes in front of you."

"Todd, are you inside yet?"

"I'm moving in now, Sam. I dropped two over here by the fence and Douglas got the one in the tower. I see movement to my right, but everything else is quiet."

Sam contemplated her options. "Frank I'm going in the farmhouse. Watch the entrance for me, will ya?" She moved closer to the front of the tent.

"Gotcha, lass. Take it slow and holler if you need backup."

Sam carefully searched the area, then sprinted toward the main house, staying low. Once there, she dropped down and waited for any signs of life from the front of the encampment. She spotted a guard leaning against a green military vehicle, smoking a cigarette, and appearing as if he hadn't a care in the world. She raised her weapon and took aim. She heard a *pop* and the guard dropped right as she was about to fire. Todd emerged from behind a metal shed and dragged the dead body into the shadows. Perfectly executed as far as she was concerned.

Reaching the top step, Sam noticed the front door to the main house was partially ajar. Several voices drifted from inside. She made out two separate voices, maybe three. Sam moved into position. Without hesitation she rushed in, weapon raised, letting her training and reflexes take control.

The first two kills were easy. Two bullets and two fallen bodies. The third man moved quicker, but still gave Sam little challenge. He dove to the right, to where his weapon and the radio system sat on the desk in the corner. She wasn't sure which item he was reaching for, and frankly, she didn't care. She pulled the trigger and her latest victim dropped to the floor.

Replacing the wipes on her suppressor, she listened for any movement and heard nothing. She pushed onward. The first door along the hall to the right was Christina's old bedroom. Sam placed her ear to the door but heard only silence. She rotated the handle slowly, opening the door enough to get her hand inside to feel for the light-switch. She counted to three and flipped on the lights, then pushed open the door and trained her weapon inside.

She took out a guy asleep in a twin bed directly in front of her with one shot to the forehead. A second man rose, half-awake, from a cot in the right corner and she greeted him with a bullet to the heart. Both men died instantly.

She detected no sound of enemies running to her, so she moved on, keeping her mind focused and her breaths even. She placed her ear to Sarah's bedroom door. This time she heard the muffled cries of a girl. Probably one of the teenagers. Sam had to fight down the urge to barge in as smoldering rage sparked inside her. Twisting the knob, Sam gently cracked the door open, and light poured from the room. A man had his back to her, no overshirt on, and his pants sagged below his waist. He backhanded the red-haired girl across the face. The hard blow sent the helpless teen flailing onto the bed.

"If I feel even the slightest hint of a tooth on my dick, I'll personally knock them all out of your fucking head!"

Sam holstered her firearm, drew her knife, and crept in. Her mind burned with hatred. She grabbed a handful of the man's hair and jerked his head back hard. Before he had a chance to defend himself, Sam brought her knife across his exposed neck in one smooth movement. His death-scream was only a low gurgle as his bloody body twitched, then fell to the floor.

She went forward, placing her gloved hand over the mouth of the frightened, half-naked teenager. "Don't scream. I'm not here to hurt you." Sam stowed her soiled knife. "I'm taking you out of here, but first I need to get to the other girl."

Once the teenager agreed, Sam removed her hand from over the girl's mouth. The girl wrapped her arms tightly around Sam's neck. "Thank you," she half-cried, half-whispered.

Sam awkwardly patted the girl before gently pulling her away. "Stay here and don't make a sound. I'll return shortly." She tossed the girl's shirt to her and left the room.

The door to the last room, Mister Dowell's bedroom, was down the hall and to the left. The deeper Sam went into the hall, the darker it became. She made a mental note to have Frank move the night-vision goggles to the top of his *must have* list.

Pulling out her pistol, Sam creeped up to the door, and listened. No commotion came from the other side. All was quiet, too quiet. Turning the knob, Sam carefully pushed the door open, keeping her body low and against the wall.

The light from the room spilled out into the dark hallway followed by a deep commanding voice from the other guard. "Drop your weapon, or I'll slit her throat!"

Keeping the bulk of her body hidden against the edge of the doorframe, Sam peeked inside. The guard used the dark-haired girl as a shield and had the tip of a bayonet pressed into the edge of her throat. Between the terrified look on the young girl's face, and the battered appearance of her naked body, Sam felt a venomous wrath snap her into action. She kept her eyes fixed on the man and placed her weapon on the floor. Standing slowly to her full height, Sam withdrew her bloodied knife as fury flooded her.

"I guess you and I are going have some fun." The man's lips curled into a sneer. He tossed the girl to the side and pointed his knife at Sam. He crossed the distance of the room in less three strides, exuding confidence. "This will not be over quickly." He thrust his blade forward toward the right side of Sam's midsection. Not to kill but wound.

She blocked the attack with her left hand while bringing the metal handle of her knife up hard into the man's face with a nose-breaking crunch. Her assailant tumbled backwards. "I agree," she muttered and rotated her body a few steps further inside the room.

He raised his free hand to his nose, then inspected the blood covering his finger. His reddened grin widened, his eyes watering from the pain. "I hope you enjoyed the hit. You won't get another." He moved, still cocky, but with more speed this time. He executed a fake sidestep to Sam's left before sending his bayonet straight in.

Sam pivoted and brought her leg up, first to block his strike and next into a smooth, powerful motion, once again striking his broken nose. He let out a pain-filled yelp. His head jerked sideways, and he threw his hands upward to cover the bulk of his face. In anguish he dropped to one knee.

"You fucking bitch!" Blood muffled his words, but Sam detected a hint of alarm in his tone.

Sam kept one eye on her enemy, the other fell on the girl whimpering in the corner. The child had her head buried in her knees as her entire body trembled. The heartbreaking sight turned Sam's blood cold. She snarled to the man. "You won't live to see another day."

He growled angrily and flung his body at Sam. She pivoted and brought a boot up, smashing him in the face. His neck snapped and he landed flat on his back in the middle of the room. His cries withered into hushed moans, and he struggled to pull himself onto his stomach while cupping his hand over his nose. Sam waited, biding her time, savoring her anger.

Finally, after much struggle, the man slowly clambered to his feet with his knife trembling in his hand. He threw Sam a humiliated glower of defeat. His eyes shot to the girl. Instantly, his lips pulled into one last sinister sneer.

The time in the room played in slow motion. Sam saw the grip of the man's hand form tightly around the handle of his blade. At the same moment, his body jolted toward the girl. Sam flipped the knife in her hand, raised it up high behind her head, and sent it with deadly force, flying at the man. The knife stuck in his side, but the man didn't go down. He stumbled, grabbed the frightened girl by the arm, ready to slice her throat in a final act of defiance. Sam frantically searched around the room for her weapon. Seeing it within reach, she maneuvered a front roll and snatched the gun from the ground. She fired off two shots. The man fell with a *thunk* at the crying girl's feet.

Sam went to the bed and yanked off the blanket. She used it to cover the shaking child.

"Jesus, Sam," Todd's voice came from the door behind her. He entered the room, lowering his weapon.

"Help me get her dressed." Sam tried hard to keep her emotions buried.

After they had the girl up and clothed and were moving both teenagers through the hallway, Todd informed the others they were coming out. A thick folder on the desk by the front door caught Sam's eye and she veered from the three to grab the file.

"Sam, we don't have time."

"Take them outside. I'll be right behind you."

She flipped through the paperwork with building excitement. The folder contained documents about other camps located throughout the United States. Sam could scarcely believe how many there were. And all appeared positioned in remote areas like this one, away from larger cities and towns. Apparently, these guys wanted to avoid detection from people like Sam's group who still gave a shit.

Folder in hand, Sam moved toward the door. A sudden thought crossed her mind. She changed direction, making her way around to the front of the desk to go through the drawers of the desk, one by one. They revealed nothing of interest. Sighing in frustration, Sam audited the makeshift office. A line of three filing cabinets in the old dining room caught her interest. She hurried over and began searching through the drawers. In the second drawer of the last cabinet, she discovered a bulky file labeled *Prison Camp Recruits*, in bold black lettering. She yanked it out and skimmed the pages. Her blood turned cold, then hot with anger as she read. Sam snatched it up and left the house.

The once-silent camp was a beehive of action. Her companions coaxed the anxious captives out from the confinements of their tents, doing their best to ease the rising tension. Sam noticed how many of the women were too afraid to grasp what was happening to them. Some were growing hysterical and gripping tightly onto one another for support. Her heart felt heavy with what they had all been through.

"We're ready to go, Sam." Douglas's eyes were moist with sadness as he signaled for her to lead the way.

"Ladies!" Sam called out. The tear-streaked faces instantly turned toward her. "Your captors are dead. You're all safe now."

The relief and excitement filling the area was thunderous, but the women and children soon calmed.

Sam said, "We're getting you out of here. We have a half-mile hike through the woods, and we need everyone to be incredibly quiet as we move. It's dark out there, so keep an eye on the children and each other."

The four rescuers positioned themselves on each side of the group with Sam leading the way. Halfway to the buses, Sam voiced her concerns to the others through the headset. "I know where the men are being held, and I have a good idea of the numbers guarding them."

Frank piped in, "Good, we can go through it as soon as we get back."

Sam said, "Once they find out about us hitting this camp, their security will rise drastically."

Douglas's voice filled the headset, "What are you saying, Sam? You want us to hit it tonight?"

"Yes, but only if we're all in agreement." Sam paused for a moment to think. "We don't have the trained manpower for another attack anytime soon if they increase their security. As of right now, they're still unaware their camps are under any threat."

"I'm with Sam," Todd cut in. "She knows what she's doing."

Frank snorted. "She sure scared the crap out of me tonight." He broke off for a few seconds, ending the silence with a sigh. "Count me in."

Douglas was the last to agree. "I'm not going to miss out on all the fun, but if we want to do this before sunup, then we need to hurry and get these people back to base."

The four loaded buses arrived at the farm at three minutes past midnight. Sam told her Uncle Phillip and the others waiting about the new plan and asked them to close the mine entrance once everyone was inside.

"Your aunt and sister will be upset with this sudden change in plans," Uncle Phillip said. He didn't seem pleased by the idea either.

Sam beamed. "That's why you're not going to tell them until we've left."

The volunteers off-loaded the women and children and moved them into the mine as Sam and her team studied the map and information on their next target. "That's Jed's farm," Frank said. "Well, it was up until the government seized it anyway."

Douglas grumbled, "Now we know why they're so eager to take everyone's property."

Sam frowned, feeling the effects of little sleep. "If this paperwork's correct, we'll be facing thirty-two guards. That's double what we've already encountered."

Frank said, "It's not too late to change your mind."

Sam gazed at the ceiling and exhaled deeply. She knew tonight would be the best time to strike, but if she led these men to their deaths, she would never forgive herself.

Douglas squeezed Sam's shoulder. "We know what we're getting into, Sam. I think I speak for everyone here when I say, if it's my time to go, then at least I go out doing the right thing."

Frank backhanded her stomach. "Come on kid, let's go raise some hell."

Chapter Twelve

Unexpected Company

After the last of the men exited the bus, Sam laid her head on the steering wheel and closed her eyes. Her bus was the last of the four to pull into the mouth of the mine. Uncle Phillip and several others closed the two reinforced metal doors behind them. Then went out and stacked hay bales on the other side to hide the entrance from trespassers.

She brought her head up as her name echoed from somewhere in the passage. The voice sounded like Rachel's. The thought of hiding in one of the seats crossed her mind, but only for a second. With a tired heart, Sam watched as two of the men they'd freed less than an hour earlier help the injured Todd from the bus parked in front of hers. At the sight Sam lowered her head once more.

"What in the hell did you think you were doing?"

Sam raised her head, feeling drained and overstretched. She knew this had been the right call. But Rachel had every right to be upset. Sam stood and slunk down the steps to where Rachel and her Aunt Agnes stood waiting. She allowed herself a darting glimpse to where Christina and Steven loaded Todd onto a stretcher before apologizing to her sister. "I'm sorry for scaring you, sis, but it worked out."

"Worked out? You did the opposite of what you said in the meeting yesterday. You went in reckless and unprepared. You're all lucky to still be alive." Rachel's body shook.

Sam handed over to Aunt Agnes the two folders she had acquired from the first camp. She pulled Rachel into a warm hug. "It won't happen again."

Rachel's struggles subsided, giving way to a frustrated sigh and a returned embrace.

Sam mouthed silently to Agnes she was sorry. Her aunt's eyes were full of concern, but also brimming with pride.

"There must be over fifty camps here." Aunt Agnes held the folder open and read as they drifted through the mine behind the fading crowd of freed captives and volunteers.

"At least, and with several hundred imprisoned at each camp, with room for more, it makes you wonder what their plans are."

Rachel asked, "What do you mean *their plans*?"

Agnes sighed. "Rachel, did you notice the people they rescued tonight? These people are not a threat to the government. They're mothers, daughters, sons, fathers, and even grandparents."

Sam thought to when these people had first arrived and been forced from the train. To her, the memory was similar to what she had envisioned the Jewish Holocaust in Europe had been like. "Maybe they are a threat."

Aunt Agnes seemed startled by the very thought, but also curious. "Go on."

Sam rubbed her neck. "I don't know. What do they have in common besides being American citizens? The government is imprisoning entire families. Maybe the threat is religion, or some type of family teachings they share. Political beliefs. I don't know, they've got to be targeting something. Plus, the people we brought in tonight are not from around here. They're from the West Coast."

Agnes asked, "Why do you think that is?"

Sam shrugged. "Maybe because if they did manage to escape, they'd be far away from friends and others who could help them. And also, because they aren't from this area it'd be harder for them to know where to go without getting caught."

"Why arrest them, though?" Rachel asked.

"I don't know, Rachel, but I do know these people here are not the bad guys. Go through the other folder and you'll see what I mean."

Agnes did as Sam instructed, flipping through photos and informational backgrounds for numerous men. She stopped walking. "Sam, were these men in the prison camps? Are they here now?"

"Those were the guards."

"The guards . . ." Agnes repeated, with disgust. "This man was sent to Leavenworth prison for life after raping and beating a female officer in Iraq and leaving her for dead."

"Yeah." She reached over, flipping the page, and pointed to the bottom. "He was pardoned six months ago. They all were." Sam wiped at her gloved hand, knowing the dried blood was his. "Tonight, I found him in a room with one of the girls. I better let Christina know some of the women will need medical treatment."

Agnes's head shook. "I'll do it, Sam. You go and wash up. You look as if you could use some rest." Agnes closed the file. "I'll send Rachel up with some breakfast later."

In a daze, Sam headed down the pathway, pushing away the memory of the lives she had ended tonight. She cleaned up and changed into jeans and a sweatshirt, debating if she should chance smoking a cigarette or two before heading to the house.

Rachel came over with Billy. The poor boy seemed half-asleep. "Could you take him with you? Mike is helping me get people checked in, and Steven and Christina have their hands full in the medical wing."

"Of course. So long as you promise to take it easy."

Rachel rubbed her pregnant belly. "Don't worry. Aunt Agnes and Mrs. Pumpernickel are keeping a close watch on everything I do."

Sam led the sleepy-eyed Billy out of the mine, noticing how quickly the boy's energy level rose as they went. "Did you beat up anybody tonight, Sam?"

"I don't know what you're talking about. I went on a drive with—"

"I'm not stupid, Sam. My friends in the mine told me what's going on."

Sam stopped and lowered herself to her knees, eyes level with the boy's. "Billy, there are many lives at stake here. If anyone finds out—"

"I know, Sam. I'm not a snitch," Billy cut in. "My parents were taken because someone snitched, and they're probably dead because of it."

Sam silently wished Rachel was here. Her sister had a gift when it came to offering emotional support to others. But for Billy's sake, Sam had to try. "Never lose hope, Billy. We don't know what happened to them, so you mustn't stop believing."

"What if we never find them, Sam?"

Her heart ached for Billy. "You and Mike will always have a place with us."

Sam was unprepared for the arms that encircled her neck. She held onto the boy for as long as he needed. He ended the embrace, not saying anything more on the subject, and continued through the pathway with Sam close behind. "Did you beat up anyone tonight, Sam?"

"Yes, Billy, I whipped them good."

Billy kept the conversation entertaining as they made their way up to the tack room in the barn. Sam closed and secured the hidden door before answering Billy's most recent question. "I've been a police officer for a little more than two years now."

"Do you like being a police officer, Sam?"

Sam squinted, noticing light spilling from the gap under the break room door. She made a mental note to remind Mike to turn off the lights when he left. She closed the tack room door behind her. "Billy, can you flip off the lights in the break room while I feed the horses?"

"Sure, Sam."

Sam was grateful for the temporary break from Billy's limitless supply of questions. Making her way around to all three stalls, Sam checked the fresh supply of hay and water already laid out for each of the horses. Maybe she wouldn't bother Mike about leaving the lights on, after all.

A female voice shouted, "Move away from the door!"

Sam spun toward the break room and froze at the sight of a woman holding a kitchen knife to Billy's neck. "If you hurt him, I swear I'll kill you." Sam's words came out in a low growl, her fist clenching.

"I don't want to, but I will. Now, move aside!"

Sam searched for a weapon of her own. Her eyes found Billy's, instantly altering her rage into the desperation of a guardian. She swallowed hard, taking a few steps to the side. "I'll give you anything you want, but please let the boy go."

"You're a cop. If I release him, you'll arrest me."

"I have money in the house. We can go inside and get it and then you can be on your way."

"I don't want your money! I only want to get out of here!"

Sam slowly shoved her hand into the front pocket of her jeans. She pulled out the keys to her truck and tossed them underhanded to the woman. "Billy, everything will be fine, trust me." Sam gave him a big smile.

Sam examined the woman holding Billy. She could tell the woman was frightened. Yet something in her eyes led Sam to think Billy wasn't really in danger. Was it regret? Sam noticed the woman's thumb resting on the blade of the knife, separating the dull edge from the boy's flesh.

A wave of hope engulfed Sam. "You're bleeding. I can help you if you let me."

The woman looked down at the circle of blood on the side of her sweatshirt. With the sudden movement, she rocked lightly on her feet. Sam took in the woman's pale complexion, figuring she had lost a lot of blood and her strength was waning.

"You're a cop."

"My name's Samantha Kelly. I was a cop, but I moved here over a week ago with my sister and a friend of ours. That boy's name is Billy. He's only ten years old. HTF agents took his parents."

"Stop talking!" The woman shouted, swaying slightly.

Sam observed the woman's eyes close, open, then close again, this time for a few seconds longer. The woman stepped backwards, off-balance. The knife slipped from her hand, and she lost her grip on Billy. The woman's knees buckled. She dropped down on all fours. Vomit, the frothy caramel color of soda but smelling of sour milk, splattered against the wood floor. Sam encircled the woman's waist, gently holding her.

After waiting until the vomiting ceased, Sam picked the woman up and cradled her in her arms. The woman's eyes rolled backwards in their sockets. She'd passed out. "Billy, get the door," Sam said, making her way back into the tack room.

"Will she be okay, Sam?" he asked, closing the hidden door behind them.

"I'm not sure, Billy."

Sam peered down at her painful, naked body, in hopes of assessing the damage, but it was too dark. She took a few short breaths before pushing herself on. She focused her eyes forward, squinting into the distance, seeing

the opening in the thick trees a little further away. Maybe Sarah had made her way out? Hope had her quickening her pace.

Her right leg caught on something hard, bringing Sam to the ground. She sprawled out on her face, fighting back the pain with a sharp cry. She laid there unmoving for several minutes in the mud, allowing her mind to concentrate on the rain as it fell on her tattered body.

Finally, after getting her breathing under control, Sam slowly moved up to her knees. She felt around for a branch to support her weight. Her fingers encountered something cold, yet familiar to the touch. She ran her fingers up slowly, along the lifeless body of the girl she loved, as fear and uncontrolled panic gripped her insides.

"Sarah," She crawled up next to the body.

"Sarah!" she shouted and shook the twisted body beneath her hands. She frantically felt for Sarah's mouth and began to perform what little she knew of CPR, as something in her head yelled it was too late.

After a few heart-wrenching minutes, Sam struggled to her feet with Sarah's naked body in her arms. She had lifted Sarah up many times before, but when it mattered, when she needed her strength the most, none came, and she fell to the muddy ground.

Fighting the urge to cry, Sam scrambled onto her feet. She dug down deep, summoning all the power her body would give, and lifted Sarah once again. She moved as fast as she could in the direction of the opening ahead, while she told her lover repeatedly to hang on until help arrived.

Every part of Sam shook as she stepped onto the concrete road. Headlights blinded her and the screeching of tires rang through her pounding head.

"It's about time you woke up." Christina held a plate of food. "I can heat it up if it's too cold."

"It's fine." Sam sat up, her mind sluggish, shaken from the nightmare. She diverted her attention to the woman on the cot next to her. She had an IV, with a clear bag of fluids hanging on a hook above her head. Her face wasn't as pale as when Sam had first seen her, but it still lacked color. "Is she going to make it?"

"I believe so. I'm worried about possible infection at this point. I gave her some antibiotics, so we'll see."

Sam surveyed the partially renovated room as she ate. "I like the changes. Feels more like a hospital in here." Sam motioned to the newly added sheetrock walls and dropped tile ceiling.

"We're supposed to have a floor put in next week, and Frank is working on getting us new equipment and more supplies."

"Nice."

"It'll make my job much easier." Christina sat next to Sam. "These are pills to help you sleep at night." She held out a small brown bottle. "You only need to take half a tablet before bed."

"I'm fine, Christina, really."

"You didn't sound fine. Sam, I'm the one with the medical degree, so here." She handed the bottle over.

Sam rolled the small, brown container around in her fingers, not interested enough to read what was on the label. "I really am fine. It's only a few bad dreams."

"Everything stays with us, Sam, the good *and* the bad. Sometimes the terrible things we work through or try to suppress resurface, especially if we're under stress or experience trauma."

"Christina, I worked through that years ago."

"Take the pills with you in case you change your mind." Christina's eyes held the love and worry of a sister. "If you need to talk to someone, Sam, I'm here. We also have a retired psychiatrist who comes in twice a week."

Sam stood, her smile forced. "Thanks, but I don't need to see any more shrinks."

"Sam."

"I'm going to have a guard posted outside the door for when she wakes up, and when she does, let me know." Sam set her half-eaten breakfast on the desk by the wall. Feeling guilty, she paused in the doorway. "I know you're trying to help, but I promise I'm fine."

"Yes, but I also know how stubborn you can be." Christina stood. "I'm worried about you."

"Don't be." Sam said, then exited the room to locate one of the guards.

After finding someone to watch over the unconscious woman in the medical wing, Sam trudged along the main pathway in search of Rachel. She found her standing outside the conference room talking to Aunt Agnes.

"You seem better. More rested," Agnes said when she spotted Sam.

"I feel better."

Reaching out, Aunt Agnes held their hands. "I know how hard these last few years have been. I'm proud of both of you. You stayed strong for one another when your parents died, especially considering the shape this country's in. You are formidable women, and I consider it a great honor to be your aunt. Without a doubt, you both have the Kelly blood running through your veins."

The three women embraced. "I say we take a few hours off, grab the boys, some fishing poles, and go to the lake like we did when you two were younger."

It didn't take long for the sisters to agree to their aunt's brilliant idea.

Sam, Christina, Rachel, and Billy returned to the house that evening for a home cooked, sit-down dinner, while Mike and Steven stayed behind in the mine to assist one of the nurses in the medical wing. Christina's next twenty-four-hour shift at the hospital was the following morning, so they ate early so she could get to bed at a decent time.

Sam was getting ready to crawl under the covers when Christina's dog let out a deep round of barks. Seconds later vehicle headlights shone through her bedroom window.

"Good boy. Bed." Sam pointed, sending the whining canine up onto the comforter while she slipped her jeans and shoes on. "Stay," she said before heading into the living room. Christina and Rachel stood at the top of the landing. She motioned for them to remain there.

The knock on the door was firm, commanding, giving Sam the impression the person on the other side demanded authority. She opened the door. "May I help you?" She kept her body in the doorway as she caught the dark eyes staring in at her. Her heart skipped a beat. For a moment she was certain Brandon Clayton was standing a foot away.

Then she realized, even though the man resembled Brandon Clayton, this agent was not him.

He flipped out his badge. "I'm Agent Brown with the HTF. May we come in?"

Sam moved over, opening the door wider for the man and his two companions. "Could I get you gentleman something to drink? We have tea, coffee—"

"No, thank you."

"What can we help you with, Agent Brown?"

He focused on Sam then scanned the front room. He spotted the two women at the top of the stairs. "We're searching for a woman in this area." He made a move to hand Sam a photo but stopped. "The last time we came through here this house was vacant."

"We recently moved back. I'm Samantha Kelly, that's my sister Rachel, and our roommate Christina." Sam gestured to the landing, praying silently Billy remained asleep in bed.

The man's eyes narrowed. "The Kellys. Yes. Well, we need to search this house for firearms." He waved over one of his agents. "Bring in the dog."

"There's no need."

Agent Brown stood straighter, and his tone deepened by his disapproval. "On the contrary, I'm afraid—"

"I have two firearms. One's in my bedroom, and the other is in a safe in the office off the dining room."

His widening eyes showed surprise mixed with confusion at her casual tone. "Guns of any kind are outlawed except for law enforcement personnel. I'll have to place you all under arrest."

"My badge is in the bedroom beside my weapon. I'm a police officer in Kansas City, Missouri, on temporary leave."

Sam could tell the man was unconvinced. "The Agent-In-Charge in your area is . . ."

"Agent Clayton, and if you don't believe me, you can call my captain."

"We know Brandon, we'll check with him." Agent Brown gestured to one of the other agents, who took out his cell phone and placed a call.

After a few moments of talking, the broad man hung up the phone. "Sir, Agent Clayton was unavailable, but an Officer Jenkins confirmed her story."

Sam made a mental note to give Jenkins a big kiss the next time she saw him.

"And you are on leave for how long?"

"A few months. Brandon offered me a job with the HTF and I'm thinking about taking it. I wanted to get my sister settled first, and the farm up to speed before I returned to Kansas City."

Agent Brown's stern face softened. "Hmm, good to hear. We do have an opening in Springfield if you choose to stay close to your family. If you do, then a reference from Agent Clayton would more than suffice." Brown handed the picture over to Sam. "To answer your question on why we're here, by any chance have you seen this woman?"

Sam forced herself to examine the picture for a few seconds. "I haven't, but maybe they have." She handed the photo to the agent by the stairs, and he took it up to Rachel and Christina. Both replied no. "Are you planning to apprehend, or is she missing?"

"Apprehend. She's a threat to the government."

"Is she armed?"

"Last we knew. She shot and killed one of my men a few days ago."

Sam squinted out the door into the darkness and shifted her weight from one foot to the next. "She's in the area?" She turned to Agent Brown, showing him her concern. "If she was able to drop a skilled agent, then she must be dangerous." Seeing the curiosity in the man's eyes, Sam knew she was on the right track. "Is there any chance you would be able to . . . no, never mind. I would probably need to call Brandon for it."

"Officer Kelly, I assure you we are as capable in Springfield as they are in Kansas City."

"Oh, I didn't mean to suggest you weren't. I don't feel like I should impose."

"Nonsense. We're all officers of the law here. Let me know what you need, and I'll see it's done."

Sam raised a brow, choosing the right words. "If you could issue a weapon permit for my aunt or her husband who live across the way, it would make me feel more at ease for their safety. At least until you caught this woman."

A smile played across Agent Brown's lips. "I can understand your worry and I assure you, your request is well within my means. It'll be no trouble at all." He puffed out his chest. "I can even do you one better. You have your sister, your roommate, and your aunt and uncle."

"That's correct."

"Come by my office tomorrow around lunchtime and I'll have four cards issued, signed, and ready to go. You'll only need to write in their names and have them sign the front of the cards, but being an officer of the law, I'll have no worries trusting you to handle it."

Sam mentally patted herself on the back. "You are a true gentleman."

Chapter Thirteen

Elaina's Story

"He simply handed these over to you?" Todd leaned on his crutch, flipping one of the permit cards around in his hand.

"Sam was in and out of his office in less than five minutes." Rachel sat at the conference room desk. She arched her back and rubbed a spot below her bellybutton.

Confused, Todd passed the permit to Sam. "The names are blank. It's virtually impossible for a person, even in law enforcement, to obtain one, and he gave you four?"

"Wasn't hard. Agent Brown has an exceptionally large ego and expects people to respect him for the position of power he holds. I played into his ego, making him believe I thought he was incapable of using his power." Sam grinned. "For our good fortune, he proved me wrong."

Rachel added. "She also wore a revealing shirt, tight jeans, and she might have suggested she really likes men in uniforms."

Sam blushed. "Whatever works, plus he offered me a job."

Todd's eyes shot to Agnes. "Really? You know, this might not be a bad idea after all."

Rachel reeled in disbelief. "Tell me you're kidding, Todd."

"It would give us an edge to have someone inside the HTF."

"Do you realize how dangerous that would be? No, Sam is risking her life enough. I'm sorry but find someone else."

Frank placed his coffee cup on the table and cleared his throat. "Todd's right, Rachel. This could provide us with a good opportunity."

"Aunt Agnes, help me out." Rachel peered across the table to the older woman, her eyes pleading.

"The decision is Sam's to make, Rachel," Agnes said.

Rachel's mouth hung open, obviously disbelieving what she was hearing.

Sam put the issue to rest. "I'm not planning on taking the job. If things change, and I feel we'd benefit from my taking the job, then I'll do it. Until then, I'm not going to put my family through the added worry."

They all knew by her *family*, Sam meant Rachel. No one argued, not even Rachel.

Christina broke the uncomfortable silence. "We attacked two camps, and yet they asked us no questions, made no hints about it. The only thing they were interested in was finding the woman."

"Those camps don't exist. At least we're not supposed to know about them." Frank leaned in closer to the table. "Their interest in finding this woman does intrigue me. Is she awake yet?"

"No," Christina said. "She lost a lot of blood, and her wound's infected, but I believe she'll pull through. I'm leaving for work shortly, but Steven and Janis are keeping an eye on her. They'll call me when she wakes."

"I would like to keep a guard posted with her until she's able to answer some questions," Sam said.

Agnes slid a list to Frank and said, "Sam, I met her in town end of last year, at Jed's store. She didn't strike me as a dangerous person."

"Do I need to remind you she had a knife to Billy's throat?"

"I don't believe she would have hurt him. She had a bullet hole in her side, was frightened half to death, and was on the run. Frightened people do desperate things, but they still know where to draw the line."

"Which is why she'll be watched. You can't know for sure what type of person she is. She might have no problems crossing that line."

Frank placed the supply list in his bag. "Agnes, Sam's right. We should keep an eye on her until we find out why the HTF wants her. She could be a danger to others, we don't know for sure. You said you had seen her before. Is there anything you can remember to help us get a better idea of her situation?"

Agnes took a moment to think. "She said her name was Amy. I don't remember her last name, but she told me she was camping."

"Did you believe her?"

"No." Agnes paused as if choosing her words carefully. "She was too hesitant for that to be her real name. Plus, the amount of food and supplies she bought suggested she was holed up somewhere with more storage than a campsite." Agnes glanced at Sam. "She struck me as a good-hearted woman. I think waking up to the sight of an armed stranger would only add more stress to her situation."

Sam stared at her aunt for a long time. Agnes had always been a good judge of character, but her aunt had not been there to see the knife at Billy's throat. If she placed an unarmed person in the room with this woman and something happened, Sam would never forgive herself. "Fine, I'll pull the guard and personally watch her. If she wakes up showing any signs of aggression, we'll go back to armed guards."

This satisfied both Agnes and Frank.

Douglas asked, "What about the other camps? We *are* planning on doing something, right?"

Agnes nodded. "We're holding another meeting tomorrow night. At which time we'll vote on positions for a committee to oversee the running of our group."

"Good," Douglas said, pushing back his chair. "Well, my cows are not going to milk themselves. I suppose I'll see you all tomorrow night."

Douglas was the first to leave the room, followed by Agnes and the others. Sam and Christina broke off from the group and headed toward the medical wing. Sam relieved the guard and positioned a chair next to the unconscious woman's bed. Christina checked the condition of her patients before leaving for work.

"You look as if you could use some coffee." A short, faintly plump, middle-aged woman, with frosty white hair handed Sam a cup, swirling steam rising from its rim.

"Thank you."

The woman said, "No, I'm the one who needs to do the thanking. If you hadn't come along, we'd all still be in the camps. I'm Janis Coddington."

Sam raised her eyebrows as she shook the woman's outstretched hand. Sam had not recognized this woman from her other trips into the mine, and now she understood why. "I figured they would give you some time to settle in before putting you on shifts."

"Oh, I volunteered. Quite a few of us have. My husband is an architectural engineer, and he's already helping with the construction of the living quarters and such. I don't know, the stuff he does is over my head. Give me a hammer and I eventually manage to break something." Janis giggled. "I'll stick with nursing, less dangerous."

Sam liked Janis. "You're a nurse?"

"Yes, an RN. I was up until two months ago when we were arrested."

Sam studied her closely, unsure what possible threat Janis would pose. "I don't mean to prod, but why did they arrest you? I mean, a nurse and an engineer, what was their reasoning?"

"I told him to get rid of his gun." Janis slumped in a chair next to Sam. "He refused, saying he had rights as an American to defend his own." Janis let out a long sigh. "I don't blame him, though. I agreed with him but didn't want to give the Task Force any reasons to arrest us, as they had done to others we knew."

Janis pointed, directing Sam's eyes to a cot two rows over. Sam's heart sank the instant she spotted the dark-haired teenager from the night before. Even though the girl was asleep, her face was tense, unsettled, as if she had drifted off into a restless nightmare. "That's our daughter over there. He blames himself for what has happened to her. I can tell it's killing him inside."

Sam moved her gaze from the girl, wishing she were somewhere else at this very moment. The room was suddenly closing in around her, making it difficult to breathe. She rose from the chair, shutting her mind off to the visions from her past. She needed air. "Would you mind keeping an eye on things, I've got to use the bathroom."

"Oh, yes of course, dear," Janis said. "Why, there's Steven now. You go do your thing. We'll manage simply fine here until you return."

"Thanks." Sam turned away from Steven emerging from one of the back rooms. His arms were full of medical supplies, blocking his view of her. The last thing she wanted was to get involved in a lengthy conversation. They hadn't had much of a chance to talk these last few days, and now was not the time.

Sam veered into a corridor off the main medical wing, staying within earshot in case something happened. After a few moments of steady breathing, Sam removed her almost empty cigarette pack from her back pocket, lit one of the semi-bent cigarettes, and deeply inhaled. She fought hard to control her coughing fit, wishing she had a shot of whisky to wash it down.

Biting her bottom lip, Sam cursed inwardly. She leaned against the wall with her eyes closed. She felt ashamed for leaving Janis the way she did. Ashamed for feeling weak, out of control with her own emotions. What happened to her was a long time ago, yet for some reason, being in their childhood home, seeing the broken-spirited girl lying helplessly on the cot, brought back a past she had fought so hard to rid herself of.

"Damn it, Sam, get a grip!" she scolded, keeping her voice to a low grumble.

Finishing her cigarette, Sam blew off the temptation to light a second one. She was running low and unsure when she would get a chance to buy another pack. She reentered the room feeling less healthy, but more composed.

Retaking her seat next to the unconscious woman, Sam said to Steven who was storing his stack of supplies into a med cart, "I like the coat."

Blushing, Steven brushed his hand over the white medical smock. "It does feel comfortable, and I like the pockets. They're Christina's idea. She says it makes the patients feel more at ease when we wear them. Something about instilling confidence with the care we provide."

"It does give off a certain air of assurance."

Steven snorted, handing Sam a fresh coffee. "Let's keep the truth to ourselves, shall we?"

"Nonsense, Steven, you're doing a wonderful job." Janis piped up from the desk where she sat writing in a file, a stack of other manilla folders sitting off to the side. Medical records, Sam figured. "He's not afraid to ask questions, and he retains what he learns. And he has empathy for the patients. A trait few doctors have these days."

Janis pointed to the woman lying on the cot next to Sam. "He hooked up her IV all by himself."

"It took me three sticks." He situated a chair next to Sam.

"She was very dehydrated. A small feat if you ask me." Janis focused on the file in front of her. "Give it time and before long you'll become proficient at it."

Steven leaned in so only Sam would be able to hear. "Once I graduate and have my own practice, I'm taking her with me."

Sam sensed his admiration for Janis. She said, "Are you planning to stay down here forever? You need rest, too."

"Oh, I have my own personal sleeping area set up in one of the storage rooms. It isn't grand, but it works. I'm sick of taking cold showers, though. If they don't get the hot water hooked up soon, I might have to head up top for a while."

She gazed at him, concerned. "You're doing a good job. But don't over-stretch yourself, all right?"

Steven said, "You have room to talk, Sam. I bet you haven't had a decent night's sleep in days."

Sam didn't argue. She couldn't, Steven was right. With everything going on, she had found little time for sleep. The few times she had managed to get some shuteye proved less than restful, thanks to her recurring nightmare.

"Where am I?"

Though the voice from the cot was scarcely above a murmur, Sam about jumped out of her seat. Steven rushed to the woman's side with Janis right behind. Sam remained unmoving, feeling awkward and out of place.

Janis leaned over, checking the woman's vitals. "You're safe, child. The bullet that hit you, thankfully, missed anything of importance, but you did lose a lot of blood and your wound is infected."

"Is this a hospital?" The woman asked. Her look of confusion changed to fear when she caught sight of Sam. "Have I been arrested?"

"Oh, no, dear, she's Sam Kelly." Janis looked over at Sam. "The one who brought you here."

The woman's voice shook, her eyes remained fixed on Sam. "Where am I?"

"You're in an underground—"

"Janis," Sam cut in, taking a step forward. "We don't have any idea who she is."

Janis said, "If she is wanted by the Task Force, then surely she's not a threat to us."

"You didn't turn me in? The boy said you were a cop." The woman's eyes shifted. "Is the boy all right?"

"His name's Billy, and yes, he's fine," Sam's temper heated up at the memory of Billy with the knife to his throat. "It's still not too late to have you arrested."

Janis pivoted to Sam. "I understand it's your job to keep us safe. But she's my patient and until I feel she's in better shape, you need to move aside and let me do my job."

Sam acquiesced, for now. "Fine. I must ask you not to give her any information regarding this place or the people in it until after I've had a chance to talk with her."

"As you wish," Janis said then she turned to Steven. "Would you go call Christiana, please?" Steven took off to do Janis's bidding and Janis bent over her patient. "What's your name, child?"

Her patient didn't respond right away, and when she did, it wasn't in response to Janis's question. "How long have I been here?"

"Close to two days," Janis said.

"Two days?" Elaina thoughts drifted to the cabin, and what she'd left hidden there. She attempted to sit up, but the nurse's hands held her down. "I need to leave. If I've not been arrested, why are you keeping me here?"

"For your safety as well as ours. Now, please rest. We'll talk later." Janis went to one of the shelves by the front desk and returned with a thick green army blanket, which she added to the one already covering her body. The additional warmth felt nice.

Rolling her head to the side, Elaina closed her eyes. She was sick of hiding, sick of running away from everyone and everything. Her life had felt over since the night of Kim's murder. These people had not turned her in. Yet, if she told them the truth and they proved to be co-conspirators, where did that leave her? Where would it leave everyone else?

Elaina opened her eyes again, her mind racing. *I cannot do this alone. I'm so sick of being alone.* "My name is Elaina Williams. I worked for a news station in New York City until the day the stock market crashed, and my life came to a sudden halt."

She spent the next hour telling Janis, Steven, and Sam her story. From the day Kim gave her the package, to Kim's death, and her own narrow escape. She talked in detail of Marcus, the FBI agent who had been helping her for the last year and a half, and her belief that he was dead.

They listened as she told them of her time in the cabin, culminating with the events leading up to her injury, and discovering the barn.

When she finished, Elaina wondered if they believed her to be completely nuts. All three remained silent, seated in chairs beside her cot. Feeling self-conscious, Elaina pulled the blankets up to her neck and waited.

Sam was the first to move, rising slowly to her feet. "I would like to see those flash drives. Can you tell me how to get to the cabin, and exactly where you hid them?"

"Those drives are the only proof I have left."

Janis patted Elaina's hand gently. "Sam freed me and my family from camps they were holding us in. You can trust her."

Elaina's eyes widened. "Camps?"

Janis said, "Holding camps. The HTF found a weapon in our home and arrested us. We were taken to an encampment not far from here."

"So, they've outlawed firearms." Elaina absorbed this information.

"What is it?" Steven asked.

Elaina shifted uncomfortably. "There's a plan, or an outline of the events this organization is planning. Some have specific dates, but not all of them. It mentions nationwide confiscation of weapons and several new laws to be enforced. It also talks of martial law and encampments where citizens who break the new laws will be held."

"All that has already happened," Sam said.

"Not everything." Elaina said. "These people . . . this organization . . . they're planning more threatening actions, including getting rid of the people in the camps."

"Getting rid of?"

"Specifics weren't defined, but the way I read it, I took it to mean the execution of every person they've arrested." Elaina's heart filled with guilt. "The Secretary of Defense was one of the names listed to oversee the camps. I'm not sure how he connects in all of this. Like I said, the information's choppy, but several other key people are also mentioned."

Elaina watched Sam pivot, move to the desk, and grab a pen and notepad. She returned, tossed them onto the bed. "I need the location of the cabin and where you hid the flash drives."

Sam drove through town less than an hour later, stopped to fill her truck's gas tank and buy a soda and a couple packs of cigarettes. She wanted to be seen in town in case she happened to run into any of the HTF agents later. The two packs of cigarettes she stuffed in the glove box so Rachel wouldn't find them. She knew for her own sake she needed to quit smoking, but the way things were spooling out, now was not the time.

Elaina's directions showed the cabin was about thirty miles north of Jed's boarded-up store in the center of town. After driving for over thirty minutes, she turned her truck around. She slammed on the brakes after five minutes of backtracking when she caught sight of the overgrown, gravel road.

Her truck bounced and weaved around dips and potholes, causing her to slow her speed to a crawl. Impressed by how thick the trees grew in the area, Sam wondered why she had never ventured out this way in her youth. This would have been a good scenic spot to ride her horse, although the woods here were too dense for her dirt bike or three-wheeler.

Pulling her truck up as far as she could, Sam climbed out, retrieving her pistol and Elaina's backpack, which she had grabbed from the office in the barn before she left. She double-checked the safety switch, tucked the pistol into the back of her jeans, and trampled through the brush. Less than twenty feet ahead, Sam stopped. The outline of a boxy vehicle, Elaina's SUV, sat hidden underneath a tarp and a pile of brush. Sam was impressed with how well Elaina had disguised her vehicle. She strode forward and pushed aside the cover. Sam peered in, nothing seemed out of place, other than an old battery sitting on the front seat. Replacing the tarp and tree branches, Sam continued up the hillside.

A copious number of trees surrounded the cabin and outer buildings hiding them from view. A good hideout for an FBI agent or someone he might want to protect. Sam waited, crouched next to a moss-covered stump, watching for any signs of life. Nothing moved so she slowly made her way around the buildings in a wide circle, scanning for any broken windows or indications of forced entry. Satisfied the buildings were unbreeched, Sam scampered cautiously into the area.

She went straight to the woodpile at the far end of the cabin and removed the key hidden underneath the misshapen log as Elaina had instructed. The deadbolt locking the door from the outside was weathered and rusted, but sturdy. Sam pushed in the key, rotating it to the right, a sharp click echoed around her as the lock opened, allowing her entry into the cabin.

The inside was clean, rustic, a cozy feeling of a vacation home for a family who sought solitude from the outside world. Sam closed the door behind her and made her way around the quilt-covered rocker, past the high-polished dining room table, to the space separating the living room from the kitchen. She bent down to inspect the floor in the corner as Elaina had directed.

"Ah," she breathed. She worked her fingers in the tiny gap and pulled the board upward exposing the stash. She removed the laptop and shoebox from the hole, then replaced the board and headed to the table. She quickly opened the box, revealing the flash drives, Elaina's wallet, and a neat stack of money tied into a bundle with a hairband. Satisfied everything was as Elaina described, Sam closed the lid, placed the items in her backpack, and exited the cabin.

Sam locked the cabin and secured the key in its hiding spot, then returned to her truck. *How did a woman from New York survive out here by herself for so long?* A year and a half in this much solitude would be hard for anyone, and Elaina had done it while appearing to have kept her sanity intact. Sam admired Elaina's perseverance.

Pulling her truck onto the gravel road, Sam thought about Elaina. She had a petite frame, and probably stood about five-feet-four-inches tall. But what had pulled Sam in was the sense of strength she'd seen in Elaina's eyes, an intensity not quite matching her delicate build.

Who was Elaina? What kept her going after being on the run alone for so long? Questions flipped through Sam's mind as she turned from the gravel path onto the paved road. When she crested the hill, less than a mile outside of town, she was met with a disturbing sight. Black SUVs with flashing red and blue lights blocked the way forward.

She had no time to turn around. An HTF agent twenty yards ahead was gesturing for her to pull off to the side and stop. Sam leaned over, grabbed the backpack, and tucked it under the passenger seat. "Damn it!" She hid her weapon inside the front waistband of her jeans, underneath her T-shirt and flannel shirt.

She counted four agents. If they discovered the backpack and the drives, she would have no choice but to shoot her way out of this mess.

"Pull over," an agent mouthed when she drew closer. The other three were busy with a vehicle heading in the opposite direction. Sam did as instructed, rolling down her window in the process.

"Routine inspection, please step out of the truck and remain where I can see you."

Sam complied, keeping the smile on her face and the driver's side door open. The feel of the cold metal against her stomach comforted her as she watched the man search the driver's seat then march around to the other side of the truck.

He pulled open the passenger door and popped the glove box. "I would not have pictured you as a smoker." He tossed the contents out onto the passenger seat. "Your teeth are too white."

"I have many secrets." Sam's words came out in a flirtatious tone. The man seemed interested.

"What secrets might those be?"

Keeping the other three agents in her peripheral vision, Sam murmured. "If I told you, they wouldn't be secrets now, would they?"

He ran his eyes down Sam's body, and slowly back up. "I guess not." He stuck his hand under the front seat, his eyes glued on Sam. "You're clean. Wait, what's this?" He yanked out the backpack from under the seat.

Sam held her breath along with her smile. *Damn it, I was so close.* She moved her hand up to her front right pocket, readying herself for the inevitable. "It's only my laptop and a few music drives, nothing exciting."

The agent grunted. He unzipped the backpack and removed the laptop.

What am I going to do, try to kill all four of these guys? And if I succeed, throw the bodies in the back, and find a place to bury them? Sam mentally answered her own question. *I guess so.* She watched the agent's hand slide inside the backpack.

"Andrews, she's clean." Another agent approached the truck.

Sam recognized the second guy as one of the agents in her house the night before last, with Agent Brown. The remaining two agents made their way over after releasing the other vehicle. One grinned as he pocketed a fist full of cash.

"How do you know she's clean? I'm the one inspecting her."

"This here is Samantha Kelly, the woman I told you about. You know, the cop from Kansas City."

The original agent assessed Sam with a more intense focus. "So, you're the one Brown gave all those weapon permits to. I can understand why." He glanced at the outline of her breasts, then replaced the laptop in the backpack. After zipping it up, he left it on the seat, seeming to have lost interest in the search. "You're right, she's freaking hot."

His words brought a reddish tint to the other agent's neckline. "We're sorry to bother you, Ms. Kelly, please continue on your way."

Sam climbed into the truck while the agent who'd inspected her vehicle shut the front passenger door. He came around to her side and gawked at the formfitting shape of her shirt as Sam buckled her seatbelt. "You know, Ms. Kelly, I have tomorrow night off and my wife's out of town."

Sam started her truck and shifted into drive. "Sorry, I'm not into married men." She pulled away to the sound of the other agents laughing at their colleague's expense.

Sam pulled into her driveway and parked at the far edge of a cornfield before she lit a much-needed cigarette. Her nerves were raw, hands shaking. She wanted to either scream, or punch something. Back in Kansas City, she could have found release in a meaningless, mutually satisfying fuck. The thought of turning the truck around and driving straight for Kansas City was tempting. Instead, she took a deep drag on her cigarette, tossed it in a half full can of soda, which had become her ashtray, and shifted the truck in drive.

She parked in front of the house, grabbed the backpack, and trekked into the mine. She debated using one of the computers in the conference room but decided not to, considering the flash drives were Elaina's to begin with.

"She's asleep," Steven was sitting behind the desk in the medical wing. "Unless you want Janis to give you a lecture, you had better not wake her."

"Where's Janis?" Sam asked.

"She took her daughter to the showers, then to get something to eat."

Sam glanced at Elaina, then to the empty cot beside her. "I'm going to try for some shuteye. Can you wake me when she gets up?"

Steven nodded.

Chapter Fourteen

The Committee

"Hey, are you okay?" Elaina knelt next to Sam's cot.

Sam blinked twice, seeming confused. "What happened?"

"I think you had a bad dream." The tube pumping fluids into Elaina's body was stretched to the max and the bottom of her hospital gown was trapped beneath her knees, limiting her ability for movement.

"I'm all right. You, however, should get into bed." Sam swung her legs to the ground.

Elaina eyed the entrance. "I'm sick of being in bed. I'd love to walk around for a bit, but I'm afraid the older nurse will make me sit through another lecture."

"Where is everyone?" Sam asked.

"Dinner. The young man's in the supply room getting me something for my headache, and your aunt came by earlier. They'd done me a favor and searched through the names of those inside the mine. My parents aren't here."

"I'm sorry. There's more camps out there. Don't lose hope."

Elaina lowered her voice. "It's hard. I've assumed they were dead for so long, I sort of adapted to the loss. Now, I'm not sure how I feel." She didn't want to talk about her parents anymore. "The other two nurses left a few minutes ago."

"Two nurses, I thought Janis was the only nurse helping Christina."

Elaina puffed her cheeks out and blew. "Janis. Yes, she's the one who's been mothering me nonstop since I awoke. The other nurse arrived about an hour ago. Tracy, I think." Elaina's eyes narrowed. "Tracy's very arrogant. I'm sorry if she is a friend of yours, but I can't stand her."

"I've never met her." Sam rubbed the vestiges of sleep from her eyes. "How long have I been out?"

"I'm not sure. It's after seven in the evening, if that helps."

"Seven p.m.?"

Elaina nodded and picked up a hint of agitation when Sam looked toward the supply room door. "It's not his fault. He was going to wake you, but Janis insisted he let you sleep. That woman's exceptionally good at getting her own way."

"She'll fit in nicely with the women here, then," grumbled Sam. "Between my aunt, sister, and old math teacher, yes, the women around here have a way of getting what they want, when they want it." Sam let out a breath, then reached a hand underneath her cot.

Elaina was amused by Sam's laundry list of the women in her life. "Are you looking for this?" Elaina pulled her laptop from the bag. "Thank you for getting it for me."

Sam exhaled. She stood and dragged a chair over next to Elaina's cot.

"Who's Sarah?" Elaina asked, keeping her eyes focused on the screen.

Sam took her seat, her expression guarded. "Why do you ask?"

"You mentioned her name several times while you were sleeping." Elaina shrugged. "Sorry, maybe I shouldn't have asked. I guess working for a news station has made me very inquisitive."

After a few seconds of uncertain silence, Sam's expression softened. "She's a memory from my past. I need coffee." Sam went over to the coffee pot. "I would offer you a cup, but Janis would probably not approve."

Elaina said, "No, she wouldn't. I've already asked her." The way Sam moved, the way she carried herself, seemed to radiate unwavering confidence, making her even more striking. The unusual spark bursting deep within was unexpected, causing Elaina's stomach to tighten, then tremble.

She glanced away before Sam caught her staring. After the laptop powered up and was ready to go, Elaina loaded the first drive and they waited.

Steven entered the room. "Sorry I took so long, apparently Tracy rearranged the meds." He removed the cap to a preloaded syringe and inserted the needle into a port on Elaina's IV line and injected the contents. "Sorry I didn't wake you up, Sam. I had my orders."

"She already told me." Sam pointed to Elaina, but her eyes remained glued to the screen.

Elaina had read the information so many times over the past year, so she focused on Sam instead. "I'm not sure why the details are so patchy. Certain events are obvious, though," Elaina said when she noticed Sam's confusion.

"It's not complete," Sam said. She tapped on the laptop and scrolled to the next page. "Probably for added protection in case the information fell into the wrong hands. What's on this other drive?"

"Financial records, and I also have a third drive with names, but those also have limited information."

Sam inserted the next flash drive. "I do agree with you on the camps. It sounds as if they're holding these people only to execute them later."

"Why not kill them right away?" Elaina asked.

"I don't know." Sam's eyes widened. She picked the computer up off the cot and positioned it onto her lap. Elaina and Steven watched in silence as she worked. After downloading the information, Sam reloaded the first drive, copied it onto the laptop, and then the last drive. "Ah. Here we go," she finally said, swiveling the laptop so they could see.

"What?" Steven asked.

"The program size, it doesn't match." She pointed to the screen. "I have all the files open, but the space used on these devices is greater than what's showing up."

Elaina felt sudden excitement. "So, this means?"

"It means there are more programs on each of the devices, but the computer isn't reading the data. The data might be encrypted. Or maybe hidden files."

"Can we download an app or something?" Steven asked.

"Nope. I'm afraid it's not that simple."

Steven stood. "How do we get the computer to read it?"

Elaina raised her eyebrows. "Wait, there is something else, maybe this will help." Elaina withdrew a notebook from the shoebox. "Kim said this read like a type of code, but she was unable to break it."

Sam shook her head. "No, I believe it's programming language."

"Are you sure?"

Steven grew animated. "Sam was working on a degree in programming when she was in the army. She would know."

"You have a programming degree?"

"I wasn't even close to finishing." Sam replaced the paperwork. "I like computer games, and the idea of making my own was interesting. I had time on my hands and the chance for a free education. This is way over my head, though." Sam held up the notebook. "This might actually help, but we'll need to find someone who understands programming language."

"Kevin."

"Who? Kevin? I don't know a Kevin."

Steven said, "You met him, Sam, the first day you came into the mine. Scared the shit out of him, I might add."

Sam stared at Steven, her expression blank.

He said, "You pushed him into a pile of boxes, crates or something. He cut his forehead and has been avoiding you ever since."

"Oh yes, him." Sam let out a hoot. "It's a good thing his weapon wasn't loaded. He could have easily shot himself."

"Some of us are not as talented as you are, Sam."

She raised her brow in surprise. "Do you two have a thing going? I mean yes, he is cute, but you and him?"

Elaina was entertained by the exchange between Steven and Sam. Steven, his hands on his hips and Sam grinning at his affront made her realize how much she missed being around other people.

"For your information we've just met, and no, we don't have a thing going. But he is a wiz with computers."

"Steven, calm down. I was only joking. I'm happy for you, really."

"We're not dating!" he insisted. "Or anything else. Get your mind out of the gutter, Sam, or I'll tell Rachel you're smoking again."

Elaina leaned in and snatched the laptop as Sam soared to her feet. "Who says I'm smoking?"

"You do." He removed a crumpled pack of cigarettes from the front pocket of his smock with a look of triumph. "These were sticking out of your pocket when you were sleeping. I didn't want Rachel to come in and see them, so I confiscated the pack for safekeeping."

Sam glared at him. "Fine, I won't tease you and you don't tell Rachel."

"I don't know, Sam. You taking up smoking again is a pretty big deal. I mean if Rachel found out—"

"Are you preparing to blackmail me?" Sam narrowed her eyes.

"Let me think about that." Steven rested a finger on his chin. "Of course, I am."

Elaina bore witness to the ensuing stare down. She could see these two had been friends a long time. Elaina set the laptop aside and awaited the outcome to the duel.

Eventually Sam sighed. "What do you want?"

Steven tossed Sam the cigarettes. "It just so happens I do like Kevin. He's not only very handsome and very smart, but he's also extremely shy."

"So?"

"I asked him out on a double date to help break the ice. I figured we could go up to the house and I can cook dinner. Maybe play some cards or something."

"Wait a sec. Are you saying you want me to find you another couple you can spend the evening with?"

"No, girl genius. I want *you* to find someone to ask out."

"I can't go around randomly asking people out. Besides, you know I'm not into dating."

He blew off her last comment. "You're hot, Sam. Women would fall down at your feet if they thought it would get them into your pants." As if to prove his point, Steven dragged Elaina into the fray. "If you were gay, you would go out with her, right?"

The question caught Elaina off guard. She opened her mouth to speak but nothing came out.

"Wait! That's right, you're gay. You said the girl, Kim, was your ex."

"Steven," Sam pinned Steven down with a glare. "She said her ex was murdered."

Steven's hope faded to embarrassed misery. "Oh, wow, I'm so sorry, Elaina. I wasn't thinking."

Elaina's insides churned at the reminder of Kim's murder. "It's all right. I've had time to make peace with the loss." She turned the tables on Sam. "Why don't you date?"

Sam jerked both hands upward. "Okay, I'm done with this ridiculous conversation." She squinted at Steven. "Can we get back to the topic of Kevin? If you would ask him to go over this, maybe he'll be able to fill in the gaps."

"Not until you agree to go on a double date. Tracy hounded me about you when you were asleep. I think she really likes you."

"Tracy? As in the nurse? You're not going to set Sam up with her, are you?" Elaina's heart fluttered in distress. Something was 'off' about Tracy, she thought.

"Why? She's attractive." Steven was nonplussed.

"I don't know," Elaina muttered. Should she tell them about her unease? Given her past relationship choice, was she really the best person to give advice? "She strikes me as a very shallow person."

Steven snickered. "A woman who offers Sam no hope for any kind of a future relationship is exactly what she likes. Tracy's perfect." He gave Sam a pout. "Please, I promise I won't tell Rachel about your addiction, and who knows, you might have a nice time."

Sam threw her arms in the air. "Fine, one date, but I need to talk to Kevin as soon as possible."

Steven jumped to attention. "I'll call him."

After he left, Sam apologized for dragging Elaina into their drama. "I guess he really likes this guy."

Elaina said, "I figured that out on my own. You didn't answer my question, though."

Placing the items in the backpack, Sam tucked it under Elaina's cot. "I have no time for a relationship."

"What a cop-out answer."

Sam's jaw muscles tightened. "It's complicated. Listen, I need to go get a bite to eat, do you want me to bring you a plate?"

Elaina opened her mouth to speak. She paused, deciding not to push the subject any further. "I would love something to eat, but I've been limited to ice chips and broth. At least until the doctor examines me tomorrow morning."

"Okay, then. I'm off. See you soon."

Elaina sat in silence staring at the entryway. She wasn't sure why it bothered her seeing Sam leave, maybe her subconscious hated being left alone after living in solitude for so long. The excitement stirring inside told her other feelings besides loneliness were inching toward the surface. Elaina tucked the blanket under her legs, trying to think back to the last time she had felt lips brush against her own.

She dropped her head onto the pillow and let out a sigh. She'd never been with anyone other than Kim, and their last kiss was almost two years before she went into hiding. Elaina gently touched her fingers to her lips and closed her eyes.

The cigarette was in her mouth and lit as soon as she left the room. Sam stood against the wall off the medical wing entrance, enjoying her tiny bit of solitude, eyes tracing the smoke rising from the ashy tip. Her mind flashed to images of Elaina lying on her cot. Sam now understood why Aunt Agnes liked her so. Elaina had a certain strength which was captivating. Yet, there was something else Elaina possessed Sam couldn't quite put her finger on. An alluring attribute which was far weightier than her shapely body and soothing voice, but Sam couldn't pinpoint the mysterious element. She did know the pull was more appealing than she cared to admit, even to herself.

By the time Steven returned, Sam was finishing her second cigarette and coughing up half a lung. Steven patted her smartly on the back until the coughing ceased. "You know, those things really will kill you." He sounded not the least bit happy.

She blew off his concern. "What did Kevin say?"

"He had to go to Kansas City, but he'll be here first thing tomorrow. I didn't tell him about the drives or Elaina over the phone, but I did tell him you had something important to run by him later." He paused, holding Sam's gaze. "You don't have to go on this date, Sam. And I won't even tell Rachel about you taking up smoking again."

"Why the change of heart?"

He propped himself against the wall next to her. "Guilt, I guess. I don't know." Sam noticed his grin falter slightly after a lengthy sigh. "When Nathan was killed, I swore I would never fall in love with anyone ever again. I was wrong. Kevin really gets to me, Sam. I'm not sure if it's his personality or his boyish charm, but I can't seem to get him out of my head." His voice took on a pleading tone. "Is this wrong? I mean, do you think I'm disrespecting Nathan's memory for liking this guy?"

"No, I don't. I know Nathan wouldn't have wanted you to be alone." Her heart felt a mixture of sorrow and happiness for him. Also a level of understanding. "You are a good man, Steven. Kevin would be a fool to pass up a chance to be with you." She squared her shoulders. "Now, I'll ask this girl out tonight sometime, but I'm not cooking. I might throw a salad together, but you'll oversee everything else."

Steven kissed Sam on the cheek. "I definitely owe you one."

Sam remained in the medical wing reviewing the data on Elaina's laptop, while Steven went to his makeshift room for some much-needed sleep.

Janis kept busy fussing over Sam, Elaina, or anyone else who was close enough to catch her attention. Sam wondered what kept the woman on her feet all day. "I really am fine," Sam said, when she took the vitamins from Janis's hand and washed them down with a gulp of water.

"Janis thinks a lot of you." Elaina seemed in better spirits after Christina, via a phone call, agreed to the removal of her IV. Coffee was still forbidden, though. "I've noticed everyone around here does."

"I have them all fooled." Sam's smile evaporated when she caught sight of Tracy. The boisterous woman had come on too strong, trying more than once to get Sam alone in the back-supply room. Even though Sam was more than ready for an intimate moment, she had learned to avoid having casual sex with a clingy woman who she might run into afterward.

Elaina had picked up on Sam's unease. "I take it you haven't asked her out yet."

Sam sighed. "No, and I hope to find a way to avoid the drama of it all." Then an idea crossed her mind. "Hey, you wouldn't be interested in a home-cooked meal and an evening of cards, would you?"

Sam waited, paying close attention to Elaina's breathing, or lack thereof. Had Elaina really stopped breathing? Sam wondered if she had been out of line for asking such an on-the-spot question? She hadn't intended to send Elaina into a state of panic.

Elaina's hands fumbled with the book she had been reading, angling it this way and that. "Are you asking me out on a date?"

Sam was baffled by Elaina's nervousness. "Sorry, I didn't mean to upset you. I was only trying to avoid a disaster and ensure a pleasant evening."

Sam stood, stretching. Across the room Tracy rested her elbows on her knees, a flirtatious smirk pasted across her face. Sam's eyes traveled downward to where Tracy's hardened nipples were visible under her too-thin, too-tight shirt.

A burning need for another cigarette lit up inside Sam, but she quashed the urge. Instead, she said to Elaina, "If you did say yes, I promise to throw in any movie you want. And also dessert."

Elaina twisted toward Tracy and exhaled. "So, you want me to save you from yourself?" Her lips pulled downward with Sam's affirmation. "Fine, I want Boston cream pie, and an entire evening of the *Lord of the Rings.*"

Sam's mood transformed into bewildered enthusiasm. "You're a woman after my own heart. I love Boston cream pie, and I have the extended edition of all three movies."

The book in her hand became the focus of Elaina's intense scrutiny.

Sam remained motionless. She debated on whether she should point out Elaina's blunder, or if she should simply walk away.

Finally, Elaina glared up at Sam. "What?"

"I've heard of speed readers and people who read books from back to front, but I've never seen anyone read a book upside down before."

Elaina flipped the book so fast, it almost jumped from her grasp.

"Hey, Sam, look what Rachel got me!" Billy rushed into the room with Christina's unclaimed dog bouncing briskly at his side.

Sam handed Elaina's computer to her and went to where Billy held out a radio-control helicopter.

"You flick the on button here," Billy's voice squeaked when he handed her the remote. "And you have to press the button on the side."

Sam followed his instructions. The miniature helicopter went straight up, did a full one-eighty, and dive-bombed the dog sending him scurrying under the nearest cot with his butt sticking out. "Sorry, boy." Sam leaned forward to pet him. "Where have you two been hiding?" she asked Billy.

"They've been with me all day." Rachel entered the room behind Billy.

"There you are! Rachel, meet Elaina. Elaina, this potbellied woman is my overly pregnant sister, Rachel."

Rachel arched an eyebrow before extending her hand to the amused Elaina. "I've heard a lot about you. Which is why I'm here. Aunt Agnes would like you to come to tomorrow night's meeting if you're feeling up to it."

Placing her book on the cot next to her, Elaina sat up. "Why does she want me to go? You have the information you need, right? My being there isn't what's important."

"We'll be electing a committee, and she feels you should be the one to explain your story to them."

Sam sensed Elaina's reluctance. She handed Billy the remote to the helicopter. "This meeting is to not only bring us together, but to give everyone an equal vote. You don't have to go, but if you plan to stay with us you might want to reconsider."

"Of course, she plans to stay," Rachel said. "Where else would she go? She's on the run after all."

Elaina cleared her throat. "Actually, I was preparing to drive to Canada."

Rachel studied the woman. "Why? You're an American citizen. This fight has to do with all of us."

"I can't. I'm ready for a semi-normal life again."

Rachel scoffed, "Yeah, we're *all* ready for life to return to normal."

"Rachel," Sam cut in. "Elaina's done her part keeping herself alive, and this information safe for the last two years. We have the flash drives and hopefully this will give us the edge we need." She spoke to Elaina, unable to imagine how difficult life had to have been for her. "If you want to go to Canada, I'll take you there myself, but I think you should at least try a meeting here. You may change your mind about leaving. You know? Keep all your options open."

Sam spent the remainder of the evening and the rest of the next day in the medical wing with Elaina. She reasoned with herself the long talks with Elaina, multiple hands of rummy, and several games of chess, were her way of being neighborly to the new resident. Deep down, Sam knew she was fully enjoying the woman's company. Plus, being in Elaina's presence made her experience unusual emotions and feelings leaving her more baffled than she'd ever been by another woman.

Sam had never stepped foot inside a union meeting, but the atmosphere in the conference room the following evening was what she assumed one would be like. The group was lively as she and Christina helped Elaina into the room. Elaina was recovering her strength, but Christina was not completely comfortable allowing her out of bed so soon, and definitely not unaccompanied.

People packed the spacious room, and over a hundred more men and women waited in a huddled mass outside, trying to hear everything being said. Agnes opened by calling out the list of positions which needed to be filled, and the duties of those positions.

"I nominate Agnes to be the Head of Committee," Frank hollered, his motion answered by a chorus of strong agreement.

"What if we came from the camps and we don't technically live here? Do we get to vote?" a woman shouted from the center of the room, causing pockets of bickering to break out.

"Everyone gets to vote." Agnes held up her hands. "We're all together in this, whether you have a residence in the area or not. As of right now, this mine is home for most of you and it's only fair you have a say."

"Then I vote for Samantha Kelly to be in charge of our training and military," the same woman called out, and Sam realized the voice belonged to Janis. The bulk of the room agreed to the nomination.

The next hour consisted of nominating and voting in the rest of the staff. Sam nominated Frank for supply and Christina for the medical officer slot. She was surprised when she heard Douglas, instead of Steven, offer up Kevin's name for the communication position. Steven seconded the motion. Agnes nominated Douglas for security, and Mrs. Pumpernickel to oversee the finances. Sam's old math teacher turned down the nomination. Instead, Mrs. Pumpernickel presented the idea of a position for the education of the children living in the mine. The masses agreed, voted her in, and Sam said a silent prayer for the kids who would be receiving their education from her. They voted a woman from the camps into the financial slot, after the woman standing next to her explained her friend had a degree in finance. Janis's husband ended up in charge of maintenance, due to his engineering degree, and the last position fell to Todd. They gave him the task of administration and record keeping of everyone in the mine. Sam enjoyed the startled look on Todd's face.

Once the voting was completed, Agnes went through the list of items that needed addressing. "For those of you who don't know Leonard Harris, he's one of Springfield's news anchors. He has brought it to my attention the HTF is now monitoring all television and radio stations in the United States. Nothing is done live anymore, and many of the stations have been taken off-air due to a so-called security threat to the government. We feel it's so those in charge can control the flow and type of information reported to the public. The less they have to monitor, the easier it will be to do just that."

"What you're saying is our First Amendment rights are completely gone?" Mrs. Pumpernickel asked. Like with everyone else, Sam's old math teacher was outraged.

"I'm afraid so. For those of you who live outside the mine, we have devised another way of keeping you updated about meetings and times. See me after the meeting, and I'll go over it with you."

Agnes finished covering the rest of the items on the list with no undo hitches, and before long, the meeting ended. It took more than half an hour for the room to clear. Sam took her seat at the table between Christina and Elaina, for the very first meeting of the newly formed committee.

"I thought these sessions were supposed to be closed," the finance woman said, with a nod toward Elaina. The woman was tall, built solid, with short feathery hair and a stern edge to her features. Sam was certain she was a lesbian, and like Sam, not the kind who carried a purse, donned makeup, or sported feminine attire.

Sam readied herself to defend Elaina's presence, but Agnes answered first. "Her name is Elaina Williams, and she has vital information you all need to hear."

The woman extended her hand across the table. "Nice to meet you, Elaina, I'm Brenda. I'll be overseeing finance."

For some reason, the way Brenda gripped Elaina's hand caused the tiny hairs on the nape of Sam's neck to stand on end. Was she put off by a sense of tenderness in the touching? Or maybe Brenda held Elaina's hand a bit past the point of good manners. Whatever the reason, Sam was on edge.

"Would you like some coffee?" Brenda asked Elaina.

"She can't have any." The words rushed from Sam's mouth, sounding the opposite of intelligent or informative. In fact, she sounded like a child refusing to share her best friend with others. "Sorry, those are her doctor's orders," Sam added.

Brenda raised her eyebrows, still holding onto Elaina's hand. "Yes, well, maybe some water, then?" she asked.

"I'm fine, thank you." Elaina withdrew her hand. She shot a quick look at Sam and her cheeks flushed.

Sam faced forward, mentally kicking herself for embarrassing Elaina.

Christina leaned over and whispered in Sam's ear, "Did I miss anything when I was at work?"

"What do you mean?"

Christina shrugged her shoulders. "You seem edgy. Are you all right?"

"I'm fine," Sam muttered.

Agnes said, "I would like to open this meeting by having Elaina share the information she has regarding a group we believe is responsible for the problems here in the United States."

All eyes focused on Elaina the entire time she spoke. She went over everything, from how she came to get the flash drives and documents, ending with Sam's concept of a hidden program, or programs on each of the drives.

"Sam's idea sounds farfetched." Brenda voiced her lack of confidence in Sam's ridiculous theory, before turning to Agnes. "Hidden files, I mean, how is that even possible?"

"Actually, Sam may be right." Kevin typed frantically on the laptop's keyboard. "It does seem like a large volume of information isn't coming up."

Sam said, "The notebook beside you might help. The writing on those papers might be a form of computer language—"

"So, you're an expert on this subject?" Brenda butted in.

"Do you make it a habit of interrupting people?" Sam countered. She thought about taking a swing at Brenda, enjoying the satisfaction it produced.

"I hear Sam's pretty knowledgeable in this area." Kevin opened the notebook, removing the papers from inside. "Yes. I see what you mean, Sam. This will take some time, but I think I can figure it out."

Brenda and Sam glowered at one another. Like two fighters ready to throw the first punch.

Christina changed the subject. "I'm putting in my notice at the hospital, but we still need more volunteers for the medical wing. Can we see if anyone from the camps has medical experience?"

"Todd, you should be writing this down," Mrs. Pumpernickel directed. "I will need supplies for the kids and textbooks as well." She cleared her throat. "Frank, I can get you a list of the things I'll need."

Face redder than normal, Frank's slouched posture snapped to attention. "If everyone would do the same, I'd appreciate it." Seconds later he returned his attention to doodling stick figures on a slip of paper. Long meetings clearly weren't his thing.

"We should also make plans for the next camp," Douglas told Sam. "Do you have any ideas?"

"I'd like to see if we have enough trained people to form two groups. If we can hit the next two camps on the same night, it'll make our travels much easier. We'll also have to go out and recon the areas first. I'm sure their security has improved since the first two camps were seized."

"You can bet they have," Douglas said. He asked Frank, "Care to go sightseeing with us tomorrow?"

The older man jerked his head up with a sudden burst of energy. "Sounds like fun. I have some brand-new equipment we can play with while we're out. How about you, Todd, are you coming?"

Todd shook his head. "I have to work tomorrow. I won't be finished until the following morning."

Christina spoke to Douglas. "We'll also need to plan a way to bring people up topside for at least an hour a day. The human body needs sunlight."

"Give me two or three days, Christina." Douglas jotted in his notebook. "I'll place security monitors and motion sensors throughout the area. I'm thinking three miles in every direction. The room behind us I'd like to use for security and communications." He gestured to Kevin. "I'll need your help in setting things up." Finally, his gaze fell on Agnes. "This stuff won't be cheap."

Frank said, "Hand me your lists after the meeting, and I'll see what I can do. What I'm unable to acquire on my own, I have several contacts who deal strictly in cash, with prices at fifty percent under market value. Do we have any funds available?"

Agnes said, "Money won't be a problem."

The rest of the meeting flew by with no unforeseen difficulties, except for Todd who continued to have his spelling corrected by Mrs. Pumpernickel. After the fourth time, he spoke to her in a polite tone, explaining he was going to use spellcheck as he typed everything into the computer.

"That does not excuse laziness, Todd."

Sam and Christina grinned at each other as the man lowered his head in defeat. "Yes, ma'am."

Chapter Fifteen

Uncertain Feelings

"You retired as a sergeant first class in the Army?" Sam asked.

"That's correct. I spent most of my time with the Tenth Mountain Infantry. I was with them during Bosnia and Desert Storm." Emmett's voice was hard, rugged.

Douglas exchanged a look with Sam before focusing on Emmett. "You Tenth Mountain guys are some crazy sonsabitches. How long were you a drill sergeant?"

"For four years during the middle of my enlistment."

Sam flipped through the pages on her clipboard. Emmett was definitely qualified to train their militia. Maybe too qualified. "You do understand these people are all volunteers. They're not military. We're not paying them. They are citizens, not soldiers."

Emmett grimaced his version of a smile, revealing a set of tobacco-stained teeth. "I know why we're here, Ms. Kelly, and it's not to hold one another's hand. You're asking me to get these people ready for combat, not a walk in the park on a warm sunny day. Give me the reins and I'll get the job done."

Douglas whispered in Sam's ear, "I like this guy. Terrifying perhaps, but I like him."

Sam slid the clipboard to Emmett, feeling somewhat apprehensive, but knowing the man was right. The tougher he trained them, the greater chance they would have for survival. "We have over a hundred and fifty volunteers so far. The first page is a list of those who have prior military service. They will help you with the training. If you feel someone is medically incapable, let me know, and I'll take care of it."

"What about weapons? Ammunition? Gear? I need to know what I'm working with here."

"Douglas will take you to the arms room when he goes over security. As of right now our outside time is limited. You'll have to make do until he finishes setting everything up. I have thirty more M-16s on order and several cases of ammo for training purposes. Give me a list of anything else you'll need, and we'll do what we can."

Emmett and Douglas left, and Sam slumped behind the desk in the conference room. Her body was sore, her mind tired. Since the committee meeting ended the day before, Sam had spent her time organizing the weapons room and setting up her office. She constructed a list of names of the people wanting to take part in the developing military group, and any experience they had. She made a list of supplies for Frank. Then she'd fed the horses and got to bed late, only to wake up early and do the same things over again before doing a recon trip to the two camps with Frank and Douglas.

Both camps were well-guarded and more than forty miles away. She, Frank, and Douglas had developed a rough plan of attack on the return ride to the mine, but it still needed a lot of work. Frank took off as soon as they arrived, to perform a much-needed supply run, leaving Douglas and Sam alone to study the map and throw some ideas around.

Her mind raced with a list of things she still needed to finish before calling it a day. Unable to focus, Sam decided to go see how Christina and the medical wing were faring. A perfect cover for checking on Elaina. A friendly check-in. Definitely not the main reason she was breaking from her scheduled tasks.

"I wondered when you'd show up," Christina said the moment Sam stepped into the room.

Sam poured herself a cup of coffee. "What do you mean? Why would you think I would be coming by? Other than a cup of coffee?" She raised the cup to her lips to take a sip.

"After the display between you and Brenda in the meeting yesterday, I had a strange feeling someone here had piqued both your interests."

Sam remained silent, not appreciating Christina's amused tone.

Christina said, "You can tell me, Sam. I promise to keep it to myself."

"I have no idea what you're talking about."

"You're serious? You don't know what I mean?"

"I *do* know you're not making any sense." Sam pulled up a chair, noticing Elaina's cot was freshly made with a book by the pillow and her belongings lined neatly underneath. "Where's Elaina?"

Christina's eyebrows arched. "Why?"

"What do you mean, why?"

"I'm simply curious. Why do you want to know?" Christina held Sam's glower. "Why not ask about one of the other patients, or Steven? Why are you interested in Elaina?"

Sam frowned in confusion. "I'm asking as a friend, nothing more."

"Are you sure about that?"

"Yes, I'm sure. What's the deal with you, Chris?"

Christina gave her one last hard stare before sitting back in her chair. "It's nothing." She waved a hand toward the supply room. "Elaina was bored and asked for something to do, so I sent her to reorganize the mess Tracy made."

Sam said, "Good. She was acting kind of restless yesterday."

Christina turned her head slightly as if checking for eavesdroppers. "Brenda came in to see Elaina twenty minutes ago. She's been with her ever since."

Sam jerked to her feet, slopping coffee on Christina's desk. "You let her back there! Why?" A volcano of anger filled her.

Christina's voice was calm, her body relaxed. "Why would I tell her no?"

Sam smacked her cup down on the desk and stomped to the supply room, suddenly hungry for a fight. Brenda's voice floated from the doorway where Sam stood, her fists clenched tight. Elaina sat on a chair sorting through a box on the floor, and Brenda stood close behind her, telling her about a vacation she'd taken three years ago. The volcano inside Sam was close to the eruption point.

"I'm telling you, Elaina, the view of the pyramids was breathtaking at night."

Elaina flicked through the contents of the box. "Why go to Egypt when you can travel to Ireland or England or someplace . . . less sandy?" She covered a yawn with her right hand. Her movement eased Sam's mind considerably.

Brenda let out a laugh, making the skin on Sam's face feel hot. "I think you would like the desert. It's beautiful in a wild, untamed sort of way. If we ever get out of this damn cave, I'll have to take you there to show you how wild it can be."

Sighing, Elaina raised her head. "I don't think I'm—" Her eyes veered to the doorway, and a smile crossed her lips. "Sam, what are you doing here?"

Sam kept her eyes fixed on Brenda. "Christina said you were here. I wanted to see if you needed anything."

"As you can see, I've already got it under control." Brenda squared her shoulders, as if guarding Elaina. "If we need anything, we'll let you know. Can you close the door on your way out?"

"I wasn't talking to you." Sam's ire ratcheted up a notch.

"I could care less who you were talking to."

"I was planning on taking a break anyway." Elaina broke in, her voice tense, almost pleading. "Why don't we go get something to eat?" Elaina reached up to set the supply box on a shelf.

Sam went over and grabbed the box. "You shouldn't be lifting. You'll rip your stitches."

"I'll get it." Brenda butted in.

The scuffle between them pressed Elaina into the shelf. "Please, it's not heavy," Elaina seemed to be doing her best to keep her footing.

The fracas morphed into more of a rugby match than a noble attempt at chivalry. Sadly, the outcome ended with angry shoves, a partially ripped box, and a surprised, yet thankfully uninjured Elaina on the floor.

"What's going on in here?" Christina stomped through the doorway. "This might not be much of a hospital, but it's a hospital, nonetheless. If you two want to act like children, take it somewhere else."

Spinning from Brenda, Sam took a step closer to Elaina, who was slowly climbing to her feet. "I'm sorry. I didn't mean . . ." She reached a hand outward, then pulled it away, uncertain. She hung her head and left the room.

Christina waited for a moment before speaking to Brenda. "You need to leave, too."

"Why should I go? I was here first."

"Because I'm in charge of the hospital, and I said so."

Brenda furrowed her eyebrows. "It's because Sam's a friend of yours." She ignored Christina and asked Elaina, "Do you still want to get something to eat?"

Before Elaina could speak, Christina cut in. "Elaina needs to rest. You can come back in an hour. After you've had a chance to cool down."

Brenda paused as if to argue further, but instead gave up and did as Christina instructed.

"I'm sorry. I didn't mean for anything to happen. One-minute Brenda was talking to me, the next thing I know, Sam came in, and both—"

Christina held up a hand. "I don't blame you for those two acting like Neanderthals." She motioned for Elaina to take a seat so she could inspect Elaina's stitches. "Unfortunately, this drama happens when two dominating women are interested in the same female."

Elaina glanced at her hands, then to Christina. "Sam's attracted to *me?*"

"Interesting how you asked about Sam and not Brenda." Christina sat on a crate next to her. Lines creased Christina's forehead. "Sam's a very complicated woman, with a past equally as complex."

"I know. The way Steven talks about her past relationships, she has definitely been around the block a few times," Elaina said. "I told myself I wouldn't get mixed up with a woman like Sam again."

"What do you mean, a woman like Sam?"

"I'm not trying to offend you or Sam, but I've already been with one disloyal woman, I don't need to make it two."

"Sam is anything but disloyal. She chooses not to be in a committed relationship. That has nothing to do with loyalty." Christina peeked toward the doorway before continuing. "I have no worries about Sam mistreating you. I am worried about Sam getting hurt." Christina hurried on when Elaina raised her chin. "I'm not suggesting you would hurt her, Elaina, at least not intentionally."

"We are talking about Sam, right? I just met her. This conversa—"

"This conversation needs to happen before Sam becomes too hung up on you," Christina said. "I'm also telling you this, so you won't be blindsided later on. As I said before, Sam's past is extremely complicated. You might decide it's too complicated for you to take a chance on getting involved with her."

Elaina felt a twinge of worry prick in the center of her mind.

"What I tell you is between you and me," Christina said. "It doesn't leave this room."

Elaina said, "Sure."

Christina said, "Sam has been the one person people could count on, even when she was young. She was always there to help her father on the farm, never gave her mother a lick of trouble, and with both of her parents' busy careers, Sam helped with the raising of her little sister, Rachel." Christina paused when faint chatting drifted in from the other room. She listened for a few seconds then turned to Elaina. "Sam has only had one love in her life, my older sister, Sarah. When they were sixteen, something terrible happened to them both. They were out one evening at the lake and two men attacked them."

Elaina shifted uncomfortably on the box, worried to hear what Christina meant by attack.

"Sam fought hard to save my sister, which was why they about beat Sam to death. They viciously raped, then stabbed, both girls and left them in the middle of the woods to die. The only thing that saved Sam was the way she was left in the mud. It slowed her bleeding."

Christina took in a deep breath, as if she were swallowing back tears. "We don't know how she did it, but Sam managed to carry my sister's body out to the road where Jed, a man from town, found them, and rushed both girls to the hospital. Sarah didn't make it, and Sam was close to death."

"You don't need to tell me anymore."

"Yes, I do. I saw the way you looked at her. You need to know. After Sam got out of the hospital, she was emotionally lost. She took up drinking and hanging out with the wrong crowd. When she hit rock bottom, Sam came dangerously close to ending her own life." Christina's head shook at the memory.

"Her mother and father packed up and moved from here to give Sam a fresh start. Sam went into the military after graduating high school, and she did her part for God and country. The hometown paper wrote of Sam's service as 'exceptional heroism,' of how she saved three soldiers, was injured twice, and earned multiple medals and awards, including two purple hearts. Agnes showed me the rest of the story in the letters Sam wrote to her. Sam saw several of her close friends die or be critically wounded. She witnessed the deaths of unarmed women and children, and other horrible things no one should ever have to live through. All of this left an even greater mark deep inside her."

Elaina's eyes were wide in disbelief, her voice barely above a whisper. "How does anyone live through that?"

"By not letting people get close to her, and by adding to the wall she had already built from her past. Her father and mother died unexpectedly several years ago, so Sam came home to take care of Rachel. She joined the police force in Kansas City, and you can figure out the rest from there."

Christina stood, placing a hand on Elaina's slumped shoulders. "Sam is neither a coward nor disloyal. She's a good woman, with a good heart. Life has dealt her some rough and painful hands, but she has persevered. Please do not make her live through another. If her road is too complicated for you to handle, I'm asking you not to lead her on."

Elaina carefully studied Christina. "You love her, don't you?"

"I would be a fool not to. But not in the way you think. I know what kind of a woman she is. I have broken the hearts of many men because they weren't able to show me even a fraction of the love Sam showed my sister." She smiled. "I love Sam like a sister, nothing more. I would appreciate it if you kept this talk between us. Sam would kill me if she knew I'd told you any of this."

Elaina agreed and Christina left the room.

Steven showed up that evening when Sam was behind her desk in the weapons room. "Agnes wanted me to get you. Frank came in early. He and Mike returned with two truckloads of supplies we need to go through."

Sam rose to her feet. "I hope he found a coffee pot for my office. I need a constant supply of caffeine to help get me through all this paperwork." She followed Steven through the passageway, surprised by the number of people heading in the same direction.

"I asked Kevin if he would like to have dinner the day after tomorrow with you and Tracy, and he agreed." His upbeat mood changed when Sam didn't respond. "You didn't ask her, did you?"

"No, I asked Elaina instead."

"Really? What did she say?"

"She said yes, but on two conditions. We have Boston cream pie for dessert and watch the *Lord of the Rings* trilogy."

Steven said, "You lesbians are an odd people, but it sounds doable." He stifled his laughter when Sam's expression turned grim. "What?"

"I might have screwed it up. I'm not sure."

"Then unscrew it. This really means a lot to me, Sam."

She forced a smile. "I will. If I have to, I'll find someone else."

Steven opened his mouth, but no words came out. Before Sam had a chance to nudge him on, Christina showed up with Janis, Tracy, and Elaina trailing behind.

"I guess you got pushed into this, too?" Tracy asked.

Sam didn't understand what she meant.

Tracy laughed, grabbing Sam's arm. "Unloading the supplies off the truck. It's where you're heading, right?"

"Oh, yes. I guess so." Sam looked over her shoulder. Her stomach plummeted when she saw the disappointment on Elaina's face. *She really is upset with me.* Sam brought her head around, missing Tracy's question. "I'm sorry?"

The woman gave a tiny giggle, not bothering to release Sam's arm. "I asked what you all do around here for fun."

"Oh, um, fishing."

Tracy scrunched her nose as if disgusted, but Sam didn't care. She was too preoccupied with glancing over her shoulder again to see if Elaina's disappointment was still there. It was.

"Fishing?" Tracy's words broke off when her other arm was yanked in the opposite direction.

Relieved, Sam stopped and waited for Elaina, who was several paces behind. "I apologize for what happened earlier." Sam fell in step with Elaina. "I had no right to barge in on you and Brenda like that."

Elaina rolled her eyes, directing Sam off to the side, away from the others. "That's not what you should be sorry for, Sam. If Christina hadn't come in when she did, you two would have gotten into a fight."

Sam crammed her hands in the front pockets of her jeans, feeling childish. "I don't like her."

"You want to fight her because you don't like her?"

"No, that's not what I meant. I . . ." *I'm not exactly sure why I don't like her.* For the most part, she had always been able to get along well with people, and the few she didn't, she tolerated. But she not only didn't like Brenda, she detested her. "I know you're upset with me. You have every right to be."

"Sam," Elaina said, "I'm not upset with you, but I don't want to see you two get into a fight. Promise me you will stay away from her."

Sam scowled. "Are you sure you're not upset? From your expression a minute ago, you looked pissed."

"It wasn't directed at you, but to that thing attaching itself to your arm."

"You mean Tracy?" Sam grinned. "Is she still annoying you?"

"You could say that."

Mike appeared around the corner of the passageway. "Hey, Sam. Do you want your stuff in the weapons room or left to the side?"

Sam realized then the passageway was almost empty. "I'll be right there," she said before shrugging her shoulders. "I guess we better go. Oh, do you still want to do the double-date thing?"

"Yes, I'm looking forward to it actually." She linked her arm through Sam's and walked with her the rest of the way.

Sam didn't care for Tracy's arm around hers, but she sure felt at ease with Elaina's. A small part of her brain told her to pull away. The rest of her mind enjoyed the closeness so much, her arm refused to let go. The short experience flooded Sam with a sense of warmth which she was sure would last through next winter.

The following evening, Steven entered the medical wing with a broad smile across his face. Sam and Elaina sat at one of the three desks, where they were engaged in boisterous conversation. A deck of cards lay scattered across the desktop.

"I'm not sure what came over me." Elaina laughed. "I pulled out as fast as I could, not bothering to say another word."

Sam had her elbows on the desk, fully engrossed in Elaina's story.

"Sounds like my first boyfriend," Steven piped in.

"Get your mind out of the gutter." Sam drained the last of her coffee and stood.

Elaina moved to rise, but Sam waved her down. "I need to see if Kevin has had any luck with the computer files."

As soon as Sam was gone, Steven filled a mug with coffee and took the empty seat across from Elaina. "Has Sam been here long?"

Elaina gathered the cards. She continued to stare to the doorway as if she could still see Sam. "She's been here off and on throughout the day," she said. "Cards mainly, but we played a few games of chess earlier."

"Who won?"

"Hmm?" Elaina jumped as if coming out of a dream. "I'm sorry, what did you say?"

Steven fought to keep his laughter inside. "Who won?"

"Who won what? Oh, you mean chess." Elaina blushed. "Oh, I don't really remember if we finished the game. We seemed to get lost in conversation. Both of us kept forgetting whose turn it was." Elaina focused on shuffling the cards. "Sam is such an intelligent woman."

Steven said, "Yes, she is."

"I mean it, Steven. Sam does more than hold a conversation. Half the time she's leading me into topics most people rarely discuss. And when I talk, she actually listens."

"As she should."

"I know." Elaina laid out a game of solitaire. "I'm not used to it. Between my parents, my ex, even at my job, I've always felt like the person standing in the shadows of others." She stopped dealing and looked up. "I'm not saying I had a bad life. I didn't. I only meant it feels nice to truly be heard."

He said, "I know what you mean." Steven tapped the cards lying face down on the desk. "Do you know how to play rummy?"

She scooped up the cards with a competitive gleam in her eyes. "Gin or regular?" she asked.

At that moment, Steven realized Elaina was the perfect woman for Sam. He only hoped Sam would eventually see it, too. "Up to you."

"Regular, and I'm keeping score."

Sam tossed and turned in bed all night, but not from the recurring nightmare she'd had since arriving on the farm. Instead, her sleeping mind conjured erotic images of Elaina. Elaina alone, Elaina with her. Elaina was standing, sitting, lying down, in extraordinary and seductive positions in every room of the house. Sam woke several times during the night feeling more frustrated and aroused than she had ever felt in her life.

"Goddamn it!" she shouted when she awoke after three in the morning. She sat up in bed, realizing her mistake. The sound of footsteps pounded down the stairs. Her door whipped opened, a worried Christina panting heavily in the doorway.

"Sam, what is it?" She flipped on the lights.

Sam squinted in the brightness and pulled the covers up around her. "Sorry, I was dreaming."

"You're drenched. Are you running a fever?"

"Hey, is everything all right?" Sam looked up toward the ceiling at the sound of Rachel yelling from upstairs.

"She's fine" Christina called out. "Go back to bed,"

"I didn't mean to wake you all. I was only dreaming."

Christina made her way over, placing her hand on Sam's forehead. "You don't feel hot. Did you take the pills I gave you?"

"I didn't have a nightmare, Chris."

"Really? Then what?" Christina sat on the edge of the bed, acting for all the world like a doctor making a routine house call.

Running her fingers through her hair, Sam winced at the thought of answering Chris's question. "I'm not comfortable talking about it."

"Sam, you know you can tell me anything."

Sam felt her face flush with heat. "No, I can't. Not about this."

"Oh, *that*." Christina stretched out the second word a little too long. "That's normal, Sam. Take care of your business and go back to sleep."

"Christina!"

"What? Oh, come on Sam, we're both grown-ups. Masturbation is not—"

"Not something I want to discuss with you."

Christina laughed. "Well, fine. Do what you need to do and let us all get some sleep, will you?" She giggled and left the room.

"Hey, Chris."

Christina stopped at the door, her brows raised in question.

"I've had dreams like this before, well not this in-depth, and each time the other woman's face wasn't completely clear."

"And your dream tonight was different?"

Sam bowed her head. "Yes."

"Was the other woman Elaina?"

Sam jerked her head up, stunned. "How did you know?"

Christina stifled a laugh. "Lucky guess. It could mean nothing, or it could be something. That's for you to decide."

Sam cleared her throat. "I'm getting these feelings, Chris. Feelings I've not felt since Sarah." She fiddled with the edge of the blanket. Thinking it and saying it aloud were two different things.

"Sam, the attraction is a good thing." Christina spoke softly. "My sister loved you very much. I'm absolutely sure she would have wanted you to fall in love again."

"I know she would have. I'm just not sure I want to."

"Also, it's your decision, but I have noticed life does seem more enjoyable when you have someone to enjoy it with." She smiled gently at Sam, before shutting off the lights, and closing the door behind her.

Sam lay in bed staring blindly up at the ceiling. She tried several times to drift back to sleep, but images of her dream kept swirling in her head, and a pulsating ache built between her legs.

Finally, after the fourth failed attempt at sleep, Sam reached reluctantly beneath the sheets and under her boxer-briefs. She felt wet to the touch, possibly wetter than she had ever been before. Closing her eyes tight, willing the images to reappear, Sam rubbed her middle finger smoothly over the center of her ache. Her mouth parted as the throbbing sensation grew, bringing with it the promise of a swift release. Her back arched, the muscles in her legs tightened as her mind soared upward toward the top-most mountain, ready for the explosion deep within. Right before reaching the peak, Sam grabbed a fistful of pillow with her free hand, bracing her body for the sweet impact seconds away.

Her breathing quickened. Her hand moved back and forth frantically beneath the sheets as the seconds passed slowly by. The release didn't come. She bit on her bottom lip as she willed the orgasm inside her to explode. More minutes ticked by, still no release.

"Crap!" She threw the blankets off her body. She knew touching herself wasn't going to work. She had known it even before she decided to try. Her feelings of frustration, her need for a release, the burning desire deep inside had nothing to do with her own orgasm. No, every part of her hungered for Elaina. The thought of tasting Elaina on her lips. Feeling the woman's climax, her head between Elaina's legs. Drinking Elaina's wetness in as her body quivered. "Crap!" Sam kept her voice low so as not to wake the others a second time.

She stripped out of her clothes and headed for the shower. The water was cold, refreshing, and she allowed it to engulf her entire body. Yet, after standing several minutes under the chilly stream, her desire remained, burning as hot as ever. Shutting off the water, Sam did not even bother to dry herself. She dressed in her running clothes and headed outside into the semi-cool darkness of the early morning air.

After a bout of brief stretching, Sam took off down the drive at a brisk pace. She would have preferred jogging on one of the horse trails in the woods, but the trails didn't get enough light this early in the morning. So, she kept her workout safe, simple. The first two miles energized her. Heating her muscles in ways she hadn't felt in months. Instead of turning around at the old oak tree she used to climb as a child, Sam kept going, deciding to add two more miles to her run.

The first slap of reality was the rough burning sensation in her lungs. She pushed herself onward. A sharp pain struck her right side less than a minute later with no warning, making the movement of her legs and her irregular breathing much harder. She slowed her pace, raising her arms up over her head to relieve the discomfort.

"Damn." She pivoted around. Her pace now became more of a haphazard limp with all thoughts of her burning desire for Elaina, or any other woman, pushed completely from her mind. Sam heard the crunching of gravel under tires behind her, then a single *whoop* of a siren.

She shuffled to a stop, fighting the urge to drop to her knees for a thankful prayer.

"Hey Sam, do you need a—"

Before Todd could finish his sentence, Sam had the door to the police car open, and fell into the seat beside him. "Drive," she gasped, shutting the door behind her.

He chuckled through the length of the drive and continued even after Sam limped into the house. Still panting, she pointed to the kitchen when he asked her about coffee and stumbled into her bedroom.

It took her longer than usual to remove her clothes, but the warm water of the shower was well worth the wait. By the time she shut off the water, her body felt considerably better. She toweled the dampness from her body, dried her hair, then dressed for the day.

For some reason, the process of selecting an outfit felt more complex than usual. Normally, the first thing she grabbed, she wore. She didn't have to worry about matching, because, for the most part, all her outfits seemed to match. Jeans, T-shirts, sweatshirts, and flannel shirts. What was there to clash? The few nice outfits she owned were still in suitcases in the bottom of her closet.

Her mind drifted. She wondered what type of clothes Elaina wore when she was not in medical scrubs. She could easily picture the woman's curvy body in sexy clubbing outfits or dolled up in a power suit. As she was imagining Elaina in skimpy, tight, see-through lingerie, reality sank in. She hurriedly threw on her clothes and joined Todd in the kitchen.

"I heard you went for a run." Christina barely hid her grin behind her raised coffee cup.

Sam narrowed her eyes at Todd. "You have a big mouth."

He cackled as they watched her fill her football travel mug with coffee.

"Where are you heading so early?" Christina asked Sam.

"I have a few early morning errands. Would you have Mike see to the horses?"

"He left last night with Frank on another supply run."

"What about the curfew?" Todd sat up straighter in his seat.

Christina lowered her cup. "Being out past curfew won't matter if they're caught with a truckload of stolen goods. Agnes gave Frank one of the weapon permits, but that won't matter either if they have to shoot their way out."

Sam screwed the lid on her travel mug. "Did Douglas okay the run?"

"Stop worrying. You both know Frank is too clever a man to get caught. I have no idea how he gets away with the things he does, but he manages." Teetering on the edge of laughter, Christina stared at Sam. "You go do your errands, and I'll take care of the horses. Next time make sure you let us know when you go running, so one of us can come pick you up."

Todd ducked when Sam sent the wet dishtowel flying at his head. She could still hear his hearty laughter as she stomped out to her truck.

Elaina awoke feeling stiff and restless. The dreams she had of Sam the entire night left her flustered. The cot gave its usual squeaking sound as she sat up rubbing her neck.

"Did you have a long night?"

Elaina gratefully took the cup from Christina's outstretched hand. "I've had better. What time is it?"

"Just after eight. Sam came in to check on you earlier, but you were still asleep."

Elaina had to fight to keep the excitement out of her voice. "Sam was here? How long ago did she leave?"

"Twenty minutes or so, I don't remember. She came by to take you to your new lodging."

"What new lodging?" Elaina stood up slowly.

"Well, you can't live here in the hospital. We'll need the bed in a few days." Christina gave her a hopeful expression. "Sam has set you up in the guesthouse, along with the committee members who've been living in the mine. The house still needs work, but some of the people have pitched in to speed things up. Douglas is working on installing alarms in the buildings up top. They will go off if anyone's in the area, giving everyone time to head into the mine."

The idea of leaving the mine was appealing, but the thought of seeing Sam was even greater. "Where did Sam go? When will she be back?"

"She's in a meeting with Todd and some of the other guys. She said she wouldn't be finished until later this afternoon. I, on the other hand, am free now. Would you like me to escort you to your new quarters?"

Elaina experienced a small twinge of disappointment, but her mood brightened with the idea of being inside a normal room again.

The sun felt warm. Elaina squinted in the brightness as she followed Christina from the barn. She wanted to bask in the beauty of the surrounding area, but the idea of a hot shower was a higher priority. Power saws buzzing, hammers banging, and boisterous voices greeted them inside the smaller of the two houses.

Brenda's familiar, agitated voice rang out as Christina and Elaina stepped through the front door. "Hey, why doesn't the plumbing work down here?"

"Sam said to do it last," said a man installing new kitchen cabinets. "Good lord, that woman complains nonstop."

"You're not kidding," a second man replied from the kitchen. "Unfortunately, I'm the one who'll be living in this house with her."

"I'll stick with the mine," the cabinet-making man said.

The second man smiled when he saw Christina and Elaina. "Ah. We've been expecting you, Elaina."

Elaina realized the second guy was Janis's husband Howard who oversaw maintenance.

He said, "Go to the top of the stairs, and your room is the last door on the right. Sam took your personal things up earlier, but your new bedroom set, and linens won't be here for a few hours."

"What personal things?"

He shrugged. "Not sure. She said they were yours."

"Damn it!" Brenda stormed from the basement fuming with anger. "Is anyone listening to me? Why can't I have the extra bedroom on the first floor?" Her mood changed the moment she spotted Elaina. "You're moving in? Guess this place doesn't completely suck." She shot the man standing beside Howard a hateful stare. "My bedroom isn't going to work."

"What's wrong with it? You have new carpet, new bathroom fixtures, a spacious closet, hell, woman, even the walls are new."

"The walls are pink!"

"Then move to one of the other rooms down there."

"They're all pink."

The man shrugged his shoulders. "It's the color Sam gave me."

"Then I want to move up here."

"Sorry, Sam made it clear the rooms on this floor are for guests only."

"What guests?" Brenda narrowed her eyes at Christina. "I see what Sam's doing. It won't work, though." Brenda went over to a collection of gallon-sized paint cans piled in the center of the unfinished living room and searched through the cans, one by one. She selected two cans and grabbed a paintbrush from a second pile. With her jaw set firmly, she pivoted to Christina. "I'll paint the damn room myself!"

The first man fought to stifle his laughter until Brenda had stomped angrily down the stairs.

"That was pleasant," Christina said. "As soon as you finish the kitchen, please hook up the plumbing downstairs."

The guy gave her a thumbs-up and went back to his work.

"I'd better go and relieve Steven. He's chomping at the bit to run to the grocery store, something about shopping for your dinner tonight."

Christina's reminder of her double date with Sam filled Elaina with excitement. After Christina left, Elaina went upstairs, clutching her backpack tight to her shoulder. She opened the door to her room and her mouth dropped. The room was bright, with so much space. But neither the walk-in closet, nor the balcony was what made her heart flutter. No, the overwhelming emotion was brought on by seeing all her items from the cabin stacked neatly in a corner of the room. Her chest swelled. Tears formed in the corners of her eyes.

She sat on the newly carpeted floor, and carefully went through her stuff. None of her possessions were extravagant or valuable, but they were all she had left in the world. The fact Sam had risked her own life for a second trip to the cabin was worth more than any gift anyone had ever given her.

Chapter Sixteen

Close Call

Sam leaned in, pointing to an area on the map hanging from a bracket attached to the ceiling. "We'll be exposed for three miles on this stretch of highway, but the rest of the trip to and from we can manage on back roads, so we should have few problems. We'll need to set up stations on each end in case there's trouble. The first bus on the way to the camps can drop off the troops, and the last bus can pick them up on the way back."

"What firepower do you want to leave them with?" Frank asked, as he watched Todd jot down the highlights on a pad of notebook paper.

Emmett spoke up. "Let's do the fifty-cals that came in yesterday and maybe a Claymore mine for both groups."

Sam leaned over Todd's shoulder. "No, better go with grenades instead of the Claymores. I don't want to waste time breaking down the mines if we don't use them."

Todd scribbled out Claymore and wrote in grenades.

Emmett spit noisily into his stained, disposable cup. "I figured we could leave them."

She glared at him. "We do not live in Iraq. Anything dangerous will not be left lying around for some unsuspecting person to find."

"Ah, wasn't thinking. Good point, Sam."

Douglas pulled his eyes off Emmett's spit-cup, trying unsuccessfully not to appear disgusted. "These camps are bigger. We'll need at least four more buses to get them all out."

"Already taken care of, Douglas." Frank tossed his reading glasses on his daily planner. "We now have four buses for each team, so transportation is more than adequate."

"Did you fix the oil leak on my bus?" Todd asked.

"Yep, and put on all new tires as well."

"Everyone satisfied with the plan?" Sam asked. When each person concurred, Sam jerked on the string to coil the map upward into its frame.

"Hey, Sam, you have a visitor." Todd said.

"I can come back later." Elaina stood, feeling self-conscious as multiple sets of eyes turned to her. She'd finished setting up her room after the furniture arrived, and she wanted to thank Sam personally before dinner.

"Nonsense, we've talked long enough." Emmett rose, removing a sizeable wad of black mush from his mouth. He tossed the glob of chewing tobacco into the cup, spit a few times, then flung the nasty mess into the waste bin beside the podium. "I want your trainees in full gear and outside within the next twenty minutes," he commanded. The group of men and women crammed around the table rose, chairs screeching on the floor. "I feel like giving the troops a little run today." Emmett followed his instructors out into the passageway.

Sam rested her elbows on the desk, rubbing both sides of her temples. "I have a last-minute change in the roster. Douglas, Todd, you two can have Emmett. Frank and I will take the kid with the nail-biting fetish."

"Hell, no! That man scares the crap out of me. I like the nail kid. He reminds me of the son I never wanted." Douglas stood, slapping Sam hard on the back. "Sorry, Sam, maybe we'll take him next time, if we make it back from this mission in one piece." Grabbing his bag, Douglas left the conference room, followed by the rest of the group.

"I didn't mean to intrude."

When their eyes met, Elaina's pulse quickened, sending an excited shiver down her spine.

A tired grin danced along Sam's lips. "You're not intruding." She stood from the table and chugged the rest of her drink.

Elaina's eyes moved along Sam's body, soaking in every nuance. Sam had her white tank top tucked neatly into a dark, well-fitting pair of boot-cut blue jeans. Elaina's eyes lingered over Sam's breasts, which appeared full yet firm. They protruded slightly from underneath an unbuttoned flannel long-sleeve shirt, which hung comfortably over the white tank.

Sam's boots were light-brown, soft leather that went well with the belt around her firm waist. Elaina swallowed, realizing the word firm had become her new best friend.

When Elaina glanced up, Sam was staring at her. Warmth flooded her body. "Sorry, I was wondering why those other men were dressed in camouflage clothing and the rest of you weren't."

Sam said, "That's one of Emmett's things. He says if you want the troops to act like soldiers, they need to dress like soldiers. He talked Frank into making a run last night to acquire enough military uniforms for every trainee to have three sets, including socks, T-shirts, and ugly green underwear."

Elaina wondered if Sam was wearing a pair of ugly green underwear beneath her well-fitted jeans. Feeling feverish, she tried hard to erase the erotic images from her thoughts.

"Are you all right? You look flushed?"

"I'm fine. I wanted to say thank you for getting my stuff from the cabin. You really didn't need to do that."

"Yes, I did. I should've done it the first time I was there, but I was more interested in finding the flash drives." Sam stepped back. "You look nice." Her throat sounded tight, almost to the point of constriction. "Did Steven say what time dinner was?"

Elaina sensed a sudden edginess in Sam. Nervously, she watched Sam walk the long way around the table. "Steven said he'll start cooking by five. Kevin's not going to show up until seven, so Steven's timing dinner around his arrival. Do you need help?"

Sam piled file after file on top of an already monstrous stack. Elaina went over, halfway leaning across the table to grab several of the folders scattered around its surface. She felt Sam's eyes on her chest. She was certain of it. Without warning, Elaina experienced an old, yet familiar, arousing sensation swell beneath her shirt. She closed her eyes tight, willing herself to focus, and for heavens-sakes, *breathe!* Her nipples were growing hard, her mind racing on a whole new level. They were becoming the perfect size for Sam to flick a thumb over, or better yet, a tongue.

Elaina's cravings flashed. She mustered all her willpower not to look at Sam but lost that battle as she and Sam locked gazes. Elaina didn't know what to do. Before she could react, Sam's expression shifted to utter panic.

Sam jerked away so suddenly, half the files in the stack tumbled to the floor. "Shit!" Sam squatted and arranged the files into two separate stacks.

Elaina had a hard time reading Sam. She could tell Sam was off, but she wasn't sure why. Was Sam experiencing good feelings or bad? Did Sam like her, or was she repulsed by her. *Damn it*, she wanted to know!

Taking the shorter path, Elana rushed around the table, and bent to help. Every time she reached for a folder, her arm brushed up against Sam's side. Sam's closeness made her ache with desire. She longed for Sam to touch her, caress her. She fought hard to keep her emotions under control, and under the present circumstances, it took all the strength she had.

Sam closed her eyes. "I can get this." Her voice was scarcely above a whisper.

The pounding of Elaina's heart made it difficult for her to concentrate. "Don't be silly."

Elaina was not sure how she made it through working so close to Sam, but in less than five minutes they had the files stacked and were carrying them to Sam's office. During the trek, Elaina found it difficult to keep Sam engaged in any form of conversation. Maybe Sam was annoyed with her. Elaina decided to keep the topics light, so she filled the air with idle chatter about the construction taking place on the guesthouse. She figured Sam would enjoy topics filled with power tools and sheetrock. After all, Sam was definitely a top.

When Elaina was about to reach her breaking point and straight out ask Sam how she felt, Sam came up with some excuse about feeding the horses and took off. Elaina ended up standing in Sam's office, alone and bewildered.

Sam entered the kitchen at half past six to the tantalizing aroma of seasoned lamb and savory flavorings, which tickled the inside of her mouth and nose at the same time. "I can't do this," she said.

Steven stood humming a lively tune as he stirred a red sauce simmering in a pan on top of the stove. He was dressed in black neatly pressed dress slacks, dress shoes, and a black, long-sleeved, button-down shirt. He had his red silk tie tucked neatly into his shirt in an apparent attempt at keeping it clean while he prepared dinner.

He rolled his eyes at the towel on Sam's head and the robe wrapped around her body. "You need to hurry and change, Sam. You're cutting it awfully close."

"You're not listening. I said I can't do this."

"Do what? Eat dinner, watch a movie, talk to people you already know, and maybe have a little fun for once in your life?" He popped a black olive into his mouth.

"You don't understand, Steven. I can't be around her."

"What?" He eyed her as if she had turned into an alien. "I thought you *liked* Elaina."

"That's just it. I can't stop thinking about her." Sam sat in a chair, her shoulders slumped forward. "Even when I'm not with her, I can't stop thinking about her. I'm so frustrated I can't even think clearly."

Sam thought about when she and Elaina were in the mine earlier, after she had made a mess of the files. She was barely able to restrain herself then, which only became more challenging the closer they were to one another. She'd ached to pull Elaina into her arms, and she had the feeling she had been seconds away from doing exactly that. There's nothing like a good slap on the face before a nice sit-down dinner, she thought.

She snapped her head up at the sound of Steven's laughter. "Sam, I think you really like this woman, and it scares the shit out of you."

"What scares me is I barely even know her."

He removed a skillet from the stove and joined Sam at the table. "All right, from what you do know, what do you like?"

Sam's knitted her eyebrows together as she considered the question. "When she smiles, the right side of her mouth goes up a little higher than the left, making her smile a bit crooked. But not when she laughs. When she laughs her lips pull slightly back causing them to be even fuller, especially in the front." Sam patted Steven's leg in her excitement. "Oh my God, she has this sort of tic thing she does when she's in deep thought, which you can spot if you look close enough right about here." Sam pointed above her left brow, indicating to Steven where the tic was.

Sam stood and paced the length of the kitchen, from the sink to the doorway. "I noticed how her mouth moves when she talks. I'm not sure how to describe it, but it drives me crazy." Sam faced Steven. "Did you know when she was younger, she wanted to be a veterinarian?" He shook his head. "Her father was a respected journalist and I believe he had a lot to do with why she changed her mind. She talks often about her father, but she's never once mentioned her mother."

Sam retook her seat. "Her favorite color is green, her favorite food is lobster, and she's the first woman I met who likes westerns almost as much as I do. Her father was a major John Wayne fan. Did you know she wrote a paper on quantum physics when she was in the tenth grade?"

"What exactly is that?"

Sam leaned back in her chair. "I have no idea."

Shaking his head, Steven returned to the stove. "Sam, you learned more about Elaina in these last few days than most couples learn after several years of being together."

He popped a black olive in her mouth and pulled her up from the chair. "I love you, Samantha Kelly, and I'm telling you this as a friend and as your unofficially adopted brother. This woman fits you like a glove. If you pass this up, you will regret it for the rest of your life."

He removed the towel from her head and draped it over her shoulder. "Now, go get ready before I kill you." He gave her a slight push toward the doorway. "Oh, and jeans are fine as long as you have on a nice shirt. And I don't mean a T-shirt."

For the seventh time, Sam examined her reflection in the full-length mirror, feeling uncertain about the color of her fitted button-up blouse. She liked the way the neckline hung low when the top two buttons remained unfastened, but she rarely wore purple, mainly reds and blacks. The doorbell chimed. Too late to change again. Sam tucked in her shirt, fastened her black leather belt, dabbed on a hint of cologne, and slipped on her black loafers.

She waved Steven back into the kitchen and went to answer the door. She assumed by the sound of Steven's wolf whistle he approved of her outfit. Steven flipped on the stereo. Soft jazz filled the air as Sam opened the door. Kevin carried a bottle of wine and red, long-stemmed roses. Crap! Sam thought. Why didn't I think of flowers? She showed him into the kitchen and made him a drink before heading off to the bathroom to splash handfuls of cold water on her face.

"Just breathe," she whispered to herself, sitting on the edge of the tub. Never in her life had she been this nervous, especially when it came to women. The doorbell chimed again, and Sam shot to her feet on a pair of wobbly legs. Lightheaded, Sam reentered the living room.

Sam held her breath and opened the door, her eyes absorbing the stunning woman before her. Elaina wore a black, strapless dress, which hung to a few inches above her knees and the neckline revealed a hint of cleavage. Elaina's shapely legs were encased in a pair of sheer black stockings, and a set of matching heels on her feet. Her hair was pulled elegantly behind her ears, completing the breathtaking ensemble.

"You're beautiful." Sam wasn't sure if she spoke the words out loud.

Elaina said, "I was thinking the exact same thing about you."

Sam tried but she could not take her eyes off Elaina, as they joined Steven and Kevin in the kitchen. Excusing herself, she prepared them each a drink, trying hard not to spill the liquor all over the drink-cart.

Halfway through the first round of drinks, conversation among the four rolled at a steady pace. The *I want to get to know you* questions were covered between bites of salad and bread. Stories of lost loves, favorite vacations, and future dreams flowed while each sipped a second drink. No one mentioned the concentration camps, the mine, Kim's death, or the terrible state their country was in. They avoided the topics of politics and religion. The unspoken agreement appeared that for this night, each desired a bit of normalcy—or at least what used to be normal.

Kevin explained to Elaina the first encounter he had with Sam, and how Sam single-handedly took out six men and several crates of ammunition. Laughter filled the kitchen as Steven served dinner, and Sam refilled everyone's glass for the third time.

"Tonight, we have rack of lamb with a red currant wine sauce," Steven placed the large serving tray in the middle of the table. The three were speechless as he dished out a generous helping to each of them.

"I've never tasted anything as wonderful as this." Elaina moaned, closing her eyes in delight.

"Watch it girl, I found him first." Kevin shot Elaina a playful wink.

Sam noted a hint of excitement flaring in Steven's eyes. Her heart felt overjoyed for his happiness.

"Let's have a toast." Kevin raised his glass in the air and the rest followed suit. "To our friendship, may it never end."

After dinner and dessert, Kevin asked Steven if he wanted to go for a walk to get some fresh air. Steven jumped at the idea, leaving Sam and Elaina alone in the kitchen.

"I want to thank you for giving me the best evening I've had in a very long time," Elaina said as she stood from the table.

Sam panicked. "You're not leaving, are you?" She almost knocked her chair over in her haste to stand. "After all, I did promise you a movie."

"I'm not going to hold you to that, Sam." Elaina came around the table, stretched up on her tiptoes and placed a kiss on Sam's cheek. "I really had a wonderful evening." She turned and walked from the room.

Sam was frozen. She felt befuddled. Had she done something to offend Elaina? All she knew was she didn't want Elaina to leave. Her body kicked into gear and Sam arrived at the front door as Elaina was reaching for the knob.

"Don't go," Sam breathed, placing her hand on the frame above Elaina's head.

"I don't need to be here. Steven and Kevin are doing well together."

"*I* want you to stay."

The sadness in Elaina's eyes cut like a knife in Sam's chest. "I'm not blind, Sam. I know how you feel about me."

"What do you mean you know how I feel? If you knew, you wouldn't leave."

"That's the alcohol talking. Today, when we were in the mine, you acted as if being near me was uncomfortable for you. Then, when you left—I'm not stupid, Sam, I knew you made up the excuse of feeding the horses to get away from me."

Sam bowed her head feeling like a complete moron. "You're right, it has been difficult being in the same room with you."

Elaina reached for the doorknob again, but Sam held the door closed, not allowing her to leave. "Elaina, please let me explain."

Elaina rested her head against the doorframe, her shoulders drooping as if weighed down.

"The reason I've been acting so odd isn't for the reasons you mentioned." Sam paused, not sure exactly how to explain her feelings. "I don't want you to take this the wrong way, and I know it's going to come out sounding degrading—No, I don't mean degrading, I mean—" Sam jerked away from the door, frustrated. "I like you a lot, Elaina. I can't stop thinking about you."

"Then why avoid me?" Elaina spun to Sam. "Why won't you look at me longer than a few seconds? Your actions are in direct opposition to your words."

Sam rubbed the nape of her neck, unsure if she was too embarrassed or too worried to speak. When Elaina made a move toward the door, Sam could only sigh. She leaned the weight of her body against the wall. "I had a hard time sleeping last night because of you. Every time I drifted off to sleep, I dreamt of you and me . . . well, I'd rather not get into the details. Just know the dream was extremely moving."

Sam paced the entryway, not looking at Elaina for fear she would lose her nerve. "Yesterday I was thinking a lot about you when you weren't around. Stupid stuff, really. Like once when you laughed, your nose wrinkled upward, and you gave a little snort. I guess it could have been a grunt, but I'm almost certain you snorted." Sam redirected her gaze to the ceiling. She couldn't help but grin. "Oh, my God, when you and Steven went on and on about the government and everything wrong with it, I didn't know if I wanted to shoot myself or record it for future enjoyment."

Sam stopped next to the banister leading upstairs and shoved her hands deep into her pockets. "But after last night it's been extremely hard, damn near impossible, to concentrate on anything besides you. I think about you constantly. A facial expression you made or something you said, or I simply think about you lying on your cot reading a book. Your hair, your eyes, your lips." Sam sulked, kicking the bottom step.

"I'm sorry, I'm rambling. To be honest, I'm having a hard time controlling myself around you. Whenever you're near me something inside my head snaps. Desire builds and all I want to do is grab you, hold you close, and caress you."

She wasn't sure why she said all this to Elaina, but as her mind spun, she suddenly felt open, exposed, vulnerable, and she didn't like it. She didn't like it one bit. She wished on all the money in her safe, on every possession she owned she could rewind time and erase the last few minutes of blabbering. "You know, maybe we should call it a night." When Sam turned, her heart leapt. Elaina stood a few inches away.

Elaina brought a warm hand up to the back of Sam's neck, pulling her gently toward her.

Their lips touched and a surge of energy ignited within Sam. She put her arms around Elaina's waist as her mouth savored the sweet taste of Elaina. Her mind shouted *more*. A shiver rippled down Elaina's body and her breathing quickened to match Sam's.

Is this another dream? Sam's heartbeat accelerated, followed by a throbbing sensation deep between her thighs. Again, her mind shouted *more*. Moving forward, Sam pressed Elaina's body against the wall. Her need for this woman grew. She brought her left hand up to the soft curve of Elaina's neck and her other hand dropped to the lower part of Elaina's back, pushing their midsections close together. Elaina's moan fueled Sam's desire even further.

Sam moved her right hand around and raised the bottom of Elaina's black dress, sliding it up past her thighs. She pressed her leg between Elaina's, as her left hand moved to unzip the dress. Grinding her leg in a steady motion, Sam felt Elaina's warmth through her jeans, and she increased the pressure.

Elaina's dress began to slip down, revealing a generous amount of cleavage. At the last second Elaina's hand shot up to stop the fabric from falling. "What about Steven and Kevin?" Elaina asked quietly. "What if they return?"

Closing her eyes tight, Sam forced herself to take a deep breath. Her heart raced so fast it made her ears ring. She backed away to steady herself, but Elaina reached for her. "I only want to move someplace more private. Somewhere that's not the front entryway."

"What if we . . ." Sam's voice came out husky. She cleared her throat. "What if we watched the movie I promised you?"

Elaina's eyes shone. "Is that what you want?"

Sam wanted desperately to take Elaina into her bedroom and make love to her, to caress every inch of her. The want was greater than anything she had ever experienced before. "My need for you is maddening."

"Then don't stop." Elaina brought her lips to Sam's for a brief taste. Her voice was a soft murmur when the kiss ended. "So, like I said, let's move somewhere else."

"Are you sure you're ready?" Sam's eyes searched Elaina's, trying to get a feel for what she was thinking.

Elaina guided Sam's hand beneath her dress to the spot between her legs. "What do you think?"

The combination of touching Elaina's throbbing wetness, and the seductive tone of Elaina's voice, pushed Sam past her limit for self-control. She pressed her body against Elaina, hungrily covering Elaina's mouth with her own. Her hand grabbed at damp panties, pulling them out of the way, almost ripping them in the process.

"Sam!" Elaina gasped, off-balance. "Sam, we can't do—we can't do this here."

All words were lost when Sam pushed her fingers inside Elaina. The amount of dampness covering her fingers was exhilarating, and she brought her mouth down tasting, caressing Elaina's neck with her tongue. Elaina spread her legs wider, welcoming every stroke deeper inside. She released her grip on the dress, allowing it to slide past her strapless bra to her waist. The only thing keeping it from hitting the floor was Sam's hand, as she slid two fingers rhythmically in and out. With her head propped against the wall, Elaina moaned.

The sensation for Sam was overwhelming, the greatest pleasure she had ever felt. Elaina spread her legs wider allowing Sam to increase the pressure of her fingers inside.

Before Sam knew it Elaina's hands were moving to the buttons on her shirt. Sam used her free hand to unhook Elaina's bra. The red, lacey undergarment floated down, revealing Elaina's full, shapely breasts. Sam increased the speed, her fingers working harder, faster. Her mouth moved to encircle a dark-brown nipple. Sam gently sucked and ran her tongue over the hardened nipple.

"I'm going—" Before Elaina could finish her sentence, her body shook.

Sam's arm encircled Elaina's waist, supporting the trembling woman. She continued to stroke and fondle, even after Elaina's muscles tightened around her fingers. Elaina held her breath, and ripples shuddered through her body.

Elaina's orgasm flowed over Sam's fingers and onto her hand. She pulled her hand out slowly and placed her dampened fingers into her mouth, savoring the taste of Elaina.

Elaina brought a trembling hand up and removed Sam's hand from her mouth. "I'm not sure if that's sexy or disturbing."

Sam smiled. "I want to taste more of you." Without waiting for a reply, Sam bent over, picking Elaina up and cradling her in her arms. Elaina's eyes were wide, her arms wrapped tightly around Sam's neck.

Before Sam could take a step toward her bedroom, Elaina patted her on the shoulder. "My bra's on the floor."

She tried to move out of Sam's arms, but Sam held on tighter. "I got it." While holding Elaina, Sam bent down, and snatched up the bra. "I like this color on you. It brings out the color in your eyes."

Elaina laughed. "You have issues."

The following morning Elaina woke wrapped safely in Sam's protective embrace. She felt Sam's chest pushed up against her own nakedness. Elaina closed her eyes tight, savoring the moment.

They had made love four times during the night, stopping occasionally for glasses of water, a shared plate of leftovers, and a quick shower. Oh lord, the shower, Elaina thought, wondering how Sam was able to make her body feel so alive in such a limited space.

Sam stirred behind her, and she held her breath, not making a sound. She didn't want to get up. She didn't want Sam to move. Elaina wanted to stay here a little longer and lose herself in the arms of the woman behind her. The powerful feel of Sam was deeply invigorating. Elaina closed her eyes reliving last night one more time.

The only small snag of the evening was that Sam would not let Elaina see her naked. Even during the shower, Sam had kept the lights off with only the glow of a tiny candle flickering in the dark room. Every time Elaina had moved her hands under Sam's shirt, Sam had stopped her. Even now as Elaina lay naked in bed, Sam wore a loose-fitting white T-shirt and baggy red athletic shorts. She was sexy, but Elaina thought Sam would look even sexier out of them.

Sam's hand twitched. She let out a tired groan and her arms tightened around Elaina. A few seconds later, Sam kissed the nape of Elaina's neck before gently removing her arms.

"I was hoping you would sleep longer," Elaina said.

"I didn't mean to wake you. I need to use the bathroom."

"You didn't. I was lying here enjoying the feel of you against me." Elaina rolled over to give Sam a good morning kiss, but Sam turned her head away. She tried again, but with the same outcome. Elaina frowned. Was Sam done with her after one night?

Sam grinned at Elaina. "It's not that I don't want to kiss you, but my breath is shockingly bad. Drinking alcohol gives me horrible morning breath, for future reference."

"Noted." Relief filled Elaina. "And I don't care."

Sam laughed. "You asked for it." She leaned in, giving Elaina a light kiss on the lips. When she tried to move away Elaina pulled her back in, her tongue urging Sam's lips apart.

The good morning kiss became a good morning orgasm. Elaina clung to the headboard for dear life, trying not to squash Sam's head between her legs. Elaina moaned as her body shook with the most glorious and intense release. Sam made her way up, pulling Elaina into her arms.

"For the record," Elaina panted, "I don't think your breath's bad."

Sam kissed Elaina's forehead. "I'm going to shower and brush my teeth." Sam held up a hand as Elaina moved to join her. "If you come in, we'll end up having sex again."

"What's wrong with that?"

"Oh, let's see. It's ten-fifteen, so I have less than an hour before I have to meet Frank in the mine."

Elaina checked the bedside clock. She jumped from the bed and grabbed her clothes. "Crap. Why didn't you say so? I was supposed to be at the hospital at ten."

The day in the hospital dragged, but Elaina's mood soared as the entire shift passed by. At seven p.m. Steven showed up looking as cheerful as Elaina felt. She hummed a lively tune while folding the freshly laundered hospital blankets.

A broad smile was fixed to Steven's lips. "I guess someone had a wonderful evening," he said.

"You have no idea."

"Actually, I might. Let's talk about your evening first then we can move onto mine." He pulled up two chairs for them to sit. "Did you make it through all three movies?"

"We didn't watch any movies. We were, um, busy."

He grinned. "Ah, so you had a *really* nice evening. What time did you end up leaving?"

"Around ten-thirty, give or take two minutes."

Steven laughed. "Ten-thirty? You lesbians don't take much time for foreplay."

"I left at ten-thirty this morning." She was giddy as she watched Steven's startled reaction to her news. She couldn't resist teasing him. "What? Still not enough foreplay for you?"

"You stayed the night with Sam? The entire night?"

She cackled. "Yes. Why do you sound so shocked?"

Steven slowly shook his head. "Elaina, Sam has never spent the night with anyone. Ever."

Elaina said, "That's not what you told me the other day. You said Sam has been with quite a few women."

"Fucking and sleeping over are two totally different things, Elaina. One is meaningless and the other, well, significant, especially for Sam. I could tell last night by the way Sam spoke about you, she had strong feelings, but *this* is different."

Elaina's heart fluttered. "What did Sam say about me?"

"Sorry, it's confidential." He stretched out in his chair. "Don't worry, Sam had nothing but good things to say."

"About what?" The sound of Rachel's voice surprised them. She struggled and finally managed to lower herself onto a chair in a semi-cocked angle.

Steven snorted. "When are you going to pop that kid out?"

Rachel massaged her belly. "In about a month, or as Aunt Agnes says, *when she's damn good and ready*. I only wish she would quit being so stubborn and move down an inch or two. My ribs need a break from her ginormous head." She studied their faces. "So, what's this about Sam?"

"It appears our Sam has gone and fallen for Elaina." Steven waved a hand toward Elaina.

Rachel wasn't smiling.

Steven frowned. "You heard what I said, right?"

"I heard you," Rachel's eyes were trained on Elaina. "The last time we spoke, you were planning on leaving. Heading to Canada I believe. Has that changed?"

Elaina's gaze ping-ponged between Rachel and Steven. Her mind raced. During the long solitude at the cabin, she'd planned out her new life, but suddenly life felt uncertain again. "I don't know. I haven't had time—"

Rachel stood with surprising speed for a woman who was eight months pregnant. "You don't know?"

"Rachel, this has nothing to do with you."

"It has everything to do with me!" Rachel yelled at Steven. "I'm Sam's sister. I'm the one who'll have to clean up the mess after this woman leaves. What do you think this will do to Sam if she ends up falling in love with her?" Rachel stamped a foot. "I don't want you to see my sister again!"

Steven sprang from his chair. "Rachel!"

"Stay out of this!" Rachel's face had grown red. She glared down at Elaina. "If you genuinely care for her, you'll let her be." With that, she spun on her heels and shuffled from the hospital.

➤◄

Standing by her bus, Sam glanced at her watch. They were leaving for the camps in less than ten minutes, and Elaina still had not shown. "Emmett, do you have the explosives?" He held up a satchel. His bottom lip bulged, probably from a wad of chew. Her stomach churned uneasily as she waved him onto the bus.

Rachel shuffled toward Sam. "Please take care of yourself and come back in one piece."

Sam said, "I will. Listen, I don't want you waiting up for us. My nephew needs for you to get your rest."

Rachel smacked Sam's arm. "For the hundredth time, I'm having a girl."

Sam shrugged. "I can always hope the ultrasound was wrong." She checked her watch. "Have you seen Elaina? She was supposed to get off work an hour ago."

"Why?"

"I was kinda hoping to see her before I left."

Rachel said, "Sam, I don't think it'd be a good idea for you two—"

"Sorry I'm late." Elaina rushed over and placed a kiss on Sam's lips. "I had to help Christina get some things set up."

Sam grinned as she pulled away. "You now have black camouflage paint smudged all over your face." She searched through the pockets of her cargo pants to find something to clean off the muck.

"I don't care, it's fine."

Remembering the item in her front breast pocket, Sam removed the black fabric and used it to wipe at Elaina's face.

"What is this?" Elaina asked, wrenching the material out of Sam's hand. "Sam, why do you have one of my stockings?"

"It's for luck." Sam gave Elaina a sheepish grin. "You dropped it in your haste to leave my room this morning." She grabbed the stocking and shoved it in her pocket.

"Time to go, Sam," Frank called and climbed onto his bus.

Sam turned to Rachel. "Remember to rest." She then spoke to Elaina. "Do you like fishing?"

"Fishing? I don't know. I've never been."

"Would you like to go tomorrow?"

Elaina smiled from ear to ear. "I'd love to."

Sam was about to lean in for another kiss, but the idea of covering Elaina with more camouflage stopped her. She made a move to board the bus, but Elaina pulled Sam to her. Their lips met. Sam's heart skipped a beat at the passion in Elaina's kiss. She closed her eyes and pulled Elaina in closer, lost in the moment.

"I'll be waiting here when you return," Elaina murmured when they broke apart. Her heart fluttered as Sam climbed behind the wheel of the bus. A heavy weight filled her as she watched the buses depart from the mine. Her eyes remained on the entrance even after the doors closed and the people around her departed.

Sensing Rachel beside her, Elaina said, "I decided to stay." She was too old to ask for permission, and too stubborn to care what others thought. When she turned, she was surprised to see a smile on the face of someone who had looked as if she wanted to kill her not more than three hours ago.

"I figured as much." She took Elaina's hand in her own. "Let's go get you cleaned up and see if there's any dinner left in the dining facility. The baby's starving."

Halfway down the hallway, Rachel locked her arm with Elaina's and giggled. "You know, I've always wanted a sister."

Startled, Elaina said, "Sam's your sister."

"Not really. Throughout my entire life, Sam's always been more like an older brother. Hell, even a second father if we're being completely honest. Case in point, twice I tried dating when I was in school, and she was overseas. I'm not sure how she found out or got their contact information, but even from a foreign country she called them out of the blue and explained what she would do to them if I was ever hurt or unhappy. Neither wanted anything to do with me after her phone calls. I eventually stopped dating." Rachel let out a long sigh. "Yes, it'll be nice to have a sister."

Elaina's cheeks blushed when she realized Rachel was serious. "I think you might be jumping the gun here."

"Oh, I'm not going to plan your wedding. Yet. I realize with my sister *that* kind of commitment will take an awfully long time, but Steven's right. She's definitely falling for you."

After Elaina washed off the black splotches from her face, the two made their way into the dining area of the mine, where several people were busy preparing a vast assortment of food.

"Why are they cooking at this hour?" Rachel asked Aunt Agnes, who stood off to the side talking to the head chef.

"We're going to have several hundred men, women, and children show up from the camps and they'll no doubt be hungry."

"Makes sense." Rachel nodded. "Do you guys need any help?"

Agnes shook her head. "You're under strict orders from Christina not to lift a finger until the baby is born. Get some food and then go rest. We can manage without you two."

They did as Agnes instructed, enjoying a pleasant meal of beef stroganoff over egg noodles, mixed vegetables, canned peaches, and a huge slice of chocolate cake. The meal was nothing compared to the wonderful dinner Steven had served the night before. In fact, the food was reminiscent of those Elaina's high school cafeteria served, but it was still tasty.

Elaina and Rachel spent an hour talking after they ate. The majority of the conversation covered Sam's amusing flaws, but they also shared stories about themselves.

"So, your mother felt you being homosexual would be bad for their social life?" Rachel asked.

"That's it in a nutshell."

"What about your father? What did he think?"

"I don't know. He was too petrified to go against my mother. Most people were."

"I'm sorry. I didn't realize people still felt that way." People started gathering around the flatscreen TV mounted on the far wall, and she turned to see what was happening.

"Hey, can you turn the TV up?" asked a man sitting several seats away from Rachel and Elaina.

Someone cranked up the volume. The voice of the President of the United States filled the cafeteria. His thick dark hair was combed neatly to one side, and he wore an expensive-looking suit. The man exuded professionalism and a sense of being in charge. "We have reason to believe the attacks will only get worse going forward. I'm sending a sizeable portion of our reserve force to assist with the immediate threat."

"What's going on?" asked one of the female cooks, clutching a large serving spoon to her chest.

Someone close to the television responded. "Some of our military bases overseas are under attack."

"Who's attacking them?"

"Terrorists, I think. I'm not sure."

Everyone watched the president. He looked as if the demands of office were wearing him thin. "Therefore, I feel we have no choice but to call for our allies in other countries to assist us with our efforts here in the United States. I'm asking for Congress to hold an emergency session next week to vote for this very thing."

"Foreign troops on American soil—they can't do that," someone close to the TV said.

"They can if both the House and Senate approve it," said someone else.

Rachel's aunt turned away from the television with her eyes closed. "Aunt Agnes, I'm sure Michael's fine." She embraced her aunt as tears slid down the older woman's cheek.

Agnes cleared her throat and patted her arm. "Of course, he is."

Mike ran in and shouted, "The buses are here!" then pivoted and rushed from the room. His words had brought movement from most of the people in the dining area, including Rachel, Agnes, and Elaina. They joined the crowd filling the entrance chamber.

The first group to pull in was Douglas's. He and Todd, with several others, removed the injured from the buses.

"What happened?" Agnes asked, as one of the soldiers from their team was carried off the bus on a stretcher.

"He was shot in the leg, but he'll be fine. Many people from the camps will need medical attention, though." Douglas rubbed his black-painted face with his hand. "It seems some of the assholes we killed tonight really got off on torturing these people." His voice shook. "Hell, Agnes, they whipped a young man within an inch of his life. He can't be more than twenty. I found him strung up and half-dead in the basement of the main building."

Agnes patted his back. "Go get cleaned up and grab something warm to eat."

Douglas slowly followed the stretcher.

"What about Sam's team. Any word?" Agnes asked.

Todd shook his head. "They must have hit a snag because they were scheduled to be in before us. Do you want me to go find them once we get everyone offloaded?"

Before she could reply, the loud reverberation of other huge vehicles bounced around the entrance of the mine. Buses pulled in one by one.

Elaina held her breath. The engines from the buses powered off and the people inside got off. "Where's Sam?" Elaina asked when she spotted Emmett behind the wheel of Sam's bus.

"We need a stretcher over here." Emmett climbed from the vehicle and headed to the bus parked behind the one he had driven.

"Where's Sam?" Rachel echoed Elaina's question.

Agnes, Elaina, and Rachel followed Emmett, who appeared too nervous to speak. Frank exited his bus and went straight for the threesome with his hands raised.

"Where's Sam?" This time Agnes was the one to voice the question.

"Sam's fine. She had a little mishap." Frank waved to two men carrying a stretcher. "She's already on the bus." He reached out, stopping Emmett from following. "You might want to stay clear of her. She's still pretty pissed at you."

"What sort of mishap?" Rachel moved closer to the bus, trying to get a peek inside. "Was she shot? Is she all right?"

"Calm down. Everything's fine. She has an injury to her backside, but she'll be okay." Frank narrowed his eyes at Emmett.

"Hey, I thought she said Halo. It sounded like Halo."

"What happened?" Agnes directed her question to Emmett, more a demand than a question.

"Well," Emmett said, "I set up explosives around the camp's command building, which I was supposed to blow after Sam cleared and gave me the signal."

Frank snapped, "The signal was *Halo*. She was calling for *Harold*."

"It sounded like Halo," Emmett cut in, frowning at Frank. "Anyway, if I hadn't set off the explosives, those men might have killed her. I saved her life."

"Bullshit, Emmett. You've seen the way Sam works. You know damn well she'd easily have taken out both those guys. If not, I had my rifle ready."

Emmett rubbed his chin. "I need a drink."

One of the men handling the stretcher stuck his head out the back of the bus. "We need a hand moving her out. I'm afraid the wood might get caught when we come down the steps."

"No." Frank waved Emmett down. "Not you. She called you every name in the book on the ride in." He climbed aboard the bus.

"The wood? Wha—what wood?" Elaina said. Her gaze met Agnes's puzzled expression. Agnes shrugged.

"Were there any other casualties?" Agnes asked.

Emmett said, "No. Other than Sam, it all went smoothly. Some of the camp prisoners look as if the guards used their faces as punching bags. So they're in sorry shape. I was impressed with Sam. She really knows her shit."

Frank hopped from the bus and called out, "Whoa! Slowly now. Watch the left side . . ."

As the men wrangled the stretcher out, Elaina saw Sam on her stomach with a foot-long wedge of wood protruding from her right glute. Blood had soaked completely through Sam's pants and the tape and bandage surrounding the projectile. She wanted to go to Sam, but Agnes held her back.

"We'll just get in the way, Elaina. Let's follow them. We can be with her while she's getting medical attention."

Emmett strode over and patted Sam's leg. "You did well out there, kid."

The stretcher bearers came to a stop as Sam glared at Emmett. "Tell that to my ass, you moron!"

Emmett shrugged his shoulders before leaning his head close to Sam's backside. "You did well—"

Sam jerked to her side and made a move for her pistol. Frank held her down and grabbed the weapon.

"Frank, damn it! Let me shoot him. He deserves it!"

Frank pocketed Sam's sidearm and slowly shook his head.

Emmett clapped his hands together and crowed with glee. "That woman has spirit!"

Frank said, "You're an idiot, Emmett. Now get outta here." He turned to the two soldiers holding the litter. "Come on, guys. Let's get her to the medical unit."

Chapter Seventeen

The Source

Kevin entered the medical wing with his laptop clutched under his arm. The entire unit, from the rich wooden floors, spacious divided rooms, and the bright drop ceiling, had been finished in record time. He stepped through the newly constructed doors. He was a man on a mission.

Spotting Steven behind one of three staff desks, Kevin's energy ramped up a notch. "Hi! Where's Sam?"

Steven glanced up from his paperwork. A grin spread across his face. "Hey, I've missed you."

"No time. Where's Sam?"

Steven's grin turned upside down and he pointed to one of the four rooms to the left.

Kevin gave Steven a brief kiss before hurrying into the room. Poor Steven was probably utterly confused by the mixed messaging of the tone followed by a kiss. But Kevin had more pressing matters to deal with at the moment.

Sam was in the back of the room, which held divided space for nine other occupants. An arrangement of hideaway beds and old-style hospital beds, which appeared to be from World War II, had replaced the cots. The room felt a little more like a hospital and less like a wall-to-wall pre-modern Red Cross infirmary located in a mine.

She was lying on her side talking to Elaina when he stepped up to the bed. "Sam, you really need to see this." Kevin situated his laptop on the ugly metal table in front of her and pushed the power button on. After the system loaded, Kevin entered in his password, *S T E V E N*.

"Great password, but not very secure," Sam said.

Ignoring her comment, he tapped his fingers along the keyboard. Soon the screen filled with lines of information.

Sam said, "Tell me if I'm wrong, but it looks the same as it did last week."

"The exact same, but now I've deciphered the information you gave me—the paperwork inside the notebook. You were right, it's a language."

"Okay . . . and?"

"I recovered the missing data, Sam."

Kevin worked the system a second time. The information didn't just change, it multiplied as soon as he pressed *ENTER*. Page after page of spiraling data scrolled right before their eyes.

"I've compiled all the data from all three flash drives and configured it into a readable format. This information shows us a detailed outline of the gradual fall of the United States which began years ago." Kevin pointed at the screen. "Read it, Sam, John F. Kennedy, this proves the CIA had a hand in his assassination. An unknown group funded a trip Oswald took to Russia a few months before the president was murdered. The funding came from a Russian bank account listed in this group's financial records. The same group also paid large sums of money to high-ranking members inside the CIA, one of the accounts they used was the exact same bank account." Kevin felt the excitement building. "Some believe President Kennedy was planning to disband the CIA. If that's true, maybe he had discovered something, I don't know, a foreign depravity buried inside a US agency."

Sam held up a hand. "Kevin, calm down. You're rambling."

He took a deep breath, steadying himself. "A few weeks before the assassination, Oswald was seen at the Russian Embassy in New Mexico. I bet the Russians are somehow involved," Kevin said. "Since then, this organization has obtained steady control over numerous American investments, banks, and assets, giving them enough power to crash the American dollar. There's a list of people they've placed inside government offices over the years, to help quietly take away rights from the people and the states, while giving more power to the government. The current attorney general and secretary of defense are two of the people mentioned. The end of the section reveals their plan for the fall of the United States government, and how a new, Unified Government is to take control."

Sam read from the computer screen. "The Trade Center, the recent riots, and attacks. This organization was funding terrorist groups to target the United States this entire time?"

Kevin said, "In hopes of weakening us, yes. It worked, too. Look at the terror and violence they sparked inside our own country. People turning on one another. Vandalizing, causing even more panic and chaos, while giving those in charge the ability to step in and take away freedoms, enact martial law, and even bring in foreign troops. All those actions veiled by the belief they're acting for the greater good, for our welfare."

Sam exhaled a huge breath. "If this doesn't change, America as we once knew it will be gone."

"I know, that's why I came right to you when I figured it out," Kevin said.

"Who's behind this Unified Government?" Elaina asked.

"The data doesn't reveal that, and there's nothing significant to 'officially' tie anyone to the organization. Over half of the names translate into sort of a hit list."

Sam scrolled further down, grasping the severity of the situation. "This makes no sense, Kevin. How's a military force from outside the United States supposed to come in without our troops, or our people, putting up a fight?"

"Sam, the president is calling for the action," Kevin said. "Last night, he announced he's sending our troops overseas, so we'll need foreign aid to protect the United States. Didn't anyone tell you?"

"No, but I was in surgery having splinters removed from my ass, and—" Sam froze. "The president's involved. . ."

Kevin gave Sam a nervous laugh. "What, the US President? Sam, that's highly unlikely. I mean, President McMullen was born here in the Midwest."

"Kevin, think about it. It *does* make sense. Almost everything new on this list was initiated the second he took office, and the amount of money this Unified Government invested in his presidential campaign is laid out right in front of us." She scrolled to the bottom of the data. "Over the years, the power of the presidential office has grown, and with the new laws, the president has almost total control."

"We still have a Congress, and they'll undoubtedly vote down the foreign aid," Kevin said.

Sam searched through page after page. It felt as if this unsettling information went on forever. She paused in her scrolling. "Alstaff, how are they involved?"

"They're a private military contractor."

Sam nodded. "I know who they are, Kevin. The military contracts with them in place of using soldiers. From cooks to base security, abroad but also at many of the bases here in the US, including Fort Carson. The ones who worked the gates at Carson were okay, but some were real dicks. It's like they had something to prove. Why is this group funding them?"

"Sam, the HTF and Alstaff are one and the same."

"Alstaff? The government hired a private military contractor for this new law enforcement agency?" Sam repositioned herself in the bed, even though her discomfort was more mental than physical.

Kevin tapped some keys on the laptop. "That's not all. They're in charge of security at the prison camps as well, but under the heading of Alstaff and not HTF."

Time stood still as Sam pondered the information. She stared at the screen not really taking anything in, until something in the wording jumped out at her. "This might be a web address. Is the security system on our computers set up yet?"

Kevin said, "I'm not quite finished with it. I've been putting most of my time into cracking this. I do have scrambling boxes we can hook up to buy us some time before they manage to trace our location. We can disconnect before they're able to lock on."

Sam said, "No, I don't want to chance it. Is there a library or Internet café still operating in Springfield?"

"One library. I don't believe it's closed yet, but both cafés have gone out of business." He snapped his fingers. "That's a good idea. We can hook up a box to one of their computers, if not then to my laptop. It should buy us forty-five minutes to an hour."

"Why would you take the risk?" Elaina asked. "What are you hoping to accomplish by snooping around in their system?"

"For starters, hopefully find out if the president is involved or not," Sam said. "If he is, we need to figure out who isn't. We need someone we can trust. Someone with enough power to stop this. I would also like to see if we can gain some insight into what the plans are for the future dates listed. One is for this next week, and it's highlighted." She directed their attention to a date, this Wednesday, showing a bold C.H. behind the numbers and dashes.

"What do you think C.H. stands for?" Elaina asked.

Sam shrugged. "Not sure." She turned to Kevin. "Tell Aunt Agnes to get the committee together as soon as possible. Let them know what's going on. Tomorrow we, you and me, will visit the library in Springfield."

"Tomorrow is Sunday, Sam, the library won't be open."

"Fine, Monday then."

"You're not going anywhere for at least a week. Christina's orders." Elaina was clearly upset by the idea.

"I can handle Christina," Sam said. "Kevin, make sure you're ready to go on Monday. Oh, and you're going to have to drive."

"Are you serious? You're in no state to travel." Elaina sounded desperate. "If you plan on doing this, I'll tell Rachel."

Sam arched an eyebrow at Elaina. "Kevin, will you get the wheels in motion?"

"On it." He closed the computer and hustled from the room.

"You're going to tell my baby sister. Wow, you've learned my one weakness. Fortunately, I can handle her." Sam slanted her body toward Elaina. "I think you're worried about me."

"Of course I'm worried about you. You're not Wonder Woman, Sam. You can't stop a bullet."

"Actually, Superman is the one who can stop bullets. Wonder Woman had the truth lasso and invisible airplane. I guess her bracelets could deflect—"

"Not funny, Sam! What you're planning to do will be dangerous. I know what I'm talking about here. These people killed Kim, Marcus, and probably many others, including my parents. Don't think they won't kill you."

Sam groaned. "Elaina, I don't mean to make light of the situation, but it has to be done."

A moment of silence followed. "Then, I want to come with you," Elaina announced.

"No."

"Why?"

"Because, if anything does happen, you tagging along will only complicate the situation. After all, the HTF is looking for you. Your presence could put me and Kevin in more danger."

"I can take care of my appearance and myself for that matter. I've done all right without your protection for the last two years."

"You had a bullet wound when we met!"

"So? You currently have a hole on one side of your ass, what's your point!"

Sam grew frustrated. When she moved to get out of bed, Elaina bent to stop her. Sam grabbed Elaina and pulled her into her arms. Elaina struggled for a few seconds, but Sam held her tighter. Elaina eventually relinquished control. Sam marveled at the way Elaina's body melted into hers.

Elaina's head came up, her eyes full of want. She placed her lips on Sam's gently, with a slight quiver. Sam closed her eyes, savoring their velvety warmth, enjoying the added stimulus when Elaina's mouth parted, welcoming her in. Their kiss was long and heartfelt. Their lips telling one another their feelings without uttering one word. Sam moved her mouth to Elaina's neck, tasting her smooth skin. Elaina moaned, sliding her body further up on the bed.

The loud beeping of Sam's phone sounded, indicating she had a message. Elaina jumped. She twisted, attempting to spring from the bed. Sam grabbed her, pulling her in, pressing Elaina's back against her chest, spooning their bodies. With one arm, Sam held Elaina close as her mouth laid sweet kisses over Elaina's soft neck. She brought her other hand around, unbuttoning Elaina's jeans. Elaina arched her back and pushed her bottom into Sam's midsection.

"What if someone walks in?" Elaina said, her head lying on Sam's shoulder.

"Does the thought scare you?" Sam asked, her words followed by the sound of unzipping jeans.

"Yes." Elaina swallowed, closing her eyes.

"Good." Sam slipped her hand inside, under Elaina's panties. Her fingers slid down through curly hair and between Elaina's soft lips. She worked her middle finger around, gliding it back and forth matching the steady rocking of Elaina's hips. Elaina's moans became louder, and her hips thrust harder.

Sam massaged the swelling of Elaina's throbbing wetness, matching the speed and pressure to Elaina's rhythm. Then Elaina went rigid, a building release rocketed out jerking her slightly forward. Sam held her tightly until Elaina's breathing slowed to normal.

"God, you're crazy."

"You can flatter me all you want, but you're still not going." Sam nibbled Elaina's ear.

"Are you always this stubborn?"

"Hmm. Only when I'm right."

The sound of voices outside the room broke the spell. With the speed of some superhuman being, Elaina fastened her jeans, tossed Sam a package of wet wipes, then threw herself in the chair beside the bed.

Sam enjoyed Elaina's unease, as if they were two teenagers about to be caught by their parents. She cleaned her hand and adjusted her butt into a comfortable position.

Frank entered the room, followed by three men and a woman. He smiled at Sam and Elaina, before turning toward the grey-haired man next to him. "Sam, Elaina, I would like to introduce you to Richard Ludlum. He's my weapons source."

Extending her hand to the well-dressed man, Sam said, "It's a pleasure to meet you, Richard." She tried to present a friendly face but remained guarded, unsure if she could trust the guy.

"The pleasure's all mine, Ms. Kelly. Frank gave us a tour of your base, and I must say it's very well organized." He quickly continued, as if he could sense Sam's skepticism on having strangers in the mine. "Your security officer, a Mister Douglas I believe, has cleared us. Plus, I can assure you everyone here is trustworthy. We're all fighting for the same thing."

Sam crossed her arms. "What exactly are *we* fighting for?"

"To end the corrupt assholes strangling our government and to restore our American freedoms."

Frank stepped forward. "Sam, I've known Richard since I was seventeen. We served in the same unit in Iraq together. Not only was he in the FBI for twenty-one years, but he retired from his career in the Secret Service less than two years ago. He has connections, Sam."

Now Sam was intrigued. "What's the FBI or Secret Service doing about this corruption you mentioned?"

"They have no proof any wrongdoing exists. Not only that, the HTF have pretty much taken over. Not much is left of the FBI, CIA, or any of the other governmental agencies as we knew them."

Sam waved a hand to the others gathered in the room. "Who are these people?"

The expression on the man's face brightened. "Ah, they're the reason I've come. They're from other groups, such as yours, located around the United States. I, with the help of a few others, provide them with weapons and military supplies. I've told them about the encampments and what you're doing, and they want to join."

"Sam, we can't fight them all on our own," Frank said. "At the rate we're going, our space here will soon be full. We have over a thousand people and room for what, five, maybe six hundred more. If we're lucky. That's two camps at the most."

The woman beside Frank stepped forward. "We all have hidden refugee camps set up, or safe areas we're constructing for people." She reminded Sam of a stay-at-home mom, or perhaps an English teacher. Either way, she didn't look as if she belonged on a battlefield. "We need to organize, though. We want to unite in one single movement throughout the United States. If we pull together, we'll be stronger."

The exhilaration churned in Sam as her hopes rose. Other like-minded groups were what they needed to build up strength, a united force willing to risk their lives for the sake of others. Sam said, "It's not only dangerous, but you'll be fighting against the government."

"We already know," a younger man off to the side said. Sam envisioned him as an accountant in a nice clean office crunching numbers. "My group was part of the uprising at the White House. Several of my friends lost their lives because of it, and others were captured and probably tortured to death by now. We're all willing to do what's necessary, Ms. Kelly. But I would like to do it in a more organized fashion going forward. With larger numbers. We want to learn your setup here and model other locations after it. We must become a united group, located strategically throughout the entire United States."

Sam gave Frank a nod of approval and then addressed Ludlum and his flock of followers. "It'll be nice working with all of you. Frank, if you haven't already, take them to see Aunt Agnes. She's getting the committee together either today or tomorrow, to go over the new information Kevin's discovered. That will be a good opportunity for everyone to become acquainted. Work out the issues for an alliance. I'm sure you'll find this new information quite enlightening."

No sooner had the group vacated the room when Steven appeared holding two crutches. "Sorry to be the bearer of bad news, but Christina wants you up and moving around as much as possible."

"It's about time." Sam tossed the blankets off her body.

Elaina remained with Sam throughout the day and into the late hours of evening watching *The Lord of the Rings* trilogy on Steven's laptop. They took several breaks to go on therapeutic walks around the hospital wing, eat dinner, and also managed to sneak away for an intimate interlude in her office. Now that the door and deadbolt were installed, of course. She still had no coffeepot.

The next morning Kevin arrived to let them know the committee meeting would be kicking off in less than thirty minutes. Sam was fast asleep.

Elaina said, "Sam needs her rest, but I'll come with you to the meeting."

By the time Elaina returned to Sam's bedside an hour later Sam was up and eating breakfast and talking to Rachel. "Did you go to the meeting?"

"How'd you know about the meeting? You were asleep when Kevin came in."

Sam pointed her forked sausage bite at her sister. "Rachel told me. I figured it would last longer."

"It's still going on. They're working out the details, especially communication between the different groups." Elaina sat in the chair on the other side of the bed, across from Rachel. She needed to come clean with what she had done, but she was unsure how. "Did you tell her?" she asked Sam, biding her time.

"What, about going to Springfield tomorrow? Yes, I did. We were discussing the trip before you came in." Sam triumphantly shoved the sausage in her mouth and chewed. "Now you have nothing to use against me."

Rachel peered at them both.

Elaina shifted in her seat. "I don't need your permission to make my own decisions."

"No, you don't. But I'm in still charge of the military aspect of the group, and I say the risk isn't justified."

"You're not going on a military mission. This has to do with security and Douglas has already given me permission to go. The entire committee, in fact, agreed to it." She watched as Sam lowered her plate to the nightstand and pushed herself up higher in bed. Her heart felt almost heavy, yet Elaina's eyes remained fixed on Sam.

"I think I'd better go see if Janis needs any help." Rachel directed a worried look between the two women before hastening from the room.

"Now I understand why you didn't wake me for the meeting. You were afraid I would prevent them from allowing you to come with us." Sam rubbed her forehead. "If it means so much to you, we'll work out the details and take extra steps to avoid detection." She dropped her hand and peered straight at Elaina. "You'll listen to me, though. No matter what I say, you'll do it. Understand?"

Elaina was breathless. "You're not upset with me?"

"I'm not pleased, but I would have done the same thing if I were you. Intimidation apparently doesn't work on you." She shrugged her shoulders. "What else can I do? You're an adult. Hell, you lived alone in a cabin, in the middle of the woods for almost two years."

Elaina hurried to the bed and threw her arms around Sam's neck.

Sam hugged Elaina awkwardly. "Give me your word you'll listen to me. And I promise to keep you safe."

Elaina released her grip, feeling for the first time someone in her life saw her as more than an anonymous woman behind the camera; the daughter who needed a husband to support her; the lover who was easily replaced. "I promise. Thank you, Sam. This means a lot."

Sam shifted to get out of bed. "You said you could shoot, and I want to see how good you are."

Elaina handed Sam her crutches. "Why?"

"If you can't handle a weapon, then you're not going to carry one. We don't need to make this more dangerous than it already is by arming someone who might accidentally shoot themselves. Or me."

"Just wait, I might surprise you," Elaina said.

"You already do. C'mon. Let's go check out your skills at the firing range."

The morning breeze felt refreshing against Sam's skin, with the crisp, clean scent of promised rain. She handed Elaina a pistol and magazines, while Kevin loaded a few items into the backseat of Sam's truck.

"Hey, where's *my* weapon?" Kevin asked, closing the rear door. "Shouldn't I have a weapon in case something happens?"

"I have an extra one for you in the glove box if you need it. I'd feel better if you didn't carry it with you until you've had more training." Sam climbed into the passenger seat of the truck and adjusted the donut cushion under her butt.

Kevin settled behind the wheel. "Our first encounter is what you're basing your decision off of?"

Sam grunted.

"I guess I don't blame you. I'll work on improving my skills."

Elaina pulled herself into the back seat of the truck. "Don't feel bad. She made me break the weapon down and put it together blindfolded before she agreed to let me carry one, and all this after she had me firing the damn thing for over an hour."

Sam chuckled. "I knew within the first five minutes you'd be fine. The rest was purely for my own enjoyment." Elaina threw her hat, hitting Sam in the back of the head. "Don't make me come back there," Sam said.

The drive to Springfield went by without a hitch. Todd had supplied them with a list of places and times the HTF was conducting vehicle checks. Yet, they were unnerved by the number of military convoys they passed along the way. When they stopped in one of the small towns to fuel up, they observed numerous armed soldiers on foot, and in vehicles, patrolling the tiny community.

After they pulled into the library parking lot, Kevin ran inside to scope out the area. He exited the building ten minutes later. "I don't like it, Sam. The building is monitored, especially around the computer stations. I think we should drive to Kansas City or St. Louis. It's only two and a half to three hours away to either."

Sam thought about running into Brandon or one of his agents and it sent a chill down her spine. "We can't go to Kansas City. How about St. Louis?"

"How do we even know if *anyplace* will be open there?" Elaina asked, sliding forward in her seat. "We might encounter the same problems."

An idea seemed to strike Kevin. "Give me a moment." He exited the truck with his cell phone. He tapped the screen and then held the phone to his ear. His call was quick and then he was inside the truck again. "I know a place we can go to in St Louis. An Internet café owned by an old acquaintance of mine."

The parking lot behind the Internet café was virtually empty, containing only two vehicles. No pedestrian traffic, no homeless folks, no one—the place was a veritable ghost town.

"Before we go inside," Kevin said, "there's something I should tell you about the owner." He grabbed his computer bag from the backseat.

Sam removed the butt cushion and tossed it on the dashboard. "Can it wait until we get out for a stretch? My ass is killing me."

"I don't want you two to get the wrong idea. We had nowhere el—"

"Sorry, sweetie," Elaina said. "I need to go to the ladies' room." She nearly dragged Sam from the truck, supporting her as they moved toward the back entrance.

"Oh, for the love of—will you just head inside and pee? You'll end up ripping my stitches—" Before Sam could finish her sentence, Elaina released Sam's arm and charged forward in search of the restroom.

Sam fell into a step-limp next to Kevin who said, "You do realize how well you two mesh, right?"

Sam grunted, trying hard to keep up with his long strides. "I like being around her if that's what you mean. She's fun and has an authenticity to her you don't see nowadays." Sam stopped abruptly, absorbing all the feelings raining down on her. Her attraction. Elaina was good-hearted, internally fierce, and genuine all rolled into one.

"Come on Sam, you can have your epiphany inside. I'm hungry."

The atmosphere of the establishment gave Sam the feeling of a laid-back bar rather than an Internet café. Dark mahogany-stained wood surrounded the baseboards and trim, burnt-orange textured paint covered the walls. Many of the pictures were black and white photos encased in fancy wood frames. Large and small dark-brown decorative planters were spaced throughout the room. The windows were multi-colored stained glass giving the interior a much-needed splash of color.

"Kevin, it's so good to see you." A tall, slender man with shoulder-length hair moved around the length of the bar and headed straight for them. He wore a black apron tied around his waist over crisply pressed khaki trousers and a fuchsia-colored polo shirt with a popped collar. "I held my breath, knowing one day I would see you again."

Sam saw Kevin rotate his cheek into the man's kiss, while keeping space between them. If the man noticed Kevin's evasive stance, he didn't let on. He ran his eyes over Sam. "Who's your friend?"

"Sam, I'd like you to meet Andrew. He's the owner of this establishment."

"Please, call me Andy."

"It's nice to meet you, Andy." Sam shook his hand. "I like your place. It's not quite what I was expecting."

"Ah, I had the café redecorated after the curfew law was implemented. I found a way to give my patrons a variety of options in one spot. I provide high-quality meals from an impeccably run kitchen, drinks from two fully stocked bars, and also connectivity, for the little Internet café."

Sam smiled. The last word she would have used to describe this place was *little*. "How do you and Kevin know one another?" she asked.

Andy guided them to a secluded booth. "Didn't he tell you? We dated for a few years. Unfortunately, he decided to break my heart and move away."

"Not exactly how the story goes," Kevin said. "I enjoyed the home life, and he enjoyed other men."

"Why don't we say we had our differences, and leave it at that?" Andy paused, then said, "But I do remember our sex-life was pretty amazing. Or have you forgotten?"

Kevin laughed. "I might have agreed with you—until last week, that is. Now I've come to realize the sex we had was . . ." Kevin shrugged his shoulders. "Mediocre." Kevin checked out the menu. "I'll have an extra-sweet French vanilla cappuccino to start."

Frowning, Andy turned to Sam.

"I'll have a diet soda and two glasses of water."

Once Andy left, Sam let out a whistle. "Telling your cheating ex, the sex was mediocre. I bet that made your day."

His voice held an air of triumph. "Truth hurts. For the record, the loaded nachos here are to die for. Want to eat before we snoop around?"

"Sounds wonderful, I'm starving," Elaina slid into the booth next to Sam.

"Do you feel better?" Sam asked.

Elaina blushed. "Yes, much better."

"That should teach you not to drink so much soda between rest stops," Sam said.

Elaina grabbed a menu. "It should, but it won't. I live for my caffeine."

"I ordered you a water and a diet soda. Kevin says the loaded nachos here are good, by the way."

"Tempting. Unfortunately, I think my arteries are about a year and a half past due for a large, messy cheeseburger."

"Good choice," Sam scanned the menu.

Elaina said, "Why don't you get the nachos, I get the cheeseburger, and we split them."

Sam tossed her menu aside. "Great idea. Damn woman, I love you."

Elaina's heart fluttered. Her mind drifted, too taken aback to comprehend Kevin's words. Her entire body felt warm, tingly, excited. She could tell Sam was unaware the effect her 'I love you' had on Elaina.

Andy returned with their drinks and took their food orders. Elaina scooted slightly closer to Sam. They gobbled their food and then Kevin got busy. He plugged in a scrambling box and laptop. Sam slid her arm around Elaina's shoulders. She bent close, wiping off a cheese spot on the corner of Elaina's mouth with her finger then sucked off the cheese.

"Oh, for heaven's sakes, Sam, you just ate."

"Sorry, I was having a little dessert." Sam smirked at Kevin's playful gagging motion. "You're only jealous Steven isn't here. You'd be doing the same thing."

Kevin peered over the open laptop. "That isn't where I would have found my dessert."

"You're both gross," Elaina elbowed Sam gently in the stomach.

"Hey, you were right, Sam. It's a web address." He angled the screen so they could see. "What do you think the password is?"

"Try *SUNKC*," Sam said. "Use all capital letters."

Kevin swiveled the laptop toward him. His fingers tapped the keys. "Bingo!" He clapped his hands together. "How did you know?"

"I guessed. It's in small print at the bottom of several of the documents. I don't know what it stands for, but—"

"Crap! I know what it means." This time he angled the laptop and slid closer in the booth so they could all see. He sounded anxious. "It stands for the Soviet Union, North Korea, and China. It's not a select group of terrorists or a government contractor doing this to us, but three very powerful countries." He glanced nervously around the room. "We can't fight an enemy this strong. Can you imagine a combined military force? It'd be impossible."

Elaina felt Sam's muscles tighten. The more she read, the more she understood why. "When this organization formed, Russia . . . or I should say the Soviet Union, and the United States were in the middle of a Cold War," Elaina said. "We were also at war with North Korea."

"These three joining forces makes sense," Sam said. "Russia, China, and North Korea are all allies, and no matter how they classify their governments, communism, indirect democracy, what they truly are is dictatorships. Authoritarianism rules. Different, but also similar in certain beliefs. US relations with these governments has been shaky over the past ten years." She took a breath. "And North Korea, they flat out hate the United States."

"Sam, check out the activity from these Chinese firms before our stock market crashed two years ago." Elaina pointed to the screen. "They dumped every stock they had, and all the Chinese companies listed on the market filed for chapter seven bankruptcy. I think this had a lot to do with our market crashing. Probably not the only reason, but I bet it pushed it over the edge."

Kevin said, "China doesn't trade in our stock exchange."

"You're kidding me, right?" Sam asked. "They've not only been allowed to trade in the US stock exchange for years, but they also have hundreds of their own companies listed. They also own a controlling majority in thousands of US companies. GE, IBM, AMC. You know Smithfield Foods in Virginia? They're the largest hog producer in the world. A Chinese company bought it."

"Sam, *a* company, not the Chinese Government," Kevin insisted.

"China's a communist-party dictatorship. A big chunk of these Chinese corporations *are*, in fact, government and state-owned. The ones who are not, with China's laws on private corporations and the power the government has, the government can force their hand on any private businesses." Sam sat forward.

The way Sam stared intently at the edge of the table, Elaina figured she was working the problem out in her head. Searching for answers, or better yet, a reason.

Kevin loaded a blank flash drive into the side of the laptop and began copying files. He opened one named 'phase two,' and they all silently read. "Elaina was right, they *are* planning on executing everyone in the camps." He swallowed hard. "We have less than six months if they stay on schedule. Once the foreign troops get here and get positioned throughout the US, they'll have the backing they need to go forward with mass genocide."

"I don't understand." Elaina's eyes moved down the screen. "They don't want to kill only the people in the camps, they want to wipe *all* American people off the face of the earth. But why? Why do they want to eradicate us?"

Sam leaned against the cushion. "Why not?"

Kevin frowned. "Are you kidding?"

"We as a nation are arrogant. Hear me out," Sam said before Kevin could voice his argument. "You're seeing this as someone who's living in a country untouched by conflict since the Civil War, and that was a war we fought against ourselves, not another country. I'm not talking about Pearl Harbor, or terrorist attacks, but an actual invasion on this very continent. A foreign military force right here in our own backyards. For some reason, we feel we're untouchable, even though countries go to war with one another all the time, for all sorts of reasons. Differences of opinions, resources, political disagreements, religious beliefs. God, do humans really need a reason to kill off one another?

"Look how many troops we have overseas and the wars and conflicts we've participated in on foreign soil. Some we're still fighting, yet most we have no business being in. Why is it so hard to imagine other countries wouldn't want to do the same to us? We have resources, land, political differences, poor foreign relations with many governments, giving them more than enough reason to want to see us and our way of life come to an end."

Sam threw up her hands. "Hell, our ancestors took this country by way of force and bloodshed from the natives who called this land their home. Then the forefathers built the foundation of America with the use of slaves purchased or stolen from a different country. But still, we don't believe the same thing could happen to us? There's a reason they call Karma a bitch."

Sam's heated focus turned toward the only other patrons in the establishment. A man and woman sat at a far table eating lunch. Even though the couple seemed content, both watched the door or peered out the window, no doubt surveying for possible threats. How times have changed.

Sam said, "They've planned this out for decades. Weakening our economy, instilling internal chaos, terrorist strikes, laws, restrictions, bringing in foreign troops." She slammed her fist down on the table. "The HTF, they're Americans."

"Sam, calm down." Kevin nervously surveyed the room. "We'll figure this out, I promise."

Grinding her teeth, Sam did as Kevin asked. She gestured for and received the laptop from Kevin, then continued to copy the files from the website.

Kevin pointed to the screen. "Open that file on the desktop, Sam. The one labeled President McMullen."

Sam hovered the arrow over the folder and clicked twice to open the file. The threesome read in silence.

Kevin scowled. "He moved here five years ago. I thought he grew up in the Midwest. Is he even an American? This says SUNKC funded everything from his schooling in Russia to his campaign for presidency. How did this happen? How did a foreigner get elected as the leader of our country? Didn't anyone verify this stuff?"

"Any record can be altered, Kevin," Sam said. "Hell, it's not hard. If I'm reading this right, all these people on here have new identities." Sam guided the cursor over the list of names in the same folder. Behind each name the file showed which position of power they held in the United States.

"Okay. Now check this file, Sam," Kevin pointed. "No, the one labeled Vice President. Damn, is everyone involved." They stared as an unfamiliar name and picture loaded onto the screen along with a separate list of hundreds of names and a capital C.H. following each one. "That man's not the vice president," Kevin stated the obvious.

Elaina shook her head. "Read what it says. SUNKC shows this man as being sworn in later this year. That's the vice president in the photo. See the gentleman standing next to him? Isn't he the guy we met in the mine? Richard Ludlum. Is he in on this?"

Feeling a new level of fear, Sam read through the file. Ludlum knew where the mine was. If he was with this SUNKC, then they were all in immediate danger. As she read her worry dissipated. "No, thank God. He was guarding the vice president and took a bullet to save his life. It's as if this group carried out the assassination attempt, and Ludlum got in the way. They wanted the vice president dead."

Kevin slapped the table. "They still do. It makes sense. They used the man with a name to help with popularity for the election, not who they genuinely wanted for the position. Once they have their president in place, they kill off the VP and replace him with their own candidate. The vice president is in charge of the Senate. That's a good position for them to have. And look at this date and the C.H. after his name. It's the same date as the one on the flash drive for C.H. Why is it connected with the VP and every name following?"

Elaina's eyes widened. "I recognize a few of the names. Two are Senators and one's a Congresswoman."

Sam pulled out her phone and did a random search on over twenty names from the list with the vice president. "Looks like they're all members of Congress and to me, it reads like a hit list, starting with the vice president. I wonder if they're planning another assassination attempt on the date listed."

Kevin fixed his eyes on Sam after she finished copying the remaining files onto the flash drive. "They all have the same date after their names. Even if you're right, they can't take out hundreds of people on the same day, it would be impossible, not to mention overly conspicuous."

"The Capitol!" Elaina shouted. Several people turned and stared at their table. She lowered her voice to an excited whisper. "C.H., Capitol Hill. President McMullen has called for members of Congress to meet on Wednesday. That's the same date by C.H." She took a breath. "Anyway, they're supposed to convene to vote on allowing foreign troops to enter the US. I bet those troops are from Russia, North Korea, and China, but of course Congress probably doesn't know that."

"Perfect time for them to wipe out the majority of the government." Sam's face went white as a ghost. "How long have we been connected to the internet?"

Elaina looked in the direction Sam was facing. Through a clear section of glass, she noticed two black SUVs had stopped across the street from the cafe.

Kevin unplugged the laptop, the scrambler, and quickly shoved everything into his bag. "Get your stuff, we're leaving."

Sam threw two one-hundred-dollar bills on the table. She followed Elaina from the booth. "Do you have your weapon?" she asked, as they moved toward the rear exit.

"Yes. Tucked into the back of my jeans."

"Leave it but be ready. I don't think they know exactly where we are yet. But I could be wrong."

Chapter Eighteen

The Fall of the Government

They remained silent until Kevin pulled into a truck stop on the edge of St. Louis. Somehow, they'd escaped undetected. He continued to scan the rearview mirror even after Sam told him three separate times no one was following them. He was anxious. They all were.

The threesome clambered from the truck. Sam stretched her legs, tenderly rubbing her butt, and lit the first cigarette since her so-called run.

Kevin took a drag off Sam's cigarette, his hands shaking. "What do we do now, Sam?" he asked between coughs.

Sam kept massaging her sore butt, contemplating. "We need to find a way to stop them."

"How are we going to do that? Who can we trust? We can't just call up the FBI. The HTF is running things now."

Flicking away the remainder of her cigarette, Sam paced alongside the truck. "We have the list of names of the people involved, and those who may be marked for death. I think the vice president looks to be our best hope."

Kevin said, "Sam, we can't walk up to the vice president and say, 'excuse me sir, we need to show you something.' He's nearly as well guarded as the president."

"Can we get a hold of Mister Ludlum?" Elaina asked. "After all, he did take a bullet for the guy."

Kevin said, "That's a great idea." He quickly dialed a number on his cell phone and waited. "Agnes, it's Kevin. Sorry, but I have no time to explain. I need Lud—"

Sam snatched the phone out of his hand and ended the call. "His name might be flagged. After all, he was on their website. If they're monitoring calls, they'll be able to trace the call. Don't use his name, and call from a burner phone."

"Jesus. You're right, Sam." Kevin grabbed his wallet from the dash and rushed toward the store. He returned less than five-minutes later. "I don't want to use a credit card and the prices here are ridiculous. I need more cash."

"I've got this." Sam hobbled inside the store. She bought Elaina a diet soda, some snacks, and two phones. Back at the truck, she handed Kevin a phone and tossed the other into the center console.

"We'll need to keep to the interstate and stop around seven to comply with the curfew," Elaina said.

"You're not going." Sam fixed Elaina with a stare. "This has become too dangerous."

"I *am* going, Sam. Please don't do this."

Sam glowered at her. "If anything happens to you—"

Elaina placed her fingers over Sam's lips. "I'll be fine. I promise to listen to you every step of the way."

"Hate to break up your moment," Kevin said, "Ludlum thinks he can get us an off-the-book meeting with the vice president. We've got to be in Pennsylvania by tomorrow evening. With curfew, we'll need to get on the road now. It'll take us a good ten hours to get there."

"Why don't you and I fly?" Sam asked.

Elaina groaned and Kevin shook his head. "It takes twenty-four to forty-eight hours for a flight pass these days. No time. We'll have to drive and find a motel before curfew."

Sam shrugged at Elaina. "You can't blame a girl for trying."

"God, you really are stubborn." She poked Sam's stomach. "You're stuck with me, so deal with it."

"Not to break up another touching moment, but we've seriously got to move." Kevin climbed behind the wheel and started the engine.

They made great time during the drive with one brief stop for Elaina to use the restroom. Then they made a slight detour to purchase hygiene items, a couple changes of clothes for each, and various supplies to get them through for a few days. At twenty minutes past seven that evening, Kevin breathed a sigh of relief the moment he pulled the truck into the parking lot of a rundown motel.

In order to facilitate rotating guard duty throughout the night they opted to share a room with two queen-sized beds. Sam took first watch.

"Want some company?" Elaina asked.

"Sure, but you should try to sleep."

"Could you doze off through that?" Elaina tossed a thumb over her shoulder to where Kevin was sound asleep, thundering snores rattling the windows.

"I've learned through my time in the military to sleep through anything. I even managed to snooze standing up a couple of times."

"Not me. I'm a baby when it comes to my sleeping environment." Elaina blew out a loud breath. "There're a few vending machines at the end of the walkway, do you want anything?"

"You have a soda in the fridge."

"It's flat."

"Not the best neighborhood to stroll around, especially at night."

Elaina did a rapid count of the remaining pile of quarters and dollar pieces. "Don't worry, it's not far. I promise not to talk to any strangers."

"Fine, get me a soda and a candy bar." Sam peered out the window one more time. "All clear."

Elaina placed a tender kiss on Sam's lips. "You're more protective than my father, Ms. Kelly."

Even after Elaina left, Sam held her smile. She liked how Elaina made her feel. But she was still bothered by her slipup at the café. Telling Elaina she loved her was an error she realized as soon as the words tumbled past her lips. She'd tried to play off the blunder and was thankful neither Kevin nor Elaina seemed to have been paying attention. She had only told one other person—other than her family—that she loved them, and that was Sarah. They had been dating for over a year before she said the words. Surely, her relationship with Elaina was too new for such intense feelings.

Sam rolled the room keycard around in her hand. She gazed out the window, then at her watch. Elaina had only been gone for five minutes, but Sam was getting restless. She opened the door, pulling it closed behind her. Keycard in her pocket, she peeked over the balcony. No movement. All was quiet. Giving her body a quick stretch, she turned, and headed for the center walkway housing the vending machines.

If only things were different, Sam thought, tossing around the image of her and Elaina on a private beach far away from here. She wanted to truly get to know Elaina. Spend quality time with her alone. Experience normal things together, not traipse throughout the United States on a task which might get them all killed.

The low sounds of a scuffle brought her to a halt. Her senses switched to high-alert, and she shifted her body against the wall. She tilted her head only enough to see around the corner and clenched her jaw when she saw Elaina being pressed up against the wall between the soda and snack machines. A hooded assailant brandished a switchblade at her throat, and two others stood close behind.

The punk and his two friends wore clothes of matching colors. Gang colors? If so, she didn't recognize them.

"All you have is pocket change? What else are you going to give us to keep me from cutting you?" His leer was revolting.

"Why don't you show us your tits," said one who wore a scraggly ball cap tilted to the side. "Or better yet, why don't you suck us off. That sounds fair." He brought his hand down and rubbed himself over his baggy jeans. The asshole standing beside him choked out a laugh as he took a generous drink from a whisky bottle.

Staying out of their sightline, Sam glanced frantically around the area. Pulling her weapon or charging in recklessly would certainly get Elaina hurt, if not killed. She needed to think of something, and fast.

Removing her cigarettes from her back pocket and lighting one, Sam unbuttoned the top three buttons on her shirt, more than enough to expose her cleavage. She took a steadying breath. Sam stumbled into the area, acting as if she didn't see the four individuals already there.

"Hey, what the fuck!" The punk with the knife snarled at Sam. His two friends jumped.

"A party." Sam gave a hazy smile and made her way over to the guy holding the liquor bottle. "I have a room." She took the bottle and ran her tongue suggestively over the rim before downing a huge swig. She took another drink, noticing the tension ease in the man holding the knife.

"You wanna party with us tonight?" asked the one with the ball cap.

Sam rubbed herself against the asshole who held the bottle. "Three guys, two gals, what more can a woman ask for?"

Sam went over to the punk with the knife, not liking how close the blade was to Elaina's throat. "I see she's not into playing. I guess we can tie her up on my bed. I like rebellious girls, they taste sweeter." When she traced her tongue along Elaina's neck to her cheek, the man holding the knife dropped his hand slightly, seeming to enjoy the display.

Sam instantly seized his wrist. At the same time, she rammed her forehead hard into his nose. He screamed. Grabbing his shirt, Sam yanked him into another painful nose-breaking, eye watering crunch. This time he dropped the knife and she let his body fall backwards to the ground. She pulled out her gun and guided Elaina behind her. Sam aimed the gun at asshole and ball cap.

"If I wasn't worried about drawing unnecessary attention to myself, I'd shoot all three of you to save the next person you meet the trouble." Sam narrowed her eyes. "As it is, tonight is your lucky night. Grab your friend and get the fuck out of here."

They moved forward, looking as if they bit off more than they could chew.

"If I see any of you here again, I swear I'll kill you," she said. The authority she intoned seemed to do the trick.

Sam put her weapon away after the idiots took off. She pulled Elaina into her arms and waited for her shaking to subside before leading her to their motel room. Neither one said a word. Kevin's snores trumpeted a greeting when they entered. Sam locked the door, sat in the chair, and tugged Elaina into her lap. Elaina laid her head on Sam's shoulder and Sam wrapped her tight in her arms. The position she was in made her ass hurt, but Sam remained still, staring out the window. Soon Elaina drifted off to sleep.

"Why didn't you wake me for the next watch?" Kevin yawned. He squinted at Elaina lying in the other bed, then to Sam. "Did you stay up the entire night?"

"I couldn't sleep."

He *huffed* out his disappointment but left it alone. "Want some coffee?"

"I would love some. Why don't you make a pot and hop in the shower? I want to let her sleep a little longer."

He gave Sam a thumbs up. He set up the coffeemaker and then grabbed his newly acquired backpack and went into the bathroom. After the coffee had finished brewing and Kevin was done with his shower, Sam went next. She finished washing her body, and was in the middle of shampooing, when the bathroom door opened.

"I want to thank you for last night," Elaina said through the closed shower curtain.

Her heart raced. "It's no big deal. Hey, why don't you wait outside. I'll be done in a moment, I promise." Sam hastily rinsed her hair under the water. She opened her eyes and saw Elaina's leg poke through the curtain. Crap! Sam rotated, keeping her back to Elaina. "Please leave. I'm not comfortable with you being in here."

"I love everything about you, Samantha Kelly." Elaina placed her arms around Sam's waist and stood still as warm water ran over them. "Inside and out, everything about you fascinates me."

Sam's shoulders slumped. Holding her breath, she faced Elaina. "There's nothing fascinating about a damaged body." She averted her eyes from Elaina's, wishing she were anywhere but in this moment. "I'm—" Her voice faltered with the touch of Elaina's hand to one of the scars on her chest. Sam closed her eyes, wondering what Elaina was thinking. She had to be repulsed by the scars. How couldn't she be?

Elaina's fingers glided over Sam's body and Sam's muscles twitched under the contact. Elaina's skin was warm, her touch, gentle. She traced each of Sam's bullet scars from battle, and the two jagged marks from Sam's childhood stabbing. "You're very beautiful, Sam."

A sob escaped from Sam's throat.

Elaina pulled Sam closer to her.

Kevin rapped on the door. "Guys, we need to leave in less than ten minutes. Let's speed things up."

"I wanted to show you days ago when we were in my bedroom, but I didn't know how. Other than Rachel, no one has ever seen them before."

Elaina leaned back, startled. "Are you telling me, no one you've been with has ever seen you naked?"

"Well, my first girlfriend, Sarah. She . . ." Sam paused, not sure how to tell the story, or if she even wanted to talk about it while she was naked.

"Christina told me what happened. Please don't be upset with her, she did it because she was worried about you."

Sam said, "Sarah was her sister. If anyone were to tell you, I'm glad she was the one."

"Is that what these two wounds were from?" Elaina gently brushed her fingers over the pale, jagged scars on Sam's chest.

"Yes. We—Sarah and I—had planned the evening several weeks ahead. That night was going to be our first time." Sam turned away. "Sarah was too good of a person to die like that."

Kevin banged on the door. "I'm hungry, and the sun's about to rise. Can we get a move on?"

"I guess I better let you take a shower before he breaks down the door," Sam murmured.

Elaina peered up into Sam's eyes. "I have never met a woman more beautiful than you. These are a part of you, and I love it all."

Sam kissed Elaina. She opened her mouth to speak, but Elaina stopped her. "I don't expect anything you cannot give. I know what we have is new, and I'm fine with taking things slow."

Sam brushed a strand of hair away from Elaina's eyes. "We're standing naked in the shower together, after knowing each other for over a week. I think we're past taking it slow."

"You know what I mean." Elaina grinned, kissed Sam on the lips, and ushered her from the shower.

The truck was packed, and Sam checked them out of the room less than twenty minutes later, giving them enough time to swing through a drive-thru for an early morning breakfast. After devouring her sandwich, hash browns, and iced coffee, Sam reclined her seat and fell fast asleep.

"Sam, we're here."

Sam blinked her eyes so as not to be blinded by the bright sunlight. The landscape was stunning. Green grass, a rainbow of wildflowers, and full leafy trees everywhere the eye could see. The truck windows were up, but the fresh fragrance of Mother Earth drifted in through the vents on the dash, and Sam was all too happy to breathe it in.

"Wow, this land's beautiful." Her throat felt dry, scratchy, and she sat up and searched for a drink. She was amused when she noticed Elaina's jacket draped over the upper part of her body. She had to fight down the urge to climb into the back seat for a kiss.

Elaina leaned forward to retrieve her jacket and softly pressed her lips onto Sam's. "Good afternoon, sexy."

Sam checked her watch. "Afternoon? I must have been tired. Do you have anything to drink?"

"Of course." Elaina passed Sam her fountain drink. "We stopped a few hours ago, but neither of us had the heart to wake you."

Sam sucked a few gulps and handed it back. "How far do you think we are?" she asked Kevin.

"If the address is right, then we're here." He slowed the truck and made a wide right turn onto a dusty, gravel driveway. It curved upward for less than a mile before inclining toward an enormous metal warehouse, which rested against acres of trees. Sam figured two Hughes H-4 Hercules would have fit comfortably inside touching nose to tail, maybe even wing to wing.

Sam recognized Richard the moment he stepped out of the smaller side door of the building. He had a huge smile on his face, as if seeing old friends for the first time in years. It was impossible for anyone, even Sam, not to return such a welcoming expression. After a brief round of handshakes, Richard ushered them inside to his so-called "humble" establishment.

Sam stopped beside the others and gawked. Richard's enterprise was anything but humble. Various crates and weaponry covered almost every inch of the warehouse, leaving barely enough space to move between the rows of pallets and larger machinery. Six brand new military tanks and several different types of artillery stood in the center of the high-ceilinged structure. More than thirty men and women, dressed in camouflage uniforms, hustled about as a person Sam assumed was a high-ranking officer shouted out orders from the side.

"Where did all this stuff come from?" Elaina asked, wide-eyed.

Richard grinned. "Why, it fell off trucks, ships, and train cars, of course. Where else?" He waved a hand casually in the air. "I've been setting up camps and supply stashes like this all over the United States. This one's smaller than the rest, but it serves its purpose."

Kevin said, "Aren't you worried about the HTF finding this place?"

"I assure you, I know how to keep my enterprise well hidden. If we ever were found out, I'd feel sorry for any HTF agents who engaged with this group. They're the best of the best. People I've had the privilege of working with throughout my career."

"So, you're a black-market, arms dealer?" Sam asked.

"Sam!" Elaina sounded shocked.

Richard said, "Yes, it does appear that way. The only difference between my group, and ones who benefit off the fighting of others, is I charge no money for my items. Yes, we have acquired equipment illegally from closed or closing military bases, along with a few other sites we've stumbled upon. But everyone is here because we believe in the protection of America and the freedom of her people, not for a paycheck. We make no money, and we lose little money, it's as simple as that."

"Why are you stockpiling so much, though?" Kevin inspected the contents of an open crate.

"There's most certainly a war coming, and it will not only be fought by us, but by every man, woman, and child strong and competent enough to fire a weapon. We have made it our mission to personally see those weapons are available, and anything else we can get our hands on." He turned his focus solely to Sam. "We're making plans for two separate attacks next week at four camps in the area. We have some last-minute snags to work through, but we've constructed cabins and shallow bunkers throughout the woods behind us in which we can house at least two-thousand refugees."

Sam said, "Sorry I doubted your intentions."

"Not at all, I would have thought the same if the roles were reversed."

Sam examined her wristwatch. "We need to leave now if we intend to make it to DC before curfew."

"Oh, didn't I tell you?" Richard asked in amusement. I called in a favor with an old friend of mine. He's providing us with a quicker means of travel." As if on cue, the sound of a helicopter vibrated the walls around them. "It sounds like our ride is here."

"Jesus, Richard! Why didn't you tell me you'd be arriving in a helicopter? I almost ordered the Second Division to shoot your ass down." The agent in a dark-blue suit motioned for the pilot to cut the engine as his hair and tie whipped wildly about.

"I radioed you when we were close."

"You were almost too close." The Secret Service agent straightened his tie. His displeasure increased the instant he noticed the three people waiting to disembark from the helicopter. "You didn't say you'd be bringing anyone with you. Sorry, but I can't clear this."

Richard jumped down. "Jeff, you know I wouldn't put him in any danger. Hell, I took a bullet to keep him safe, what more do I need to do—"

Jeff held up his hand. "Yes, yes, yes, I know the story. You tell it every time you want something from me, or the department." He narrowed his eyes at Sam, Elaina, and Kevin still waiting to exit the helicopter. "Are they armed?"

"I don't know. I forgot to ask." Richard turned to them, his voice chipper. "Well? Are you carrying?"

Sam and Elaina removed their pistols from behind their waistbands and laid them on the floor inside the helicopter. Kevin was not so graceful. He opened his backpack and fished around for a few seconds. When his hand gripped the butt of the weapon, he automatically pulled it out with the barrel pointing toward the agent, as if saying *See, I have one, too.* Richard reacted quickly, preventing Jeff from unholstering his firearm.

Sam yanked the gun from Kevin's shaking hand and placed it beside the others. "Sorry, he's not very skilled when it comes to handling firearms."

"You're going to have to leave." Jeff's hand rested on his holstered gun.

"Jeff, you know as well as I that our government is dying. Hell, so does the vice president. That's why he refused to take any HTF agents onto his security detail. Which is why I brought them." He inclined his head in the direction of the threesome. "They have the proof we need to end this."

Jeff glared from Sam to Kevin's frightened face, and then to Richard. "You're a piece of work, you know that, Ludlum?" He waved off a group of agents running toward them. Jeff thoroughly patted down Sam, Elaina, and Kevin. He then checked the contents of Kevin's backpack before speaking to the other agents. "They're clear. Could you tell the vice president Mister Ludlum has arrived?" Jeff furrowed his brow. "And that he's brought guests."

Richard grinned at Jeff before motioning for the three to follow him from the helipad.

Four stories tall, with brick walls and bright white windows and trim, the vice president's estate looked more like a mansion than a house. It sat on top of a hill with a great view of the city lights shining below. A side door opened, casting even more light out into the well-lit walkway, and two robust Great Danes bounded toward Richard.

"Oh, my," Elaina gripped Sam's arm.

Kevin sidestepped, using Sam's body as a shield.

"Brutus, Pepper. Did you miss me?" Richard greeted the dogs as if they were his own.

"They don't take kindly to strangers, so you three might want to keep your distance," Jeff said. "Down, Brutus," he ordered in a commanding voice as the stout, fawn-colored male approached. The dog immediately lowered himself to the ground with a deep throaty snarl.

Sam stepped forward, Elaina and Kevin remained behind. Jeff gawked at Sam as if she were crazy. Richard watched with his brow raised, while rubbing Pepper's chest.

"I warned you," Jeff said.

Sam kept her voice steady. "He'll either bite me or he won't."

"Sam, are you crazy? Come back here," Elaina's voice was raspy.

The dog stood when Sam approached. She stopped, didn't say a word, only acted as if the dog didn't matter. Brutus huffed a bark and tilted his head. Eventually he stepped forward and bumped his snout into Sam's leg.

"A fellow dog person, I take it." The voice came from the side door.

Sam glanced up to the man standing in the doorway. "I grew up on a farm, Mister Vice President." She nodded to the dogs. "They sensed Richard and Jeff didn't see me as a threat, so they fed off that, and not my arm."

His tossed his head back and laughed, then whistled. Both dogs ran to him. "Come in and let's talk about why Richard has brought you here to see me."

They followed him in, along with Jeff and two more agents. The grand entryway was elegant, with stone-statues, pricey artwork, and a granite fountain to give those who entered the correct impression someone of importance resided there. Shooing the horse-sized dogs away, the vice president directed them into a library with a sitting area in the center. Flames danced in a stone fireplace, casting light around the room, as everyone, except for the three Secret Service agents, took a seat.

"It's good to see you, Richard. It's been too long." The VP's eyes were warm, honest. "How's the shoulder doing?"

"I can't complain." Richard said, then he formally introduced his three companions.

"So, why have you come?"

Sam motioned for Kevin to open the backpack. "Frankly, to save your life, and to stop the slaughter of most of Congress."

The vice president uncrossed his legs and scooted forward. "You have my attention."

Sam explained what they'd discovered, and what they assumed was going to happen tomorrow morning when Congress convened. Kevin opened each file they'd copied while at the Internet café the day before.

After the explanation was complete, the vice president stood. He strolled to the fireplace with his head lowered. After close to three minutes of glaring into the flames, the vice president spun on his heels to where Jeff was standing. "Go through each list, every file. Find out who in Congress was marked like me, and the names of those here in the United States these foreign governments are financially supporting. I want to know everything, including who we can and cannot trust. We need to stop this, but I don't want to risk going through the wrong channels to do it."

He turned to the agent by the door. "Pack up my wife and kids and escort them, and two agents, to the safe house until this mess is over. Take my dogs as well."

"Yes, Mister Vice President."

Richard stood. "Sir, your life's in danger. We need to get you out of here, too."

"No, I'll see this thing through. We have a corrupt president, presidential cabinet, and what, three countries trying to topple our nation. I'm staying."

"Sir," Jeff said, "Richard's right. If you fall, we all fall."

"Please concentrate on the lists, Jeff."

Sam listened as the third agent called for reinforcements. After a half-hour of silently watching the growing commotion, she made a unilateral decision and returned to the helicopter.

"What's going on?" the pilot asked. "This place is crawling with men. Is Richard still here? I saw a car pull out twenty minutes ago with two big dogs."

"You better come inside. This might take a while." Sam retrieved the three weapons still lying in the middle of the helicopter. She tucked one in the front of her jeans and another she hid in her jacket. Back inside, Sam handed Elaina her weapon and told her to keep it on her.

By midnight, she'd seen a score of additional personnel report in. She had no clue how many more agents were stationed around the perimeter. Food and drink trays were regularly set out. Agents were sifting through the data, others conducted regular security rounds inside the dwelling, and the vice president sat with Ludlum and his Chief of Staff, who Jeff had sent for the second he'd been cleared.

Jeff made his way to the vice president's desk in the corner. "Sir, the list of everyone who checks out."

"Good, get a team together and place some calls. I don't want a single member of Congress to enter the Capitol."

"My cell phone went dead," Jeff announced a few minutes later.

One of the female agents said, "Here, use mine."

"It's dead too," Jeff tossed the phone back to the woman.

"Don't you guys charge your devices?" Richard pulled out his cell and threw it to Jeff.

Jeff tapped the screen. "Sorry, old man, yours isn't working either."

Suddenly everyone in the room dug their phones out. Sam and Kevin were both unsuccessful in getting theirs to work.

Jeff made his way over to the landline phone sitting on the desk. "See if we're still connected to the Internet," he said to the agent closest to him. "Landline's down, too." He replaced the receiver into the cradle.

"No Internet connection," the agent said to Jeff.

Sam stood. "They know someone hacked into their system. This move is their way of making it hard for us to raise the alarm."

The vice president inhaled as if to shout. In a controlled voice, he said, "Jeff, take some agents and head to DC. I don't care what you have to do but make sure no one steps foot inside that building."

"Yes, sir." He summoned three agents and they followed him out the door leaving everyone in the room quiet and worried.

The picture window in the library framed a beautiful dawn sky of vibrant shades of red and blue, as if mocking the treachery raging throughout the dying democracy. Sam shifted her weight to the side and moved in order to lay Elaina's head on the pillow she had been sitting on. She stood, rubbing the spot on her butt cheek.

"Does it hurt?" Elaina's voice drifted up from the couch.

"No, but it itches like a mad dog." She smiled at Elaina. "Want me to get you something to drink?"

"Um, a diet soda would be wonderful, but I'll settle for sweetened coffee if you can't find any soda."

The Secret Service agents Sam passed seemed tired, but alert. She found the kitchen. Richard stood by the stove talking to a few agents.

"Do you have any soda?" she asked.

An agent opened one of three massive refrigerators. Sam joined him and pulled out two twenty-ounce bottles of Elaina's favorite. "Thank you."

"Ludlum said you rescued some people from prison camps."

"Yes."

He withdrew a photo of a young woman standing next to him on a beach. "She's my little sister. Her name's Nicky. Well, her legal name's

Nakasha, but I call her Nicky. My family hasn't heard from her or her husband in some time. They were vacationing in Branson, Missouri, when they went missing."

Sam inspected the picture closely. Something clicked. "Is she pregnant?"

His eyes widened. "Yes! You've seen her?"

"I have," Sam said. "She wasn't one of the people at the camps, but I did see her in the mine. She's safe and in good care. I'm not sure about her husband, though."

The man clutched the photo as tears streamed down his face. "Thank you."

Sam's throat tightened. She placed a hand on the man's arm, unsure of what to say or do. The agent standing closest to Richard joined his colleague. He gave Sam a friendly nod before guiding the emotional agent onto the screen porch off the kitchen.

"He's a good man," Richard said. "They all are."

Sam threw Richard a curt nod, then hurried to the library before her emotions got the better of her. "Still no word?" Sam cleared her scratchy throat.

"No. Why are your eyes red?" Elaina opened her soda.

"Someone's peeling onions in the kitchen. What's the plan?"

Kevin said, "Wait and see is really all we have. There's less than two hours to go until Congress assembles." Kevin stood and gestured to Sam. "Do you want to go out for a smoke?"

When Sam got up, so did Elaina. "You two are not leaving me alone."

Over the next hour and a half everyone grew more restless. Sam went in search of Richard and found him by the front door staring vacantly outside. "You need to make plans to get the vice president as far away from this city as possible. There's a good chance this won't end well."

Richard's sigh was drawn out, his rugged face, worn with exhaustion and stress. "The vehicles are packed, and the helicopter's ready. If this goes bad, I want him moved into your family's mine. At least until we can get this figured out," he said, not taking his eyes off the view.

"Are you transporting him in the helicopter?" Sam asked.

"Yes, with a few of the men, and you three. The rest of the agents will drive." Richard suddenly shifted his attention to her. "You know, before going to the mine I read your military file. Reclassed to an 18 Echo once your waiver was approved. You had over a year of intense Special Forces training, including the Free Fall Parachutist Course. First thing I thought was you must have a death wish or something."

Not sure how to take his abrupt shift in conversation, Sam studied his features. He wasn't revealing much, maybe a pinch of curiosity, or possibly amusement. "Great recap of my career. Did you have a question?"

He peered out the window, then to her. "Frank, and the others in the mine I've talked with, haven't a clue what you did in the service. Most believe you plugged in cords and powered up radios for eight years."

One of the agents came up behind them. "Richard, it's time."

Sam and Richard followed the agent into the library where everyone was gathered around the wall-mounted television. A woman with a microphone was on the screen standing in front of the Capitol. "—As for the issues with the nationwide communication outage, we would like to assure everyone this should be fixed by this evening. Since we're the only station currently able to broadcast, we'll air regular updates. Consider this an exceedingly small taste of what Y2K would have been like if it actually had happened." She paused, then went on to explain to the viewers the issues Congress would be voting on today. After a few minutes passed she touched her hand to her right ear and her eyes widened. "I've been told several Secret Service agents have been shot while attempting to assassinate the vice president. No word yet on whether the vice president was killed."

"They didn't make it." Richard spoke to the vice president. "Sir, we have to leave now. They'll make the connection if they haven't already."

"It's Agent Dixon!" A man shouted.

Sam glanced at the screen in time to see a paramedic covering Jeff's face with a white sheet. The view switched to the woman in front of the Capitol. "We still do not know the reasons behind the attempt—"

The rapid reverberation of three explosions from the Capitol was greater than anything Sam had ever seen before, even during her time in combat. Everyone in the room jumped backwards as if they could feel the effects of the eruptions first-hand. The last explosion blasted the reporter into the camera a split second before the station went off the air.

The next explosion felt as if it shook the foundation of the house. No one moved.

"Someone blew up my fucking helicopter!" A rain of gunfire from outside followed the pilot's shout, and he dove headfirst to the floor.

"Get the vice president into the safe room!" Richard bellowed.

Sam ran, taking Elaina by the hand and yelling for Kevin to follow. They went with the agents and the vice president into a hidden, reinforced room off the kitchen. "Stay with the vice president and we'll come get you when it's safe. Keep your weapon ready, you might need it." Sam squeezed Elaina's hand and then stepped away and waited for the thick steel door to close and latch. She was grateful Elaina kept her word and didn't argue.

Sam followed two agents through the kitchen, with her weapon out and ready. They met up with Richard, then moved swiftly through the back door and around behind an all-white wooden shed in the backyard. "If we get to the tree line maybe we can flank them," Sam said.

Richard pointed to the agents. "You two go to the east side, and we'll take the west. Watch your crossfire when you move to the front."

Both hurried off without a second's hesitation.

"You ready?" Richard asked.

Sam said, "You first."

He crouched low and ran, with Sam on his heels. They took cover behind a large pillar. He motioned with his hand, directing Sam's gaze to the two HTF agents along the southwest corner of the house. "I'll take the one on the right," he announced, bringing his weapon up and taking aim. They fired almost simultaneously, dropping both HTF agents dead right outside a bay window. They moved forward.

Sam was not sure if her stitches ripped open or if the right side of her butt had decided to sweat profusely, but the area on her ass felt warm and wet as she ran, and a sharp pain shot through her butt cheek. At least it doesn't itch anymore, she thought, throwing her body on the ground next to Richard.

He glanced back. "Are you all right?"

"I'm fine, out of shape." She lied.

"You're butt's bleeding. You ripped your stitches open, didn't you?"

Sam shrugged her shoulders. "I'll live."

He laughed. "Frank said you were a badass. I think he meant to say you had a *bad* ass."

"Anymore jokes like those and I'll stand up and let them shoot me."

Richard pointed to the grouping of HTF agents fifty feet from the front of the house.

"I could sure go for a grenade right about now," Sam grumbled.

"No kidding. Hey, do you think we can make it to those bushes without being seen?"

"Not sure, but I'm game if you are."

"That's the spirit," he said. "Let's go."

They sprinted forward as fast as their legs would carry them. By this point, Sam's butt was completely numb from the pain. When she dove behind the bushes, she heard, more than felt, the final rip from her stitches, along with a fresh stream of moisture flowing over her right leg.

A bullet soared past an inch above Richard's head. Sam turned and fired. She hit the first man in the chest and the second in the throat. The dying HTF agent dropped to his knees and Richard sent a final round between the man's eyes. Then, all hell broke loose. Bullets flew around them from all directions, and they pressed their bodies tight to the ground.

"Shit, Sam! This was a stupid idea!" Richard said.

"Hey, this was your idea! I'm only a guest here, remember?"

"Guests first." Richard waved a hand for her to precede him.

"You're too kind." Sam surveyed the area. "All right, tell you what we're going to do. We're going to shoot at the agents behind us and pray your friends in the house take out the ones in front." Sam reloaded her weapons.

"What kind of a plan is that?"

"You have a better idea? Maybe you would like to try and make another run for it?"

Richard let out a long dramatic sigh. "Fine, let's roll over on our backs and start shooting. Maybe we'll get lucky and hit something."

Sam wasn't sure how they managed to shoot anyone, but somehow, they had taken out a handful of HTF agents. Before long, the two agents Richard had sent the opposite direction came around and supplied reinforcements. Agents from inside the house came outside, taking cover behind the bricked barrier on the wrap around patio. Within minutes, their cascade of bullets drove what was left of the HTF into a retreat, giving Sam and the other three Secret Service agents perfect targets to hit.

Richard shouted to an agent ten feet away. "Try to wound that one there. No, not that guy, the tall lanky one with the red hair." He grinned to Sam. "He looks like a chatty individual, and we need to get some intel out of these fuckers."

Chapter Nineteen

The Rise of Dictatorship

The man relaxed into the comfort of the soft leather chair, as the woman worked the light foundation into key areas around his nose and chin. The office was chaos, but he tuned it out, not wanting to spoil his feeling of victory. This moment belonged to him. His place in time, separating him from the line of so-called *great men* before him. He was in control and more powerful than he could have ever dreamed possible. Soon, what was left of this nation would fall, and he would be there on the grand day to see it happen.

His office door burst open, and a short, anxious man with a high-pitched voice entered. He hated the voice, detested everything about it and the man who owned it, but he wasn't the one who picked the members of his cabinet. No, *they* had chosen for him, his superiors, but after the explosion this morning, he should now have a say in the way the country was run, should he not? After all, he *was* the president.

"Mister President, I have urgent news."

Adam sat up and waved the makeup woman and her brushes from the room. He removed the catchall cloth from around his neck. What is it?"

"The agents we sent have been killed. All but one, and he's missing."

"What of the vice president?"

"He's gone, sir, along with a number of his Secret Service agents."

Adam slammed his fist against the surface of his highly polished desk, causing everything on it to clatter. "Who did this? How could this have happened?"

"We don't know, sir. The security tapes at the VP's house were erased."

The president lowered his head and rubbed his temples to try and relieve the developing headache. "It would be so much easier to blame all of this on the vice president instead of having to track him down and assassinate his ass."

The squeaky-voiced man nervously cleared his throat. "Mister President, I'm afraid the public wouldn't believe the vice president would be capable of these allegations."

"Of course, they wouldn't believe it, you jackass!" The president shouted. "He's a fucking goody two-shoes, who's incapable of harming a fly, let alone a human being. Jesus, he's even a God-damn vegetarian!" The president narrowed his eyes. "How much of our information did they get a hold of? How much of our plans do they know?"

The short man's irritating voice rose an octave. "We don't know, sir."

"Is there anything your incompetent agents do know?"

The high-pitched response caught on a stutter. "We know the ones who helped him are probably the same people who hacked into our system a few days ago."

"They are *probably* the same ones?" The president sprang to his feet, sending his chair backwards into a shelf of pricy knickknacks. They clattered in protest, but thankfully, no shattering crash followed. "No shit they're the same ones, you moron! Get the hell out of my office!"

Half-tripping, the man scurried from the room.

The president grumbled to the four men sitting off to the side. "See what happens when you don't let me pick my own people! I'm surrounded by complete idiots! Total incompetence."

"We'll find the vice president and those assisting him. You have an announcement to make in a few minutes. I suggest you calm down."

"Don't give me orders. I'm the one in charge here!" When the man sitting on the couch stared into his eyes, Adam realized he had overstepped his boundaries. "I didn't mean—look, Viktor, I'm worried, that's all."

"Would you gentleman please excuse us for a moment?" Viktor didn't take his eyes from Adam.

Once the room cleared, Viktor stood from the couch and made his way slowly over to where the president stood. He placed a hand on Adam's shoulder. His fingers dug in, swiftly sending Adam to his knees in agony. "We're not doing this for the power of one man, but for the good of several nations. You will remember your place in the future, or I'll see your reign here is short lived."

Adam whimpered and bobbed his head up and down. Viktor released his grip.

He helped Adam to his feet. "Now, you will sit behind that grand desk of yours and prepare for the speech we rehearsed."

"I didn't mean to talk out of place."

"I know, Adam. I know." The man almost cooed his words. "You were raised for a grand purpose, and soon, after the fighting is over, and this great country is ours, you will get your just reward."

Adam nodded before taking his place behind the desk. His legs felt weak. He carefully sat on the chair, which now felt hard as a board. He shifted uncomfortably, trying to find a tolerable position, then finally signaled to the still-smiling Viktor that he was ready.

Viktor left the room. He returned a moment later, followed by three news station reporters and their camera crews. The camera lights flipped on, temporarily blinding the president. He barely recovered in time for his cue.

"I come before you tonight with much sorrow and worry in my heart. An act of hatred and terror shook this great nation of ours in an explosion this morning, claiming the lives of many great men and women." He paused appearing disheartened by the gravity of it all. "This horrific act of terrorism has left us weak and vulnerable. It has torn through the very fabric holding us together, and I for one refuse to let the incident go unanswered." His sorrowful demeanor changed to controlled anger. He did his best to convey outrage. "Which is why I'm calling for foreign aid to help us through this crisis. We are not sure, as of yet, how long it will take before our allies can respond, but when they do, I am positive I will be able to count on each and every one of you to show them the gratitude they deserve."

He glanced down in defeat, then to the camera. His head shook, and his movements played to his frightened citizens. "It has been confirmed the men responsible are Secret Service agents. We're not yet certain of the identities of all those involved in this horrendous attack, but we have strong reasons to believe several other agents of the Secret Service as well as other high-ranking officials of the FBI and CIA, are also involved. Until we can conduct a full investigation into this matter, I'm ordering the temporary suspension of those agencies. The Homeland Task Force will take over all duties until we deem it safe to resume normal operations."

He watched Viktor write on a notepad. The cameras were still on, but he was unsure of what the man with the ugly scar over his right eye wanted. He continued to speak into the camera. "I know we will see each other through this difficult time."

Viktor casually walked over and handed the president a folded sheet of paper, keeping his body out of camera shot. Adam opened it and read. *Brilliant!* He peered up at the camera with a serious expression. "My staff has received confirmation the vice president is alive, and he's been abducted by members of his own security staff. If anyone has any information regarding his kidnapping, please notify the local HTF Agency in your area. My prayers are with us all."

When perimeter alarms in the mine went off, Agnes flew from the medical wing. Swarms of people hurried about as Emmett's commanding voice echoed loudly throughout the passageway. Frank entered the conference room at the same moment as Agnes, both moving toward the security monitors in Douglas's office.

"What is it, Douglas?" Agnes asked, assessing each of the eight monitors.

"There are six vehicles approaching from the south. I think they're heading straight for the south entrance."

She followed his finger with her eyes. Sure enough, six black SUVs with tinted windows barreled down the long gravel drive. "It's the HTF. Radio Emmett and tell him to meet us there with his troops in two minutes!"

Frank followed Agnes from the room. "How do you think they found us?"

"I don't know, Frank." But deep down, she thought she knew. The last time they heard from Sam and the others was three days earlier, and with everything she'd seen on the news within the last twenty-four hours,

Agnes was already on edge regarding the welfare of Sam and her companions. Even though she argued with the committee, she believed they were still alive and safe, this new development was proving she might well be wrong.

She knew Sam would never give away their location, even under torture. As for Elaina and Kevin, she didn't know either of them well enough to be certain. In addition, she heard the HTF used means of torture most civilized nations wouldn't even consider doing. She pushed the thought from her mind. The idea of their deaths was hard enough. Imagining brutal ways in which they died was unbearable.

"We're ready Agnes," Emmet said when she entered the tunnel by the south entrance. The movement in the mine by the south entrance settled and all weapons were aimed at the barricaded metal door.

"I have over one hundred armed soldiers here and several hundred more on standby to replace them if they fall." Emmett shifted his stance and directed a small group carrying a weapon and ammo. "I want the fifty-cal set up in the middle."

Agnes moved forward, glancing up to the monitor by the door. She watched as the vehicles stopped right outside the barn. Several men dressed in dark-blue suits exited the vehicles, took out their handguns and semi-automatics, and took positions around their convoy. "I'm thinking twenty-five, maybe thirty."

"They probably have more on the way."

She studied Frank closely. His eyes seemed to hold the same fear she was feeling. "We should relocate people down into the cave while we still have time."

"It's not set up yet."

"We don't have a choice." A movement on the screen caught her attention. She stepped closer to the monitor. "Emmett, stand-down your troops."

"What's going on?" Frank didn't need to wait for her reply. His lips formed a wide grin the moment he saw the woman waving into the monitor from the opening of the barn. Two others came alongside her. "Yep, she sure is a tough one, your niece."

"She's a Kelly." Agnes's eyes were moist, and her voice filled with pride. "Emmett, call Douglas and tell him to turn off the alarm. Sam's home."

It took them close to twenty minutes to get a team outside to open the doors. For Sam, smelling the familiar air of her family's farm was well worth the wait. After the last of the vehicles were safe inside, Sam limped over to her aunt, where she received a heartfelt embrace.

"I see you ripped your stitches out. Rachel's not going to be happy."

Sam glanced around. "Where is she? I assumed she would be here."

"Your sister's been in the medical wing since four this morning. Contractions."

Sam's throat went dry.

"Don't worry, she's fine. Christina says she still has a few more hours before the baby comes."

Feeling somewhat relieved, Sam directed Agnes to the man approaching. "Sir, I would like for you to meet my Aunt Agnes. Aunt Agnes, the Vice President of the United States."

Agnes's eyelashes fluttered and she brought a hand up to straighten her already tidy hair. She blushed while shaking his hand. "It's a pleasure to meet you, Mister Vice President."

"Please, call me Ben." He grinned broadly, revealing a perfect set of white teeth. "Sam has told me so much about you on the ride here, I feel we are somehow related." His laugh was genuine, and Sam could tell Agnes liked him straightaway.

"So, I take it my niece did not kidnap you after all."

"Kidnap? Oh, heavens, no. Actually, she saved my life."

Sam had no doubt this man had been a people-loving politician for most his adult life. "Aunt Agnes, a lot has happened in the last few days." She waved over one of the agents. "But first, his sister Nicky is here." She showed them the photo the agent handed to her.

"Oh, yes," Frank said. "She's in the medical wing with Rachel. She had her baby two days ago."

"How is she?" The agent seemed as if he was deciding whether to cry or shout out with joy.

"She's fine. I can take you to her. It's not far."

Sam waited until Frank guided the man down the passageway. She turned to her aunt.

Before Sam could speak Agnes said, "Why don't you have Elaina take you to the medical wing, and let Christina re-stitch you? Kevin and I will accompany these men to the dining facility, and they can fill me in on what's going on. I'm sure you are all quite hungry."

"I could go for a bite to eat." The vice president flashed his smile once again, offering his arm to Agnes.

"I'll have someone send you some food," Agnes said to Sam and Elaina, before locking arms with the vice president.

Sam crossed her arms as Agnes and the vice president walked away. Agnes was acting odd, and Sam wasn't sure if she was comfortable with the arm holding thing or not. "Does she seem all right to you?" Sam asked Elaina.

Elaina let out a tiny laugh. "Of course, Sam, she's fine." Elaina reached up and rubbed at the wrinkles between Sam's eyes. "How often does someone famous come around to visit?"

"That's it!" Sam snapped her fingers as Elaina directed her through the wide tunnel.

"What is?"

"Aunt Agnes is acting like a groupie."

Elaina laughed. "She's entertaining a very important guest."

"They're not guests. That's the Vice President of the United States and we're hiding him for his protection."

Elaina stopped Sam and pulled her head downward, for a warm kiss. "Your aunt is a big girl, Sam. Stop worrying, she's happily married. They both are." The second kiss was more passionate. Sam's focus centered on Elaina in her arms.

All thoughts of Agnes vanished, as her body burned hot with desire. When her hand moved underneath the front of Elaina's shirt, Elaina quickly yanked it out. "Are you crazy? Someone's bound to walk by and see us."

Sam leaned in and whispered, "Are you scared?"

"Oh, no you don't, Sam. We're not doing this here." Elaina pulled a pouting Sam with her as they continued along the passageway.

"You're no fun."

They decided to let everyone rest that evening and schedule a committee meeting for the following morning. Douglas, Frank, and several men began the task of getting the old farmhouse, which once belonged to Sam's late uncle, fixed up for their new guest. The two-story dwelling was a good, strong structure with a solid foundation and quite a bit of living space, but not yet an adequate place for the Vice President of the United States, or his agents.

Janis's husband, with the help of a second team, worked at reopening the entrance to the mine which ran underground to a secret door in the basement of the house. They estimated the project would take a week to complete, but with the way Agnes drove them, they'd likely be finished in half that time.

"We've got to go." Christina removed her long white hospital coat and draped it over her chair.

"You did good, sis." Sam kissed baby Jennifer softly on the forehead and gingerly handed her to Rachel. "I love you both very much." She kissed her little niece again, then her sister, before grabbing her crutches and leaving the room with the others.

"I believe that girl already has you wrapped around her little finger," Elaina said.

Sam smiled. "You might be right."

They stopped by the next room and informed the Secret Service agent sitting with his sister that the meeting was about to start. He was happily doting over his sister and three-day old nephew.

The meeting lasted well into the morning, with the entire committee, the vice president, and all the Secret Service agents in attendance. They discussed the most recent events and tossed around different ideas on what to do.

"Everyone involved with this organization, who holds a high office must be assassinated." Richard directed his words to the vice president. "Sir, they're too much of a risk to the government if we keep them alive."

"What government?" Brenda questioned. "The government fell the moment the members of the Senate and House of Representatives died. The few politicians left are probably as involved as the president."

"The government lives as long as there are people still fighting for it." Richard shot Brenda a glare.

"How many corrupt politicians are we talking?" Frank asked.

The agent standing within arm's reach of the vice president said, "Twenty-seven, maybe twenty-eight, but there are a couple of names on the list we're still not sure about."

"We need to hit them at the same time, you realize that, right?" Sam asked. "If we don't, warning flags will go up, and we might not get a second chance."

Richard said, "I agree. The only problem we have is finding them all. The information regarding the location of the president and the members of his Cabinet is not easy to come by. You can also bet their security has increased. Especially now they know someone's onto them."

The vice president asked, "Who will have access to the information?"

"Presidential Cabinet members who we're targeting, the leaders of SUNKC, and high-ranking agents of the HTF. Sir, as of right now, we're stuck. Too bad our damn prisoner died on the way here."

Sam shook her head in response to the unasked question on her aunt's face. "You don't want to know," she mouthed.

"Agent Brown would probably have access. He's in charge of the entire Midwest," Todd informed Richard, yet he was eyeballing Sam.

"Who's Agent Brown?"

Before Todd could answer Sam spoke. "Apparently, he's my new boss, if we can overcome one little snag."

Richard straightened against his chair. "I'm not following."

Sam explained to Richard and the others the job offer Agent Brown had made to her.

"That's exactly what we need, an informant!" Richard about jumped at the good news.

"The problem, though, is he wants a letter of recommendation from Agent Clayton in Kansas City. That's not going to happen."

The vice president didn't hesitate. "Sam, that's not a problem. I can send out my two best men to take Clayton out of the equation. But, just so we're clear, you do realize the amount of danger you'll be putting yourself in by taking the job."

"My sister has already informed me of the dangers, and I assure you, the greatest danger I'll be facing is telling Rachel I took the job." She turned to Richard. "I guess we have the beginnings of a plan." Her gaze drifted over to Elaina, but Elaina looked away.

The muscles in Sam's stomach tightened. She couldn't tell if Elaina was upset with her or not, but Sam could tell Elaina's mood had suddenly shifted. If she could take Elaina away from here and try for a normal life, she would. In a heartbeat. But Sam knew a normal life would not be possible until they ended this, and it would take time and many dangerous challenges on everyone's part.

Sam adjusted the pillow on her seat, unable to concentrate on what Richard was saying. *What will happen if SUNKC's troops do make it here to the US?* She closed her eyes tight, wishing the war-torn images away. Cursing under her breath, Sam forced herself to focus on the issues at hand.

"So far, they have confirmed over three hundred members of Congress died in the explosion, and they're still going through the wreckage searching for more bodies, and with any luck, survivors."

The vice president slowly exhaled. "Of those select few elected officials who were not caught in the explosion, how many of them are not a part of this conspiracy?"

"Only twelve, sir," the agent said. "Like I said before, sir, there are a few names on the list we are still checking into, but twelve have been confirmed."

"Jesus, twelve?" The vice president paused, appearing to weigh his troubled thoughts. "What is being done for their safety?"

"Several trustworthy members of the CIA and FBI we've recruited are moving them to a few of our protected encampments," Richard said.

"And what of my family?"

"They will be here sometime next week once we feel it's safe to transport them," Richard told the vice president.

The instant the meeting ended, Sam pulled Elaina aside and waited until the room cleared. "I thought maybe we should talk," Sam said. She searched Elaina's eyes for clues to what she was thinking. With everything Elaina had already been through, the people she had already lost, maybe she would view this relationship, and Sam's own willingness to leap without looking, too challenging to take on. "Are we okay?"

Elaina melted into Sam's arms. "I'm worried for you."

Sam was surprised by the tender reaction, and by how wonderful it felt. She breathed a sigh of relief. "You're not upset?"

"I'm not upset." Elaina's smile wavered. "I don't want to lose you, Sam. Not after I just found you. I've already lost so many people in my life because of the HTF, and now you'll be working with them every single day. I cringe to think of the dangers you'll be in." Elaina tightened her arms around Sam's waist.

"I promise you won't lose me." Sam gazed directly into Elaina's eyes. "I'm actually quite tough when I want to be." Sam tilted her head down and their lips came together. It felt natural, perfect, as if some higher being had made one specifically for the other.

Elaina broke away. "Why don't we go say goodnight to Rachel and Jennifer before we head up to your house?" She pressed her lips against Sam's neck.

Sam's libido snapped to attention. "That sounds like the best plan I've heard all night."

To be continued . . .

Author's Afterword

An earlier version of this book was originally published in 2011. Who knew that my imaginary world would so closely mimic the events of today, over a decade later! Back then, I wrote this book because I felt the power our government holds over us had been steadily growing, and the number of countries at odds with America could one day be our downfall. I put that together and created the conspiracy for *Veiled Conspiracy*.

As an American, I feel we have a false belief that our country is untouchable. A few of the countries we have unstable relations with are World Powers. Those countries may be allied with one another, share similar anti-democratic political views, and have a common dislike for the West. If they combined their fighting forces against the United States, the outcome would be disastrous. I don't feel a nuclear war would happen—at least I hope not. The consequences would be devastating for anyone left standing. I feel this is the main reason the Cold War ended. Those in power realized, even if victorious, in a nuclear war everyone would suffer. But there are also other ways to weaken a Nation.

This is Book One in what I intend to be a three-book series. I've already written the second book, and it's in production for publication while I work on Book Three.

Thank you for going on this journey with me toward liberty. Please bookmark my publisher's page where you can keep track of the publication of all my titles.
www.LaunchPointPress.com/books CHELE.html

Michele L. Coffman
Kansas City, Missouri
May 2022

About the Author

Michele L. Coffman lives in the Kansas City, Missouri, area. She's an Army Veteran with fifteen years of service where she froze in Germany, sweated in Kuwait, sought shelter from the noon rainstorms of Panama, almost got bit by a poisonous snake in Ecuador, and even unknowingly bedded down with a tarantula in Nicaragua. She currently works in the field of medical care.

Michele has two wonderful children and is a proud grandmother of one incredible child, also named Michele. She is a passionate writer, has an untamable imagination, and enjoys writing sci-fi, conspiracy thrillers, and—well, just about anything that strikes her fancy.

Acknowledgments

A big thank you to my sister, Ruth, for your direction and guidance, and for the gift of your poem. Another big thanks to my publisher Lori L. Lake and to my editors for this edition, Judy Kerr and Kay Grey, both of whom were a joy to work with.

Because of the hard work and dedication from each of you, I'm able to do what I love and share it with others.

www.ingramcontent.com/pod-product-compliance
Lightning Source LLC
Chambersburg PA
CBHW070519100726
47907CB00004B/895